Scion

Scion

B.A. Seloaf

SCION

iUniverse books may be ordered through booksellers or by contacting:

iUniverse
1663 Liberty Drive
Bloomington, IN 47403
www.iuniverse.com
1-800-Authors (1-800-288-4677)

ISBN: 978-1-5320-1878-7 (sc)
ISBN: 978-1-5320-1879-4 (e)

Print information available on the last page.

iUniverse rev. date: 03/08/2017

~ 1 ~

This story begins with the sun rose.

No, that wasn't a case of careless grammar or an inability to find the correct tense of a fairly uncomplicated verb. Rather, it refers to the ancient flora of Africa, where, as most educated people know, the whole catastrophe known as mankind began.

The sun rose, yes. It was a delicate and very rare flower with the amazing ability to change colour as the sun passed across the bright African sky. In the morning its petals were a soft pink, which changed to a bright yellow at noon, and then to a flaming red and deep purple as the sun sank towards the western horizon.

No one knew what colour it took on during the night, as it was too dark to see anything then. People had tried to light fires to provide the light necessary to obtain the answer to this ancient question, but the sun rose only grew in places far away from trees or any other inflammable objects, so by the time the people involved managed to gather enough wood for a fire, the sun had risen anew. Thus the mystery of the sun rose's colour at night remained unsolved, and most people thought it was an ugly little flower anyway.

Not Marsha, though. She watched it with amazement in her dark brown eyes as the little flower turned as yellow as the yolk of an egg, stretching itself up towards the warming rays of sunlight. Actually, the midday sun was hot enough to burn most other growing things into oblivion, but the sun rose was a damn resilient bugger of a plant. Nobody screwed with the sun rose, as we will see in just a little while.

But first, let's have a look at Marsha. This section would not be necessary if there'd been a photo of her at the bottom of this page, but unfortunately cameras were in short supply during this primitive period of African history. At least I believe they were. There are no clear indications as to exactly how old this story is, so theoretically there might have been cameras around. If there were, Marsha didn't have one among her possessions.

Marsha was a woman of average height and slim build. She had long, black hair reaching all the way down to the small of her back. Her figure was leaning a bit toward boyishness, which had led to much debate among the men of her tribe. Some found her incredibly sexy, while others would rather shag a gnu. Being the chieftain of said tribe, she was in her full power to exact punishment on those with such a disrespectful opinion of her, but for some reason the thought had never occurred to her.

She was the head of the Khadal tribe, in more than one sense. Besides the title's more obvious meaning, she was also in possession of the tribe's most highly developed brain. Not that there was much competition, of course. Most members of the Khadal tribe were so stupid they had trouble carrying out a coherent conversation, which might have made them a very quiet tribe if not for their unfortunate love of blabbering themselves silly whether they had anything interesting to say or not.

Listening to their imbecile chattering for more than a few minutes would probably be enough to cause mental breakdowns among the (mostly) more intelligent people you and I are used to dealing with. This would've made them a very efficient means of torture, as most anyone would gladly sign any confession placed in front of them just to put an end to the insufferable noise.

The Khadal tribe lived to the south of the mighty jungle to the north, and east of the great savannah to the west. They had little or no contact with other human or sub-human creatures – not because they were socially awkward in any way (at least not more awkward than what was considered normal at this time), but because something in their subconscious told them such contact usually ended in bloodshed.

Some of the older tribesmen claimed there'd been a time when the Khadal was a thriving people, unchallenged in wisdom and culture throughout all Africa. The majority of the people regarded this as foolish old tales, and the storyteller usually ended up getting a good whipping for mentioning it. Marsha liked whipping old people. It made her feel pleasantly drowsy.

She was wide awake now. Watching the tiny, incredibly bright flower, she felt an irresistible urge to possess it, to have its beauty by her side, always and forever. It was vaguely like the way two people in a romantic movie feel when their eyes meet for the first time. That the main character in a romantic movie would only be interested in a one-night stand is as unthinkable as a poem making sense.

Not that Marsha had ever experienced any such desires, of course. She was a completely asexual person, which was very uncommon among people who dressed suitably for an average temperature of over forty degrees centigrade. Some members of her tribe whispered that she fancied various kinds of animals, but there was no more truth to that than to most other things the Khadal men and women said. Anyone who knew her well - which was basically no one at all - would know she was terribly afraid of any animal larger than a bug, and bugs made her quite uneasy as well.

The thought of bugs halted her for a moment. What if there was a bug on the flower? A small, nasty bug with bright red eyes, grinning at her with sharp, white teeth while its long, thin legs coiled around her helpless body. In her mind, the bug grew to many times the size of the plant, and kept growing until it covered the whole world. She thrashed about wildly with her arms, which would have looked incredibly odd to a person watching her. Fortunately, there wasn't anyone within sight at the moment.

When she'd calmed herself she bent down and took the sun rose between her two fingers. She had only two fingers on her left hand – a reminder of an encounter with an alligator a couple of years ago. The tribe's medicine woman had tried sewing fingers taken from a dead old man onto Marsha's maimed hand, but after a few days they'd started smelling so badly it made Marsha dizzy and everyone around her nauseous, so she'd had to have them removed again. She'd thrown them into the lake where she'd gotten her fingers bitten off, and two days later another member of her tribe found a dead alligator lying on the shore.

When Marsha touched the flower's delicate stem a sharp pain jolted up her arm. She jumped several feet into the air, screaming her agony in a way that would have fooled some smaller kinds of monkeys into believing it was mating season. Marsha kept jumping up and down, sucking her aching fingers between fits of moaning and sobbing. She didn't notice the other woman's approach until she was standing right beside her.

"What's wrong, chief?" Gemma asked, worry distorting her elfin face.

"The sun rose!" Marsha pointed – by pure accident - towards the eastern horizon.

The other woman looked confused. "Yeah, but that was several hours ago. Why so excited?"

"No, no." Marsha managed to keep her feet steady on the ground, but her arms kept flailing about madly. "The flower. I tried to pick it, and it stung me. Felt like a viper, or a scorpion."

"Whoa!" Gemma exclaimed. "You've been bitten by a viper *and* stung by a scorpion? How can you still be alive?"

Marsha glared at her. "Of course I haven't. I simply imagined it'd feel something like this."

"You have a very vivid imagination," Gemma complimented her. "I've never thought about how something like that would feel. Think you could describe it somehow?"

Marsha grabbed her arm and bit it as hard as she could. Gemma shrieked like a bat. She was one of very few women who could produce a sound that high-pitched. Marsha stepped back, satisfied with herself.

"It felt like that, only about twenty times worse," she said, looking at Gemma as the other woman rubbed her aching arm.

Looking at Gemma was something many men enjoyed doing. Her dark, silky hair fell in glossy waves to her shoulders; her skin was soft as a midnight breeze, her body tall and slim and sexy. Her garments were made of water buffalo hide - a tight vest with a matching thong that bared her round, firm buttocks, burned nicely brown by the hot African sun. She moved with the grace of a panther, except at food time when she was more like a charging rhino.

Many of the Khadal men had tried to get her to spend the night with them, each advance ending in failure and – more often than not – with a black eye for the man in question. Gemma's only true passion was hunting, and she kept saying her spear was the only lover she'd ever need. People had often speculated whether they should take that literally or not. In the end, most had decided the question was better left unanswered.

"I see." Gemma sucked the place where she'd been bitten. "Why touch it if it hurts that badly?"

"Because I didn't know it'd sting," Marsha snapped. "I wouldn't have done it if I'd known." That was a lie, but she hoped the other woman wouldn't detect it. The urge to pick the flower had been so strong she wouldn't have cared if it had killed her. She spared a brief moment to wonder at that, then went on. "Let's go back to the camp. The sun has already begun its descent, and we wouldn't want to be late for dinner."

Gemma shook her head, causing her hair to swirl around it. "No, and then I must hunt buffalo," she said.

Marsha raised an eyebrow. She had two of those, and there was nothing weird about either one. "How's that? The others have probably gathered food already."

"I don't know. I do know. I'm not sure."

Marsha frowned. She was used to odd behaviour from the members of her tribe, but this was unsettling. Perhaps she'd bitten the girl too hard.

"What is it you do and don't know, Gemma?" she asked.

Gemma's beautiful face went through a number of grimaces. Some made Marsha flinch; others made her wish she was a spear.

"I don't know why, but I know I must hunt buffalo," she finally said. "It's like when you have to pee really badly, except that you can't do it behind someone's tent. I must head off, search for the..." She trailed off, a distant look in her bright eyes.

"Search for what?" Marsha asked.

The other woman blinked. "Huh? Have you lost something?"

"Er, no. It was you who said you were going to search for something, but you didn't say what."

"I said I was going to hunt buffalo. That's all."

Marsha scratched herself behind her right ear. It always seemed to itch more than the left one. Sometimes she wondered if she should ask the medicine woman to remove it so she could throw it into that lake and see what washed up.

"You said... oh, never mind." Marsha let out a long breath. "Go hunt buffalo, then. Just don't leave until you've drunk my luck potion."

As the two women began the long walk back to the Khadal camp Marsha tried to put two and two together. Gemma was hopeless at mathematics, even by the standards of their very primitive tribe, so Marsha knew she'd get no help there. When she finally succeeded, another thought struck her. She stopped, causing Gemma to walk right into her.

"Ow, my nose!" Gemma complained. "Why did you stop so suddenly?"

Marsha was too distracted by her new realization – things like that didn't happen very often to members of the Khadal tribe – and completely forgot to apologize. This made Gemma slightly ticked off, but knowing she could beat the other woman up quite easily she didn't bother with making a scene.

"Something struck me," Marsha said, her voice distant.

"That's not possible," Gemma said. "There's only the two of us here, and it sure wasn't me."

"What? Oh, not like that. It was a thought. You know, the kind that feels like a spark suddenly turning into a blazing fire."

Gemma stared blankly at her.

"Anyway," Marsha went on. "Didn't you find it strange that you suddenly got that notion about having to hunt buffalo even though we already have food for at least two days?"

"Huh?"

"Indeed. And at the same time – or rather, just before – I got that intense urge to pick the sun rose. I don't even know what you're supposed to do with a sun rose."

Gemma scratched her head. "Neither do I. Do you think Emkei knows?"

"I suppose we could ask her when we get back to our camp," Marsha said. *If we ever do...*

"Yeah, but what if she says one of those weird things nobody understands?"

Marsha shrugged. "Then we'll ask Pebe. Come on now."

They were delayed further by a group of lions who'd strayed off too far from the savannah and now walked around aimlessly in circles between two green hills. Gemma was a little tempted to engage in a fight, but after some persuasion from Marsha she agreed hiding was a much better option.

The lions took their time about doing nothing, so it was almost dark when the two women got back to the camp. The campfires were already lit and food was prepared in large cook pots. The smell of stew reached them long before they were able to make out the camp itself.

The tribe's huts were dotted like mushrooms around an open space of hard-packed dirt. There were about fifty of them, each containing one family. The empty area in the middle of the camp was where all important events took place - weddings, funerals, executions, public announcements and other things people found more or less (usually less) interesting. Marsha's voice had a tendency to become shrieky whenever she had to raise it, so most members of the Khadal found it vexing to listen to her for any length of time.

There was a lot of activity in the camp when the two women entered. Children were running about, being generally annoying, and women were preparing meals while their husbands pretended to do something useful. Marsha was greeted with respectful bows and polite words, while Gemma received a lot of whistles and indecent offers. All in all, it was an evening like any other.

They seated themselves on the ground outside Marsha's hut, which was the camp's biggest. Not because she was the chieftain - the Khadal made no such distinctions between people in important positions and the common rabble - but because she was a bit claustrophobic. The disorder originated from a childhood incident, where a group of troublemakers had locked her in a barrel and sent it rolling down a hill. This had also resulted in a fierce hatred of dancing and anything else that involved whirling and spinning around.

Some of her friends had the kettle boiling already. Pebe, a boisterous young man with a nose that looked as if it'd been intended for something completely different, sat cross-legged and talked to Amanda - a beautiful, voluptuous woman with an obsession for weird rhymes. On the other side of the fire slouched Emkei, an immensely fat, middle-aged woman who claimed to be a seer. No one could remember if she'd ever predicted anything useful; usually she just spoke in riddles no one understood.

Sometimes Emkei's predictions had devastating effects. Take the day the alligator maimed Marsha's hand, for example. On that morning Emkei had told her "Never plunge your head into the water unless you have one to spare". So when Marsha dropped her dagger into the shallows of Lake Montaught she used her hand instead of her head to search for it, a mistake that resulted in three of her fingers ending up in the alligator's belly. After that she'd sworn never to heed the old woman's advice again.

Marsha sat down next to Emkei, while Gemma showed some children how to cartwheel over the cookfires. This made the tribe's medicine woman very happy, not because she got to show off how skilled she was at treating burns, but because a kid she hated got his hair burned off. When the kid's mother brought the screaming boy to her she put the fire out by emptying a pot of almost-boiling water over him. That made the kid scream even louder, and Ginger - as the medicine woman was called - to chuckle happily.

"Mmmmm... zebra stew," Amanda said, putting her wooden spoon into her mouth.

"No, silly," said Gemma, who'd rejoined them after getting a bashing from some of the children's parents and a cookie from the medicine woman. "That's a spoon; the stew is in the pot."

"Oh, sorry." Amanda took the spoon out and began filling her bowl with steaming stew. "*A spoon of stew in your ear, and zebras neighing you will hear,*" she added.

"I killed the zebra myself," Pebe said with a satisfied and slightly arrogant expression. "I had forgotten my spear down by the river, so I had to jump onto its back and bite it to death. It fought like a maniac, and if I hadn't been such a mighty warrior it'd probably have thrown me off and trampled me to death. Not that I'm complaining, of course. I'd gladly risk my life every day if it meant my people didn't have to go hungry. I hope you appreciate my efforts, Marsha."

"Of course I do." Marsha put a spoonful of stew into her mouth. She knew perfectly well that Gemma and Amanda had killed the zebra that morning. They were all used to Pebe's boasting, the same as with Emkei's riddles. Both were a natural part of life, just like haemorrhoids. At least that was the case for Emkei.

"Did you find anything on your expedition, Marsha?" Amanda asked. She was a very talkative woman, a trait that annoyed many people. Not because they thought she said stupid things, but because it made it more difficult to make their own stupid things heard. People usually have an aversion to those most alike to themselves, probably because they see their own weaknesses reflected back at them.

Others found Amanda annoying because she, like Gemma, often drew the men's eyes. No one dared throw bawdy comments at her, though, because of her inhuman strength. Once she'd thrown a loaf of bread at a man who'd asked her if she wanted to go for a swim with him, in the nude. He'd been unconscious for three days, and she claimed she'd done it playfully.

"A sun rose," Marsha informed her.

Amanda blinked. "Another one? Where did it come from?"

"No, silly," Marsha said. "It was a flower. I tried to pick it, but it stung my hand quite horribly. Do you know anything about them, Emkei?"

Emkei looked up from her stew. "If you touch the sun you will get your wings burned. If you don't have wings you won't reach the sun." She returned her attention to the food.

"I once picked a sun rose," Pebe said. "It hurt a lot, but I endured it. I can endure more pain than any man who ever lived. Once, when I shaved..."

"Do you still have it?" Gemma asked him, her eyes sparkling with excitement.

Pebe shook his head. "Why, no. I was on my way back to the camp when I was attacked by a score of cannibals. I killed them all, of course, but when I looked for the flower it was gone. Bloody shame."

"I don't believe you picked one," Amanda said. "You're a wimp. *A wimp, a wimp, a wimp with a limp.*"

This might've made Pebe look as guilty as a child caught with its hand in the cookie jar, but being a man of very limited mental stability he burst into a convulsive fit of crying instead.

"I really did pick one," he whined. "You're mean. I'm no wimp. I'm a great warrior, and a damn good botanist."

"Oh, well," said Marsha. "I'm sure Amanda didn't mean to hurt you."

"I didn't," the other woman said. "If I wanted to hurt him I'd punch him in the nose."

That made the young man look even more miserable.

"I bet your hands are itching to do just that," he moaned. "What did I ever do to make you hate me so much?"

"Hey, I was joking," Amanda said. "You know I don't hate you. I might not feel more than a moderate fondness for you, but I'd never want to see you get hurt. We're friends, aren't we? Well, sort of..."

Pebe glared at her, which might actually have made him look fierce if it hadn't been for his red-rimmed eyes and glistening wet cheeks.

"I don't believe you," he grumbled. "You just called me a wimp and a liar. No true friend would do that."

"I said I was joking. I'm sorry."

They continued arguing until Amanda finally gave up and turned her back to the young man. Emkei momentarily took her attention away from her food – she was on her third bowl – and gave the two of them a puzzled look.

"What's up with you guys?" she asked.

"They were arguing about whether Amanda wants to hurt Pebe or not," Gemma said. "In the end Amanda threw up her hands and said discussing things with him was as pointless as getting you to wash."

The seer gave Amanda's back an indignant frown.

"She shouldn't eat so much, then," she muttered. "Only amateurs eat until they throw up."

"Er," Gemma said, but Emkei was already busy spooning more stew into her mouth. It looked like the fat woman hadn't grasped the concept of chewing, or if she had she'd probably dismissed it as too time-consuming.

When all of them had finished their meals Marsha cleared her throat, made sure there was a nice canopy of stars above her, and said in a voice sounding like she was announcing the arrival of some long-expected messiah: "Gemma will hunt buffalo tomorrow."

No one answered.

Marsha looked at her friends. All of them seemed lost in their own thoughts – a considerable achievement given the simple nature of most Khadal minds. Suddenly irritated by their lack of attention, she picked up an empty kettle and placed it in her lap.

"I'll start working on that luck potion," she muttered to herself.

"You're going to make a luck potion?" Amanda asked, suddenly all ears. "That's amazing! Who's it for?"

"It's for me," Gemma said. "I'm going to hunt buffalo tomorrow."

"That's exciting, Gemster!" Pebe exclaimed. "When did you get that idea?"

Gemma frowned. "That was the weird bit. I didn't really think of it; the thought was just there, as if someone had put it into my head. It was more like an urge than a thought, actually. I knew I had to do it, or... or..."

"Or the world would end?" Emkei nodded, as if everything Gemma had said made perfect sense. "That happens every now and then."

"The world ending?" Amanda said. "That can't be. It's still around."

"What your eyes perceive may only be a vague reflection of the splendid thing we so insufficiently name reality. Never presume to understand the fullness of events, lest your ignorance consume you. Ah, that stew was really good." Emkei slapped her ample belly, emitting a happy belch.

The other four might actually have understood her words if not for the bit about the stew, which they thought to be part of the message. Amanda wondered if it meant the stew hadn't really been there; Gemma wondered whether hunting buffalo would cause the world to end; Pebe got an uneasy feeling that Emkei knew he hadn't killed the zebra and would make Amanda hurt him. Marsha wondered if the seer thought her an incompetent leader and planned to make stew of her.

No one dared ask what Emkei had meant, however, so the matter never got cleared up. Because of that, none of them ever looked at stew the same way again.

"Okay," Marsha finally said. "Potion time."

The ingredients in the luck potion were zebra blood, elephant testicles, ostrich guano and sweat from a drunken man who'd sat in a tree for three days. These were mixed in a small kettle while the maker chanted silly stuff that not even the most imbecile child would find entertaining. Amanda sometimes used these verses as inspiration for her poetry.

Gemma had drunk the luck potion many times, so the foul taste didn't bother her. Marsha had only tried it once, by accident. She'd asked Gemma what it tasted like, and the slim woman had replied with "Foul". Marsha had thought she said "Fowl", and had been sick for three days. When she finally recovered she decided that no luck in the world could be worth going through that ordeal again. Besides, if Gemma drank the potion Marsha could send her to do the more important tasks - and others which required luck - and thus didn't need to taste the foul stuff herself. This was about as smart as a member of the Khadal tribe ever got.

A while later, when Gemma had gone off to throw up and prepare herself for tomorrow's hunt, Marsha got a brilliant idea.

"Let's make a fertility potion," she suggested.

"No need," Pebe said. "I only need to think about pulling down my pants, and half the camp gets pregnant. Just tell me how many you want."

"Er, no thanks," Marsha said. "I think this tribe has enough of your genes as it is."

If you wonder how Marsha knew about a modern biological term like *gene*, you'll have to keep wondering. Perhaps she used a more primitive expression that somehow got lost in translation over the years. Perhaps she said the tribe had enough of Pebe's germs, and whoever put together the chronicles from this time misheard it.

"Why a fertility potion?" Amanda asked. "There are lots of children about already."

"Yes, but none of them are mine," Marsha pointed out. "One day I might want someone to pass on my vast stock of knowledge to. You know, helping the Khadal into a better and more enlightened future."

"Enlightened in what way?" Pebe asked, still sounding displeased about the rejection of his genes.

Marsha tossed her head impatiently. "These matters are too deep for you to understand, Pebe. I'm talking about new technologies, new approaches to life. Have you ever thought about why we're here?"

"I'm here because of the food," Emkei said, once more patting her ample stomach. Amanda laughed.

A sudden upwelling of desperation caused tiny beads of sweat to appear on Marsha's forehead. She didn't have anything to back up her last statement with, and was afraid she'd look like a fool if her friends continued to question her. She turned to the seer, hoping for some support.

"Emkei, you have gazed into the future countless times. Certainly you must be familiar with the things I speak of."

"What?" The fat woman blinked. "Oh, yes. Of course. Know them all."

"And?"

"And I think you should start working on that fertility potion. It's getting late."

"Just tell us what the future of the Khadal looks like," Marsha prompted.

The seer yawned. "I can't speak for the rest of you, but I see myself nicely wrapped up in warm blankets, dreaming of handsome young men who think big women are the most attractive thing in the world. It shouldn't be long until that vision comes true."

"You know, Marsha," Amanda said, eyeing her chieftain with curious interest. "If you want a child, the first step usually is to find a suitable man. You're a young, healthy woman. There'll be no need for a fertility potion."

"A man?" Marsha glared at Amanda as if she'd suggested she'd mate with a baboon. "Why would I want a man involved in this? He'd just get in the way."

"Surely you must know that it takes both a man and a woman to make babies?"

Marsha began putting new things into the empty kettle. "Not if I make it strong enough," she said, her face shining with determination.

Sighing, Amanda leaned back. "*A potion so strong, instead of a dong,*" she mumbled to herself.

When Marsha had finished mixing the ingredients, she leaned forward and sniffed the air above the kettle.

"Strange," she said. "It smells kinda sour, but I'm sure all the ingredients were fresh."

"It smells here too," Amanda said, pinching her nose between two of her fingers.

Marsha looked at Amanda. Amanda looked at Marsha. Then both of them looked at Emkei.

"It must come from one of the other campfires," the seer said innocently.

"*A seer's fart goes straight to the heart,*" Amanda said, waving her hand in front of her face. "At least you won't have to worry about the potion being bad, Marsha."

Marsha drank the potion. The taste was peculiar but far from unpleasant. There was a tingling sensation in her stomach. Could she be pregnant already? The sensation grew stronger, rising through her body until it reached her throat. Suddenly she couldn't breathe. Her eyes bulged, her face feeling like it was about to explode.

"Marsha?" There was sudden alarm in Amanda's voice. "What's wrong? Emkei, do something!"

Something large and soft filled Marsha's mouth. She emitted a strangled sound, then convulsed as half a dozen chickens popped out. Pebe yelped and shuffled backwards, as if they'd been scorpions rather than birds.

Gasping for air, Marsha looked down at the last drops of potion left in the kettle.

"Oops, I must've gotten some ingredient wrong," she said.

"More likely you had the wrong recipe to begin with," Amanda said, catching one noisy bird with each hand. "Or do you think you accidentally made a fertility potion for hens?"

"At least we have food for tomorrow now," Emkei said, giving the chicken she'd caught a hungry look.

Some of the chickens managed to escape and started causing disorder among the nearby groups of people. Marsha ordered them to catch the unruly birds and bring them back to her, and, as she was their chieftain, a few actually obeyed her. Others seized the opportunity to run around the camp, causing their own measure of havoc. Marsha and Amanda got up, yelling and – in Amanda's case – dealing out a few well-aimed punches.

They'd just managed to establish some resemblance of order when Emkei suddenly spoke, this time in the menacing voice of prophecy.

"What once was may come again, but beware the insect."

~ 2 ~

Marqamil was woken from his meditation when a voice called his name. Well, to be honest, the voice said "High Priest", followed by some other stuff he didn't quite get. Slamming his fist down hard on the even harder stone table - a course of action that put his hand in a state of mind-numbing pain - he stood up and glared at the intruder. It was Chrisox, one of the clerics.

"What have I told you about disturbing my meditation?" he thundered. His voice was actually very thin and brittle, but the cave's acoustics made it sound quite impressive.

He now saw that there was another man with Chrisox - a young fellow, his face tanned dark brown by the accursed sun. Marqamil eyed him suspiciously.

"Who's that?" he asked.

"This young man wants to be initiated into our cult," Chrisox said. "He claims to have travelled for years, both day and night, through fire and water and countless dangers, making it here only by the grace of the Raven God and a pair of very good shoes."

"Those must be some very good shoes indeed." Marqamil scratched his thin brown hair. "What's your name, son?"

"I'm Drunk," the newcomer said.

"Oh? This early in the morning?"

"No, sir. My name is Drunk. Drunk of the seven rivers. I've travelled through fire and water, through blood and death, through..."

"Yes, yes, I know," Marqamil interrupted him. "And it was all thanks to the shoes. Why do you want to be initiated into the Cult of the Raven?"

The young man thought for a while, looking rather peculiar as he did so because of the way his mouth hung half-open.

"Because it's my destiny," he finally said.

"What do you mean it's your destiny?" Marqamil asked, his frown deepening.

The man named Drunk shrugged. "I dunno. It seemed like the thing to say."

The High Priest smiled. "That's a good, honest answer. I've always liked my men honest."

Chrisox emitted a choking sound.

"What's the matter?" Marqamil asked, shooting the cleric a worried look.

"Er, sir..."

"Speak up, man! I don't have all day."

Chrisox took a deep breath, his eyes fixed on a spot a few feet left of the High Priest's face.

"Well, sir, what you said clearly had sexual implications. Saying that you like your men a certain way does, well, make it sound like you're experienced with..."

"That's the most ridiculous thing I ever heard," Marqamil said. "But I'll be considerate and rephrase myself. The sight of a new recruit gladdens me. We haven't had one in a long time."

Chrisox produced a demonstrative cough.

The High Priest sighed. "What now?"

"Er, you made that sound as if we were going to eat him, sir," Chrisox said. "Like *we haven't had pepper stew in a long time.*"

Marqamil's eyebrows narrowed. "We're not cannibals, Chrisox. We don't even eat meat. How can you even think of having this young man for dinner?"

"Well, perhaps because we haven't had any good food in a long time, and most of us would welcome any change in our diet..."

"That's enough!" Marqamil snapped. "This young fellow hasn't been here two minutes, and you've already accused me of both cannibalism and sodomy. What will you do next, suggest I torture children while I pretend to meditate? We're a religious cult, sure enough, but there are limits!"

As opposed to most religious fanatics, Marqamil had never been drawn towards cannibalism, sodomy, or harming innocent children. He had practiced celibacy for most of his life, but that had mostly been a result of his geeky personality and far from fetching appearance.

In fact, the cause of his irritation regarding Chrisox's interruption was that he'd been dreaming about Lizbug - the hot, young apprentice who showed so much promise. Marqamil had spent countless hours trying to think of a reason to get rid of the traditional black robes of the Raven Cult. The problem was that all the holy scrolls emphasized that the members of the cult had to cover their bodies to protect them from the evil eye. With *the evil eye* they meant the sun, but the robes were just as resilient to the eyes of horny, middle-aged men.

The easiest way for him to make his wishes come true would have been to point out that the deep, dark caverns where the Raven Cult resided weren't exposed to sunlight, and thus the members should walk around naked. Unfortunately, Marqamil hadn't thought of that solution yet. In his dreams, though, Lizbug's body was fully visible in the flickering candlelight, shadows playing across its delicate curves, his hands around her soft waist, her warm lips pressed against his…

"My lord?"

Marqamil quickly wiped the drool from his mouth and tried to resume an expression of dignity, which failed monumentally.

"Yes?" he croaked.

Chrisox had begun moving restlessly from one foot to the other. "Will you have any further need of me, sir? I really need to… pray."

The High Priest made a dismissive gesture with his left hand. "No, I'll be fine. What will you be praying for?"

"Ummm… a kind of release," Chrisox said. "Removing base urges and finding contentment for both body and mind. That sort of thing."

"Ah, that sounds nice," Marqamil said. "I should try it some time. Off with you now."

"Enjoy your piss," Drunk called after the cleric.

When Chrisox had disappeared the newcomer took a few cautious steps into the High Priest's chamber.

"It's a pretty nice place you've got here," he said, examining a box of random junk sitting on a low cupboard.

"Huh?" The High Priest had gone back to fantasizing about Lizbug. This time she wore sexy black lingerie and – for some inexplicable reason – a pair of much too large rubber boots. Muddy tracks followed her into his chamber.

"I said I like your place," the new recruit said. He picked up a small ivory statuette depicting some strange, gangly bird standing on one leg with its wings tucked close against its sides. "Is this supposed to be the Raven God?"

Marqamil frowned. "That ugly little thing? I've no idea where it came from. You can have it if you like."

Drunk quickly put the statuette back into the box. "Does that mean you'll have me? Not for dinner, but as a member of your cult?"

"I don't know. You've been touched by the evil eye. Why should we risk having such a creature among us?"

"Well, I did go through war and famine, battling the forces of..."

"Yes, yes, I know that." Marqamil waved his hand as if trying to get rid of a very persistent fart. "I'll need something more concrete than that."

"I will help you find your heart's desire."

That took the High Priest aback.

My heart's desire, he thought. *To learn to call upon the Raven God to free my people from the burning gaze of the evil eye, to allow them to walk freely under the black skies, to rule the world under His hand, forever and ever.*

That was what all the members of the cult prayed for, what they'd happily give their lives for any day except Fridays, when there was dancing. That was his heart's desire.

Or rather, it should have been. What popped into his mind was the image of Lizbug's naked body in his arms - to spend eternity in bed with her, not giving a flying fuck about the bloody Raven God or that ugly thing in the sky. That was all he desired, the only thing he was willing to risk his life for. Once he got her he'd be content. If he got her he'd never wish for anything else in his whole life.

His expression must have revealed something, for the young man's face broke into a wide grin.

"I knew that'd work," he said triumphantly. "Where do I begin?"

Marqamil rummaged through his papers until he found what he looked for. He put away the erotic story he'd written the previous night and picked up one of the cult's application forms, handing it over to Drunk.

"Here. Fill this out. You'll begin with washing dishes for three days, then you'll do the laundry, dust the floors, and clean out the privy. In your spare time you'll have to read a couple of thousand pages on the history of the cult and its most prominent leaders. Once or twice a week you'll be tested to see if you've learned anything. Failing the tests will result in death. Any complaints?"

The young man looked as if he'd rather be killed at once.

"Is that all?" he asked listlessly.

"Yes. Oh, and you'll have to sleep with me tonight."

Drunk's face lit up again. "Really? I thought you said you didn't do that kind of stuff. Not that I have any objections, of course."

Marqamil shrugged. "It's just part of the ritual. All new initiates have to do it."

"It's a good tradition. What position do you like best?"

"Position?" Marqamil said, frowning the way he always did when he didn't comprehend something. "I'm the High Priest. I quite like that position. It's the highest rank a member of the Cult of the Raven can obtain."

The young man laughed. "I was talking about tonight. You and me. What position would you like?"

"Oh." Marqamil wondered why the man hadn't expressed himself more clearly. Perhaps it had something to do with him being an outsider. The relentless gaze of the evil eye must make people's minds dull and hazy.

He pointed to the extra bed on the opposite side of the room from his own. "You'll sleep over there. I hope you won't be noisy."

Suddenly Drunk looked very disappointed. "I suppose not," he mumbled.

"Good," Marqamil said. "You'd better get on with your chores now if you want to get any sleep at all. And don't neglect your reading. It's very important."

"Why is it so important to learn about old leaders who've been dead for hundreds of years?"

"Because the rest of us have forgotten everything we learned when we were novices," the High Priest explained. "It's been almost thirty years since I read about those things. You can hardly expect me to remember anything at all."

"Haven't you read any of those books since you were a novice?" Drunk asked, disbelief showing in his eyes.

Marqamil emitted a derisive snort. "Of course not. Why on earth would I want to do that? Those books are boring enough to make a mule cry. No, it's much better to have the new initiates read them. Then we can ask them if there's anything we need to know."

"I see."

"Good," Marqamil said. "You seem like a fast learner. Keep an extra eye out for anything to do with these thick robes we wear. If there's any mention at all of not having to wear them I'd like to know immediately."

"Oh? Why's that?" Drunk asked.

"It'll be the first step towards me finding my heart's desire. Find that, and I promise I won't be too harsh when I question you about the boring stuff. Get going now. There's a studying chamber farther down the hall. It's usually empty."

When the young man was gone the High Priest sat in silence for a moment, staring straight ahead of him. What did all this mean? How was this new initiate going to grant him his heart's - and other parts of his body's - desire? It would require a miracle to make Lizbug fall in love with a smelly old fart like him. This Drunk person might not be stupid, but Marqamil sincerely doubted his competence went that far.

He thought of Lizbug again. It was almost as if he could see her, standing there right in front of him, her beautiful, dark eyes regarding him quizzically. This was the most lifelike picture of her his mind had ever conjured. He could almost…

"Hello," said Lizbug.

Marqamil blinked. The young woman really was there, looking as breathtakingly beautiful as always even with that accursed robe on. Her long hair was dark and fine as spiderweb, her face pale - completely untouched by the evil eye. She was the most perfect woman he'd ever seen (out of a total of six, including his mother, grandmother, and wart-infested aunt Marbolonia). He would happily have given up his right hand for a single grope.

"Yes, child?" he managed, his voice so strained it almost trembled. Sweat had broken out all over his body, making his skin itch slightly.

"I was just wondering who that new recruit was," Lizbug said. "He walked past me in the corridor, looking like he was headed for his own execution. Who is he?"

"He's the new recruit."

"I know that. Does he have a name?"

"Yes."

"What is it?"

"Drunk. It must be some kind of foreign name. Like Skunk, or Stunk. Very odd, really."

She looked at him as if he was an idiot, which made him very excited. Not because it was a rare and special occasion – it happened almost every time she looked at him - but because everything Lizbug did, no matter how trivial or repulsive, tended to arouse him. If the woman had scraped guano from the floor with a dead rat he would probably have found it erotic.

He continued, "Don't you approve of him? He seems nice enough."

"He's touched by the evil eye," she said heatedly. "I don't appreciate having to live with such a foul being."

A pang of jealousy struck Marqamil like a two-thousand-pound hammer. Well, a two-thousand-pound hammer hitting him very lightly, for he wasn't turned into a bloody spot on the floor.

"I-I didn't know the two of you were going to live together," he stammered.

She drew herself up, giving him a haughty look. Her voice was cold as ice when she replied.

"How dare you insult me in such a fashion? A creature as pure and noble as myself, allowing someone like that near me? Next you'll suggest I take the evil eye itself into my bed!"

"I-I'd never… What would you have me do?"

"Send him away. I don't want him here."

Marqamil took a deep breath. He hated when he had to speak against the woman he loved, but sometimes his station forced him to.

"There isn't a rule against admitting people with tanned skin into the cult," he said. "Remember that the founders of our society had lived their entire lives under the evil eye when they dedicated themselves to the Raven God. This aversion of yours is completely uncalled for."

"But you saw his face! He's *tainted*! *Unclean*! What if he infects the rest of us with his disease? I've come too far to let some outsider lay waste to everything I hold dear."

The High Priest leaned back, suddenly feeling very tired.

"I know you've worked hard here, Lizbug," he said. "We all have. But we can't throw this young man out simply because he's an outsider. I mean, I don't know where you lived before you came here."

She hesitated for a moment, then spoke in a calmer voice. "I lived below ground. It was dark and humid and nice, just like here. I don't want that to change."

"Neither do I, my child. But I don't think we have anything to fear from Drunk. I'm sure you'll change your mind once you get to know him."

She did something with her clothing then, and suddenly it seemed to cling to her body in a way Marqamil wouldn't have thought possible a minute ago. His mouth went dry and he stared at her, unable to do anything else.

"Please do this for me," she said, her voice low and husky. "I'll make sure you won't regret it."

Marqamil would've run straight to Drunk's chamber, grabbed him by the scruff of his neck, and thrown him back out into the blazing sunlight from which he'd come, but Lizbug's little performance had made it impossible for him to breathe, so a few seconds later he fell off his chair and collapsed on the hard stone floor. He didn't hear Lizbug curse furiously where she stood in the doorway.

~ 3 ~

Gemma's feet moved without making the slightest sound. She'd always prided herself in her stealthy way of moving. Singing loudly, she proceeded deeper into the jungle, her eyes darting this way and that as they searched for signs of buffalo presence.

You may wonder why she'd gone into the jungle to hunt buffalo, when everyone knows the big, smelly animals live on the savannah. There's no answer to that question. Some would call it fate; others would say plain airheadedness. Both suggestions are legitimate in Gemma's case, as we'll see in just a little while.

Despite being very hungry, she hadn't opened the bundle of food she carried across her shoulder. This was due to the lingering effects of the luck potion – the most effective crash diet method of the time. Gemma could be quite the glutton at times, keeping her slim figure only thanks to her constant running about without accomplishing much. The more she ate, the more she ran. Today she hadn't eaten much, and hence she walked at a slow pace.

Suddenly she detected movement in front of her. Raising her spear, she readied herself for the kill. A charging buffalo wasn't something you wanted to fight with your bare hands when you hadn't had anything to eat since last evening. Unless you were called Amanda, of course. That valkyrie of a woman could probably stop a whole herd of the beasts with a flick of the wrist.

But the beast that emerged from the undergrowth was no buffalo. It was short and broad, with thick limbs and thick body armour. It moved towards her, seemingly in slow-motion, with its head thrusting out like the head of a homing torpedo. Gemma watched it approach, too terrified to move.

When the beast was ten paces from her she threw her spear at it. She wasn't less afraid than when she'd been too afraid to move, but when your life is threatened you tend to move no matter how afraid you are. It was a fairly good throw, not good enough to bring down something of buffalo-size, but very straight and with a lot of force behind it. Unfortunately, the spear bounced off the beast's hard armour and fell to the side.

Gemma would have peed her pants if she'd worn any. This didn't really make sense, as it'd be far less messy to pee in the tiny outfit she was wearing, but that somehow didn't seem like the thing to do. The beast moved closer, menacing hissing sounds emerging from its half-open mouth.

Then Gemma heard the sound of a macaque somewhere ahead of her. She quickly forgot about the tortoise, picked up her spear, and ran towards the sound. No living woman - and very few dead ones - could run as fast as Gemma. She'd probably have caught the small monkey if she hadn't tripped on a root and fallen face down into a small but sticky mound of monkey droppings. She gurgled and spluttered, making enough noise to scare the shit out of any poor beast within earshot. Fortunately, the only beast close enough was the aforementioned monkey, and its stomach was presently empty.

By the time Gemma regained her feet the macaque had fled up a tree and begun leaping from branch to branch. It chittered maniacally as it flung itself through the air, landing in the next tree. It continued its flight, and Gemma knew she had to move fast if she wasn't to lose sight of it.

She placed her spear between her teeth and, grabbing a liana, swung herself nimbly up into the nearest tree. After sprinting along a thick limb, she grabbed another liana and swung across to the next tree. She kept moving in this way, sometimes more than twenty feet above the ground. The sight would have made Pebe green with jealousy.

In this way she managed to gain ground on the monkey, using the momentum created by her weight and strength. She felt the ecstatic joy of hunting bubble in her heart (and the last of the luck potion bubble in her stomach). Only a little farther, and she'd catch the annoying little thing. If she reached out she could almost grab hold of its tail...

BANG!

She had only lost concentration for the merest instant, but that had been enough. Instead of catching another liana she slammed straight into a thick trunk, knocking herself senseless. Groaning softly, she slid down the tree, the rough bark scraping against her face and hands. When she reached the ground she collapsed in a motionless heap.

While she lay like that a group of small rodents came trotting by. Their leader cautiously stepped up to her and poked her butt with its nose. Gemma stirred, suddenly caught in a disturbing dream involving two grinning men and a very large sausage.

The rodent soon lost interest, but because it had a clear sense of which way it was going it didn't step around Gemma. Instead it climbed onto her back, waited a few moments while it listened for alarming sounds, and leapt down on the other side. The rest of the small animals followed.

When Gemma finally woke up she only remembered dreaming about being overrun by a herd of rampaging elephants. This, combined with the intense throbbing in her head, left her with a sensation of overwhelming misery. She crawled over to a rock and sat down, supporting her aching head with her hands.

She'd sat like that for some time, the bruises on her face and hands throbbing steadily, when the boulder began vibrating and then rising slowly, lifting Gemma into the air. She quickly leaped off it, landing softly on her feet. From the ground emerged a huge shape, vaguely human-like, but over ten feet tall and seemingly consisting of solid rock.

Gemma tried to locate her spear, but it was lost somewhere in the undergrowth. *Oh well,* she thought, *if I must fight this thing with nothing but my bare hands and feet, then so be it.*

That she'd probably have no trouble running away from the creature didn't occur to her. Courage and folly usually walked hand in hand. Last time Gemma had walked hand in hand with someone she'd almost ended up pregnant. If the person hadn't been another woman she'd probably be stuck with a whole bloody family by now, instead of standing face to face with this horrifying monster.

If Gemma had been given the opportunity to choose she would have picked the monster any day. The thought of taking care of children scared her more than any demon the dark caverns of hell could ever spew out.

The big creature fixed its hollow eyes on her.

"You sat on my face," it rumbled.

"Errr... sorry?" Gemma stammered. "I thought you were an ordinary rock. Big mistake, it seems."

The creature gave a sound like an enormous rockslide. Gemma realized it was laughing.

"Don't worry. It was an interesting and far from unpleasant experience. I've never had a human sit on my face before. Women of my own kind, of course, but never a human girl. I'm Tai-X, by the way, of the stone giants. And you are?"

"Ummm... Gemma. Gemma of the Khadal tribe." She didn't want to think about what it'd be like to have one of these things sitting on your face. The image got stuck in her mind anyway, and for some disturbing reason it made her oddly excited. She shook her head, seating herself on another boulder, after first giving it a close look to make sure it wasn't a living creature. "Where are you from?"

"The stone giants live on the great island to the southeast (Madagascar, for those of you not familiar with African geography). I've travelled far across the sea to get here. Or below it, to be exact. We prefer to move through the ground instead of on top of it."

Gemma was speechless. Well, almost speechless.

"Why?" she managed.

The stone giant sat down on a large boulder across from the one Gemma was sitting on. The movement looked more like a stone wall collapsing than what humans generally think of as *sitting down*. Gemma wondered what would have happened if she'd chosen to sit on one of these ordinary rocks instead of on the stone giant's face. Before she could pursue the thought Tai-X spoke again.

"I don't know. We feel naked when we walk through this thin thing, what do you call it?" The creature made a vague gesture.

"Air."

"Yes, air. Thanks. I don't know why we feel this way, but it's pretty damn embarrassing."

Gemma thought for a while. "Perhaps it's because you don't wear any clothes?" she suggested. "We humans feel embarrassed too, if we walk around with no clothes on."

The stone giant looked down at its huge body. "I'll be damned. It seems you're right. I wonder why no one ever thought about that."

"Yay!" Gemma clapped her hands, laughing happily. "Now you'll have to go back and tell your people they should wear clothes. Perhaps they'll make you their king, after solving this eternal mystery all by yourself."

She winked at Tai-X, as if to say she didn't want any credit for herself. The stone giant didn't seem to notice, however. It looked far into the distance (as far as you can when you're surrounded by trees on every side).

"No," it said solemnly. "My destiny is to lumber around aimlessly until I've found the answer."

"The answer to what?"

"I don't know," Tai-X said, looking confused. "I have this irresistible urge to find an answer, but I don't know to what. All I know is that it's very important, and that I must find it or all my kind will perish."

"Awww, that's sad." Gemma patted the stone giant's hard, rough cheek. "You should make a lot of babies, so your people will live on."

Tai-X gave her a puzzled look. Gemma didn't notice because of the way the creature's eyes were set so deeply in their sockets. She kept grinning like a fool. Or rather, like someone who thought they'd just said something incredibly witty. Fools seldom do that, so the expression was not very fitting.

There were no fools among the stone giants, so Tai-X never made the simile in the first place. Another thing the stone giants didn't have was toothbrushes, but that's not relevant to this story.

"You don't make babies," Tai-X said, sounding as if it explained the most trivial matter in the world, like that you don't drink water (you don't if you're a stone giant). "At least we don't."

By then the stone giant's voice had taken on a slightly insecure tone. Its brain - which wasn't obtuse, but terribly insular due to being isolated on an island its entire existence - was just beginning to realize that there might be species that actually *made* babies.

"We just grow from the rock," it continued. "That's the problem I've come here to solve. There hasn't been a new stone giant born in hundreds of years. We're a dying breed."

It was silent for a moment, then its eyes widened (only a fraction of an inch, but that was quite spectacular for a stone giant).

"Rust and splinters! That's it!"

"What's what?" Gemma had been thinking about what it'd be like to be born out of a rock. She wondered if it would hurt to push one's way through such a hard thing. This made her realize that she was very uncomfortable on the boulder she was seated on. She shifted her weight, trying to find a better position.

"The question I came here to find the answer to!" the stone giant exclaimed. "I must find out how to make babies. Of course! Why didn't I think of this earlier? I must be off at once. Farewell, Gemma of the Khadal tribe."

"Well, I could..." Gemma got no further. The large creature had already risen to its feet (or its equivalent of feet) and lumbered off into the surrounding trees. She followed it with her gaze, then shrugged and went to look for her spear. It was past time to move on.

Her hunting went badly after the encounter with the stone giant. The dizziness she'd felt after hitting the tree had left her, but she still had trouble concentrating properly. She went deeper and deeper into the jungle, until she reached its deepest place. After that she continued towards the less deep parts on the other side.

This would've been pretty interesting if Gemma had been moving into a river instead of a jungle. Imagine what it'd be like to reach the river's deepest place - the bottom - and then, by continuing in the same direction, move towards another surface. This wouldn't be possible unless the bottom went away, and then it would no longer be a river.

If Gemma had thought about this she'd probably be so confused she'd fall into a week-long thrashing seizure. Fortunately she thought about less complicated things, like how many beans you could stuff into your mouth without having to swallow, or how many times she'd be able to jump around the Khadal camp on one leg between sunrise and sunset. These thoughts kept her occupied for quite some time.

It was getting dark between the tall trees when she saw something that looked like a large cliff ahead of her. Excitement spread through her body like a fatal disease. She crouched low, spear held ready in both hands as she crept closer.

Perhaps a large, smelly beast lurks in some hidden cavern in there, she thought. *With its red eyes shining in the dark, its sharp teeth waiting for a juicy piece of human flesh.*

Most people would have run away at the thought of facing such a creature, but Gemma only felt an irresistible urge to kill it, whatever it was.

"Let's see who'll be the juiciest when this is over," she whispered to herself. She didn't know it, but that was the first time anyone had used that phrase anywhere in the world.

When she got closer it became apparent that it wasn't a cliff, but a ruined building. Or rather, it would've been apparent to a person of normal intelligence. Gemma, who could be a bit of a dumbass at times, continued as if some fierce, roaring monster was about to jump out of it at any moment.

Incidentally, a big, hairy monster jumped out from the shadows to her left and emitted terrifying roars while it waved its arms in a menacing fashion. Its eyes weren't red and its fangs were only moderately sharp, but it was still a very scary thing to behold.

Luckily for Gemma, she was so intent on the stone structure before her that she didn't notice the apparition. As the beast in question only attacked things that oozed fear, she soon lost her status as potential victim/dinner. Producing low growls of disappointment, the monster lumbered off into the jungle hoping to find someone more receptive to its little performance.

Gemma went through a gap in the outer wall and into a tunnel completely devoid of light. She used one hand to feel her way along its rough wall, wondering at the odd formations carved into the rock. Some of them made her blush, even if she couldn't see them. A more dirty-minded person might have spent all night in this tunnel, but as mentioned before Gemma didn't care much about such things. She went on, deeper and deeper into the darkness.

After a few minutes the tunnel widened into a spacious cavern. A dim light entered through holes in the ceiling, making it possible for Gemma to distinguish broken stone formations all around her.

"Whoa!" she whispered to herself. "This looks like some sort of temple."

She wasn't sure what a temple was, but for some reason the word popped into her head and seemed to insist on being spoken.

"I AM DEAD, I AM DEAD, I HAVE NOTHING IN MY HEAD."

The loud chanting took her completely by surprise. She looked around to see where it came from, but saw nothing out of the ordinary. She scratched the back of her leg with her spear butt, wondering if she could've imagined it. She'd just decided that must be the case when the chanting came again.

"I AM DEAD, I AM DEAD, I HAVE NOTHING IN MY HEAD."

It came from somewhere above her. The natural reaction would've been to look up, but instead Gemma sat down on the cold stone floor and rummaged through her pack for something to eat. Halfway through her meal of dried zebra uterus she chanced to look up, and what she saw made her choke on her food.

About ten feet above her head hung a skeleton, a rusty chain connecting it to the stone wall. Its empty eye sockets seemed to stare straight at her. Gemma frowned at it. Why would a skeleton chain itself to a cave wall?

"I AM DEAD, I AM DEAD, I HAVE NOTHING IN MY HEAD."

Suddenly Gemma realized that this ugly thing might be of a hostile nature. She jumped up from her sitting position, sprang several feet into the air, and drove her spear in between the creature's ribs. It passed straight through and out through its back. When she pulled it back she made the skeleton swing in its chains, which produced a sharp creaking sound that cut into Gemma's ears like a rusty dagger. She landed on the hard floor and took a few staggering steps back.

"I AM DEAD, I AM DEAD, YOU CAN'T KILL ME WITH YOUR... fuck, that won't rhyme. You should've used something that rhymes with *dead*." The skeleton's voice had changed to a normal, if somewhat vulgar, tone. Gemma looked at it thoughtfully.

"How about *I am here, I am here, you can't kill me with your spear*?" she suggested.

"That's brilliant!" the skeleton exclaimed, its white-glistening teeth grinning down at her. "How did you learn to rhyme so well? I've been here hundreds of years, having nothing to do but make up verses and chants, and still I never thought of that."

Gemma shrugged. "I have a friend who rhymes a lot. I suppose I picked up a thing or two."

"Why have you come here, huntress? No one has dared enter the Temple of the Hippo in a long time. Our cult was vanquished long ago. I am the last one alive. Well, not alive, but the last anyway."

"I... umm... I thought it was some beast's hiding place. And my name is Gemma. Who are you?"

"When I was alive my name was Tom-Tom," the skeleton said. "I suppose it still is, as no one has informed me otherwise. Gemma, would you please help me down? My feet are getting numb."

"Really?" She looked up at the thin, white bones of his feet. They looked perfectly fine to her.

"Of course they aren't. Will you still help me down?"

Gemma regarded the thick iron chains with a frown. "I doubt my spear could cut through those even if I managed a good swing. Considering how far up they are I'd be lucky to give them a half-decent one."

"Oh, that's bad," the skeleton said mournfully. "Don't you have any other sharp objects?"

She thought about this for a while. "Marsha, our tribe's chieftain, always said I have a sharp tongue."

"Then use it."

She did.

Once back on the ground, the skeleton dusted himself off with his bony hands.

"That's one sharp tongue you've got there," he complimented her. "Don't think I've ever seen anything like it."

Gemma was used to having men compliment her, but this was the first time a dead man had done so. It almost made her blush. When he asked her what was wrong she was reluctant to answer.

"I've never met a dead man before," she finally said. "It feels kind of awkward. Besides, you're naked."

Tom-Tom looked down at his body. "Am I a man?" he said, his voice suddenly filled with deep sadness. "Look at my body, Gemma. Where can you find proof I'm a male creature?"

"Umm..." Gemma said. Her eyes found Tom-Tom's pelvic bone, lingering there for the briefest moment before quickly moving away. She blushed again.

"That's right," the skeleton said. "Nowhere. But do you know what the worst of all is?"

She didn't.

"It's that I don't *feel* like a man. Everything that made me a man is gone. I look at you, and judging from my memories you're a very beautiful woman. Still, I don't feel drawn to you the way a man should be drawn to a woman like you. I don't feel anything. Hunger, thirst, lust - they're all gone. Even pain is gone. Can you imagine someone longing to feel pain, simply because it's better than feeling nothing? If I had known death was like this I would never have died."

His words filled Gemma with pity. She hugged the poor creature, telling him she'd try to think of something, some way to give him back his manhood. She wished she'd known how to make Marsha's famous fertility potion. A strong dose of that might have turned this skeleton into a raving sex machine.

The thought made her blush for the third time in a very short while. Thankfully, Tom-Tom didn't notice this time, or if he did he managed to hide it. One of the advantages with being a skeleton is that it's fairly easy to hide your feelings, as you have no facial expressions. This is one reason skeletons are so good at poker.

When they'd finished hugging Gemma returned her attention to the temple.

"What are we going to do about this?" she asked, making a sweeping gesture with her spear.

Tom-Tom thought for a while, and when he spoke again he sounded more cheerful.

"If you like, we can restore the Hippo Cult. It was a glorious society once. Its members were strong in both body and spirit, as wise as they were prosperous. Well, almost, at least."

"I like that," Gemma said, her eyes sparkling with excitement. The light had vanished almost completely, so her eyes might as well have been closed. "I'd like to hear more about this Hippo Cult. What was it like? What happened to it?"

It took Tom-Tom a while to tell her the whole story of the cult. The members had devoted their lives to worshipping the great Hippo God, and this temple had been the centre of that mindless bowing and chanting. The Hippo God (who was a big one for flattery) had granted his disciples wealth and wisdom far beyond anything the African continent had ever seen. There was more food than anyone could eat, more wine than anyone could drink without dying from alcoholic poisoning. There was music everywhere. The cult's members dressed themselves in silk and lace and jewels. The men were extremely handsome, the women hotter than a dragon's breath after it's had Mexican food.

"But how could such an extraordinary people be destroyed?" Gemma asked.

"We were too well off." Tom-Tom sighed. "When our enemies came we were too fat and too drunk to fight. Even so we sold our lives dearly. The ground before the temple's gates was red with enemy blood. Our last stand was in this very chamber, but not even the Hippo God could protect us then. We were slain, one by one, until only one remained. Me. They took me alive and chained me to the wall, where I was left to starve. The power of the Hippo God kept me alive for close to a month. I don't think I even noticed when I died. How 'bout that?"

Gemma thought about that for a while. What if people really didn't notice when they died? What if she was dead herself? She didn't think so. She was young and healthy, and had sustained no major injuries recently.

Emkei, however... The seer was old and fat and didn't smell that good. She'd have to return to the Khadal camp and warn the woman. She had the right to know if she was dead. There were lots of things she wouldn't need to do anymore - eating, sleeping, breathing...

The dead Hippo Cult man made her forget about Emkei when he spoke again. "Oh well, no use mourning what once was. We have a lot of work to do if we are to get this cult going again. The first thing we'll have to do is start a fire. There was always a fire burning on the altar over there." He pointed, but no one saw because of the darkness. "The Hippo God speaks to us through the fire."

"He does?" Gemma said, astounded. "That must be very hot."

"My dear young woman, this is a god we're talking about. They don't feel heat and cold like we do. Well, like you do."

Of course Tom-Tom had no idea what he was talking about. He'd never spoken to a god, and had no idea what it was like to be one. Anyway, they collected some firewood and lit the holy fire on the altar. Because of the divine power of this place, or the skill of the craftsmen who'd manufactured the brazier (Tom-Tom didn't know much about craftsmanship, so he claimed it was the Hippo God's power), the fire would burn for weeks without more firewood being added.

In the light of the fire Gemma could see the large statue of the Hippo God behind the altar. The fire made its ruby eyes seem to shine with a light of their own. Suddenly the large chamber got a completely different feeling to it. It was no longer a ruin full of broken things. No, it was a place of power with memories more ancient than she could imagine, memories that had been awoken from their slumber by herself and this dead creature. It made her feel both big and small at the same time, like a mighty river suddenly being faced with the immensity of the ocean. Or something like that.

"What do we do now?" she asked.

Tom-Tom's hollow eye sockets turned to look at her. "We go find the cult some new members, of course."

~ 4 ~

Bathora woke from her dreams soaked in sweat. Not because she'd had nightmares, but because it was forty-three degrees centigrade in her tent. Having lived in this heat all her life, she didn't think much of it. What she did think of, and not kindly, was the smell that filled her nostrils the way snot did when you woke with a really bad cold. The only difference (except for a number of minor things like Bathora not having a fever, a cough, or even knowing what a cold was) was that she couldn't get rid of it by blowing her nose.

By complete coincidence she attempted to blow her nose into the crook of her arm (she always slept without any clothes on because of the immense heat), and wondered why she'd done such a strange thing. It would obviously not make the smell go away. Muttering to herself, she put on her garment of office and went outside.

It took her a while to locate the source of the bad smell. Actually, it was very obvious from the moment she emerged into the bright morning light, but a number of things distracted her, pulling her attention in a dozen different directions at once.

One was the tall, black man standing about ten paces from her tent, banging a wooden pole into the ground with a stone club. Winston had changed a lot since the last time she saw him. He was three feet taller, had four arms instead of two, and a long tail lashed the ground behind him. He was so intent on his labour he didn't notice her presence.

The sky was green instead of blue, but she dismissed that after only a few moments, deciding it would have no effect on today's work.

One thing that did worry her was the feeling of unease that seemed to crawl up her leg like a small, hairy bug. When she looked down she noticed that there really was a bug crawling up her leg. She brushed it away with her hand and prepared herself to enjoy the wonderful feeling of not having any bugs crawling on her skin.

The uneasy feeling was still there, though. Bathora searched her entire body to see if there were any more bugs, but found nothing. She looked around to see if she could find the source of her unease somewhere in the camp.

At this moment she might have decided to investigate where the nasty smell came from. Instead, she was interrupted by the sound of running footsteps. The sound seemed to come from every direction at once, and when she looked closer she realized why. Today was the day of the yearly running competition, when the members of her tribe - the Telu - competed to see who could run ten laps around the camp in the shortest time.

As the participants began the race whenever they felt like it and there was no way of measuring time, there were always endless hours of discussion about who had actually won. More than once the argument had ended in bloodshed, making it all but impossible for someone to win the race more than once.

One man ran straight into the camp. Bathora pointed at him with a long, accusing finger and yelled furiously.

"Hey! That's cheating! Go back and follow the track, or you'll be disqualified."

The man didn't obey her, a thing that always made her mad. She clenched her fists, threw her head back and screamed her outrage into the unnaturally coloured sky. The running man stopped and regarded her quizzically. The transformation from being a running man to a non-running man could easily lead to confusion, especially among primitive tribes like the Telu.

"What are you doing?" he asked when his mind finally cleared enough to allow him to speak. "Why are you yelling like a maniac?"

Bathora struggled to get the words out between her fits of mad screaming. "You... didn't do... as I said... That... made me... mad...You must... do... what I tell you... to do..."

"Oh. What did you tell me to do, then?"

"I... don't remember..."

Bathora lowered her head and stopped screaming. The man who'd been running a few moments ago but wasn't any longer opened his mouth to say something, but Bathora's madness quickly moved into its next stage. She began spinning round and round while croaking like a frog. It was a very odd thing to behold, and even Bathora's crazed mind registered that it could have devastating effects to her station as the tribe's leader. It would probably be months before people showed her proper respect again.

The non-running man thought for a moment, then said, "Tell me something new, then."

"Like... what...?"

"I don't know. Something. Anything."

All the screaming and croaking had made Bathora's throat sore. The spinning made the world blur around her, and she was beginning to feel sick. She realized that the madness was likely to kill her if it didn't pass soon. *But how do I stop it?*

The Telu had many traditional ways to cure madness. Most of them involved hitting the mad person really hard on the head. Very few people woke up after going through that treatment, so it was deemed very efficient.

It's strange how efficiency loses its appeal when you're waiting for a club to connect with your skull, Bathora thought.

It must be said that thinking wasn't one of Bathora's most prominent skills. Her mind operated at the speed of a continental shelf. A very stable continental shelf.

Right now she needed the continental shelf to leap across a chasm and bring her back to the relative safety provided by sanity. For some reason this non-running man wanted her to say something to him. She tried to come up with something interesting.

"The sky... is green... today," she finally managed.

"I know," he replied. "No need to tell me that."

"But... you asked me... to tell... you something..."

"Yes, tell me to do something. That's the only way to get rid of your madness."

"Oh." Bathora was so surprised she forgot to spin. The world settled around her again, her mind returning to its usual hazy state. She blinked a few times, wondering at what had just happened. The madness appeared to be over, but she wasn't sure how it'd happened. Had she done something to make it stop? Nothing particular popped into her mind. It was simply not there anymore. She stared dumbly at the young man.

"Well?" he said, regarding her impatiently.

"Well what?"

"Tell me what to do."

Bathora shrugged. "Do whatever you want."

The non-running man glared furiously at her. "Is that all you have to say? I'm doing this for you, you know."

"Oh?" Bathora raised an eyebrow. "And why's that?"

"To get rid of your madness, you fat-arsed fool! There are much more pressing matters I should attend to. The least thing you can do is show me some gratitude. It's not like I'm demanding a chest full of gold or some sexual favours."

The insolent rebuke filled her with such rage she almost burst into another fit of mad hollering. She stepped over to the non-running man, grabbed him by the collar of his primitive vest, and forced him down into a kneeling position.

"You're not in a position to demand anything from me," she said, her voice cold as ice. It brought a pleasant chill to the air around her.

The rage instantly drained from the non-running, kneeling man's face. He bowed his head in sudden deference, touching his forehead to the ground.

"I know, Mistress," he said weakly. "Please accept my forgiveness."

"What are you doing here anyway?"

He looked up. "Strange," he said.

"What?"

"The sky is green."

"I know. We discussed it earlier. What of it?"

The kneeling, non-running, upwards-looking man was still looking up.

"I've never thought about how odd a green sky looks until now," he said slowly. "I wonder what made it turn green all of a sudden. Do you think it'll be this way from now on, Chieftain?"

As you can see, Bathora had completely forgotten about the original purpose she'd had when she left her tent. That might in part be because the smell wasn't as bad out here in the open - in fact, she barely noticed it at all. For someone who knew Bathora, however, it came as no surprise that she could only keep a thing in her mind until something new arrived to claim her attention. After that it had to place itself last in line and wait for her to notice it again.

She was still blissfully unaware of the most critical of these matters.

"Did you want anything?" she asked the non-running, kneeling, upwards-looking, wondering man.

"Oh yes." The man looked at her again. "My name is Gideon. I'm one of the hunters."

"So?" Bathora wasn't very interested in hunting. As long as there was food on her plate whenever she was hungry she didn't care how it got there. Or what it was, for that matter.

"My lady, I was journeying through the outskirts of the jungle to the south when something really strange happened."

Bathora chuckled to herself. "What? A naked woman leapt out from a bush and asked you to have sex with her?"

That made Gideon's mouth drop halfway to the ground. This wasn't a mere saying; neither was it the effect of a physical abnormality. He was simply still kneeling with his face fairly close to the ground. Anyway, the reason for his astonishment was that Bathora had just inadvertently described his greatest fantasy.

"No." His voice was barely a whisper.

"What then?"

He cleared his throat. "It was a vision, a revelation. A mist rose up from the river, and from it a voice spoke to me."

Bathora was suddenly all ears. Supernatural mysteries had always fascinated her. Winston's shape-shifting, for example, tended to unnerve most of the Telu members, but for some reason it always made Bathora feel slightly horny.

"What did it say?" she asked.

Gideon shrugged. "It told me there were zebras further to the west."

"Zebras?"

"That's what it said." Gideon frowned down at the ground. "I don't know if I believe it. There haven't been any zebras this far north for as long as anyone can remember."

This conversation continued to make Bathora more and more confused, drawing her further and further away from the problem she'd come here to deal with.

"Why would it tell you there were zebras if there weren't any?" she asked. "That's one poor excuse for a revelation voice. We have soothsayers here in the camp who can do better than that."

"Yes," Gideon said, executing a nod that almost made him smack his head into the ground. "Perhaps it was trying to deceive me. You know, like directing me to a place where I'd never find my true destiny."

Bathora snorted. "Whatever. So, was that all you wanted to tell me?"

"Of course not," Gideon said, finally deciding it was safe to get back to his feet. "As I didn't believe the strange voice, I went east instead of west. And then I turned south."

"Why?"

"Because I ran into a cliff and couldn't continue further east. Anyway, my new route took me close to the old temple of the Hippo Cult."

Bathora hissed at that. The Hippo Cult had been the Telu tribe's deadliest enemy throughout its history. There had been generations of war between them, and more people than one could count had been killed. Bathora could only count to six, but that was of no importance here.

The Hippo Cult had finally been destroyed and the temple was now no more than a hollow ruin. Its very name still brought acid to her mouth, though. She spat on the ground, and her saliva burned itself smoking into the dirt.

"I hope you didn't enter the temple," she said reproachfully. "There may still be evil at work there. Such a foul place can never be fully cleansed."

"I didn't," Gideon said. "I turned back when I was about a hundred paces from it. That was when I saw the smoke."

"Smoke? What smoke?"

"The smoke rising from the temple. That was why I came here, to tell you about it."

Bathora felt all cold inside. It was a breathtaking contrast to the heat she felt on the outside. The day grew hotter with every minute. Some of the participants in the running competition had collapsed and lay panting on the ground. Bathora made a mental note that perhaps there wouldn't be any bloodshed this year.

"Why didn't you tell me this at once?" she demanded.

Gideon shrugged. "I tried, but you kept interrupting me."

"I did not!"

Sighing, Gideon gave his mentally deficient chieftain an impatient look. "Are we going to stand here and argue all day, or are you going to do something about the Hippo Cult?"

"We're going to argue. No one throws accusations like that at me and walks away unpunished."

"Watch me." Gideon turned and began walking away, seemingly without effort.

"Wait!" Bathora ran after him and grabbed him by the back of his buffalo hide vest. "How did you do that?"

Gideon turned his head and regarded her curiously. "How did I do what?"

"Walk away from me unpunished. I told you you couldn't do that."

"Well, maybe it was because I didn't throw anything at you."

Bathora's forehead furrowed into deep creases. It made her look several years older than her actual age of twenty-four. Strangely, it didn't add any wisdom to her features. Many people claim to get wiser with age, but very few actually manage it. Bathora had never made any claims about wisdom, probably because she found the word very difficult to pronounce.

"Why would that be of any importance?" she asked with the frustrated tone of someone who felt the conversation was about to slip out of their hands.

Gideon spread his arms in a placating gesture. "You said no one threw accusations at you and walked away unpunished. I merely spoke the accusation, never threw anything. So why shouldn't I be able to walk away?"

"Hmmm." Bathora rubbed her chin thoughtfully (if such an expression could be used on a member of the Telu tribe). "I suppose you have a point there. I should think of some other threat to use on you."

By now, Bathora had forgotten not only about the bad smell in her tent, but also about the alarming news regarding the Hippo Cult. She would probably have spent the rest of the day trying to come up with a suitable threat for the young man if he hadn't incidentally brought her mind back to her initial concern.

He looked past her, eyes suddenly widening. "There's a man pissing on your tent!"

Bathora turned around, but the vehemence of her movement left her looking in the wrong direction. Her eyes fell on one of the runners, lying senseless in the dust. She gave him a disapproving frown.

"What a pitiful excuse for an athlete," she muttered.

"Hey! That's not a very nice thing to say," the runner gasped. "I did my best. As our tribe's chieftain you should be more supportive."

"I'll be supportive to those who deserve it!" Bathora snapped. "And to those who call me slim and beautiful. Now, where was I going? All the mess I've had to endure today has made me dizzy."

Gideon pointed to her left. "That way, Chieftain."

"Thank you." She turned and began walking back towards her tent. Before she'd taken three steps she noticed the strange-looking man standing by its side, spraying urine all over it. She turned to face Gideon, who'd been following close behind her, but because of his longer legs he was still on his second step.

"There's a man pissing on my tent!" she exclaimed. "Why is he doing that?"

"Probably because he needed to," Gideon said.

Bathora moved swiftly towards the stranger. "Hey! You there! Stop that!"

The stranger looked up. "It's not that easy, you know."

She regarded him closely, so closely her nose sometimes touched his robe. It was a very peculiar garment - a long, brown thing looking like it was made of some sort of hide, but thinner and softer than any animal hide Bathora had ever seen. Whatever animal it was taken from must be a pretty small one, for it was made of a multitude of patches sewn together with sinew. The patches varied in size from that of her forearm to something that might match her back. Bones of all kinds had been sewn all over it, so many the cloak rattled softly as the man moved. Bathora took one of the bones between two fingers and tugged softly. It didn't come loose.

The stranger sniffed the air between them, then licked his lips. "You smell nice," he said. "And you have beautiful eyes."

"Thanks." Bathora said, smiling happily. "They change colour depending on what mood I'm in."

"Really?"

"Yeah. They're usually dark brown, but when I get angry or excited they glow like amber."

The stranger was still emptying his bladder all over her tent wall. "That's fascinating. I've never seen eyes like that before. They make you a very desirable woman."

"It's very kind of you to say so," Bathora said. "Not that I haven't heard it before, of course. Lots of men find them attractive, same as with my bum. What do you think of that piece, by the way?" She turned sideways to expose the half-moon shaped protuberance her plump hip-section made.

The stranger sized her up with his eyes as if she was a prime cut of meat. "Very nice. Perhaps I can get to know that part of you better later on. Right now I have more important business to discuss with you."

"Such as pissing on my tent?"

"No." The stranger put his thing back inside his cloak and leered even more intently at her. Bathora suddenly felt as if she had no clothes on. Or rather, as if she didn't have any skin anymore. At first it made her uneasy, but she got used to it after a while. She wondered if you could get used to not having any skin. She decided to try it some day.

"You're Bathora, right?" the stranger continued. "Chieftain of the Telu tribe?"

"Yes, and you are?"

"Samoul, of the shamans. I've come all the way from my people's home in the swamplands to discuss a matter of utmost importance."

Bathora scratched her head. Her long, dark hair was tangled and clammy with sweat. She'd have to wash it in one of the mountain streams some time soon. It must've been a year since last time. Or maybe two.

"You must have come to the wrong place," she told him. "We live a quiet and peaceful life here. What could possibly be important enough for someone to travel halfway across the world to find me?"

"Lots of things," Samoul said. "And the swamps really aren't that far away. Anyway, are you sure there isn't something you've been worrying about? Some piece of news unsettling your stomach? A shadow from the past, suddenly come back to haunt you?"

Bathora thought for a moment. "Well, there was an unpleasant smell this morning, but I think that's just been sorted out. No, nothing out of the ordinary in a long time."

"What about the revival of the Hippo Cult?"

"It's been revived?"

The shaman blinked. Actually, he'd been blinking throughout their conversation, but no one saw fit to mention it until now. Bathora, however, hadn't blinked in nearly twenty minutes. Her eyes were beginning to water. She wondered where she'd put her handkerchief.

"You were told about the Hippo Cult less than half an hour ago," Samoul informed her. "It made you really upset. You were trying to think of a way to obliterate the cult once and for all. Your ancestors thought they succeeded in doing that, but they were obviously wrong. The cult has risen again. The deadliest enemy ever known to the Telu tribe is back, looking for vengeance."

Bathora waved her hand at him. "Yes, yes, I know that. I would have found a way to deal with this damnable cult if you hadn't kept me occupied with your endless talk about eyes and bums and swamps."

"Would you now?" Samoul looked amused. "Well, then. Tell me."

"Tell you what?"

"How you plan to deal with the Hippo Cult."

"I haven't thought of anything yet."

Samoul shook his head ruefully. "And you never will. The Telu tribe is too weak for another war. Most of your men can't even run ten laps around your camp. Their wisdom is but a shadow of what it once was. Soon the Hippo Cult will have gathered enough strength to crush you in a single blow. Only I can save you."

This time Bathora blinked. "You? How?"

"I will show you the way to the swamplands. There you will find the answer."

"What answer?"

The shaman was markedly impatient now. "The answer to how you'll defeat the Hippo Cult."

"Why do I have to go to the swamplands to do that? Swamps are smelly, and full of rats and snakes and lizards. What if I'm eaten?"

He laughed. "You won't have to worry about any rats or lizards or snakes eating you. I'll make sure you reach our dwellings safely. That's a promise, on my honour as a shaman."

"What kind of honour do shamans have?" Bathora asked, suddenly suspicious.

"Err... pretty much the same as everyone else, I suppose." The shaman donned his most charming smile. "Don't worry, fair Bathora. My people are very concerned about your health and well-being. They'd grieve deeply if any of your parts were lost on the way."

"Thanks." She smiled at him. "That's very kind of them."

Samoul gave her a satisfied nod, then allowed his eyes to examine her from top to bottom. She was a very beautiful woman, he noted. The round, fleshy curves of her body made his mouth water.

She must've noticed the look in his eyes, because she suddenly asked. "Would you like something to eat before we leave?"

"I would, but there's no time," he said, voice heavy with regret. "Every moment we waste gives the Hippo Cult time to grow a little stronger. We must leave at once."

"Okay. Just give me a moment to gather some men."

She looked at the participants in the running contest, lying scattered all over the camp. Not a single one remained on the track. It looked like she'd have to literally gather them up.

"No," Samoul said. "You must go alone."

Bathora raised a questioning eyebrow. "Oh? Why's that?"

"Because." His voice sank to a whisper as he leaned closer to her. "If you don't, you'll be betrayed."

She turned her head slightly, putting one hand behind her ear. "I didn't get that. Speak louder, please."

"IF YOU DON'T, YOU'LL BE BETRAYED!!"

Bathora jumped back, startled by the shaman's suddenly booming voice.

"No need to shout," she said reproachfully. Then a slight smile suddenly curved her lips. "So it'll only be you and me, huh? I must warn you, I snore something dreadful."

The shaman frowned. "I'll have to find something to put in my ears, then. I'm very sensitive to sounds when I sleep. My own breathing woke me up once."

They decided to think of a solution to this problem on the road. Bathora went over to where her camel was tethered and tried to mount it. She failed. Frowning, she tried again, but with the same result. The damned thing seemed to have grown taller since last time she rode it. She took a step back and glared at it.

"What the hell is wrong with you?" she shouted.

Samoul had caught up with her. He eyed the animal, scratching his chin with a long fingernail. "That's a giraffe, my lady. The camels are over there." He pointed.

"Oh." Bathora wondered why she hadn't noticed this before. It seemed so very obvious now that the shaman had pointed it out to her. What if her perception had played other tricks on her as well? What if this man wasn't a shaman at all, but some sort of dreadful monster? What if she was a monster herself?

After some consideration she decided that to be very unlikely. People would have screamed and run away if she'd been a monster. She wasn't too sure about that shaman, though. It was something about the way he stood there, looking at her as if she was a complete idiot. It wouldn't surprise her if he suddenly transformed into a twelve-foot demon right there before her eyes. A twenty-foot demon, now, that would have been a surprise, or if he'd transformed behind her eyes instead of before them. She reminded herself she'd have to look at things more closely from now on.

"All right, lead the way," she said when she was finally seated on her camel's back. Samoul had thankfully brought his own riding animal, or Bathora might've had to nick one from one of her tribesmen. She didn't want to think about all the explaining she'd have to do if someone caught her stealing camels from her own people. Even an intelligent, good-looking chieftain like her might have trouble getting out of a fix like that.

As the sun climbed towards its noon peak the two riders set out westwards across the barren, rocky landscape surrounding the Telu camp. Behind them, some of the runners had recovered enough to get up on their hands and knees.

As they watched their chieftain vanish into the distance they wondered if they'd ever see her again.

They wouldn't, and no one could even begin to fathom the effect her departure would have on the tribe's future.

~ 5 ~

People have always wondered what makes a group of humans suddenly decide to settle down together and become a tribe. Some have compared it to people meeting for the first time in a bar. At first they more or less refuse to acknowledge each other's existence, but after a certain number of pints they suddenly realize they have a lot of things in common and sit down at a table to discuss them.

Seeing as this would never have happened if the people involved were sober, the theory has been discarded as having nothing to do with the natural behaviour of humans. The scientists responsible of this unjust dismissal belong to the kind that vigorously advocate the theory that humans demonstrate irrational behaviour when under the influence of alcohol, refusing to consider the possibility that it might actually be the other way around.

Another theory is based on the need of getting things done that you can't (or don't want to) do yourself. We can demonstrate this theory with a very simplified example:

Imagine a man and a woman meeting randomly at a pub (night clubs are usually too noisy for conversations involving more than one word at a time). The woman might ask, "Do you know how to fix cars?" If she's lucky, the man will reply, "Yes, I do. Do you know how to cook?" If the woman possesses this skill so uncommon among the male part of the population, the two might agree they complement each other well enough to start a family and will go home to begin work on their first unit of offspring.

This theory could successfully be applied to a group of primitive people a couple of thousand years ago. Take a couple of good hunters, a few builders, a glutton or two talented at both preparing and consuming food, plus someone who knows how to take care of all the injuries the aforementioned people are likely to inflict upon themselves, and you have a nice little tribe. Most of these characters can still be found in most of today's pubs, and their behaviour has changed surprisingly little over the millennia.

Marsha wouldn't have enjoyed a night at the pub very much. It was bad enough to be in charge of a bunch of nutcases leading fairly uncomplicated lives. Having to look after them while they yelled for more beer, ran off to stuff their mouths full of kebab, or randomly passed out while visiting the rest rooms would've been too much for any one person. The noise and cigarette smoke would also be very annoying to someone used to the lucidity and stillness of a jungle glade.

Most of her fellow tribesmen were more likely to have enjoyed a night out, and would probably have fit right in among the pub crawlers of today (or any period of time, for that matter).

She looked at the bowl of stew in her hand. Today it had been Pebe's turn to hunt for food, which always made things interesting in a somewhat scary way.

"What's this?" she asked, pointing at what looked very much like small pebbles.

"Pieces of antelope meat," Pebe said, somehow managing to keep a straight face. "They'd be more tender if I'd cooked them longer, but I didn't want to keep you waiting. The spinach got nice and soft, at least."

Marsha examined the long, green things. They were definitely grass. The thought of what this so-called stew would do to her digestive system made her shudder. Not wanting to hurt the young man's feelings, she put a spoonful of it into her mouth and swallowed without chewing.

She glanced at Emkei, who ate with a healthy appetite. "Is the food to your liking, Emkei?" she asked.

The fat woman nodded vigorously while chewing for all she was worth. "Yes, I needed something solid to steady my bowels. You'll have to give me the recipe, Pebe. We should have this more often."

Putting down her bowl, Marsha made a mental note never to eat anything the old seer cooked.

They'd spent three long days looking for Gemma. When the young woman didn't return from her hunting expedition Marsha grew worried and started to ask the other Khadal people if they'd seen any signs of her. Most of them seemed to have forgotten about Gemma altogether, forcing Marsha to describe her in shameless detail before they showed any sign of recollection. After some additional inquiries Marsha concluded that no one had seen Gemma since the night she went hunting for buffalo.

She'd decided to arrange an expedition to search for the beautiful young woman. Consulting her friends, she quickly realized she wouldn't get much help there. Pebe claimed he'd better take care of the rescue operation himself, seeing as Gemma might have journeyed into dangerous territory where only the bravest of warriors (like himself) should set foot. Emkei said travelling made her joints ache and that she'd heard the food was terrible in other parts of the country. The only one providing some vague resemblance of useful advice was Amanda, who had no reason to worry about either dangers or the supply of food.

"We should divide the tribe into smaller parties," she said as she brushed her long, dark hair with a bone comb. "That way we'll be able to search a larger area."

"I'm not sure," Marsha said thoughtfully. Her inner vision pictured a scenario where Khadal people ran around all over the surrounding countryside, no one remembering where they were going or where they'd come from.

Then she imagined what would be written in the chronicles about this period of time. *During the incompetent leadership of Marsha, chaos and division fell upon the Khadal. The tribe scattered across the African continent, and a few years later all memory of them had been lost.*

"No," she said more firmly. "I think we'd have a better chance of success if only the four of us left. There'd be no way for the different groups to communicate with each other once they were out in the wild, and many would probably get lost. The four of us ought to be enough to find Gemma."

Amanda had nodded in agreement. "You have a point there, Chief. I wouldn't want to be in a company with Pebe in charge."

So the four of them had set out alone. Some of the Khadal children had come to witness their departure, but most had lost interest pretty quickly. The tribe's adult members barely seemed to notice that something out of the ordinary was happening.

Because Marsha was uncommonly clever for a Khadal member, she went to look for Gemma on the savannah, the place any sensible person would have chosen for a hunt. She'd underestimated Gemma's airheadedness completely, never considering the woman to be stupid enough to go hunting in the thick, dark jungle. Thus her mission was doomed to fail before she'd taken a dozen steps.

There was no need to dig a latrine pit after Pebe's indigestible food, so the four travellers went to sleep early. They didn't post a guard, and escaped being eaten by a flock of lions by pure luck. The lions had had a fat, juicy buffalo for lunch, but because of the chemicals in the shrub the buffalo had eaten its muscle tissue had turned into highly alcoholic beef. The lions, who were on their way to the place where Marsha and her friends chose to make camp, got seriously inebriated and began quarrelling about who had slept with each other's wives.

The argument culminated in a big fight where all the lions were killed, except one who later fell into a river and drowned. A short time later a large number of dead fish were found floating on the surface. The members of a primitive tribe living mostly on fish the river provided suddenly found themselves feeling very frolicsome one night after dinner. Some began dancing naked in the firelight and many women ended up pregnant. Afterwards all agreed they'd had one hell of a night.

Marsha awoke at dawn the next day. Her stomach still felt full, so she decided to skip breakfast. She woke Amanda and Emkei and sent them to fetch water. Pebe seemed to be deep in some dream, for when she shook him he moaned and said, "Get the oranges out of your nose and put your head back on so we can finish planting the shoes." She didn't ask him about it when he finally opened his eyes and sat up.

They continued west across the savannah, looking everywhere for signs of Gemma. Marsha called her name over and over, sounding very much like someone looking for a runaway dog. Amanda made up appealing verses like "*Gemma, Gemma, come back here! We are running out of beer*!" and "*Where is Gemma, where is she? Is she sitting in a tree? Please come down and have a nap. Pebe wants you on his lap*!"

The latter one caused Pebe to sulk for an hour, walking by himself and kicking the tall grass that covered the ground. When he was done sulking he spent quite some time asking if the women thought Gemma would consider sitting on his lap for a while. They told him she probably would, and after making them reassure him some twenty-odd times he decided she would and was content.

In the afternoon they decided to split up in order to cover more ground. Marsha pointed at a grove of tall trees a few miles ahead of them and told them to regroup there. She took the southernmost path, looking for Gemma under stones and behind large plants. She found a lot of worms and two eggs, but no Gemma.

The alarming call of a flock of birds made her look around, and suddenly she was stiff with fear. A leopard was running towards her at full speed, its red tongue hanging out between sharp, white teeth. It emitted low, hungry growls as it sprinted closer.

She started running but knew it'd do no good. There were only two known cases in the history of the Khadal tribe where a human had outrun a leopard. The first was when the leopard had gotten its legs entangled in some sticky, snake-like plant and kept falling over, allowing the group of chased hunters to stop and have a good laugh at the poor, struggling beast.

The other case was when a terribly witty woman named Balooetta had tied the tails of two sleeping leopards together. When the animals woke up she and her friend Leena ran in opposite directions. The leopards decided to go after one woman each, and naturally didn't come very far.

Some people argued that this should count as two cases, as two leopards were involved, but they were overruled because it was decided that because the leopards were tied together they should count as one animal. After that some people tried to escape taxes by tying themselves together and claiming to be only one person.

Marsha ran as fast as she could, but the leopard was soon on her. It jumped, knocking her down with its paws. She lay there in the grass, waiting for the animal's cruel teeth to cut into her flesh, but instead it stroked itself against her, licked her face and purred like a tame kitten. Marsha didn't believe her eyes, but managed to pat the creature on its head, saying it was a good boy. The leopard beamed with happiness.

Pebe and Emkei made big eyes when they saw her new companion. Amanda had gone off to hunt for food and would rejoin them later in the evening. The leopard let Marsha ride on its back, which was very uncomfortable in the beginning but got more and more pleasant as she got used to it.

Emkei also wanted to ride, but the animal collapsed under her weight and walked with a heavy limp for over an hour. Pebe found this unbelievably amusing and teased Emkei endlessly about it. Finally, she grew angry and sat on him too. After that he didn't find the idea funny anymore.

When the sun sank towards the horizon like an orange on an acid trip they made camp. The leopard had recovered from Emkei's unsuccessful attempt at riding and was wrestling playfully with Marsha. Pebe was still suffering from the seer's ungentle treatment and lay groaning on the ground, claiming his back was broken. Emkei herself was knitting.

Somewhere in the distance a bird was attacked by a furious swarm of mosquitoes and fled screaming in search for a river where it could submerge itself. The mosquitoes shaped a mocking formation and laughed scornfully at it. Unfortunately, their laughter didn't sound very different from the sound their tiny wings normally made, so the effect was more or less lost.

Suddenly the leopard was lifted six feet into the air. Astonished, Marsha looked up. Amanda, newly returned from her hunting trip, had taken the large animal by its tail and was now swinging it in circles above her head. The fear-stricken beast screamed and waved its paws like a small kitten who'd been taken away from its food. Amanda prepared herself to slam the animal down on the ground with uncompromising force.

"No!" Marsha jumped to her feet. "Amanda, don't!"

The young woman gave her chieftain a puzzled look. "It was about to kill you," she said.

Marsha shook her head. "No, we were only playing. It... it's sort of like a pet."

"Oh." Amanda put the leopard down. It quickly slunk away and hid behind Marsha, whimpering softly. Pebe exchanged an understanding look with the poor animal. Marsha squatted beside it and began scratching it behind an ear. Emkei blew her nose into her knitting. At that moment the small group of people looked incredibly odd.

The food that night turned out to be infinitely better than the night before. Amanda had caught an ostrich and carried it back beneath one arm. The meat was delicious, and there were fresh, crispy vegetables to go with it.

They ate with good appetite while the leopard gnawed the bones clean. It growled when Emkei leaned over to snatch back a wing bone for herself, but when the seer moved her humongous rump as if to seat herself on it again it yelped and hid behind Marsha. Pebe quickly busied himself with collecting the bowls, eager to get as far away from Emkei as possible.

The next day was very much like the day before, except that their bowels felt a lot better. Well, except Emkei's, of course. Her healthy appetite combined with the digestion of a dead panda kept her in a constant state of indescribable bubbling gases and sour regurgitation. This might explain why she'd never got married. Grass died where Emkei sat, and Marsha had seen insects drop dead after passing too close to the seer's mouth when she belched.

In the afternoon they suddenly heard faint booming sounds that made the ground shake beneath their feet. At first Marsha thought they came from Emkei, but the complete absence of smell eliminated that possibility.

The sounds came closer, until they suddenly saw large, hulking shapes atop a low ridge ahead of them. Loud, trumpeting sounds were mixed with shrill screams. It sounded like a jazz festival gone completely off the wall.

"It's the Elephant People!" Pebe yelled. "We're doomed!"

Marsha felt a chill run down her spine. She'd heard frightening tales about the Elephant People all the way from her childhood. They were said to be a barbaric people with half-human faces, fighting with spears of fire. In battle they rode large, monstrous beasts that couldn't be killed, blood-thirsty zombies who did everything their masters commanded.

Many mothers used these tales to frighten their children into doing things they didn't want to do, like being silent so the grown-ups wouldn't miss any of the important gossip that dominated their evening conversations.

"The Elephant People never existed," Amanda snorted. "They're just phantasms out of legend."

"They're not!" Pebe protested.

"Oh? Do you know anyone who's actually seen them?"

"Are you mad?" Pebe shouted, panic making his voice shrill. "No one who's seen the Elephant People lives to tell others about it!"

Amanda laughed. "That's the classic excuse. All sensible people know there's no such thing as an Elephant People. Or if there was they must have died out hundreds of years ago."

"It looks like all those sensible people were wrong," Marsha said. "Remind me never to trust the majority again."

Her companions turned to look the way she pointed. The huge creatures were now so close their elephantness couldn't be questioned. There were almost a dozen of them, curved tusks pointing majestically into the air as their massive legs plodded through the tall grass.

"So?" Amanda said defensively. "They're just large beasts, not fire-breathing demons. Nothing to be afraid of."

"What do we do?" Pebe sounded as if there were more than enough things to be afraid of. "Marsha?"

Marsha's first impulse was to shout "*Run*!", but she soon realized that wouldn't do them much good. The elephants were already halfway down the hillside, lumbering on at a speed Marsha and her friends wouldn't manage to keep for more than a few hundred meters. Emkei wasn't likely to manage much speed at all, and she wasn't too sure about Pebe, either. Rumour said Emkei had once beaten the young man in a running competition. It sounded too unbelievable to not be true.

The elephants closed in, and before Marsha knew it she was looking at a scene taken from a madman's fantasies.

Pebe was standing in front of one of the huge animals, shouting and waving his spear at it as if trying to chase off a hyena. The elephant looked at him, then grabbed him with its trunk and lifted him thirty feet into the air. Pebe's screams, which had at least been vaguely threatening at first, now changed into boyish shrieks of blind terror. The elephant shook him mercilessly while its rider laughed like a mad demon watching two clowns throw pies into each other's faces.

Another beast had wound its trunk around Emkei and struggled to lift her. After a while it gave up and lumbered away with its head hanging in shame. Emkei took a wedge of cheese from her pack and began devouring it happily.

Off to the right Amanda stood, one hand holding down an elephant's trunk while the other delivered hammer-like blows to its head. The poor animal tried desperately to get away, but Amanda kept a firm grip on its trunk while the blows kept falling. The animal's rider let out screams of outrage from its back.

A big elephant charged in Marsha's direction, trumpeting as its rider urged it forwards. The beast towered above Marsha like a mountain on four legs. She watched it approach, every muscle in her body paralyzed by fear.

A mighty roar answered the elephant's trumpeting as the leopard leaped in front of Marsha. It looked terribly small compared to its enormous opponent, but appeared intent on defending Marsha to the death. The elephant looked down at it, more amused than threatened.

Baring its teeth, the leopard jumped at the elephant's foreleg. The huge animal stomped down on it with all its brutal force, crushing the poor thing to death. This woke Marsha from her numbness, and she screamed in anger and grief. Raising her spear, she went to avenge her brave pet.

She ran between the elephant's legs like a rat in a labyrinth, stabbing here and there without causing any harm worth speaking of. The elephant lowered its head and gave her a curious look, apparently uncertain what to make of the silly little creature at its feet.

"Stop it, you fool! All of you, stop it!"

The voice came from the large beast's rider. It was so commanding that everyone, both atop elephants and on the ground (and Pebe still in mid-air), stopped and turned. The rider climbed down the elephant's side via a rope ladder. Marsha saw that it was a tall woman, wearing a mask resembling some vaguely elephantine demon. Her clothes were made of brown leather and showed off her slim figure very nicely. She took off her mask and smiled at Marsha.

"Greetings, honoured travellers," she said, her voice as chirpy as that of a bird who'd gotten vodka in its water. "I am Tiwi, by the grace of the gods queen of the Elephant People. Well, more of a goddess than a queen, if I may say so, and I'm not just talking about my beauty. I can start a thunderstorm just by waving my hand slightly, and slay monsters by the wink of an eye."

"Oh yeah?" said Pebe, who'd been put back on solid ground. "That doesn't make you a bloody goddess. I can do things you've never even dreamed of."

The beautiful young woman turned her large, gleaming eyes to regard him. "I doubt that, my lowly friend. All you seem able to do is produce girlish screams when lifted off your feet. Or were you trying to defeat us by making us laugh ourselves senseless?"

Pebe's face turned as red as a potato painted the wrong colour. "I can do mighty and powerful things," he murmured.

"Yeah? Like what?"

He thought for a moment. "I can eat a hundred grapes in fifty seconds."

Tiwi feigned astonishment. "Really? That's very impressive."

"Without using my hands."

"That's still nothing," Tiwi said. "I've drunk the milk from twenty coconuts in thirty seconds. Through my *nose*!"

"I don't believe you," Pebe snorted.

Tiwi's pretty face was outraged. "What do you mean you don't believe me? I'm the most divine creature on this earth. Doubting me is like the worst kind of blasphemy imaginable. I would have you executed if you weren't such a pitiful little thing." She looked down at Pebe, who was a head shorter than her. He took a step back.

Marsha cleared her throat. "Well, if the two of you have nothing more to say we'd appreciate it if you let us continue our journey. We're looking for one of our friends. I don't suppose you've seen her? Young woman, nice butt, carrying a spear?"

"No, we haven't," Tiwi said, turning back to Marsha.

"Oh, okay. I suppose we'll have to keep looking, then."

"I'm afraid you can't," Tiwi said, shaking her head. "You'll have to come with us to our camp. It's not far."

"But we don't want to..."

"Perhaps not, but you have to."

Marsha frowned at the tall woman. "Are you saying we're prisoners?"

"No, it's just that you can't leave."

"That sounds very much like being a prisoner to me."

Tiwi shook her head again, making her glossy black hair swing around her shoulders.

"Not at all," she said. "A prisoner is imprisoned. You're just not allowed to go where you want. That's a restriction, not imprisonment."

"I'll show you what I think of your *restrictions*!" Amanda took a few steps forward, fists raised in a menacing gesture. Marsha stepped in front of her.

"No, Amanda. They have archers with bowstrings drawn. We'll go with these people. It's obvious they don't intend to harm us."

"That's right," Tiwi said cheerfully. "We just want you to come with us. We'll show you all the hospitality you require. Hannah! Embolo!"

Two elephants came closer. Atop one of them was a man with a dark cloth covering his eyes, on the other a woman with strange sounds coming from her open mouth. Tiwi smiled when she saw Marsha's confused expression.

"Embolo is blind," she explained. "Hannah is our gargling woman. What is it you polish your throat with today, sweetheart?"

The gargling woman swallowed, then spoke. "Gorilla brains mixed with rhino urine and vomit from a man who's been fed his dead mother's liver." She took a bottle and refilled her mouth. The gargling resumed.

"The gargling woman is in contact with the Elephant God," Tiwi informed them. "It's a very important position in our tribe. Not as important as mine, of course," she added self-assuredly.

"I'm not going anywhere near that woman," Pebe said. "If she hiccups I might get that stuff all over me, and I'd rather have Emkei sit on me again than that."

"Emkei and Amanda will ride with her," Marsha declared. "And Pebe and I will ride with the blind man."

"Right." Tiwi nodded. "Embolo, you're taking these two on your animal."

"I see," the blind man said.

"No, you don't, but that's not important right now." Tiwi began climbing back onto her own mount. Pebe followed her every move with his eyes, no doubt enjoying what he saw. Marsha shook her head. If there ever was a people more insane than the Khadal, this had to be it.

The Elephant People's camp was a tight cluster of tents, surrounded by the tribe's sacred animals. There must've been fifty of the huge, grey beasts, fettered to thick iron poles dug deep into the ground. Marsha suspected the elephants were strong enough to pull up the poles and escape, but obviously they weren't smart enough to realize that. Some of them trumpeted when they saw their friends arrive.

The journey back to the camp had taken more time than expected, as Emkei had proved too heavy to get up onto her elephant's back. The old seer had had to walk the entire way, and once she had to take a half-hour break because her bowels made themselves reminded. The pile she left behind was larger than the one the elephant next to her produced.

When they'd dismounted the four of them were split up and taken to different tents. Tiwi brought Marsha to a big, dark one. When her eyes had adjusted to the dim light inside she saw several large, black men with broad-bladed spears in their hands. She was completely surrounded. Outraged, she turned to Tiwi.

"You said you wouldn't imprison us! You're a liar!"

The queen smiled and shook her head. "You're not imprisoned. We just have to keep you in this tent while I take care of some business. These men will look after you."

She left the tent. The armed men closed in on Marsha, delight gleaming in their dark eyes.

"Come, little woman," one said. "Let's play."

~ 6 ~

The Cult of the Raven God is an old society, and by old I don't mean old as in "The milk has gone old", nor as in "Marqamil is too old to date the sexy Lizbug". No, I mean *really* old. Its roots go all the way back to the days of Hippodemus IV - a man who, in his own time, was known mostly for his huge appetite and equally huge girth.

No one back then could have imagined that this fat oaf would ever make an imprint on history. If he hadn't – by pure chance – chosen the chamber that later became the High Priest's office as the residence for his huge bulk, he'd never have ended up as the cult's founder in the chronicles dealing with its early days.

The cult's real founder was a young woman named Marydette. As opposed to Hippodemus she actually knew something about the Raven God, and if she hadn't died at such a young age she'd probably have turned the Raven Cult into something worthy of its name.

Unfortunately Hippodemus managed to ruin most of the work she'd done, even robbing her of her place in the history books. This was a bloody shame, because Marydette was a really clever girl, far from bad-looking as well as an excellent kisser.

Ashlob, one of the cult's initiates, was only a half-decent kisser. This was mostly an effect of her joining the Raven Cult at a very young age and hence never got many opportunities to practice. She was short, nice, and at the moment slightly drunk – a result of having had no one to share her bottle of wine with at lunch and therefore drinking it all herself.

Standing in the doorway to his office, she regarded Marqamil with dark brown eyes while twisting a lock of dark brown hair between her fingers. Her eyes looked almost black where they peered out from her pale face, but surprisingly her hair looked as it always did where it framed that same face. If Ashlob had known about this she'd probably have considered it a phenomenon no one but the Raven God himself could've explained. What she didn't know was that the Raven God didn't care how her eyes and hair looked, as long as she didn't look at him while he was peeing.

She'd stood like that for almost an hour, not because she waited for the High Priest to notice her, but because she waited for the universe to move into the right spot. Twisting her hair helped her perceive the intricate patterns of existence that most people were unable to see or understand. She didn't think any less of them because of those inabilities, of course. Some people were born with this talent and others weren't. It was as simple as that. She twisted her hair some more and waited for the signal.

As you may have guessed, Ashlob suffered from as many mental disorders as there were stars in the sky. This had totally ruined her childhood dreams of becoming a healer. People had bled to death while Ashlob waited for the molecules in the air to stop bouncing and allow her to pick up the bandage. Once she was summoned to help delivering a baby, but by the time she'd finished all the rituals that process demanded the child had learned to walk and speak three dozen words.

A religious cult had been the perfect place for a woman suffering from this extreme form of compulsive behaviour. Ashlob quickly learned to blend her own personal rituals into those associated with worship of the Raven God. No one would find it strange when the member of such a cult walked in circles while muttering obscure things to herself. Most wouldn't be able to distinguish it from what generally passed for normal cult behaviour.

Ashlob had drawn the eyes of many of the cult's male members until the day Lizbug appeared, about six months ago. Since then everyone had ignored her. This didn't upset her in any way, seeing as she was a devoted worshipper of the Raven God and cared nothing about romance or sex.

This would've made her a suitable choice for the position as High Priest. Even with the multitude of mental illnesses she suffered from she'd probably do a much better job than Marqamil. It was also likely that her fellow cult members would have supported her had she chosen to challenge the current High Priest.

This idea had never occurred to Ashlob, who was completely satisfied with her life as a cleric. The only thing she wasn't satisfied with was the food, which was quite tasteless and lacked both variation and class.

Suddenly the electric signals found their way through the tangled thicket of her mind and she jerked into receptiveness.

"High Priest," she said timidly. "I'm sorry to disturb you while you work, but your presence is required."

Marqamil looked up from the report he'd been pretending to read.

"Ah, so there was something you wanted to tell me," he said with an amused smile. "I was beginning to despair. How come it took you so long?"

"I waited for the correct time, sir. Everything must be done at the right time, or chaos and disorder will corrupt the universe and nothing will be done properly."

The High Priest emitted a dry laugh. "I'm afraid you're deceiving yourself there, my child. Each single point in time is too short and passes too quickly for even a sharp-minded woman like you to make them out. Millions of them would come and go in the time you spent inhaling before speaking to me. Can you imagine how infinitely small the probability of you finding the exact right time to speak would be?"

This made Ashlob confused. As a person suffering from compulsive behaviour, she always knew when the right time had come, and knew better than to question the source of that knowledge.

"I..." she began, but the High Priest interrupted her.

"If the correct time was indeed at the very instant you uttered the words, which I find highly unlikely, then now would be too late. In fact, you should announce the correct time well in advance, so I'd have time to reply and take whatever action the situation required, maybe even visit the privy in between. But the probability of me finding the exact point of time you referred to would be as good as non-existent. My only chance would be to guess and hope for the best."

"Sir, I'm not... I'm not sure I understand what you're trying to tell me," Ashlob said. "All I know is that there was something I had to tell you, and that I had to wait for the right time to do it. It's impossible for me to tell when the right time for you to reply would be, but I'm sure it'll make itself known when it does arrive. What significance does all this talk about probabilities have?"

"My dear Ashlob," the High Priest said patiently. "I'm sure you'd understand its significance if you tried to look at things my way. What I'm trying to say is that it's virtually impossible to find a single point in time, even if you knew what you were looking for. So, instead of spending half the morning trying to achieve this, you could've told me what you came here to tell me right away. Doesn't that sound sensible?"

Ashlob pondered this for a while. "Umm... maybe. But I'd have to spend the rest of the day trying to put the universe back into place."

"Well, do you have anything else planned for today?"

"Not really, but..."

The High Priest flashed his teeth in a triumphant grin. "See? Next time you'll deliver the message first, and we'll worry about the universe later. What was it you came to tell me, by the way?"

All the talk about probabilities and going to the privy had almost made Ashlob forget. She had to tap each side of her nose a fixed number of times (in this case sixteen) before recollection came to her.

"It's time to initiate the new member into the cult," she finally said.

The High Priest nodded as he rose from his seat. "I should have guessed. Shall we go?"

As they left his office Marqamil gave the discussion they'd just had some befuddled consideration. He wasn't sure where all those deep thoughts had come from, and how he managed an analysis based on physics tinged with philosophy was completely beyond him.

Truth was, he'd felt a bit odd ever since his fainting incident on the day Drunk had arrived. He'd spent most of his time daydreaming, which wasn't unusual in itself, but he'd found that he had trouble remembering what the dreams had been about. The only ones he remembered clearly were the ones involving Lizbug, and even those had been full of strange thoughts and happenings.

I hope I'm not becoming as mad as Ashlob, he thought miserably.

Ashlob might be one of the cult's most capable members, but her severe case of compulsive behaviour brought along a few limitations. When she walked down a corridor, for example, she had to take two steps ahead, then one step back, followed by three steps ahead and two steps back.

Thus it took the two of them almost half an hour to walk the fifty meters from the High Priest's office to the Hall of the Raven, where the initiation rites took place. Marqamil wondered how someone with a problem like that could do *anything* at the correct time.

She must be extremely good at planning, he mused. *Or just plain nuts.*

The Hall of the Raven was a large, cavernous chamber, looking somewhat like a railway station. There were no trains, of course, and no rails, low-quality shops or drug addicts (unless you counted the still half-drunk Ashlob). At its far end was a large stone statue of the Raven God - a tall, manlike shape with the head and wings of a bird of prey. Its eyes were garnets, reflecting the light from the candles and torches which spread a dim luminance in the chamber.

There was no altar in the sacred hall. The old chronicles hadn't mentioned anything about sacrifices being necessary to please the cult's patron deity. Hippodemus always had his subjects place a large tray of food and drink outside his chambers at night, and seeing as it was always gone by morning the cult members saw it as a sign that the Raven God was pleased with their service.

A few of the cult's more psychotic leaders had suggested human sacrifices, but they'd always died mysteriously in their sleep before any victims could be collected.

Some more junk lay scattered across the floor, but none of it has any importance to the story.

Of the three people already present in the room Marqamil noticed only one - Lizbug, looking more beautiful than ever with the candlelight sending shadows dancing across her pale face. Her big, dark eyes looked both beautiful and dangerous, like a twilit pool full of crocodiles. Lips the deep red of fresh blood were parted ever so slightly, as if preparing for a kiss. The voluminous black robes the members of the cult wore hid her body completely. Marqamil cursed this tradition, not for the first time. He'd happily swap brains with Ashlob if it allowed him to see what Lizbug had underneath that robe.

The other two people were Chrisox and Drunk. They were currently in the middle of a conversation that seemed to involve card tricks, beer and chasing people through the headquarters' tunnels. Lizbug managed to look incredibly busy, even if she did nothing except staring blankly into the shadows.

Ashlob walked backwards three times around the assembled company, after which she patted each one on the head. Seemingly satisfied, she placed herself between the two men and the young woman, at exactly the same distance from each of them.

The High Priest cleared his throat. "We're gathered here today to initiate a new member into our cult. Our new member is Drunk, and will hopefully remain so for the rest of his days."

Chrisox sniggered.

"What?" Marqamil glared at the cleric.

"Oh, nothing. Just the elation you feel when someone makes a grammatical mistake involving a reference to the wrong noun, especially when it makes it sound as if it isn't a noun at all. You know what I mean."

"What?" Marqamil said again.

The cleric waved his hand. "Oh, never mind. Please proceed."

The High Priest felt his authority decrease with each passing moment. All the others were looking at him, not a single one showing any sign of respect for his station. In desperation he turned to Lizbug, hoping to find a little compassion in her dark, enchanting eyes. To his dismay, she appeared to ignore him completely. Instead she was looking at the statue of the Raven God, frowning slightly. Marqamil swallowed, then continued in a stammering voice.

"I-I believe you've learned about the purpose and rules of our cult. You'll have to abide by those rules if you're to stay, Drunk."

Chrisox burst into a violent fit of laughter.

This time the High Priest almost ran back to his chamber to hide under his blankets. Luckily, the brown-skinned youth answered him before he had time to put his feet into motion.

"Yes, High Priest. I've studied them closely."

"Would you mind repeating them, my son?" Marqamil said. "Some of us may have forgotten them."

Drunk took a deep breath. "The cult's purpose is to serve the Raven God and pray for Him to release us from the tyranny of the evil eye, to prepare for His arrival, so He may rule the world through peaceful, eternal night." He turned to Chrisox. "I believe that was all?"

"Yes, probably," Chrisox said. "Oh, and when you reach two hundred pounds you get an extra talent."

The young man blinked. "I do? I didn't find anything about that in any of those boring scrolls you made me read."

The cleric shrugged. "Times were hard back when those were written. The only one fat enough was Hippodemus, and he couldn't write. The knowledge has passed from member to member through the centuries."

"You must be kidding," Drunk said incredulously. "What sort of talents are those?"

Chrisox ticked them off on his fingers. "Being able to drink beer for twelve straight hours without going to the bathroom, not having to brush your teeth in the morning, looking through women's clothing..."

"Hey!" Marqamil exclaimed. "Why wasn't I told of this? Someone get me a sausage immediately!" He shot Lizbug a wishful glance.

"We don't have any sausages here," Chrisox said. "No meat products, remember?"

"I don't care!" the High Priest snapped. "It takes forever to get fan on beans and maize. I need protein, dammit! And you'll be punished for not telling me earlier."

"It doesn't apply to High Priests," the cleric informed him.

"Well, let's find ourselves a new High Priest then. Any volunteers?"

No one replied. Ashlob looked at Chrisox, then yelped and hid behind Lizbug. The dark-haired woman met the cleric's eyes as if it were a challenge to single combat.

The High Priest struggled to force the thoughts this new revelation had filled him with out of his mind. There were more important matters he should focus on. There'd be plenty of time to deal with those other things later. Still...

There must be a way to achieve this talent. Surely it can't be out of reach for someone as important as a High Priest?

He felt his heart beat faster when he thought of the new, exciting life that awaited him - a life full of small, lacy pieces of cloth that barely hid what they were supposed to hide. He suddenly knew he'd get very little sleep tonight.

"Shall we continue?" Chrisox suggested.

"Continue what?" Marqamil had completely forgotten why he was there.

"Er... I'm about to be initiated into your cult," Drunk informed him.

"Oh, yes. Well, do you agree to dedicate your life to serving the Raven God, to fighting the evil eye and protecting people with no underwear?"

"I do." Drunk chose to ignore the part the High Priest had gotten wrong.

"Good. Kneel before him, then, and put your hands on his mighty feet."

The young man knelt before the statue, reached out his hands and slowly placed them on the Raven God's stone feet. Marqamil opened his mouth to chant the ceremonial words.

His mouth remained open, but no sound emerged from it.

There was another sound, though. A deep rumbling that seemed to come from everywhere at the same time. The cavern's walls and floor shook slightly, as if some monstrous giant had decided it was time to have some fun with them. Ashlob screamed, but the sound was almost lost in the sudden turmoil.

"What's happening?" Chrisox yelled.

For once Marqamil knew exactly what was going on.

"His hands are touched by the evil eye!" he shouted. "By putting them on the holy statue he awoke the Raven God's wrath. It's the worst kind of blasphemy. Well, apart from pissing or scribbling obscenities on it, of course."

"Then why the hell did you let him touch it?!"

Because he said I'd get Lizbug, the High Priest thought, but of course he couldn't say that. Drunk's promise of giving him what his heart desired seemed like a bunch of useless parasols right now. How would that young man manage to make a girl like her want a guy like himself? He had to provide some kind of explanation, however, so he said what Drunk had said when they'd first met.

"It was his destiny."

"Fine." Chrisox rolled his eyes and tried to keep from falling as the ground heaved beneath his feet. "It was his destiny to destroy this cult and its members, so you did what you could to assist him. I wish I'd thrown him back out into the accursed sunlight. That'd serve him right. Come to think of it, it'd serve you right as well." He glared malevolently at the High Priest.

Marqamil opened his mouth to order the cleric to stand back, but right then one last, violent convulsion went through the cave, knocking all of them off their feet. There was a sharp popping sound, and everything was still.

The High Priest had ended up face down on the stone floor. There was blood in his mouth, and something that felt like a piece of his tongue. He spat it all out, then lifted his head, wincing as a jolt of pain shot through it. The stone had cracked in several places, he noticed. His shaking fingers found one of those cracks, and he slowly pulled himself to his hands and knees. It was an arduous task, seeing as Chrisox had fallen over him and temporarily lost consciousness. The other members of the cult groaned and struggled to get back on their feet.

Drunk still knelt in front of the statue, but his hands were no longer empty.

"What's that?" Ashlob asked, staggering towards him.

"It-It's an egg," the new initiate stammered.

"Yay! Pancakes for supper, then?" the young woman said excitedly.

"Move aside, child," Marqamil said sharply as he stepped up beside them. "How did you get that, Drunk?"

"Well," Ashlob said. "I was having lunch, and there was no one to share the bottle of wine with. You know I can never leave a bottle half-empty. It makes me feel like my head's gonna explode. Like when I walk, if I don't step backwards..."

"Shut up! Drunk, where did you get that egg from?"

"It-It came from the statue, High Priest. Right into my hands. It's a miracle!"

"Indeed it is!" Ashlob exclaimed. "I haven't had pancakes since before I joined this cult, and that was almost fifteen years ago. I'll get the frying pan."

"No!" The High Priest stared at the egg. It was large, at least a foot long, and covered with intricate patterns in many different colours. Drunk held it the way you hold a poisonous snake, equally afraid of crushing and dropping it.

"This is a miracle, true enough," Marqamil continued. "But it has nothing to do with food. This egg was sent to us by the Raven God himself. It must have a deeper and much more important purpose than being eaten. We must leave these caves, expose ourselves to the evil eye, and travel until we find the answer."

"What answer?" Ashlob asked grumpily, still thinking pancakes a much more appealing idea.

"I don't know, child. It's just what you do when things like this happen. You travel across the world, looking for the answer. We won't know the question until we find it. It could be anything. Why did the Raven God give us this egg? What are we supposed to do with it? Will our cult get a new purpose now?"

"Why can't we have pancakes?" Ashlob whined.

Marqamil patted her on the head. "You might find the answer to that question as well, my child. But enough talk for now. We must get ready for our journey. It'll probably be a very long one, filled with dangers and strife. Go on now, back to your chamber and start packing. You too, Drunk. Lizbug..."

"Can I guard the egg while we're travelling?" the beautiful woman asked.

The High Priest looked from her to the egg. Drunk had handed it over to him as carefully as if it'd been a newly born babe. It felt cold and heavy in his hands, and somehow filled with power. He suddenly felt a strong reluctance to let anyone else touch it.

"No, child," he said. "This egg is for me to carry and watch over. This is what it means to be High Priest. Guarding important stuff and not getting to see through women's clothes. It's a cruel fate, but someone has to do it. I'm sorry."

"That makes two of us," Ashlob muttered, giving the egg one last hungry look before scampering off towards her chamber.

Lizbug's dark eyes didn't leave the egg. For a moment Marqamil thought he saw uncertainty flicker through them, and then something else. Could it have been fear? It was gone as quickly as it'd appeared, leaving only inscrutable darkness. He clutched the egg closer to him and repeated, more to himself than to any of the others.

"Someone has to do it."

~ 7 ~

The big, black man in front of Marsha rolled the dice for the third time.

"Three sixes!" he exclaimed, as happy as a small child who just got a lollipop from his aunt. "That's eighteen points for me. Now I got you all!" He chuckled.

Marsha picked up the dice. She'd been relieved when she found out all these men wanted was to play Yahtzee with her. She'd even put some of her soul into the game (a part of it she could do without). For a time it'd been fairly enjoyable, but after a few hours it started getting deadly boring, until she almost found herself hoping they'd change their minds and decide they wanted to rape and torture her instead.

She threw the dice on the ground in front of her, examined the result, picked up two and threw them again. Then she threw them a third time.

"I'll put this in the Chance box," she announced. "That makes nineteen. Two better than you had," she added, winking at the man who'd played right before her. He scowled at her, the ring in his nose making him look like an angry bull.

The next man - Ogian, she thought his name was - picked up the dice, put them in his mouth, rattled them a little and spat them out again. They fell into a perfect pattern on the ground. Ogian was a big one for show and artistry. He wasn't as good at counting, though.

"Three of a kind!" he chirped. "Three fours, a six and a two. That's twenty-four points."

"Twenty," Marsha corrected him.

"Twenty-four," Ogian persisted. "Three times four is twelve, times six is sixty-four, divided by two is… twenty-four. Or maybe twenty-six. I'll settle for twenty-four, though. I'm not a greedy man."

"It's twenty," said the man who got the three sixes earlier. His name was Kharuba. "You have to count the pips. See. One, two, three, four, five…"

They waited for him to finish. The other two men agreed Ogian should be awarded twenty points. Ogian wouldn't agree to anything less than twenty-two, so the argument continued. Marsha took the opportunity to ask Kharuba some questions.

"You Elephant People seem to travel a lot. Are you looking for something?"

The man frowned. "The Queen says we have some great and important purpose in this world. Well, at least she does. We're only here to assist her."

"Ah, so you're moving around until you find out what this purpose is?"

"No, it's because our elephants eat so much. We can't stay in the same place for long, or they'll be without food."

Marsha digested this information for a while, then spat out the result.

"Are your elephants part of this great purpose?"

"How should I know?" Kharuba said sourly. "Ask the Queen, or maybe Hannah. They're the ones supposed to be in contact with the gods. All I get to do is shovel the dung into heaps. Big heaps. I can show them to you if you like."

"No, thanks," Marsha hurried to say. "Tell me some more about this gargling woman. Does she receive messages from this Elephant God of yours?"

Beside them, Ogian had agreed to lower his score to twenty-one. One of the men seemed content with this, but the other continued to argue. Kharuba glared at them before turning back to Marsha.

"Yes, she does, but the Queen usually changes them before telling us. Says Hannah interprets some things the wrong way. Somehow the messages she gives us always include lots of praise for her own beauty and wisdom. Last time she said the Elephant God told her he should be worshipping her and not the other way around, that he was nothing compared to her, and that there was no one, man or god, who was worthy of her love."

"Did the Elephant God say if there was a woman worthy of it?" Marsha asked.

Kharuba thought for a moment. "I don't think women were mentioned. Maybe next time. I'll remember to ask about it."

"Good." Marsha noticed that the Yahtzee game had been resumed and that Ogian looked very disappointed. "Did you only get twenty points?" she asked, trying to put some sympathy into her voice.

"Eighteen," he replied. "Bunta-koop says I have to pay two points for trying to cheat. Me, cheat? It's an outrage! I take great pride in my playing, just like in everything else I do. Did I tell you about the time I made the elephants dance?"

Marsha shook her head.

"It was quite a performance," Ogian said proudly. "The Queen gave me a pat on the head afterwards. Ask any of these louts if they'd ever been granted such an honour."

"She gave me a pat on the ass once," said the one called Bunta-koop. He was chewing something that looked like old leather. Marsha had watched him put it in his mouth, contemplated for a while, and decided it was best not to ask.

"I gave *her* a pat on the ass once," said Kharuba.

"The hell you did!" Ogian exclaimed. "She wouldn't let you do something like that and remain alive. No one touches the Queen, not even the Elephant God."

"Oh, I did it all right," Kharuba said, smiling happily as he relived the event in the murky hollows of his brain. "We were out on a mission - just me, her, and old Balambarou. We got pretty drunk, and the Queen started crying and complaining about what a lonely life she had, being the most divine creature on the planet. So we tried to comfort her and one thing led to another, as old Balambarou could've told you."

"What happened to old Balambarou anyway?" Ogian snorted.

"He got squished under his elephant's foot," Bunta-koop said.

"See?" Ogian's voice had a hint of triumph in it. "The Elephant God punished him for his blasphemy! It's only a matter of time before his wrath falls on you, Kharuba."

Kharuba threw the dice.

"Yahtzee!" he exclaimed, and rose to perform some ridiculous celebratory dance. Marsha had to throw herself to one side to avoid ending up the same way as old Balambarou, except it'd be under a mad dice-player's foot instead of an elephant's.

The other men glared angrily at the dancing Kharuba.

"So much for the Elephant God's wrath," muttered Bunta-koop.

"Oh, I'm sure he'll get what he deserves," Ogian mused. "He'll probably turn into a lunatic and run madly into the jungle. Then, after a day or two, he'll fall victim to a bunch of incredibly mean and hungry leopards. That's usually what happens when you grope your queen."

"Err... excuse me," Marsha broke in hesitantly. "I'm a queen, sort of, and I've been groped once or twice. No one went mad or got eaten."

Ogian reached out a hand towards her rear end.

"But there must be a first time for everything," she hurried to add.

The black man snatched back his hand and hurriedly reached for the dice instead. He was just about to throw them when there was a loud noise from somewhere outside the tent. Marsha looked up in surprise. It appeared someone had tried to walk through the tent wall. She gave her companions a questioning look, but none of them seemed surprised.

"Further to the left, Embolo," Kharuba called.

There was the sound of someone muttering, and then the blind man stumbled through the tent's entrance.

"Is the one called Marsha here?" he asked.

"I am," Marsha said. "What's going on? Where are my companions?"

"The fat woman is with Hannah," Embolo said. "It appears they have a lot in common, both regarding hobbies and tastes in food and drink. The man was in a bit of a shock after all the excitement earlier today and had to lie down for a while. The one called Amanda is with the Queen. You are to join them at once."

"Has any harm been done to any of them?"

The blind man shrugged. "I think the Queen gave the young fellow a smack on the bum, but that's about it."

Ogian grunted something and looked extremely jealous. Kharuba winked at the other Yahtzee players. They all laughed.

Marsha rose and brushed off her clothes.

"Take me to your queen, then," she commanded.

"Follow me," the blind man said sourly, then turned and made for the tent's entrance.

"Embolo! Further to the ri..."

Before Kharuba had time to finish his warning the blind man bounced against the tent wall and fell backwards onto the ground. His head struck a hard object someone had used to kill a scorpion with earlier that day, and with a sigh he passed into a state of physical and mental motionlessness. There were a few moments of silence.

"Yahtzee!!" Ogian yelled, fake elation filling his voice like the smell of rotten fish.

"Shut up!" Bunta-koop growled.

"It's true! Five sixes! It's a miracle."

"You didn't even throw the dice."

"I said it was a miracle, didn't I?"

The fourth man, who had some strange name like Xyrophlectius or Zurophadiarus or something, frowned at the dice.

"Those are the same five sixes Kharuba just got," he said. "You just picked them up and put them back down the same way."

"Right," said Bunta-koop.

"Right," said Kharuba.

"Right," murmured Embolo, who'd emerged into a semi-conscious (or more like quarter-conscious) state. "Further to the right..."

"Err... I'll find the way to the queen on my own," Marsha said and left the tent. No one appeared to notice.

Queen Tiwi's tent was, well, Marsha wasn't sure how to describe it. The Elephant People didn't seem to possess much in the way of jewellery, so the queen had covered it with whatever ornaments she'd been able to find. There were various sorts of greenery, some dry and yellowed, old clothes and woven things that couldn't possibly serve any purpose other than taking up space. Tools and other objects (often only parts of them) hung from strings tied to the ceiling, and there was so much useless junk on the floor that Marsha had to step carefully not to tread on anything.

Tiwi herself sat at a wooden table, doing her best to ignore Amanda, who seemed tremendously bored. It was obvious the two women didn't get along very well. When Marsha entered the tent the queen looked up and smiled brightly at her.

"Ah, Lady Marsha, how nice to see you. Do have a seat. Is there something you'd like to eat or drink? The fruit pie is particularly delicious today."

"No, thanks," Marsha said. "How's Pebe doing?"

"Oh, the poor young man." Tiwi smiled sympathetically. "I think it was too much for him to be faced with such a formidable creature as myself. You know what it's like to stare into the sun on a bright day. Not that even the brightest sunlight could rival my own brilliance in any way, of course."

Amanda snorted.

Marsha went on, "How long will you keep us as... umm... non-prisoners?"

The queen seemed to find this an incredibly difficult question to answer.

"Dear me, I have no idea. Until I've decided what I think of you, I suppose."

Marsha opened her mouth to ask what the hell that was supposed to mean, but another man of the Elephant People entered the tent and addressed the queen.

"Glorious Queen, I'm sorry to inform you we've had to put down one of the elephants. Its funeral will be held at noon two days from now. We'll eat as much of it as we can in that time, of course." He licked his lips hungrily.

Tiwi jumped to her feet, her face taking on an outraged expression. "What? Why? What was wrong with it?"

"It appears its brain got damaged somehow. It started to behave oddly a few hours ago, and then it collapsed and lay on the ground with its eyes rolling and froth dripping from its mouth. It was not a nice thing to see, not nice at all. So we had to put it out of its misery."

"Don't you have any idea what happened to it?" Tiwi asked.

The man shook his head. "Its jaw was cracked, but no one can recall seeing it fall or do anything else that might have caused such an injury. It requires a fearsome blow to crack an elephant's jaw, Your Grace."

Amanda blew on her knuckles nonchalantly, then began cleaning her fingernails. Marsha said nothing.

"Was there nothing you could do to save it?" the queen persisted.

"You could have used some of your divine powers," Amanda muttered.

Tiwi ignored her, or perhaps she hadn't been listening. The man lurched into an incoherent explanation about the complexity of brain damage. Marsha didn't pay much attention to him. A large spider had caught her eye, crawling harmlessly across the tent's floor but still making her skin itch.

"Amanda?" she said faintly.

"Huh?"

"Would you please kill it?"

The voluptuous woman blinked. "They already did. It'll be buried two days from now."

"No, not the elephant. That spider over there. You know how I hate bugs and spiders."

"Oh, okay." Amanda went over and put her foot down heavily on it. The squishy sound should have been sickening, but Marsha could swear she felt better the instant the spider died.

"Nasty creatures," she muttered to herself.

Amanda grinned at her. "How about hiding it in Pebe's blankets? Imagine the squeals he'd produce."

"No!" Marsha said, more firmly than she'd intended. She shrugged when Amanda raised a questioning eyebrow. "It wouldn't be hygienic," she hurried to explain. "Those things carry diseases sometimes."

The man had reached the end of his extensive and completely pointless lecture on the structure of the elephant brain.

"I'm terribly sorry, most godlike Queen," he finished.

Tiwi nodded thoughtfully, or at least the way people capable of thinking tend to nod.

"Fine," she finally said. "Things like this happen when you lead such an imperative and precarious life as I do. You may go now."

When the man had left the queen took up an old mirror from the table and began admiring her reflection. Marsha cleared her throat as politely as she could.

"Umm...Your Grace?"

"What?" Tiwi looked up, obviously very annoyed at being disturbed during such an important task. "Oh, Lady Marsha," she said in a more pleasant tone. "I had forgotten you were here. What was it you wanted?"

"Err... I don't know. You were the one who sent for me."

"I did? That's odd. Why would I have done that?"

Marsha took a deep breath. "Perhaps you wanted to talk about what will happen next?"

"Oh? And what will that be, pray?"

"I don't know." Marsha had a feeling this conversation grew more pointless the longer it went on. Unfortunately, she couldn't think of a way to steer it into more sensible subjects.

"Well, then it wasn't a good idea to bring you here, was it?" Tiwi said. "If you wanted to talk about what's to happen next the least thing you could've done was bring me some information. I'm a very busy woman, you know." She went back to examining herself in the mirror, making small sounds of approval now and then.

"Err... I might have an idea," Marsha said.

"*An idea so bright, to cast some light on the path of the brainless one*," Amanda intoned.

"Huh?" said the queen, looking up from her mirror.

"I said I..." Marsha began.

"*Her figure is slim, but wits so dim, all full of elephant dung*," Amanda finished.

Marsha made a new attempt. "What I thought, Your Grace, was that we're looking for our friend, and you're trying to find your great purpose. Why not combine those two quests? Who knows, perhaps we'll find the answer to both in the same place."

Tiwi frowned at her. "Is this the woman you talked about before, the one with the nice butt? Do you think the Elephant People will find its great and glorious purpose in her butt?"

"Well, no," Marsha said. "What I meant was..."

"A *butt so nice, to draw the eyes of gods and men alike*."

"Shut up!" Tiwi snapped.

Amanda rubbed her knuckles again. The anger on the queen's face slowly turned into hesitation, and then to unease. She turned her back to the voluptuous woman and fixed Marsha with her piercing gaze.

"What did you mean, Lady Marsha?" she asked. "Think carefully before you answer. Your life may depend on it."

Marsha blinked. "Are you threatening me?"

"No, silly. I meant in the long run. What we decide here and now may put you in a situation that might prove fatal to you. So don't suggest anything foolish, like having Embolo use his sixth sense to guide us on our search."

That made Marsha frown. "He has a sixth sense? Does that have anything to do with his blindness?"

The queen shook her head. "He only has four senses. A sixth would mean he'd have to have a fifth, and with his vision gone I have no idea what that would be. Anyway, are you going to suggest anything, or will you just sit there leering at me like a fool? You Khadal people seem a bit slow, if I may say so. No offence meant."

Marsha realized this woman had a way of messing up her thoughts in some weird way she couldn't really put a finger on. She wouldn't call Tiwi particularly smart, nor extremely stupid. It was just that her way of random thinking made it difficult to carry on a meaningful conversation.

She didn't know it, but this talent made it close to impossible for other members of the Elephant People to rebel against their narcissistic queen. After a few minutes of talking to her they had usually forgotten completely what they were unhappy with, and any plans and schemes they'd made suddenly seemed hard to remember.

"We should travel together," Marsha finally managed. "Join our forces, that sort of thing. United we stand but divided we fall. You probably know all about it already."

"I do?" Tiwi looked puzzled.

"Well, perhaps not, but it seems like a good idea anyway. Neither of us has had much success in their search so far, right? I think it's time to try something new."

"Sounds good to me," Tiwi said, scratching the back of her head with the mirror. "But where will we go? This continent is vast, and our goal might lie anywhere. I think we should go..."

"West," said Marsha.

"East," finished the queen.

They glared at each other.

"Well, that was a good start to our joint venture," Tiwi said after a while. "Any more great ideas, Lady Marsha? Like how we're to decide which way to go, when we obviously have very different ideas about which direction would be the best."

"Why not let the gargling woman decide?" Amanda said absently.

There was a moment of silence.

"Brilliant!" Tiwi exclaimed. "Absolutely fucking brilliant!"

She hugged Amanda so fiercely the voluptuous woman almost fell off her chair. Marsha gave her head an incredulous shake.

Well, at least we've agreed on something. Let's hope it'll continue that way.

~ 8 ~

Being chieftain of the Telu tribe has often been compared to being a hen in charge of two hundred unruly chickens. In fact, most of its chieftains have had a level of intelligence equal to or slightly lower than that of a hen. That the tribe managed to function properly despite this is considered one of the greatest miracles in the history of the world, outshone only by the taste of a nice hippo stew and the luscious body of the woman Bathora.

Some people claim that relieving yourself after having drunk an immense quantity of water should be counted among the world's most awe-inspiring phenomena. This has, however, never been commonly accepted, probably because water has always been in scant supply in this part of the world.

Sex has never been considered to be a particularly good thing, which has resulted in a dwindling of the Telu population. The reason sex isn't very popular in this tribe is that most of its male members are completely besotted with their chieftain, hence displaying very little interest in their wives. As a result of this, the wives have developed very advanced methods of masturbation, which in turn has made them lose interest in their husbands. Nature has an amazing way of adapting to new situations.

Bathora herself had her own way of adjusting. This was mostly a product of her inability to remember something for more than two seconds after it had vanished from sight. She had completely forgotten about her tribe's war with the Hippo Cult when the young man Gideon reminded her of it, and when Gideon was out of sight she forgot about it again. Fortunately, the shaman Samoul informed her about the resurrection of the Telu's ancient enemy, bringing Bathora along in the search for a way to extinguish the hippo cult once and for all. Or at least that was what she thought.

The moment they lost sight of the Telu camp Bathora forgot all about being its chieftain. She had probably forgotten her own name if Samoul hadn't used it with regular intervals. The only thing that stayed in her head was a vague notion about being on a quest to wipe out some stupid religious sect from the face of the earth.

When she'd asked Samoul five times why she had to fight the Hippo Cult he got tired of explaining, only replying with a simple "You just have to". Fortunately this was enough to keep Bathora satisfied.

"There's another thing I don't understand," she said. There were lots of things Bathora didn't understand, like why you fell downwards instead of upwards, or why water quenched your thirst when gravel didn't. Anyway, this was what occupied her mind at the moment: "How am I to find the answer I'm looking for in your marshlands?"

The surprise at getting a relevant question from his companion startled Samoul so much he fell off his camel. Bathora's annoyance grew when she didn't receive an answer, until she turned to assail the shaman with a look of blazing fury. That was when she became aware he was no longer on his riding animal.

"Hey!" she exclaimed. "What kind of a gentleman are you, leaving a poor, defenceless woman alone in the wilderness like this?" She didn't consider the fact that if Samoul had actually left her he wouldn't be able to hear her complaint. Furiously, she turned her camel around to return home. That was when she noticed the shaman lying unconscious on the ground some fifty paces away.

"Oh dear!" She jumped off her camel and ran to help her companion. Unfortunately, she tripped and fell over him, breaking two of his ribs in the process. This was the only injury Samoul suffered from the incident, apart from a small bump on the back of his head.

The pain this mishap triggered made him regain consciousness. He gasped, partly from the pain and partly because Bathora was sprawled across his chest, making it difficult for him to breathe. Some men might have found this a pleasant experience (having Bathora on top of you, that is, not getting your ribs cracked), but Samoul wasn't one of them. He did his best to keep a happy face, though, and decided to offer Bathora a compliment.

"Oof, you're much heavier than you look," he grunted.

Most women wouldn't accept this as a complimentary thing to say, but Bathora was not like other women. In fact, many people would say she resembled a five-year-old boy more than anything else, a thing that most five-year-old boys would take as a grave insult. Anyway, she merely rolled off the shaman and inspected him with the kind of look a man uses when he's trying to fix his car but has no idea how to do it.

"Are you hurt?" she asked.

Samoul tried to rise to his feet, grunted with pain, and lay back down again.

"Somewhat," he conveyed. "Will you help me rise?"

Bathora giggled. "Don't you think it's a bit early for that? I mean, we've only just met. I like to know a man a little better before I, you know, get intimate."

Perhaps it was because he'd hit his head on the hard ground, but for the first time since they met Samoul felt the woman had said something he was too slow to comprehend. This resulted in an alarming drop in his self-confidence, so overwhelming it might have short-circuited his brain and left him a drooling vegetable for the rest of his life if his inborn defence mechanisms hadn't instantly kicked in, blotting out the sensation. He shrugged, as well as someone can shrug when lying flat on his back.

"I'll do it myself, then," he said.

Bathora shrugged, a much more graceful gesture than what the shaman had managed. "Enjoy yourself. I'll tend to the camels while you're at it."

Let's move back to the topic of Bathora's sex life for a moment. I'm sure most readers would rather hear some more about that than listen to a description of how she groomed and fed the camels. Unfortunately, there isn't much to tell. As many offers as she might've had, Bathora had only gone through the physical act of love once in her life. The lucky fellow was called Winston. He's made a short appearance earlier in this story, and will appear some more before the end.

No one has been able to explain why Bathora chose Winston of all people to be her first and - so far - only lover. By the time of their romance he was a short, thick-bodied man with hard, lizard-like scales covering his skin, bristling hair sticking up between them. His hands had been covered with something that looked like a mix of mould and moss, and his head looked like a big mushroom that had been digested for three days and then thrown up.

He'd made Bathora with child that night, but when the foetus became aware of its genetic prospects it tore off its navel string and starved itself to death.

The two travellers continued their slow journey until dusk, when they made camp in a hollow basin filled with boulders of various sizes. Bathora thought it looked as if a bunch of giants had used it as target in a game of rock-throwing. Samoul didn't light a fire. Instead, he took some dried meat from his pack and divided the strips between them. Bathora realized than that she had forgotten to bring provisions, but that didn't affect her mood in any way.

"What kind of meat is this?" she asked, chewing enthusiastically with her mouth wide open.

The shaman smiled slyly at her. "You like it?"

"Yeah." She burped. "If I could get my hands on one of those animals I'd grow a whole herd of them."

"You can't grow a herd from only one animal, Bathora. You need at least two."

Bathora stared blankly at him for a while. Then comprehension dawned on her.

"Ah, yes, that's me. Bathora. Sorry, for a moment I thought you were talking to someone else."

"I should be the one to apologize," Samoul said with all the patience of someone who's only known Bathora for a very short time. "I'll remember to remind you of your name more regularly."

"Great! So what's the beast called? Is it dangerous?"

"It could be. Its name is…" He spoke a combination of random syllables.

Bathora's forehead creased in concentration. "I don't think I've heard of it. It must be uncommon in these parts."

"Not quite," he said, swallowing the meat he'd been chewing. "You can find some nice, fleshy specimen if you know where to look."

She nodded. This shaman was a pleasant fellow to be around, she decided. He talked about interesting things and seemed to know a lot. She'd never liked people who knew too much (too much knowledge by Telu standards could be compared to a normal four-year-old). Those people usually walked around with their noses pointing up into the air, and Bathora had a strong aversion to larynges (or throat-bumps, as she called them).

Winston had turned out to be such a man. Bathora had noticed that the morning after their night of passion. Winston had begun talking about the future they were to share, and had annoyed Bathora immensely when he claimed to know which part in it would be best for her. So she'd dumped him and they hadn't spoken to each other since.

That night Samoul dreamed about walking through a forest of very tall and thick trees. There were strange sounds all around him. He was alone. Where were the other members of his tribe? He shouted as loudly as he could (which wasn't very loud).

"Hello?! Lulu? Doggy? Where are you?"

But the only response he got were the strange sounds, and they kept growing louder.

He looked around for the source of the sounds and gasped in sudden fear. The huge trees were swaying, some of them falling with an impact that made the ground shake. He started running. The forest seemed to be without end. Finally, he tripped and fell.

As he lay on the ground, unable to move, he saw a tree - the biggest of all - topple and fall towards him. He screamed. The tree landed straight across his body, crushing him to the ground. There was pain.

He awoke to find Bathora sitting on his stomach, bouncing slightly up and down.

"Get up, you lousy camel!" she shouted angrily. "It's morning, and we have to be off. You can't lie here all day. Get up! I'm not going to walk the rest of the way." She bounced some more.

Samoul groaned. "It's me, you stupid pork chop. The camels are tethered by the big boulder over there."

"Oh." Bathora looked confused as she rose to her feet. The shaman followed, massaging his aching abdomen. The sky was overcast, the air a little cooler than normal. They were soon back on the road - if there'd been a road in this god-forsaken wilderness.

Around noon they came to a huge ravine, its cliffs sloping almost vertically down towards a small river surrounded by rocky ground. The non-existing road continued on the other side, about a thousand feet away. Bathora stared at the empty air before her.

"How do we get across?" she asked.

"We can't." The shaman looked troubled.

Bathora thought for a moment, if what went on inside her brain could be called thinking. Spontaneously, she said, "But you came this way on your way to the Telu camp, didn't you?"

"Yes, I did."

"Didn't you get across then?"

"I did."

"How?"

He pointed. "I went across the bridge. You can see the remnants of it down there by the river, and over there on the other side."

Bathora frowned. "But it's broken. How did you manage to get across on a broken bridge?"

"It wasn't broken when I used it."

"But why is it broken now?"

Samoul sighed. "I don't know. Does it matter?"

She snorted and scratched herself on one of her plump buttocks. "How am I supposed to know if it matters? I wasn't here when it broke."

"Okay," the shaman said, rolling his eyes. "The problem remains, though. We can't get across, and there's no other way to the swamps. So what do we do?"

Being a woman in a leading position, Bathora was used to making decisions like this. Usually, however, the questions she faced were more along the lines of "How do I get this pebble out of my ear?" or "Do you remember which of these women is my wife?".

This was a bit trickier. She looked once more at the empty space.

"Hey, what's that?" she asked, pointing with a long finger.

Knowing Bathora's tendency to pay attention to random and completely unimportant things, the shaman didn't bother with looking too closely. "What's what?"

"There's something down there, not far away. It looks really odd."

Deciding there could be no harm in finding out what had caught the inbecile woman's eye, Samoul squinted to see better in the bright noon light.

"Hallelujah!" he exclaimed. "You're right. It's a rope. No, two ropes, stretched across the ravine."

"Really?" Bathora said. "What do you think they're there for?"

"We can use them to cross the ravine," Samoul said. "We'll have to leave the camels behind, though."

"Noooo!" she moaned, stroking her camel's fur affectionately. "I don't want to leave old Betsy. She's served me well for many years."

"And still you couldn't tell us apart," the shaman muttered under his breath. Then, louder, so Bathora could hear, "The ropes can't take their weight. They'd break and we'd plunge down to get smashed against those rocks down there. Even if it's just the two of us, we'll have to cross one by one. I'll go first. Wait until I'm across before you follow. Get it?"

"Get what?"

"What we're to do."

"Yeah, think so. I may need to pee before I go, though."

Samoul shrugged. "Fine, be my guest."

While Bathora went looking for a bush to relieve herself behind, the shaman made his way down the treacherous cliff to where the ropes were fastened. His camel looked indifferently at him, not the least bit sorry about losing its owner. It looked forward to a new life of gluttony, laziness, and sex with lots of young females. Basically what any human coming out of a long-term relationship would want. If camels could grin, this one would have done so.

Samoul tried the ropes' strength. They seemed very solid. He took a few steps, moving sideways with both hands firmly on the upper rope. The wind picked up as he progressed further out into the ravine, making the ropes sway slightly. He tried not to think about the vast drop below him, but somehow he kept hearing the nauseating sound his body would make when it hit the ground.

Considering his current position, he would've landed in the river with a not-too-loud *splash*, but that didn't occur to his frenzied mind. His knees started to shake, a little at first and then more and more violently. Enormous gases formed in his stomach.

Finally, he reached the other side and turned to see if he could make out Bathora's pleasantly rounded form. She wasn't down by the ropes. For an instant he feared the imbecile woman had forgotten what she was supposed to do. If so, he decided to leave her there and return home alone. There was no way he'd go back across the ravine and fetch her, no way in the entire world.

Then he spotted her, and his fear and disbelief rose to hitherto unknown heights.

Bathora sat on the back of her camel, obviously intending to ride the animal across the rope.

"*Nooooo!!!*" Samoul shouted and began waving his arms furiously. "You utterly stupid woman! You can't do that! It'll be the death of both of you! Get off the camel now! Off, I said!"

The Telu woman didn't seem to hear him. She rode the camel down the rocky slope until she reached the ropes. Samoul stared wide-eyed as the beast took one hesitant step onto the top rope, then another, and another.

When Bathora rejoined Samoul he sat slumped with his back against a rock, folded arms hiding his face. She smiled happily at him from her position on the camel's back.

"Ah, there you are," she said. "Shall we continue?"

The shaman didn't reply. Soft, whimpering sounds barely made their way up to Bathora's ears. She gave him a concerned look.

"Are you crying?"

There were some more sobs. Bathora dismounted and crouched down by her companion's side, putting an arm around his shoulders.

"There, there," she said softly. "What's wrong? Did your mother die or something?"

Samoul shook his head. "I've just realized there's no hope whatsoever for mankind."

"Aw, don't say that," Bathora said, having absolutely no idea what he'd meant. "I'm sure everything will turn out well in the end."

"What point is there in trying to learn things about life and the world, to organize societies with laws and morals, to invent tools to facilitate tasks great and small, when a person completely without brains can perform miracles like this without having the slightest idea how unique they are?"

"That's a very good question," said Bathora, who hadn't understood it or realized it referred to her. "How about we discuss it while we're travelling? There are many hours of daylight left, and I can't think of anything else to talk about. What say you?"

The shaman moaned. There were a million things he wanted to say to this woman, a million questions he wanted to ask, but in his bewildered state of mind he only managed the most obvious one.

"How did you do it?"

"Do what?"

He gave up.

"Can you get my camel over too?" he asked.

Bathora looked back across the ravine. "Nah, I don't think so. He looked very crossly at me when I took Betsy away from him. Besides, I think he's run off. He didn't seem too sorry about you leaving him."

"What are we going to do, then?" Samoul asked, slowly climbing back to his feet. "I won't be able to keep up with you on foot, and your camel can't carry both of us. You'll have to walk beside it."

Bathora stared at him with an outraged expression. "*Walk*? *Me*? I'm the chieftain of the… of the…"

"The Telu."

"Right. The Telu. How dare you make such a foolish suggestion? Only simple people walk. Chieftains *ride*."

The shaman shrugged. "Very well. Can you ride slowly enough for me to keep up?"

Bathora looked up at her camel. "I don't think so. Old Betsy only has one level of speed. I could ride in circles around you, but that'd make me dizzy. No, you'll have to find some other way."

The shaman thought for a while. "A way for you to ride at the same pace I walk…"

"I know!" Bathora exclaimed happily. "If I ride on your back we'll keep the same pace. That would solve everything. Down on your knees with you!"

Samoul wasn't happy with the prospect of carrying Bathora on his back. He recalled all too well the last time he'd had Bathora's weight on him. The woman must have really thick bones or something, because she seemed to be twice as heavy as she looked. It certainly couldn't be her brain adding any extra weight.

He judged the distance they had left before reaching the marshlands. It was still pretty far. He tried desperately to find another solution, but his thoughts kept moving in circles, the way they sometimes do when you're asked a really simple question in a quiz competition. Eventually, he gave up and bent down so Bathora could climb onto his back.

"Good boy," she said as his back creaked under her weight. "Let me find myself a more comfortable position."

She moved a little, and Samoul swore he could feel his vertebrae grinding against each other. He groaned and staggered to one side. Bathora frowned down at him.

"Got any complaints?" she asked.

Do I have any complaints? Samoul thought. *It feels like I'm carrying a whole mountain on my back. I should tell this fat cow of a woman to walk on her own two legs, or I'll leave her here to starve.*

But what he said was, "No, of course not. I just stood on a patch of uneven ground, is all."

"Ah, that's always a problem when you're out in the wild like this. Now, you can use your hands to support my legs. Don't touch my bum, not unless I specifically tell you to. I will know it's intentional if you do, so don't even think about claiming it was an accident. Let's see what speed those skinny legs of yours can manage!"

The camel watched them with a strange mix of amusement and disbelief. At least it was a strange mix for a camel, whose thoughts usually revolved around more simple matters like where to find shade or if it'd be a good idea to get your teeth into that thorny thing claiming to be a plant. Betsy wished she had someone to make a bet with. She judged the man wouldn't be able to carry the woman more than three miles before dusk. She was willing to bet one of her humps on that.

It was lucky for Old Betsy she didn't have anyone to bet against her, because when the sun sank behind the western horizon Samoul had carried Bathora a little more than four miles. The last few hundred meters had been unimaginably painful, as he'd had to crawl on his hands and knees while the woman's fat bum did its best to cause irreparable damage to his back. Finally he collapsed on the ground, and might never have got up again if Bathora hadn't decided to haul him back upright, if only to tell him it was his turn to groom the camel.

As they sat around a small fire he tried to calculate how much weight Bathora would lose if he didn't give her any supper, but seeing as he wasn't a very good mathematician he got the result completely wrong and gave her almost all the food. Bathora gobbled it down, burped a few times, and said she looked forward to tomorrow's ride. Samoul went to sleep hoping he'd never wake up again.

He did wake up, though, and had to endure another few hours of carrying Bathora across the barren wasteland. As noon approached the landscape around them grew more soggy. Puddles of stinking water lay bubbling all around like pots of very bad pea soup. Frogs croaked and they heard the sound of crickets from thick stands of swamp greenery. They had reached the marshlands.

"We've reached the marshlands," Samoul announced.

Fine, thought the camel. *Time to get outta here.*

"Hey!" Samoul said, pointing the way they'd just come. "Your camel ran off."

Bathora gave a loud snort. "Of course it didn't. Old Betsy is much too faithful to ever leave my side."

"Perhaps it got jealous because you abandoned its back for mine." *Though I doubt even a camel can be stupid enough to actually want to carry this fat oaf of a woman on its back.*

"Don't be absurd," Bathora retorted. "She knew I only did it to make things more convenient for you."

Samoul rolled his eyes. "I bet she knew exactly how I felt. Anyway, she's over two hundred meters away now, and still galloping."

"She isn't. Look, she's right here." Bathora reached out to pat the camel. "Betsy? BETSY! Come back here, you filthy, ungrateful animal! I won't accept this kind of behaviour from you! Come back, I said!"

"It's no use," Samoul said dourly. "We'll have to continue without it."

Some of the more romantic and naive readers might hope Bathora's camel reunited with Samoul's and that the two lived happily ever after. Unfortunately, reality tends to be much harsher than that. The camel reached the aforementioned ravine, and in a fit of hubris it tried to cross on the rope once more. Without the protection of a mind without the slightest hint of perception it toppled over almost immediately, experiencing a quick, painless and very gory death at the ravine's bottom. The sound it made when it was crushed would have kept Samoul firmly separated from his appetite for at least a month.

The shaman's village was situated close to a muddy brown river which appeared to crawl rather than flow across the land. In some places it was difficult to see where the marshlands ended and the river began. The mud splashed around Samoul's feet as he entered the village and put Bathora down. She giggled with delight as her bare feet sank into the soft ground.

"What's wrong with your earth?" she bubbled. "You can't walk on it. It's more like you walk *in* it. It's hilarious."

"Have you never been to any of the more damp parts of this continent?" Samoul asked.

"What? No, of course not. Our land is all hard and dry. Some people say there are wet parts in the jungle to the south, but I don't believe them. I never go there anyway. Look, there's people coming. Are they your friends?"

The village - a small cluster of tents that looked to be made of the same hide-like material as Samoul's cloak - had been silent when they approached, but now there were people moving towards them. All wore the same garment as the shaman, with various amounts of bone-white ornaments. A beautiful young woman and a young man with long, dark brown hair came up and greeted them.

"This is Lulu," Samoul said. "Lulu, meet Bathora, chieftain of the Telu tribe."

"Hello," Bathora said. "Nice to meet you."

"Likewise," the woman said, in a way that made it very clear she didn't mean it. Bathora was, of course, too stupid to notice, but some left-over instinct told her she wouldn't like this Lulu. She wasn't sure what the cause of the aversion could be. Perhaps the woman was jealous because Bathora was more beautiful and intelligent than her? Or that she was a chieftain and Lulu only an ordinary citizen? Whatever it was, it didn't matter. She was pretty sure she'd be able to kick the woman's ass if she needed to.

The man stepped forward. "I'm Dogshit."

Bathora blinked. "Good for you. Must have been a pretty big dog." She reached out a hand and squeezed the man's thick arm. Lulu shot her a venomous glare.

Dogshit smirked. "No, that's my name. Actually it's Doucheet, but Dogshit is easier to say. You can call me Doggy if you like." He winked at her.

"Oh. Well. Fine. Nice village you've got here. But can you really drink the water in that river?"

"We don't drink water," Lulu said acidly. "Water is for the weak."

"Oh, so it's weekend now?" Bathora said. "I didn't know. What do you drink during weekends, then?"

The swamp people looked confused. After a while Doggy seemed to reach comprehension.

"Oh, now I see," he said. "That's not what Lulu meant. She meant we don't drink the water because all the dirt in it weakens us. We drink other things instead. If you…"

"That wasn't what I meant, and you know it," Lulu snapped. "Stop sucking up to this water-filled piece of pork. It's disgusting."

"Isn't that too early to tell?" Samoul put in.

Lulu chuckled softly. "Very funny, Sam. Oh well, at least the supply is plentiful."

"Yes," Dogshit agreed. "The whole village will meat her."

Bathora looked from one to the other. "What are you talking about? I seem to have trouble understanding your dialect. Besides, I'm hungry. When will there be food?"

"Oh, right after you've had a bath," Samoul said, smiling happily. "You must feel very dirty after the long journey."

Bathora had never thought about things that way. While she lived with the Telu there had been other people to take care of such matters. Some days there'd been someone wiping her skin clean, other days there hadn't. She did feel a bit unclean after having been in contact with Samoul's strange cloak for a day and a half, though, so she nodded her agreement.

"A bath sounds good, as long as I don't have to wait too long for the food."

"Don't worry," Doggy said, taking her by the arm. "We're all pretty hungry, and we'll give you something to munch on while you soak. What's in the usual recipe, Lulu? Carrots, turnips, onions, what else?"

"Only meat and spices," the woman said sourly. "Lots of spices, in case the meat is bad." She gave Bathora a look full of disapproval.

The swamp people seemed like an efficient lot, for by the time Bathora reached the centre of the village they'd already prepared her bath. A large, black kettle hung between two poles. The water in it must've been filtered several times to get rid of as much of the mud as possible. Bathora looked at all the people assembled around the thing.

"Am I to have my bath with all of them watching?" she asked.

Dogshit folded his arms across his chest. "Are you afraid of showing your body, chieftain? I thought you were proud of it. You have very good reason to be."

Bathora grinned happily. "Of course I'm proud of my body. Any sensible woman would be. Not that I've ever met a woman, sensible or not, who looked this good."

The man kept standing there, eyeing her expectantly. When it became apparent he wasn't about to say anything more, Bathora shrugged.

"Well, I suppose it's not every day your primitive tribe gets to see a woman of such beauty. No groping, though."

Lulu snorted and turned around, as if the look of Bathora's naked body made her sick. Dogshit, on the other hand, made no attempt to hide his interest as Bathora removed her garment of office and climbed into the kettle. The water was pretty cold.

"Any chance of getting some heat?" she called over the rim.

"One moment." It was Samoul's voice. Bathora heard someone rummage around on the ground beneath her. A faint smell of smoke drifted up into her nostrils. Soon afterwards the water began heating up into a more pleasant temperature. Bathora sighed happily and splashed a little with her hands.

Something hit her head and fell into the water in front of her. She picked it up and looked at it.

"Ah, carrot. Thanks a bunch." She munched it hungrily. More vegetables kept dropping into the water all around her. It wasn't long before she'd eaten as much as she could.

"It's all right," she called. "I don't want any more. How big a glutton do you think I am?"

There was no reply. Bathora splashed some more, but more out of annoyance than joy this time. The water was getting too hot. She shouted once more to the people on the outside.

"Can you put out the fire, please? I don't want it any hotter."

She waited for them to carry out her request, but nothing happened. Instead the water grew even more scalding. Bathora tried to stand up, but the kettle's inside was so slippery she kept falling over. She shouted again, louder and angrier this time.

"Can't you hear me out there? I said I didn't want any more heat. Have you all gone deaf?"

She thought of various reasons for the lack of response. Was it possible that some outside threat – either a rivalling neighbour or a flock of wild predators – had struck the village and killed everyone in it? Surely she would've heard screams and the sound of battle if that was the case? Or could some strange illness have fallen upon them and put them all to sleep or death? She'd heard of such things happening, but not to an entire tribe within a few minutes.

The water was so hot it hurt her skin. The fumes it gave off made it difficult for her to breathe. She gasped a few times to gather enough air for another shout. This time her voice came out as a shriek, thin and desperate.

"Stop it! You're hurting me! Stop it, I tell you! Help! Help!"

Suddenly she detected motion to her right. Turning her head, she saw Samoul the shaman peering at her over the rim. The relief of seeing her companion's face made her forget about her nakedness. She reached up a hand towards him.

"Samoul! Help me up, please. I'm being boiled alive here."

The shaman didn't reply. Instead, he looked over his shoulder to speak to someone behind him.

"She's doing fine. Nice and red. I think she'll be ready in another hour or two."

Bathora's eyes widened. "What are you talking about? I can't sit here another hour. If you don't put out the fire I`ll be dead in a few minutes. You must… oh."

It appears that some extreme situations, or series of events full of clichés, can be comprehended even by a person of minimal intelligence. One of these typical situations would be to find yourself in a kettle of almost-boiling water, surrounded by chopped vegetables, while people of a foreign tribe watch with hungry eyes and watering mouths.

There was something so unmistakable about the whole thing, even if the person in the kettle was someone like Bathora, who usually couldn't grasp why you couldn't see things when it was dark. Some human instincts are inborn, and knowing when you're about to be eaten seems to be one of them.

"You're not a shaman!" she exclaimed. "You're a cannibal!"

Samoul gave her a mirthless smile.

"You brought me all the way here so you could eat me?" Bathora continued. "Wow, wasn't there anyone else closer at hand? I could've helped you, you know, if you'd just told me what you were after. There are some people in my tribe I'd love to be rid of. Oh well, I suppose you wouldn't settle for anything but the best. Is this some special feast day? One that happens only once in a thousand years?"

Lulu's voice came from somewhere outside the kettle. "She's making an awful lot of noise. Isn't it time to knock her unconscious? I'll be happy to do it. I won't even need a club."

"Soon," Samoul said. "Let me explain a few things to her first. I owe her that much, at least."

"I can do the explaining myself," Bathora snapped. "That cloak of yours. Is it... is it...?"

"Human skin, yes, and the ornaments are parts of human bone. And you're right, of course. We're a tribe of cannibals. In fact, we're the last one. That's why I was sent to fetch you. We knew we were a dying breed, so we called upon the Cannibal God to ask for advice. He told us, while munching on a leg of some very large human, that we had to devour the flesh of one of the great leaders of this land - a queen, a high priest or priestess, or a chieftain of some ancient people of power and wisdom."

"Right, and which of those applies to me?"

"I`m not sure," Samoul said. "Maybe one, maybe all of them. When I saw you, I knew at once you were what we needed. Getting you here was quite easy, even if it almost cost me my poor back. Once you're dead and eaten the future of our tribe will be secured. It'll live forever, while ages come and pass around it. I'm not happy about this, but it has to be done."

"I'm happy," Lulu chirped behind him.

The water was close to boiling now. Bathora had to use all her willpower to keep from crying out in pain. She knew she'd die here, in the cook put of the cannibals. She made one last desperate attempt to rise and leap out of the kettle, but her feet only slipped on its inside. There wasn't much strength left in her limbs, and her head was spinning. Sweat and tears mixed on her face, blinding her eyes.

You might have wondered why the Telu tribe chose a brainless goof like Bathora to lead them. It wasn't, as might be suspected, because of her good looks, nor was it because she belonged to the family which had led them for generations. No, it was due to a completely different reason. Bathora had power.

She wasn't aware of it herself, nor did the other members of the Telu understand much about it. She had a vague idea she wasn't like other people, that there was something special about her. This could be a sign of common arrogance, which Bathora indeed possessed a great deal of, but the notion had much deeper roots than that.

She'd never spoken to any god or goddess, nor had any of them spoken to her in a language she understood. There'd been no need for her to use magic or perform miracles to maintain her dominion over the Telu tribe. Its members didn't even find many virtues to admire in her. They simply thought it'd be best for everyone to have Bathora as their chieftain. And that had worked out well so far. No one had needed her to do anything else. Not until now.

Someone with a more normal level of stupidity might have called upon the gods when faced with a situation like the one Bathora was currently in. The less arrogant ones might have tried some sort of prayer, while the ones too full of themselves to humiliate their pride in such a way were more likely to shout a demand to whatever deity they'd chosen to attach themselves to. The result would be the same. Gods usually have better (or at least what they consider to be better) things to do than listening to humans incapable of taking care of themselves.

No, if you want to use a god's power the thing to do is to just take it and worry about the consequences later. The gods are usually too busy (or too scatterbrained) to pay much heed to whoever's using their power. Someone gifted with sharp wits would recognize this, and someone totally bereft of wits would do it from pure instinct. I don't think anyone requires an explanation as to which group Bathora belonged to.

She raised her arms, hands clenched into fists, and screamed out her rage and frustration at the top of her lungs. The power surged through her like a wild torrent, making her skin tingle and her eyes glow like smouldering embers. She let it all out in one great eruption, and the kettle blew apart around her. Hot water splashed onto the ground, making it even muddier than before. Bathora tumbled out with it.

The air on her bare skin felt pleasantly cool, and the power had relieved her of all fatigue and dizziness. She rose to her feet like some mad, sexy demon and searched for her next victim.

It happened that Samoul was the one closest to where the kettle had been. The blast had thrown him flat on his back, and he was still struggling to get up when Bathora stomped her foot down on his chest, cracking a few more ribs. Then, without a word, she let the power slam into the cannibal like a bolt of lightning. Samoul turned into a crispy piece of meat that he himself was likely to have found exceptionally appetizing.

The village was in turmoil all around her. Children were screaming; men were shouting at each other. Bathora saw some trying to run. She reached out her hand, striking them down with great hammerblows of power. She'd allow no one to get away. These people had planned to have her for dinner. *Her*!

The chieftain of the mighty Telu tribe! Now they had to taste her revenge. She wouldn't rest until every single one of them was dead.

"Stop her!" Lulu shouted, her shrill voice piercing through the din. "Gather together! Attack her from all sides!"

Snarling, Bathora hurled a lance of power at her. Lulu threw herself to one side and rolled behind a bush. Before Bathora could pursue her she was attacked by a number of cannibals waving knives, forks and clubs made of bone.

She swung her arms around, knocking one of her attackers out of the way by accident. More power shot out from her outstretched hands, and bodies erupted in clouds of fire and smoke. That made the last of Bathora's attackers lose their courage. As they turned and fled she laughed hysterically, allowing them to get about halfway to the village's edge before striking them down.

Bathora continued to blow up people and tents and everything else she could find. Somewhere along the way she found her old robe and put it back on. It was dirty and had spots of soot here and there, but it was better than nothing.

At last there were only smouldering piles of ash left of the cannibal village. Bathora looked around. A wooden raft with two people, a man and a woman, was slowly making its way down the river. She regarded it for a while. It wouldn't be too difficult to catch up with them, but that meant she'd have to jump into the muddy water and she had no swimsuit. She shrugged and began walking in another direction. A short time later she'd forgotten all about the raft, the village, and the tribe of cannibals.

~ 9 ~

"Can you see her?" Lulu asked, trying to find a comfortable position on the small raft. It was a task that should have been impossible, but somehow she managed to seat herself sideways between two logs in a way that wouldn't kill her ass for at least a couple of hours.

"No," Doggy said.

She glared at him. "You're looking the wrong way, stupid. That's the way we're going." She pointed to the north. "Look that way."

"Why don't you look yourself? I prefer looking this way."

"Because I've just found a comfortable position. You're standing up, so you should do it. Now, is she following us?"

Reluctantly, Dogshit turned his head and scanned the ground along the river's western bank. "No. I can't see her. She must have given up."

Lulu let out a relieved breath. "Good. I can't believe Sam brought her to the village. All our people are dead because of him."

"Everything went as planned until she blew up the kettle," Doggy said with a shrug. "If Samoul hadn't insisted on talking to her instead of knocking her on the head we'd have our bellies full by now."

"She was a very repugnant woman. I bet we would've gotten sick if we'd eaten her."

"I don't know. I think she looked quite tasty."

For some reason that statement annoyed her. "What's happened to your taste in food? You used to find the best pieces, and always shared them with me. That Bathora woman was foulness itself. How could you even consider eating her?"

He looked down at her, his long hair moving softly in the light breeze. "I wasn't talking about food."

It took her a while to comprehend what he meant. When she did, her face took on a deep red-brown colour. She bared her teeth in a snarl worthy of any feral dog.

"Tell me you're joking."

"I'm joking."

Lulu relaxed. "Phew! For a moment there I was worried. You promised me never to look at another woman."

He laughed. "You know I've broken that promise a thousand times. I can't hunt for food with my eyes closed."

They chuckled together as the raft made its way downstream. After a couple of hours the water got clearer as they left the swamplands behind. Suddenly Lulu's stomach rumbled.

"I'm hungry," she announced.

"Me too," Doggy said coldly. "But we can't go ashore to hunt for meat. We have no weapons, and I know nothing about these parts."

Lulu began laughing hysterically. Her lover glared at her, suddenly filled with the anger you feel when people laugh at something you don't understand. For some reason it always feels like they're laughing at you. In this case the suspicion was justified.

"What?" he demanded.

She pointed at him, still shaking with suppressed mirth. "When... when you said you didn't... didn't know anything about these parts... you... hahaha... you held your hand on your crotch. It just looked so damn funny."

That didn't amuse Dogshit. Very few things did, in fact. Most people considered him a complete bore. Lulu had found a way of using this to her own advantage. By keeping close to Doggy she could draw attention to her own sense of humour, which was quite good at times but quickly grew repetitive. Her jokes usually brought more laughter from herself than from her audience.

Being a very self-centred woman, Lulu rarely noticed the mellow response her jokes received. On the few occasions she did, she dismissed the others as being "as dull as Doggy". This didn't increase the cannibals' appreciation of her sense of humour in the least.

"Well," Dogshit went on, pretending he hadn't heard her words. "We still need something to eat."

Lulu fingered one of the large hoops hanging from her right ear. "That's right. We'll starve if we don't eat."

"Got any suggestions, then?" he asked.

She thought for a few more moments. "Hmm... if you die first I could eat you. Then I wouldn't have to bother with hunting for at least two weeks. Perhaps we don't need food after all. Tell me, are you beginning to feel faint?"

"Not at all. I feel so strong I could kill someone on the spot." He tried to give her a menacing look, but instead his eyes fell on her long, shapely legs, which she'd stretched out in the warm afternoon sunlight. Suddenly the thought of making love on a raft slowly moving down a river seemed unbelievably appealing to him.

He was just about to ask if she felt the same way when she brushed a strand of some sort of weed from her foot.

"Wait!" he said. "I have an idea. Let's do some fishing."

She frowned at him. "But we don't have any..."

"Watch me," he interrupted her.

"Watching you won't get us any fish. You need rope, and a hook, and something to tie it to."

"No, you don't. Just cover your nose." Smiling, he bent down and took off his boots. Lulu quickly put two fingers into her nostrils, but in the fraction of a moment this took her she accidentally got some air into her lungs. The smell was like nothing she'd ever experienced before, like hundreds of corpses rotting in a huge pile of excrement. She felt her head spin, and almost lost consciousness for a moment. Gasping, she tried to push the nausea down.

"So this is why you always keep your boots on when we make love?" she asked.

"Of course. What did you think?"

"I don't know. Maybe you had a deformity you were ashamed of, or something."

This seemed to make him angry again. "I don't have any deformities!"

She tilted her head to one side, making her ear hoops sway a little. "What about that big boil on your..."

"Silence!"

She chuckled softly, then leaned back and watched as he plunged his bare feet into the river. An instant later dead fish began popping through the surface. Lulu laughed and clapped her hands (or rather, slapped her knee with one hand while the other was busy protecting her nose from the terrible smell). Soon Dogshit had gathered enough fish to last them three or four days. He put his boots back on, and Lulu could breathe normally again.

"We'll have to cook these," she said, examining one of the fish. "Get us ashore."

Doggy looked confused. "How? We don't have anything to steer with."

"I don't know. Use your hands to paddle with, or something. Just keep your feet inside those boots. I'm surprised they haven't corroded yet."

"Me too. They've endured a lot of acid from your mouth."

"Oh?" Lulu said, giving him an affronted glare. "So now you complain about my mouth being foul? I'll remind you of that the next time you try to put your tongue into it. I'm pretty sure I haven't had any complaints about that before, from you or anyone else."

Doggy suddenly looked jealous. "What do you mean *or anyone else*?"

"Never mind. Are you going to get us ashore, or do you plan to spend the rest of your life on this raft?"

Dogshit went down on his knees and began paddling vigorously with his hands to get the raft to change direction. Lulu watched him labour with an amused smile on her lips. There weren't many things she enjoyed more than watching a man work, especially when he wasn't very good at what he did. Sometimes Doggy had to crawl over to the raft's other side to stop it from moving around in a circle. Soon his cloak was completely soaked, as was his long hair. His mood was sinking like a drunken hippo in a lake.

"Paddle faster!" Lulu urged him. "And stop splashing. I don't want to have to dry my hair again."

Doggy doubled his efforts, whipping the water around with both hands. The raft moved a little closer to the eastern shore. Lulu moved a little to avoid the water Doggy kept splashing around despite her complaints. The raft reeled violently, almost causing her to fall off. There was a loud splash and a mass of water cascaded over her. She coughed and spattered like a cat.

"What the hell do you think you're doing?" she yelled when she'd got all the water out of her nose and mouth. "Are you trying to drown me?" When there was no answer she looked around. "Doggy? Hello?"

With a shock she realized she was alone on the raft.

"Doggy!" She bent down to look into the water. "Where are you? I'm sorry for yelling at you. Here, take my hand!"

She reached down into the water, moving her arm around in search for her lost lover. There was nothing there. As panic started to fill her, she lay flat on her stomach to reach further into the depths of the river. Tears stung her eyes, but she never admitted that afterwards.

"*Doggy*!" Her voice was reduced to a whisper now. Her arm hung limp, all strength gone from it. The river lay still all around her. The raft barely moved. Lulu almost fell asleep, exhausted from all the excitement she'd been subjected to that day.

Suddenly something touched her arm, jerking her senses back to full alertness.

"Doggy! Here!" she shouted, groping as deeply into the water as she could. Where was he? She couldn't make out any shapes in the dark water. What if he'd hit his head on something and lost consciousness?

Something touched her again. A wet hand grabbed hold of her arm and pulled. She braced herself to haul the man back onto the raft, but the hand only pulled her closer to its edge. Her legs kicked in a desperate attempt to find something to hold on to.

"Doggy!" she screamed. "I can't hold on..."

SPLASH!

You might have gotten the impression that Lulu was a spoiled and lazy brat. This is completely true, but it didn't mean she lacked strength and flexibility. On the contrary, she was a rather fit woman, always keeping a close watch on her figure to ensure she received the proper amount of attention from the male members of her tribe. She was also a good swimmer, which is a very useful trait when you've been pulled head first into a river.

She wrenched herself loose from the hand's grip and kicked herself back to the surface. Once again she fought to get some air back into her lungs. It worked eventually.

"Blimey," she said. "Now look what you've done to my clothes. Not to mention my hair..."

She automatically blamed Dogshit for this mess, which was completely unfair. She'd blamed the man for a lot of things over the years, most of which he wasn't guilty of. He'd never have tolerated this if it wasn't for all the good sex he got out of their relationship. After all, cannibals aren't all that different from other people. They just find more than one meaning to the expression "carnal lust".

Lulu floated there, wondering what to do next, when she felt something touch her leg. This wasn't something she was unused to in any way. Lots of men (and a few women) had tried the same thing ever since she was twelve. Most had been repaid with a slap, one ended up with a crushed skull, another got his manhood chewed off, and two lucky fellows ended up in her bed. None of this would be the outcome today, though.

"Doggy..." she purred, forgetting that the man wouldn't be able to hear her beneath the water. "I know it's you. Get back up and I'll think about it. I suppose I don't have anything else to do while my clothes dry."

The hand moved further up her leg. Lulu started giggling.

"Kinky. I like that. Did you pull me into the water just so my robe would get wet and clingy? The hem is halfway up my thigh, it seems. Clever boy. Very clever, indeed."

A monstrous, vaguely human shape burst through the surface in a cloud of water and mud. It seemed to be made of mud or clay, with black hollows where its eyes should have been and a mouth full of sharp teeth. Its face was twisted into a terrifying grimace, radiating a primal will to hurt and consume. It resembled the look some people have when entering a pub.

Lulu screamed as the mudman reached out its slime-dripping arms toward her. She tried to hit it, but it was like hitting the muddy ground in the swamplands, the holes her fist made in the monster's soft body closing themselves immediately as she withdrew her arm.

Her punches didn't appear to cause the creature any harm at all. Its hand caught her hair and pulled her head closer to its open mouth. She could feel the stench of decay even if the mudman seemed to have no breath. It was nauseating, almost as bad as Doggy's farts the morning after a very long and hard night of drinking.

Closing her eyes, she waited for the creature's sharp teeth to sink into her flesh, wondering briefly if this was how her own victims had felt just before they ended up in her stomach. It almost made her feel a bit guilty, especially since the creature seemed in no hurry to finish her off. Did the slimy thing toy with her? Could it sense her fear and somehow find pleasure in it?

Then she heard a wet sound and mud splashed across her face. At first she wondered if the mudman had spat on her, but then she heard a familiar voice calling from some distance away.

"Lulu! Get away from it! Swim ashore!"

Another rock came flying, this time hitting the creature's shoulder. The strong, wet hand released its grip on her hair, and Lulu managed to kick herself away. Dogshit stood on the shore some twenty paces away, another rock ready for the throw should the mudman attack her again. Right now it seemed too busy with recovering from its injuries. Doggy's first throw had smashed its head into nothing, and it struggled to repair the damage. It seemed able to take parts of its body mass and use them in other places the way you can do with a snowman.

Lulu swam the short distance to the eastern shore and climbed out of the water. Doggy helped her back to a standing position.

"Are you hurt?" he asked, eyeing her dripping form closely. "I was so afraid I'd hit you with one of the rocks. It was quite a long throw."

She wrung some water out of her clothes and hair. "I'm fine. Will it follow us?"

"No, it can't leave the water. It'd get dry and crack before it got very far. But let's get away from the river, in case there are more of them."

They left the river behind and moved on into the jungle. Lulu kept complaining about being hungry, berating Doggy for having lost the fish along with the raft. It required a lot of arguing and an even greater amount of sulking to get him to go look for something to eat, and all he found was some fruit that didn't taste very nice. Lulu munched one of them grumpily.

"Where will we go now?" she asked, wiping some juice from her chin. "Our village is gone, our people dead. There are only the two of us left. It's horrible!"

He swallowed, grimacing at the unpleasant taste. "Well, at least I won't have to worry about you cheating on me."

"Hey! You were the one who couldn't take his eyes off that fat Telu woman."

"She wasn't fat, just curvy. Anyway, we'll have to look for some other place to live. Somewhere we can find lots of good meat. Do you know how far this jungle stretches?"

"Of course I don't!" she snapped. "Why would anyone care about that? It's ugly and smelly and boring. Pretty much like you, actually."

"Perhaps you'd like to go back to the river instead," he shot back. "It's slimy, full of shit, and smells of fish. For some reason it reminds me of you."

She threw a mango at him. It hit him straight in the face.

"Let's continue south," she decided when she'd calmed down a little. "It's too cold in the north, and that Bathora woman came from the east, which means it's probably not very nice over there. We'll have to cross the river with all its muddy horrors if we're to go west. That leaves south. Aren't people supposed to be very juicy down south?"

"No idea. Where did you hear that?"

She shrugged. "Somewhere. Or nowhere. It doesn't matter. We'll find out when we get there."

They spent the rest of that day travelling through the jungle. When night arrived Doggy put together a narrow bed of foliage. It wasn't very comfortable, but he was so tired he could've fallen asleep on a jagged outcrop.

Lulu seemed inclined on keeping him awake, though. She tossed and turned, elbowing him in the side several times.

"What the hell are you doing?" he growled when she almost poked him in the eye.

"I keep getting bugs in my hair," she complained. "It's disgusting."

He turned his head toward her, white teeth gleaming in the dark. "Are you talking about the hair on your head, or somewhere else?"

She was silent for a moment, then burst into a hysterical fit of giggling. It was that contagious kind of giggling you can't protect yourself against, and soon the two of them sounded like a pair of young girls. When their mirth finally subsided they fell into a deep sleep.

The following afternoon they emerged onto the savannah. Neither one had heard the name savannah before, so Lulu chose the very intelligent name "grass-thingy" for it. They continued their journey south without finding any nice places to stay. Dogshit muttered something about how it had been a bad idea to go south and ended up getting all the blame for it himself. There was very little to eat, which - after some loud arguing - he was also blamed for.

The sun had begun the last part of its lazy descent towards the western horizon when they reached the top of a tall hill. A little to their right the river wound its way through the (somewhat) lovely landscape. Lulu raised a hand to shade her eyes when she looked in that direction. Yes, she'd been right. There was a small company of people making their way across the river on the backs of shaggy camels. The country they came from looked more barren than what lay on the opposite side of the river. She turned to Dogshit.

"Do you think they're edible?"

He frowned, not because of her question or because he had to gaze into the sun, but because she'd just released a very foul-smelling fart. She waited for the wind to blow it away before speaking again.

"Well?"

"They look unnaturally pale, except for that young lad over there," he said. "That might mean their meat is a bit tasteless. The major problem, however, is that they're many. At least ten, perhaps as many as a dozen."

Lulu counted. "They're eight, you moron. Five men and three women. And yes, they are pale, and wearing a lot of clothes. Black clothes, in this heat. They can't be very smart."

"Smart enough to put up a pretty good fight, I'm sure," Doggy muttered. "I think we should go talk to them. They might share their food with us if we convince them we're friendly."

She looked confused. "How do we do that?"

"We don't try to eat them."

The newcomers turned out to be some odd sect called the Cult of the Raven God. They came from some caves in the mountains to the west, and were on a mission to put out the sun, if Lulu understood things right. Their leader was an elderly man called Marq-something, and the rest were members of his cult. They wore the large amounts of clothing to protect themselves from the sun, which they called *the evil eye* and seemed to hate more than anything in the world.

"The evil eye," the cult leader said solemnly, "is the root of all evil. Its gaze taints the mind and body, filling us with indecent thoughts and desires."

"Really?" Lulu said. "Like what?"

"Like..." The Marq-fellow hesitated, obviously not used to having his faith questioned.

"Like wanting to have sex with someone?" Lulu suggested.

The High Priest's face took on a ludicrous shade of pink. Lulu realized he was blushing. His reaction made her feel incredibly pleased with herself.

"No, not at all," he mumbled. "Love is a good thing that we of the Raven Cult encourage. Right, Lizbug?"

"Huh?" The female he'd addressed blinked, then turned to glare with disapproval at the High Priest.

"Isn't love a wonderful thing?"

She shrugged. "Sure. As long as it's kept below ground."

The man laughed. The sound had a slightly nervous tone to it.

"Lizbug is a very devout member," he explained to Lulu. "She wasn't happy about journeying into the lands exposed to the light of the evil eye. Said it'd stain the cult's purity. I told her we'd be fine, with these robes protecting us and all. *Never fear the enemy*, I said. *Stand proud and face him down. Let him fear you instead of the other way around.*"

Doggy didn't pay much attention to the High Priest's words. His eyes were fixed on the young woman Lizbug, who was very beautiful and possessed a great deal of sex appeal.

Lulu's face darkened when she saw the worship with which her lover looked at the woman. That she was unable to deny Lizbug's beauty made her even angrier than when Doggy had flirted with the Telu bitch. She pushed the jealousy aside for the moment, but promised herself she'd give the man a piece of her mind later that evening. She might take a piece of his liver in return.

"But I'm sure you're not interested in hearing about our internal affairs," said the High Priest. "Why don't you tell us about yourselves instead?"

"We're... um... travellers," she managed. "Looking for nice stuff."

The High Priest nodded, then his expression grew more serious. "You've been touched by the evil eye. That's not good. How do we know you're not demons from its fiery domains?"

That was a question she'd never expected someone to ask her. It took a while to think of a suitable answer.

"Well, wouldn't we have killed you already if we were? Thrown bolts of fire at you or something? Besides, it's often cloudy where we come from. Which is nice, of course. Much better than this blazing sunlight." She grimaced, hoping to express genuine revulsion.

That seemed a good enough explanation for the old man. Or maybe it was the setting sun shining through Lulu's robe and outlining her slim figure against its fluorescent light that made him discard the doubts he'd had about them. He nodded to himself, patted his old camel gently, and spoke for the whole company to hear.

"These two travellers will share our camp tonight, and continue with us tomorrow if they so choose. I want you to treat them with hospitality and kindness, despite the touch of the evil eye on their bodies. You, fair Lulu, I invite to my own tent."

"And I invite myself to Lizbug's," Dogshit said.

"In your dreams," the young woman replied sourly.

"Fair enough."

Lulu thought this a good opportunity to repay her lover for the jealousy he'd made her feel. She moved closer to the High Priest and gave him a radiant smile.

"I'd be happy to share your tent, High Priest," she said. "Perhaps the touch of your gentle hands will purify my poor, tainted body. And when your hands grow weary I'm sure there are other parts you can use."

She glanced sideways at Doggy, awaiting his retort, but to her dismay he didn't even appear to have heard her. His attention was focused so intensely on Lizbug she thought him unlikely to notice if the earth suddenly opened itself to swallow him.

Standing there, she wished it'd do just that.

~ 10 ~

It is not always easy to make a distinction between a language and mere sounds. A monkey emitting an alarm call, for example, can hardly be accused of using a proper language. But what if it has different sounds to indicate lions, snakes and humans? If a monkey can do that it should (if it's not incredibly stupid even by monkey standards) also be able to invent sounds meaning *two lions*, *big snake*, or *a bunch of loud, messy humans probably under the influence of alcohol.*

This is probably how the most primitive forms of human language were developed. Someone might have used the word *ugh* when seeing another member of the same species. Then, after a while (probably several years, considering how slowly we humans tend to learn new things), extending it to *ugha* (two people), *agh* (hello) and *oy oy oy oy* (look, hot female over there!). After a few thousand years the language will be advanced enough to allow people to write limericks in it.

What Gemma looked at now, however, could not be described in any language so far invented.

"How does that feel?" she asked cautiously. "Do you feel like a man again?"

Tom-Tom looked down at the gnu genitals she'd sewn onto his pubic bone. Blood still dripped from them, they didn't smell very nice at all, and a multitude of flies buzzed around them. If a skull could frown, Tom-Tom's did.

"I'm not sure," he said, touching the thing with a long, bony finger.

Gemma scratched her head and got gnu blood in her hair. "Perhaps you need a woman to practice with. Er... one of your own kind, I mean."

"Maybe. Do you know where I can find one?"

She thought for a while, then shook her head. "No. We used to dig holes in the ground and put our dead there. Perhaps some of them are still able to move. But I suspect those might already have dug their way back to ground level and walked away."

The skeleton shrugged and rose to his feet. They'd found the remains of a black cloak in the Hippo God's temple, and it now hung across Tom-Tom's shoulders like a bat's wings. He turned to gaze across the barren plain to the north.

"We must continue our search," he proclaimed. "The Hippo Cult needs a lot of new members. How many do we have so far?"

"None, unless you count the two of us," Gemma said. "Are you sure we should go that way? It doesn't look very nice."

"The road to accomplishment and wisdom is seldom a comfortable one," Tom-Tom said solemnly. "I suspect there'll be nothing but tears, pain and despair until we've managed to revive the cult."

"Will things get better once it's revived?"

"That depends on how many enemies we've gotten ourselves in the process," the skeleton said, pulling his cloak tighter around him. "My guess is there'll be a few decades of war, possibly famine, diseases and other terrible things."

Gemma looked shocked. "But why do we want to revive it if it will only bring us misery?"

"It's our duty, Gemma. Many people will die, yes, but in the end the land will flourish the way it once did, many years ago. All evil will be driven out; there'll be happiness and love and peace. Don't you think that's worth fighting for?"

"I guess." Gemma didn't sound at all convinced. After a while she shrugged. "Let's go, then."

They set out across the northern plain. It was a dry, barren landscape, very different from the savannah to the west of the Khadal camp.

The savannah! Gemma suddenly remembered. *That was where I was supposed to go, not to the jungle! Why would anyone hunt buffalo in the jungle*? She muttered something under her breath.

"What?" The skeleton turned his head, eyeing her questioningly.

"Oh, nothing. Just amazed at how stupid people can be sometimes."

"Do you mean me?" Tom-Tom asked, the dismal tone back in his voice.

Gemma gave his arm a reassuring pat. "No, silly. You're good company. I'm not sure if you count as *people*, but that doesn't matter. I like you the way you are."

"Really?" Tom-Tom's whole visage brightened, making him look like a young boy who'd asked a girl out for the first time and received a *yes* for reply.

"Yeah. I like how you're so devoted to our cult, that you'd willingly give your life... err... death for it. I think my old tribe could use some skeletons like you."

"That's nice of you to say, Gemma. What are the people in your tribe like?"

Gemma shrugged. "Some are really dumb. You know, going into the jungle to hunt for animals everyone knows live on the savannah and such."

"Ha ha ha. That's pretty dumb, yes. No wonder you left them. A clever girl like you should be able to find better company than that."

Gemma said nothing, only stared intently right ahead of her and hoped the skeleton wouldn't notice the slight flush to her cheeks.

They'd been on their way a couple of hours when a small shape suddenly burst from a bunch of bushes to their left. It only took Gemma an instant to point her spear at the odd-looking young woman standing before her, waving a thin branch as if it were some mighty weapon. After a short time the woman stopped and grinned at Gemma.

"Hi, I'm Fae. I hope I didn't frighten you... much."

Gemma regarded the woman closely. She was quite lovely - her skin tanned nicely brown, her small body well-proportioned and sensual. She suspected most men (and a fair amount of women) would find her attractive. The woman's hair looked odd, though. It was formed into a dome atop her head, with long, thin bones sticking out in every direction. A leather pouch hung from one of them. Gemma wondered if the woman had forgotten about it.

"Hello there, fair lady," Tom-Tom said cheerfully. "Isn't this a lovely day? Perfect for two people to meet and fall in love." He grinned like a fool at Fae.

"Forget it," Gemma whispered in what would've been his ear. "Not bony enough for you."

The skeleton looked disappointed. "We could starve her for a bit," he suggested.

"No." Gemma shook her head. "She'd die."

"That's what I meant."

She sighed, trying to be patient. "You might have forgotten this, but people don't want to die. Starving someone to death is a terrible thing to do. I don't think anyone would even *consider* dating you if you did that to them."

"But being dead isn't really that bad," Tom-Tom protested. "I'd be perfectly fine with it if I had someone to share my death with. Don't you think I can convince her...?"

"No."

"But..."

Gemma silenced him with a sharp look. Turning back to Fae, she tried to think of something constructive to say.

"Would you like to join our cult?" she finally managed.

The small woman beamed at her. "Sure. I was thrown out of my last one. What's yours called?"

"The Hippo Cult," Tom-Tom said, giving her a suspicious look. "Why were you thrown out?"

Fae shrugged. "I called our chieftain a fat cow. She really is one, you know. Except most cows are smarter. Did you know that once she chased her own shadow for three days, claiming someone was following WHAT THE HELL IS THAT?!"

Eyes wide with fear, the young woman pointed at Tom-Tom. The skeleton's robe had blown apart, and the things Gemma had sewn on to him were clearly visible.

"Errr..." Gemma said. "We were trying to make him feel more like a living man."

"And *that* was the best you could think of? I mean, what woman would find that desirable? You're more likely to kill them than excite them, by the pure shock of seeing that, that..."

"That's a great idea!" Tom-Tom exclaimed. "Why didn't I think of that before?"

"Huh?" Gemma gave him a confused look.

"I'll scare the women to death first, and after that I can focus on exciting them. Brilliant! But wait. You didn't die, and neither did Fae. Am I not scary enough? I can do grimaces, you know. Want to see?"

"Tom-Tom," Gemma interjected. "You can't go around scaring people to death. There'd be no one left to join the cult. I think we should take those things off. They might be a problem when we try to recruit new members."

"But I want to be a man!"

"Didn't you hear what Fae said? Not even dead women would find that sexy. We'll think of something later. Perhaps the Hippo God can perform some sort of miracle?"

She didn't know that the most miraculous deed the Hippo God had ever managed was standing on his hind legs for fifteen seconds without falling over.

"Ok, then," the skeleton said with a sigh. "Fae, I'm sorry if I frightened you. I hope you still want to be part of the Hippo Cult. I-I sort of think you're very cute."

Fae gave him a thumbs-up. "Now, that's the way to talk to a girl. Some more training and I might even feel a little faint when you look at me with those big, dark sockets. And it's about time I found myself a husband, so who knows? You might be lucky." She grinned at him.

"Why do you have those bones sticking out of your hair?" Gemma said in a desperate attempt to change the subject.

The girl turned her smiling face to Gemma. "I think they're pretty neat, and when there's lightning I get this incredible light show in my head - green, yellow and purple lights, all swirling and twinkling and bursting into wonderful shapes. And afterwards I glow in the dark for two days, like a big, sexy torch. Have you never experienced that, skeleton man?"

"Umm... no, I don't think so," Tom-Tom said. "Did I glow in the dark, Gemma?"

"Nope, but there hadn't been any lightning for a couple of days. We'll check next time. It does sound quite spectacular."

"Yeah," said Fae. "But it kinda sucks when you try to hide. There was this time when I had an affair with my friend's husband, and when she came home I tried to hide under the bed. It didn't work out very well."

"Would women find glowing skeletons exciting?" Tom-Tom asked.

Fae patted him on the head. "I'm sure you'll find a way to use it to your advantage, dude. I once tricked this guy into believing I was a goddess and demanded he give me some sweets. I could've gotten all he owned if he'd been more religious. Now, where are you two headed? If we continue this way we'll bump straight into my old tribe, and that wouldn't be a good idea. They're not a very nice bunch."

"Perhaps we can turn their souls away from their evil paths and lead them into the Hippo God's light," Tom-Tom intoned.

"Right," Fae muttered. "It'd be easier to lead them into the river. Better, too. But I'll let you try, if you feel you must. Don't blame me if it ends in disaster, though."

It took them two more days to cross the dry, barren wasteland north of the jungle. Fae turned out to be a very companionable person, good at telling jokes and making a fool of herself. She wasn't very good at hunting, though. Her strategy seemed to rely on finding animals who got scared to death when small human girls shouted and waved their arms madly at them, or beasts with bodies so fragile they died when someone threw a stick at them. Unfortunately they didn't encounter any such creatures on their journey, which meant that Gemma ended up doing all the hunting.

Tom-Tom tried to eat, but the food just went straight through him. That led to another discussion about what being a man was like.

"A man eats large steaks and drinks strong beverages," he whined as Gemma wiped his bones clean of badly chewed meat. "I remember that. Large bowls of fruit and other delicious things. What does delicious mean, anyway? I remember the word but can't recall what it stands for. Is it a colour? Or a shape?"

"No, silly," Fae said between slurpy sounds. "It's a taste. Like the meat on this leg. It's delicious. What kind of animal was it, Gemma?"

"No idea. Never seen one like that before. It was about five feet long, looked somewhat like a small gnu but with warts all over its head and upward-pointing tusks. Quite a fierce little fellow, really. Almost tore the skin off my leg." She pointed to her thigh, where a long, thin scratch ran across her brown skin.

"A warthog," Fae explained. "Yeah, those buggers can be a bit nasty when they're threatened. That's why I never go near them. I knew a guy who tried to ride one once, though. I still don't know who made the loudest noises, he or the hog. Ha ha ha, that was a lot of fun." She burst into fits of chuckling laughter.

"I didn't taste *anything* when I ate the meat." Tom-Tom's voice was even gloomier than before. "At least I don't think I did. I can't really remember how you do when you taste things."

"You do it with your mouth," Gemma explained. "Put the food on your tongue and you can usually tell what it is even if you didn't look at it before."

"What's a tongue?" the skeleton asked. He put two fingers into his mouth and explored the inside of his jaw bone.

Fae stuck out her tongue as far as she could. "Wis is a towwg!"

Tom-Tom gave it a tentative look. "And all humans have those?" he enquired.

"As far as I know," the young woman said when her tongue was safely back inside her mouth. "You use them for kissing, too."

"Kissing..." the skeleton said wistfully. "I think I kissed a woman when I was alive. Or maybe several of them. Gemma, do you think you could find a tongue and fasten it to my mouth?"

Gemma choked on her meat. "I don't think that'd work any better than the gnu genitals," she said when she'd stopped coughing. "Putting a dead animal's tongue into your mouth wouldn't make you taste the food. As for the kissing... no, not recommendable. Right, Fae?"

"Not recommendable at all," the girl agreed.

Tom-Tom seemed to sink even deeper into his state of post mortem depression. For a moment Gemma thought she saw damp spots on the bone below his eye sockets. *Skeletons don't cry*, she told herself, but the anguish in Tom-Tom's voice almost made her believe it possible.

"I felt there was something in my mouth, but it could just as well have been a piece of cloth," he moaned. "This is horrible! The more time I spend in the world of the living, the more dead I feel. It was better back in the temple. There was no one to remind me of everything I've lost." He took a discarded bone from the ground and threw it into the fire. "I hate life," he whimpered. "Dead people shouldn't be alive."

Gemma tried to think of a way to comfort the skeleton. "But you have an important task to carry out," she said, trying to sound cheerful. "Without you there'll be no more Hippo Cult. You can't give up now, Tom-Tom. The world needs you."

"Yeah," Fae put in. "And there are all these nice, dead, rotting women waiting for you. You don't want to miss out on those, would you?"

Despite their efforts, Tom-Tom stayed in his sulky mood the rest of that evening, forcing Gemma and Fae to entertain themselves as best they could. Gemma asked the other woman about the tribe she'd been thrown out of, so she'd know what to expect when they reached the place of its camp. What she learned didn't increase her faith in the Hippo Cult's future.

"Our... I mean, their chieftain is called Bathora. She's got an ass the size of a continent and is probably the most stupid creature ever to walk on two legs, or any number of legs for that matter. The members of the Telu, which is the name of the tribe she rules - or whatever you call the pointless strutting about she usually does - don't have much more in the way of intelligence than their chieftain. How they've managed to survive this long is beyond me. I can do more in one day than the entire tribe usually accomplishes in a week."

"You mean they're lazy?"

Fae shook her head, causing the leather pouch to swing back and forth.

"Oh, no," she said. "They do all kinds of stupid things, like running around the camp until they pass out, or digging holes that they fill up again the next day. Anyway, what I was trying to say is that it's impossible to get them to do anything useful. They might be willing to join this Hippo Cult, but they're also very likely to ruin it from sheer stupidity."

"But are they evil?" Gemma asked.

"Not really," Fae said, drawing circles in the dirt with a stick. "There are good and bad people among them. Most are somewhere in between. They can be selfish and callous, sneaky and pretentious, but also honest and helpful. The only one who might cause some real trouble is that Bathora woman. Her mind is like a rhino - it may seem slow, simple and harmless, but once it's put into motion it can cause severe damage before someone gets it to stop."

Gemma thought about this for a moment. "But why did you make her your chieftain if she's that stupid? Wouldn't it be better to pick someone smart?"

Fae shrugged. "It's not that simple. I think she was chosen to be chieftain because a chieftain isn't really supposed to do anything. If she'd been put to hunt or build things she'd cause much more harm than she'd do as a ruler. You need some skill to carry out most tasks, but anyone can be a chieftain. It's probably the best way to keep a person away from the important decisions."

Gemma thought about the chieftain of her own tribe. Marsha was a good woman, both friendly and clever, and they hadn't made her chieftain just to get her out of the way. She wondered what Marsha was doing now. Several days had passed since Gemma left the Khadal camp.

They must be really worried by now, she thought. *Pebe's mind is of a rather fragile nature, and if Emkei spews out one of those cryptic messages that no one understands things could get really bad for them.* She promised herself she'd go back once this Hippo Cult business was finished.

Fae wanted to put on some sort of disguise so the members of her old tribe wouldn't recognize her. There were very few useful things in the wilderness, though, so the best she could come up with was to put dirt on her face and cover the bones in her hair with whatever greenery she could find. When she was finished she turned to Gemma.

"What do you think?"

Gemma looked at her thoughtfully. "I'm not sure. You still look like yourself, somewhat. I could kill another warthog and cut the hide loose for you, if you like."

"Hide," Tom-Tom muttered. "I wish I had hide."

"It's called skin on humans," Fae pointed out.

"It doesn't matter what you call it. I'll never get mine back. Dead people never get anything."

"At least you don't have to worry about stomach flu," Fae grumbled.

"The chieftain of my tribe is very good with potions," Gemma said. "Perhaps she can mix something together that'll make your hide grow back.

She once gave Emkei a draught that made tusks grow from her jaw. Some of the men still say they made her look better. Anyway..."

They found nothing better to distort Fae's appearance with, so after some heated discussion they decided she'd stand behind Tom-Tom when they entered the Telu camp. They did that a little after noon.

"Hello, Fae!" one of the tribesmen called out cheerfully. "Where have you been? I missed you loads."

Gemma and Fae exchanged a look. Fae shrugged.

"Hello, Joz. Err... I was driven away. Didn't get along too well with Bathora. I don't think she'll be happy to see me here. Do you know if there's some place I can hide?"

The man bared his unnaturally white teeth in a wide smile. "You don't have to. She isn't here anymore. Just left one day and never came back. Winston and Gideon are leading us now. The two of them have been sharing a tent for a couple of days. Never saw that one coming?"

"No one ever thinks very much around here, Joz," Fae said. "That's probably why we're still alive. So Bathora left, huh? I pity the poor people she's gone to pester now."

"Perhaps she couldn't find her way back," Joz said. "Her memory isn't all that good. Anyway, we're doing quite well without her. Who are your companions, by the way? Aren't you going to introduce us?" He gave Gemma a long, appreciative glance.

"Sure." Fae pointed at each of her friends in turn. "This is Gemma of the Khadal tribe, and this is Tom-Tom, chief skeleton of the Hippo Cult. He may seem a little whiny, but he's quite nice once you get to know him. If we only manage to find him a wife I'm sure his mood will improve."

The Telu man frowned as he contemplated this. "A wife for a skeleton? That won't be easy. There's Marya, of course. She says she likes slim men."

"Is she dead?" Tom-Tom asked, not sounding too hopeful.

"Why, of course not. None of the women in our tribe is dead. A few might be deadly boring, but I don't think that's what you're looking for."

"He's just spent several hundred years alone in a dark cavern," Gemma said. "So I'd say he's familiar enough with boredom. We were looking for someone dead, though."

"Well, Shelma is quite old," Joz said. "So if you have the patience you can wait for her to pass away. She seemed healthy enough the last time I talked to her, though."

"We'll deal with that later," Fae said. "Right now we need to get everyone together. There's a very important announcement we have to make."

Joz nodded slowly. "Right. Get everyone together. I'll see what I can do. Please sit down while you wait. I'll be right back."

It turned out it took half the afternoon to get all the people of the Telu together. Most were running about all over the surrounding country, as if intent on showing everyone and everything the meaning of the word purposelessness. They even had to get a few down from the distant mountains, where they'd gone in a desperate attempt to find a woman's lost eye.

That the woman in question appeared to have been born without it hadn't done anything to lessen their enthusiasm, and as they were dragged back to the camp they kept asking how long it'd be before they could continue their search.

Gemma didn't like the look of this Winston who'd taken over the task of leading the Telu. Fae had told her he changed appearance from time to time. Gemma had thought she meant he changed his hair style or dressed a different way, but when she saw him she understood the changes were far more complicated than that.

The man had two thin wings on his back, and a sharp sting growing from a point just above his buttocks. The skin on his arms was striped in yellow and black, so sharply it hurt her eyes to look at him. She was filled with an intense urge to swat him, but what really brought a sour taste to her mouth was the expression on his face. She couldn't put a finger on what it was she didn't like about it. It just wasn't a nice expression.

Gideon looked much nicer. His body was lean and athletic, and his face quite handsome. He also appeared to be somewhat smarter than the rest of the tribe (which didn't say much, to be sure). The other men and women looked like common idiots.

Winston eyed the newcomers. "What business brought you to our camp, strangers?" he said haughtily. "I don't suppose you have news of our former leader, the woman Bathora?"

"No, sir," Gemma said after a moment of hesitation. "We've come to ask you to…" She broke off as something hit her softly on the shoulder. She turned to see what it was.

Fae's pouch had fallen from the bone it'd been attached to and now lay on the ground at her feet. Gemma bent down to pick it up.

She almost dropped it again when the air around them erupted with gasps and exhilarated outbursts. The storm of sound was so sudden and so forceful it almost made her sway. She stood there, holding Fae's pouch in one hand as she looked at the Telu people, most of whom had now fallen to their knees with their eyes fixed on her. The look of them made her frown.

"What's going on?" she asked.

It was Gideon who answered. He and Winston were the only ones who'd remained standing.

"This is a miracle! The gods have sent us a ruler who will stand above all our former chieftains. For the first time in hundreds of years the Telu tribe will have a queen. This heralds the beginning of a new age, a time of greatness for our tribe. It's an apocalypse, a rebirth. Command us, Your Grace. We're your humble servants."

Gemma waved her hands, feeling very embarrassed about this new situation.

"Hey, hey, calm down a little, you lot," she said. "I'm just a member of the Khadal tribe who got lost in the jungle. I'm no queen, and I'm not going to do any of this apoco-stuff. Please get back to your feet and stop this silly bowing and scraping."

Some of the people obeyed this, her first command as the queen of their tribe, but most remained on their hands and knees. They were obviously too overwhelmed by her presence to carry out their duties as her subjects. Even Winston looked a bit taken aback. His wings fluttered restlessly on his back, producing a soft humming sound. He finally decided the situation called for some explaining and started to speak slowly.

"There's an old prophecy among our people," he said. "Stating that when the thonged woman appears among us there will come a new age of glory and power for the Telu. Whatever chieftain is in charge of the tribe at that time will have to renounce his leadership and become a servant of the new queen."

The tone in his voice made it clear he wasn't at all pleased with this prospect. Gemma suspected he'd planned to spend the rest of his life as this tribe's ruler, and now, after only a couple of days, he found himself once more reduced to a lowly servant. She listened carefully as he continued speaking.

"The entire tribe will be at her command as she leads us into a future of endless victories and wonders. When you turned your back to us we saw the sign we've been waiting for, and I have to admit it was a very pleasant thing to behold. So, the prophecy has been fulfilled and we have our queen. What would you like us to do, Your Grace? The Telu awaits your orders."

Gemma's face split into a wide smile. This was an unexpected twist of events. She didn't believe all this nonsense about a prophecy and a time of glory and miracles, but if these people thought her thong made her some kind of semi-goddess, well, that was just great. Now the rest of their mission would be as easy as making Pebe blush. Well, almost as easy.

"I command you all to join the Hippo Cult," she announced. "Tom-Tom here is an old member, and we're going to revive the cult and bring it back to its former greatness. The Telu will be the first people to join, which is a great honour."

She added the last as a way of showing how gracious a queen she'd be. It didn't have the effect she'd hoped for.

The members of the Telu stopped their acts of worship and stared incredulously at her. A soft murmur arose, disapproving voices that'd been filled with admiration and awe only a moment ago. Winston's features were distorted with rage and disgust. Gideon's pleasant smile had changed into a terrible rictus, his white teeth looking more like fangs ready to bite. Gemma looked at all the hostile faces, then leaned close to Fae.

"What did I do wrong?" she asked.

"I'm not sure, but I'd have that spear ready if I were you."

"I had my doubts the moment I saw you," Winston growled. "It was like a voice from inside, telling me you'd bring nothing but trouble to our tribe. And see now what's happened. You're trying to turn us over to our ancient enemy, to make us slaves to the Hippo Cult. I should've had you killed the instant you set foot in this camp."

"Hold on a sec," Gemma said, trying to sound calm. "I`m not trying to turn you into slaves. You told me yourself that I would lead you into a time of greatness. What does it matter if you'll achieve that as members of the Hippo Cult?"

"It does matter!" Winston's voice had risen to a roar. "Our tribe has fought endless wars with the Hippo Cult over the centuries. Thousands of us have died. Tens of thousands. A member of the Telu would rather swallow his own mother than become part of that, that *filth*!"

"Hey!" exclaimed Tom-Tom. "The Hippo Cult used to be the centre of wisdom and prosperity on this continent. I won't stand here and listen while such blasphemies are brought down upon its name. I might be thin, but I'm hard, and I'm not afraid to die. I'm used to it!" He clenched his fists and held them up like a boxer.

"I'm your queen!" Gemma shouted, sounding more and more desperate despite herself. "Look, I wear the thong. You must obey my commands!"

"Be silent, false queen!" Gideon roared. "I don't know what devil sent you here, but we'll send you straight back to him. The true queen of the prophecy would never suggest such a thing as you just did. You're just trying to mislead us with your nice, shapely rear. Well, we're not fooled that easily. We know a fake when we see one."

"This is even worse than in Bathora's days," Fae muttered.

Tom-Tom took a step closer to Gemma. "I think it's time for us to leave," he said in a low, urgent voice. "We won't accomplish anything here. I remember now. The people we fought, who ruined the Hippo Cult and laid waste to our homes, was called the Telu."

She blinked. "You were defeated by people like *these*?"

"Not really. They were a much more powerful people back then. And I think they had a queen - a woman of incredible slyness and malicious power. The prophecy must have something to do with her."

Gemma nodded. She wanted nothing more than to get out of there and forget this nasty tribe ever existed. The only problem was that its people had formed a circle around them and were closing in, slowly but steadily. Gideon had found a spear somewhere and was now advancing in Gemma's direction. She looked around for a way out, but saw only dark eyes in dark faces. Eyes wanting to see blood, demanding to see blood. *Her blood.*

They were saved by a mere accident. Dark clouds had drifted in from the east, and thunder had begun echoing between the mountains. Suddenly a bright flash of lightning burst from a cloud that looked like a rampaging beast, bathing the camp in white light for an instant. There was a deafening boom, and the ground shook slightly.

Fae cried out, a mix of terror and delight in her voice. Alarmed, Gemma turned to see if the girl was alright. Blue sparks ran back and forth along the bones in her hair, and her face glowed with a bright light that shifted from green to orange to purple. But it wasn't the young Telu woman who made her gasp and open her eyes wide.

Tom-Tom had turned into a pillar of light and electric sounds. It was as if the lightning bolt was racing through every bone in his body, crackling and hissing. A cloud of multi-coloured sparks surrounded him, blue and silver lightning erupting from his outstretched hands. It was a glorious show of flashes and explosions, more spectacular than any fireworks the world would behold in later days.

Naturally, it drove the primitive members of the Telu tribe wild with fear.

The circle of murderous faces that had surrounded Gemma and her friends dissolved, and instead there was a camp full of running and screaming lunatics. Gemma grabbed her spear, shouted for Fae and Tom-Tom to follow her, and set off towards the wilderness they'd come from earlier that day.

Before she left the camp she looked back over her shoulder to see if anyone followed them. No one did, and there was only one person who stood silently, untouched by all the panic, and watched her go with expressionless eyes.

Winston.

~ 11 ~

Marsha had a nightmare.

As chieftain of the Khadal this was something she was quite used to. Every week in that tribe contained at least three or four days she'd remember the same way you remember a really bad dream. People often forgot whether it was lions or zebras who ate people, and the most insignificant problems were likely to cause a turmoil that could take hours to sort out.

It had, for example, happened several times that someone had accused a fellow tribesman of having put maggots in their stew, and even if Marsha knew it was always the man's own short-sighted mother who'd done it, mistaking the slimy little creatures for sausages, it always took all her authority and experience to prevent the outbreak of a war between the families in question. The stew usually ended up in front of Emkei, who wasn't touchy about what kind of dead animal she put into her mouth.

Another incident that left her wishing she were dead was when Pebe had lost his little rag doll (this didn't happen back when he was a small child, but less than two years ago) and the entire camp had to search the surrounding countryside for two days. Finally the doll was found under a pile of laundry, where Pebe himself had put it to protect it from the evil ghosts he believed to roam the camp at night.

Amanda had shaken her head and muttered, "*No one can boast like Pebe bold, but the thought of ghosts will get his pants soiled.*"

This nightmare had nothing to do with trivial matters like these, however. In the dream Marsha was walking through a strange land, searching for something she couldn't remember but knew was of great importance. Like in most dreams, she paid no attention to the fact she had no idea where she was, or that she didn't know how she'd ended up there.

She stopped to look at a big rock. *Funny,* she thought. *It looks almost like a head. I wonder if there are rocks shaped like other body parts as well.*

After considering this for a while she found herself blushing fervently. *What would happen if there were rocks shaped like men and women, and they tried to mate*? Something told her that might actually happen, even if it hadn't in a very long time.

"They've forgotten how to do it," she said to herself. "Just like I've forgotten what I'm searching for."

As she walked on, trying to remember what she was looking for, a demon appeared atop a hill a couple of hundred paces ahead. It was a horrifying thing, taller than most trees and surrounded by flames. Its roar made the ground shake, forcing Marsha to cover her ears with trembling hands.

The demon threw its head back, lifted its dark arms to the sky and bellowed its rage into the heavens. Lightning struck the ground around it, causing tons of earth and rock to erupt into the air.

Marsha turned and fled.

The demon's red, glowing eyes spotted the fleeing shape far below. It roared again and lumbered after her, strong legs carrying it across the ground at a fearsome speed. Marsha knew she wouldn't be able to escape it, but still she ran. She ran like she'd never run before in her life.

Where were her friends? She had to warn them, tell them to escape while she tried to draw the demon's attention away from them. She was their chieftain. It was her responsibility to make sure they were safe, to sacrifice herself to save their lives. Where could they have gone? They'd been at her side only a short time ago.

She spotted Pebe among the trees to her left. The young man was hanging out washing, tying the clothes to a length of rope dangling between two trees. He glared at Marsha when she came running towards him.

"You stole my doll!" he shouted, pointing an accusing finger at her. His other hand was gripping a bunch of towels. "You gave her to the ghosts!"

"I did not!" Marsha said between gasps of laboured breath. "Pebe, forget the doll. There's a monster coming this way. You must run, quickly!"

The man seemed not to have heard her. "Give me my doll. I saw the ghosts take it and give it to *her.* It is not hers. She should get one of her own."

Marsha was confused. "Who? Who did they give the doll to?"

"She says she's the greatest, but that's not true. I'll kill her elephant to prove it. That won't make her happy, of course, but that's not my problem." He chuckled happily.

"I don't know what you're talking about," Marsha said. "But it doesn't matter. You have to get out of here. The demon will appear any minute now. Go! Run!"

Pebe took one of the towels and wiped his face with it. "Amanda will take care of it. She'll take care of everything."

Marsha thought about this for a moment. Amanda really was freakishly strong, but was she strong enough to defeat this demon? She'd seen the power it wielded - a force more fearsome than anything she'd seen before. Well, there was no one else to help her. She had to find Amanda.

She left Pebe and ran into the woods. Behind her she heard the sound of the demon's progress, closer now, so close she could feel the ground shake with each of its mighty strides. The heat it radiated was carried on the wind, touching her skin and making her sweat. She ran on, wondering how much longer she'd manage.

Emkei was stirring a large, black kettle with something that looked like an elephant's tusk. The seer's heavy bosom bounced up and down as she worked. Marsha thought she'd never seen the fat woman display such energy.

The steam the kettle's contents gave off was so acrid it made Marsha's eyes run and her nose itch. It didn't seem to bother Emkei, who was leaning slightly forwards so she could look down at the brew she was stirring. Holding a hand over her nose and mouth, Marsha went closer.

"Emkei, have you seen Amanda? There's a huge demon coming, and I think she's the only one who can defeat it. I must find her, and quickly."

"Shhh," the seer cautioned. "It'll soon be ready now. It must be done the right way, or everything will be lost. So much is at stake, and there are strong forces working against us. They weave their webs all around us, but if we keep them boiling they'll lose their stickiness. They don't like heat, oh no, be it sunlight or fire."

"The demon was surrounded by fire," Marsha said, not sure what to make of the woman's inane rambling. "But I'm certain it hasn't come to help us. We must either defeat it or run. I don't think we can run away from it, though. It moves so fast."

Emkei didn't lift her eyes from the kettle's contents. "It will help us in a way, but it's true that we can't escape it. It'll kill us all if we don't stop it, and then our mission will be doomed to failure. Amanda will take care of it. She's a good girl. She'll take care of everything."

Yes, but how can she do anything if I don't find her? Marsha thought with growing desperation. She racked her brain, trying to find some clue in Emkei's cryptic words, but it was no use. The seer's words simply made no sense at all to her.

The demon will help us, but it'll kill us if we don't defeat it? How would that be possible?

Suddenly Emkei dropped the elephant tusk and picked up a small cup. She dipped it into the kettle, then lifted it to her mouth and emptied it. She didn't swallow. Instead she gargled, producing a thick, bubbling sound that made Marsha feel sick.

The seer continued her gargling, eyes shining with delight. Finally Marsha overcame her revulsion and stepped close enough to look into the kettle. It appeared to be filled with muddy brown water, with something that looked like spiderwebs floating here and there. In the middle lay one large object, and somehow she knew it to be the core of everything, the foundation stone upon which the future of her people rested. It was the goal of her mission, the thing she'd been searching for.

It was an egg, large and oblong, its surface covered with intricate patterns. It seemed to look up at her, as if asking for help.

"I'll return to you," Marsha said, feeling as if talking to an egg was the most natural thing in the world. "I'll have to deal with the demon first, but then I'll come back to you. Don't worry, you'll be safe here. They don't like the heat, remember?"

She had no idea why she'd said that last thing about the heat, but she knew it was true. Stepping away from Emkei and the kettle, she looked around. Where was Amanda? She had to find her soon, or the demon would lay waste to everything, including the egg.

And that would mean the end for the Khadal, and all other good-hearted people on this continent. That was clear to her now. How could she not have seen it all along?

The demon was very close now. She heard its roaring mixed with the noise as it trampled down trees and bushes. Had it killed Pebe already? The poor boy would never get his doll back. What had happened to the bloody doll anyway? She shook the thought away and started running again.

She found Amanda at the foot of a steep cliffside. The woman was beating a large, grey elephant with a very small stick. The beast had a black cloth tied around its face, covering its eyes. Amanda was shouting at it furiously.

"Bad elephant! Didn't I tell you what would happen if you cheated again? You're only allowed to throw the dice *three* times! That's zero points for you, and don't try to argue! I don't care if you didn't get to touch the queen's ass.

Give me the dice now and let's continue this farce of a game. What?! You gave them to the gargling woman? Have you lost your mind? I'm not touching them after they've been in *her* mouth!"

"Amanda!" Marsha called. "You have to help us! There's a large demon coming, and you're the only one strong enough to defeat it. Let go of the poor elephant. It didn't mean to steal the skeleton's manhood. The demon..."

She turned around. The demon was approaching, long arms outstretched before it. It was still wreathed in flames. The heat was so intense it made rivulets of sweat run down Marsha's face. She wondered what would kill her first, the heat or the demon's sharp fangs. Desperately, she turned back to Amanda.

"Stop it, Amanda! It'll kill all of us, and then we won't be able to protect the egg! Stop it!"

Amanda frowned at the approaching monstrosity. "It's only a demon," she muttered.

"You must stop it!"

The demon was only a dozen paces away. It stopped for a moment, regarding the two small shapes before it. Marsha tried to back away, but she only bumped into the elephant.

"Oops, sorry," she said without thinking.

"This will teach it a lesson," Amanda said. She lifted the elephant into the air, held it over her head for a moment before flinging it at the demon as if it'd been a loaf of bread. The demon toppled over backwards and landed on the ground with the elephant across its body. The impact of the fall made the ground shake and cracks opened all around them. Marsha was thrown off her feet as well and landed on her butt. That didn't make the ground shake.

"There," Amanda said, sounding very satisfied with herself. "That should keep it occupied for some time. Now, where's Gemma? I got a sudden craving for roasted buffalo."

Marsha frowned. "How am I supposed to know where she is? I haven't seen her since..."

She couldn't remember when she'd last seen Gemma. As a matter of fact, she had trouble remembering what Gemma looked like. Did she have bones in her hair? Or bones sewn onto her clothing? She wasn't all bones, was she? She had a very disturbing image of a very bony figure with something unspeakable sewn onto its loins. No, that couldn't be her. Gemma was a good-looking woman - all the men had agreed on that. But why couldn't she remember her face?

There was a deafening roar right beside her. The demon bent down, picked up Amanda by the hair and threw her hundreds of feet into the air. Marsha saw her vanish into the distance. It was only her and the demon now. The elephant was nowhere to be seen.

The demon turned to her. Its face was ghastly, like a mix of all nightmares ever dreamed throughout the history of mankind. It was a face more horrible than anything she could have imagined, and yet it looked oddly familiar when she saw it this close. She couldn't bring herself to look away. The demon leaned down, the stench of its breath making her dizzy.

A giant pair of dice rolled down the cliffside and tumbled onto the ground between them. The demon gave them a puzzled look as they rolled away across the ground.

"YAHTZEE!!" someone called. The voice seemed to come from very far away, but was still strong enough to fill the air around them. Marsha pointed an accusing finger at the demon.

"You cheated!" she shrieked. "It wasn't your turn! Give me the dice!"

The demon let out an infuriated roar, obviously none too pleased with being accused of cheating. Its bestial face came closer to Marsha until it seemed to fill the entire world around her. She screamed and put her hands over her eyes, but the face wouldn't go away. She was still screaming when she woke up.

"Calm down, dear lady," said Ogian. He was leaning over her bed the same way the demon had loomed over her in the dream. There wasn't anything scary about Ogian, though. The man's mind was as innocent as that of a child, and probably less intelligent. There was genuine concern in his eyes as he looked down at her.

"You must've had a nightmare," he continued. "That happens to me too, sometimes. Once I dreamed that Bunta-koop didn't let me play Yahtzee with him. I woke up soaked in sweat and wouldn't stop shivering until they put the dice in my hands. Was your nightmare like that, too?"

Marsha shook her head. "Not exactly, though there were dice in it. Big dice."

She glanced around, half her mind still caught in the nightmare. It took her brain a few moments to remember where she was.

The camp of the Elephant People, yes. I'm in one of their tents, and there's no demon anywhere. We're all safe here.

The gargling woman had decided they were to head south, so south they'd headed. Emkei had tried out some of Hannah's brews, finding them both pleasant-tasting and good for the mind. That she hadn't heard any gods speaking to her didn't bother her much. What was truly important was that her bowels felt better than they had in a very long time, which brought a lot of inconvenience to Kharuba and the others who were in charge of shovelling the dung together.

"What was your nightmare about, then?" Ogian enquired.

"An egg," Marsha said absent-mindedly. She never paid much attention to her dreams, but the image of the large egg lingered in her mind even though the rest of the nightmare was fading.

The egg is important. I must find it and protect it. But where do I look? There's a whole continent out there, and it could be anywhere.

"An egg?" Ogian sounded puzzled.

"Yes, a large egg. It's very important. I must find it."

The black man thought for a moment. "I think there are ostriches on the plains to the north. They lay pretty big eggs. But we're going the wrong way if you want to find them. The gargling woman said our goal lies to the south, so that's where we're going."

Marsha nodded. She doubted the egg she was looking for was an ordinary bird's egg anyway.

But how do I find it? And who are those other people looking for it? What was that thing about them not liking fire?

Ogian seemed to have gone back into his own thoughts, so she poked his arm softly.

"Was there something you wanted to tell me?"

He blinked. "Oh, yes. The Queen wants to see you. She's waiting right outside."

Marsha rose and went out into the fresh morning air. The sun was just making its way over the eastern horizon, painting the sky in shades of pink and orange. Tiwi stood atop a small rise, looking out over the landscape to their south. She smiled when Marsha joined her.

"G'morning, Marsha. Isn't it a lovely morning? I hope you slept well."

"I did," Marsha said cautiously. She saw no reason to tell this woman about her dream. Tiwi had treated the Khadal people well enough since they became part of her camp, but Marsha wasn't ready to trust the woman with her more personal thoughts yet. They had assumed their quests had nothing to do with each other, but Marsha didn't doubt the queen of the Elephant People would do anything to protect her own interests if a conflict arose. So she said nothing about the egg or how she'd learned about its existence.

"What were you looking at before?" she asked instead. "What kind of land lies ahead of us?"

Tiwi pointed into the distance. "Do you see that mountain over there? We'll set our course towards it today. It's further away than it looks, so it'll take us a few days to reach it. The legends say a deep and ancient power lives inside it. It'll be a good place to look for the answers to all our questions."

Marsha looked at the mountain. It had a menacing look to it. White smoke rose from its top and she thought she heard a faint rumbling sound coming from it. Looking at it made her queasy, so she turned her eyes back to Tiwi.

"What's this mountain called?" she asked.

"It's called Mount Azagh," Tiwi said. "Named after the ancient Demon of Fire."

~ 12 ~

The subject of love has been widely debated ever since human languages became advanced enough to express more intricate thoughts than *I want food* or *I want sex* (even though a brain belonging to a body which had just consumed fourteen pints of beer is highly unlikely to manage thoughts more complicated than those two examples). Is there really such a thing as love? Or is it simply a combination of feelings with names much less suitable for soppy songs? Is "love" an excuse humans use to cover up needs and wants they'd rather not admit to having?

These questions might make some of you uncomfortable. *Of course there's such a thing as love*, you'd say. *It's in all the movies and songs and books. What more than a woman's love could drive a man to walk through fire and water, risk his own life and act like an utter fool in general? What is left to live for when love has abandoned you?*

Well, most people who've just broken up with someone wait for the next weekend, then they go out and find someone new to "love". So there really isn't any reason to be all devastated when you've lost your "special one". There are plenty of them out there.

But enough of the cynicism for now. Let's instead look at a few situations where the word *love* can be applied rather safely.

First, imagine a married couple who've lived together for forty years. The love they feel for each other is very different from what two drunk teenagers experience when they head off towards the nearest bush. Love, to these old people, is more a feeling of trust and safety, a knowledge of what your partner feels and wants. They've long since learned to respect each other's differences and to treasure the things they have in common. One of them may even have had a well-paid job, which probably added a warm and fuzzy feeling of safety to their relationship.

Then there's the love a man feels when he has a newly poured pint of Guinness in front of him. This situation often inspires a sense of perfection - you know that you have the entire glory of the drink ahead of you and that the glass won't get any fuller than it is right now. True love is worth fighting for, and what is more likely to cause a fracas than when some idiot spills out your beer?

There's also the love Marqamil thought he felt for Lizbug, which is pure sexual attraction bordering on obsessive madness. If you compare him to the man with the Guinness in front of him, Marqamil would have swallowed it all in one huge gulp, including the glass and half the table. You might be able to imagine the emotional hangover he'd get after losing the object of his desire.

The love Lulu felt for Dogshit had a little of all the three cases mentioned above in it. She knew him well enough to know exactly how to bend and twist his mind into a shape she liked, and just like a pint of Guinness the man tended to leave a bitter aftertaste in her mouth. The moments of desire were there too, often preceded by some intense squabbling and a few thrown objects.

Lulu was ready to accept both the good and the bad parts of their relationship as long as she managed to get the last word in their arguments. Arguing with Doggy could be quite enjoyable, and even if the man drove her nuts sometimes she had a hard time picturing life without him.

But things had begun to change in the past two days. Doggy had started to act strangely the moment they joined the Raven Cult people, and his behaviour had continued to get worse with every hour spent in their company. It wasn't like all the other times the man had gone sulky on her. She'd always given him a good reason to, and she'd always been able to get him out of it when it got annoying.

This time, however, she'd done nothing, and nothing she did seemed to affect him. It was as if she'd stopped existing, at least as far as he was concerned. Every time he saw her he seemed to have to think hard to remember who she was, and when he did remember he looked like he wished he hadn't. She'd done all she could to provoke him, as even an angry outburst would've been better than this new indifference, but the man seemed more concerned about the flies buzzing around his head. The whole situation was so frustrating she wanted to scream.

"I know where the problem lies," she said aloud when she sat by herself on the evening of their third day with the Raven people. "It's that trollop Lizbug. She's caught him in her web like a cunning, vicious spider. He's done nothing but stare at her since we hooked up with these people. I really don't understand what he sees in her. She's pretty enough, I'll give her that, but so pale and cold. She'll turn him into an ice sculpture if I let her have her way with him."

That last thought stirred another voice inside her to life.

"At least that'll make him stiff," it pointed out. "The way he is now he wouldn't even get aroused if you did the *kahoula* dance for him. He'd be more use to you as an ice sculpture."

"Yes!" the first voice agreed. "He'd always be ready to pleasure me then. No whining about having a headache or not being in the mood. Only hard, stiff manliness." She chuckled.

But what could she do to win him back? She'd tried everything to catch his attention, failing miserably every time. Sexual invites hadn't worked, nor had her attempts to make him jealous by flirting with that old geezer of a High Priest. Marqamil himself seemed as obsessed with Lizbug as her lover had become. She wasn't even sure he'd noticed her attempts.

She sighed. Her life had turned into a pitiful, miserable shadow. Even the food was bad. The Cult of the Raven God only ate vegetables; everything else was considered extremely sinful. She wondered what they'd think if they knew what usually made up hers and Doggy's diet.

The only one in the company who seemed fairly normal was the cult's most recent recruit, the young boy Drunk. His face wasn't as pallid as those of the other members, and he actually had a sense of humour. The others seemed to regard the two cannibals with a mix of discomfort and contempt. If they hadn't looked so damn tasteless she would've considered eating them, just to rid herself of their endless frowns and stares.

"You look like you've swallowed a lemon, my dear."

She looked up. The High Priest stood over her, with an expression that lay somewhere between amusement and reservation. Lulu had noticed several times how this man appeared to be full of conflicting emotions - his reverence for the Raven God contra his blatant coquetting of Lizbug, his deep hatred for the sun giving way to his even deeper fear of the night sounds of the savannah, the way he despised people who'd consider eating any part of an animal while he continuously picked his own nose and put whatever he found there into his mouth.

There was contradiction in the way he looked at her, too. She knew he thought her attractive, and yet he'd rather jump off a cliff than touch her skin, tainted as it was by the evil eye. Lizbug's pasty white skin was another matter, of course, but there he was prevented by the thick cloaks the Raven people had to wear when travelling beneath the sun. Besides, the woman ignored him as fiercely as Doggy ignored her. That almost made her feel sorry for the man.

No wonder he looks so miserable most of the time, she thought. *His life seems like a never-ending series of denials. Every time he wants something the cult has some impediment waiting for him. I bet he curses the Raven God more often than he praises him.*

"I'm sorry," she said. "I suppose you're referring to some fruit again. We don't have many of those where I come from. They do terrible things to our stomachs."

He sat down beside her. "I'd like to know more about the place you and Dogshit come from. I've spent my entire life in the temple of the Raven God. It's difficult for me to imagine a life under the constant influence of the evil glare."

"It isn't that bad, really," she said. "We lived a very peaceful life. The sun didn't do us any harm as far as I can tell. The meat went bad if you left it too long in the sunlight, of course."

Lulu gave herself a mental slap when she saw the grimace of disgust on Marqamil's face. She knew his attitude towards meat and those who ate it. How revolting wouldn't the thought of it, rotting in the light of the sun he saw as his greatest enemy, be to him? She quickly tried to think of a way to change the subject.

"I always liked walking at night, with only the stars to guide me," she managed.

He looked up at the night sky without much approval. The people of the Raven Cult mistrusted the stars, believing them to be spies of the evil eye, charged with keeping an eye on its enemies when they thought themselves safe from its burning gaze. Lulu wondered if she'd made things worse by including them in their conversation. Marqamil's voice was still pleasant when he spoke again, though.

"Does your people have a god?"

She nodded. "We do, but we don't pay much attention to him, or he to us. He's usually too busy taking care of his own business."

"What's he like, this god of yours?"

Lulu frowned into the fire. Lizbug didn't like fire, she remembered. The fool woman claimed it was a thing related to the evil eye, sent to devour the souls of the faithful the way it devoured wood. She'd tried to persuade the High Priest into forbidding campfires, but Marqamil had just laughed and said they wouldn't be able to see without them. Besides, he'd never heard of a fire that would darken the skin the way the evil eye did, and until he found one that did he saw no harm in lighting them at night.

Lizbug had given him a furious look and stormed back to her tent. That'd been the only pleasant moment Lulu had experienced since joining the Raven people.

"He's a bit of a glutton," she said in answer to his question. "He seems to eat constantly. Perhaps that's why he has so little time for us. Eating seems much more interesting than taking care of his people."

"Why not choose another god, then? One that does care about his people?"

She shrugged. "I think it's better to take care of yourself and not wait for some god to do the job for you. I've seen people call out to different gods before we... before they were killed. It never helped them. And look at yourself. You're a High Priest, but did your god ever give you any of the things you wanted most?"

A sudden flash of firelight seemed to catch something in Marqamil's eyes, and his face blushed slightly.

"No," he murmured. "Not really."

"That's what I meant. You've never thought about abandoning the Raven God, even if you haven't gotten anything back for all your devotion, right? You just keep doing what you've always done, just like my people. We're not that different from each other."

The High Priest contemplated her words in silence. Then, as if the notion had struck him like a blow from above, he turned back to her, face beaming like a child who'd just been given a lollipop.

"Have you seen the egg?" he asked, his voice full of enthusiasm.

"Egg? No. What about it?"

He jumped to his feet and stretched out a hand to help her up. "Come, I'll show it to you. I've kept it hidden until now, not knowing if I could trust you. But I believe now that you're a woman of good intentions, even if you've lived your entire life under the influence of the evil eye. The Raven God sent it to us, so serving him has yielded a little after all. It's quite a miraculous thing, really. I'm sure you'll like it."

She followed the High Priest back to his tent. For a moment she felt like a silly young girl who'd just fallen for a well-prepared pickup line.

But what kind of a pickup line is "Have you seen the egg?"

She let go of the thought and reached for another one, but all she got was the sensation of the soft night breeze against her skin. It was a very nice feeling, and together with the stars above and the distant murmur of voices it put her in a mood where she might actually have fallen for a pickup line as non-erotic as "*Have you seen the egg?*" Fortunately she was unaware of this, or the shame might've driven her to commit suicide.

Marqamil always put up his tent some distance away from the others. The light from the campfires didn't stretch as far as this, and Lulu could only see its outline vaguely against the pale stars.

As she waited for the High Priest to invite her in she thought she saw something move to one side. She squinted to see better in the faint light. Yes, there was definitely something there - a black shape, darker even than the shadows behind the tent.

There wasn't enough light for her to make out whether it was a human or some other creature of the night. Its movements appeared tentative, as if it was searching for something. For a moment she thought she heard a sniffing sound, like a wild animal trying to pick up a scent.

"*There's something there*!" she hissed, grabbing Marqamil's robe with one hand and pointing in the direction of the dark shape. "*Can't you see it*?"

"What?" The High Priest looked around. "I see nothing. The darkness must have played a trick with your imagination, sweet Lulu. Hold on a second, I'll find a torch."

The moment he spoke the dark shape stiffened. An instant later it was gone, as if swallowed by the night. Lulu thought she heard a soft rustling sound in the knee-high grass, but that must've been her imagination. She frowned into the darkness.

"It was there!" she insisted. "I think it was looking for something."

The High Priest chuckled softly. "Perhaps it was your boyfriend checking if the two of us shared a bed. Not that you were very convincing in your attempts at flirtation. You kept turning to scowl at him, usually after each sweet word to me. That's not rational behaviour for someone trying to seduce another man."

She ground her teeth so loudly it might have woken a sloth. So the man *had* noticed her efforts. Noticed and ignored them. Well, not exactly ignored - he had studied her with the same interest a scientist would show a new and somewhat amusing species, noticing the mistakes she'd made and probably thinking of ways to correct them. That was even worse than simply ignoring her. It bordered on *ridiculing*.

She felt tempted to sink her teeth into the man's puffy flesh right then and there just to get back at him, but with some effort she forced herself to refrain. There'd be plenty of time for epicurean pleasures later. Besides, she had a peculiar feeling there were more important matters at hand than avenging minor slights.

Another, more disturbing thought seeped into her mind. She realized she was actually enjoying the High Priest's company at the moment. For the first time in days she didn't feel lonely or miserable. Perhaps eating him wouldn't be such a good idea after all. Unbelievable as the thought was, she wondered if she wouldn't miss this pale old fool more than she'd miss Doggy, if she'd been forced to give up one of them.

The inside of Marqamil's tent looked rather pleasant when illuminated by warm torchlight. There were soft, colourful carpets on the floor, a low wooden table with matching chair and various other items, many of which she couldn't identify. The deep smell of incense filled the air like a persistent fart.

The High Priest moved over to a simple wooden chest marked with a sign saying "dirty underwear". He smiled when he saw the look of doubt on Lulu's face.

"No one would search for it in there," he explained.

Slowly, as if still not convinced, she moved over to his side and looked down into the chest. There was no underwear in it, dirty or clean. Its bottom was covered with soft cloths, made of a material she hadn't seen before. Atop them lay the egg, looking as pompous as a cat on a velvet pillow.

"What do you think?" he asked her.

"It's *beautiful*!" She wiped away the tears that had suddenly filled her eyes, then grabbed the hem of his robe and blew her nose in it. The egg truly was a magnificent thing, its surface covered with intricate patterns in colours that could only be found in a winter sunrise. She reached down a hand to touch it.

"It's so hard," she established. "Do you think it'd break if I sat on it?"

The High Priest gave the egg a measuring look. "It feels incredibly solid. I doubt anything could break it."

She scratched her head. "I once met a woman. Her name was Bathora. She was so fat she could probably break a rock by sitting on it. I hope she'll never get anywhere near this egg."

"So do I, my dear Lulu. So do I."

Lulu felt a weird mix of pleasure and sadness when she left Marqamil's tent. It was almost like after you've had a night of exceptionally good sex with a person you knew you'd never see again. This had happened to Lulu a few times, not because she travelled a lot and had many brief acquaintances, but because she sometimes liked to sleep with a man before eating him. Some of her people claimed this to be against morals and ethics, but Lulu dismissed them as old-fashioned and self-righteous.

It was late now and most of the Raven people had returned to their tents. Lulu went to put out her fire, which seemed all too interested in the dry savannah grass. After that she returned to the tent she shared with Dogshit.

Lulu didn't know it, but the tent had once belonged to Lizbug. Marqamil had given it to them in the hope that Lizbug would agree to share his. Strangely enough, the woman had produced an extra tent from somewhere in her pack, forcing the High Priest to return alone to his own tent with a look on his face resembling that of a small child who'd been denied the right to play with the others.

She stopped outside the tent and listened. There were voices coming from inside it, low and murmuring. She couldn't make out who they belonged to, but she had an idea or two. Donning her most fearsome scowl, she jerked aside the tent flap and barged in. The sight that met her left her speechless, even if she knew she should have expected something like it.

Doggy stood in the middle of the tent, engulfed in a passionate kiss with Lizbug. One of his hands was clutching her back, the other grabbing one of her buttocks. The woman had both hands entangled in his long, unkempt hair, pulling his face closer to hers.

Lulu stared at them for a few moments, not knowing what to say or do. The two lovers didn't seem to notice her, not until she sidestepped and accidentally kicked a small tin jar. When they heard the noise they turned to look at her, not stepping out of their embrace. Lulu wished she would've been spared this sight.

Her former lover looked blankly at her, without the slightest hint of recognition in his eyes. Lizbug, however, smiled rapturously at her. The pale woman's blood-red lips seemed to speak soundlessly to her, words of triumph and malicious pleasure.

You seriously thought you had a chance against me? Can't you see he belongs to me now? You lost, bitch! You lost bad!

~ 13 ~

High above the brown, barren ground a small bird soared, searching for something to eat. It was very hungry, and very annoyed.

"Have all bloody flies gone on strike?" it said to itself. "Or is there something good on TV I don't know of?"

The last thought made it crease its forehead, or would have if that was the sort of thing birds did. A TV? What above earth was a TV? Could it be short for Tiger Warner? No, that would've been TW. Turbulence Velocimeter? The bird shook its head. No, that wasn't even a word. It decided it must mean Troublesome Vertical Wind, even if the short form of that logically would be TVW. Perhaps it had made a mistake, and thought about TV when it actually *meant* to think about TVW. *Yes! That must be it.*

So, it thought. *Let's take this from the beginning. There are no insects because there is something good on TVW.* The bird frowned for real this time. That didn't make sense at all. Come to think of it, it wasn't sure it understood the thought in the first place. It certainly couldn't remember ever having any similar thoughts before. And insects didn't watch TV, or TVW, so why bother?

Damn, it was hungry.

Something was moving on the ground to its right. The bird focused its eyes. It was a human female, hopping forwards like a frog. Making a quick comparison of the creature's brain size and the amount of intelligence it showed, the bird decided this must be the biggest pinhead ever to walk this earth, or fly above it. It quickly set course in the opposite direction, afraid of what coming too close to this human airhead might do to its health.

Bathora fell backwards and landed on her ass. Fortunately, it was a very soft thing to land on. She lay on the ground for a while, gazing up at the light blue sky where a single bird flew at high speed towards the horizon. Her legs ached from all the hopping, so she stretched them out until they felt better.

"Oh, my," she panted happily. "That was fun. I must do it again tomorrow."

She looked around. There was nothing but barren wasteland around her. The ground was brown and dry, scattered with pieces of broken rock and clay that had dried hundreds of years ago. It wasn't a very hospitable landscape, but not too different from where Bathora had grown up.

"I wonder where I am," she said aloud. "There's nothing here I can use to find out which direction I should go. It wouldn't have done much good even if there was, because I have no idea where I'm going."

No matter how much the bird might despise Bathora, the two had something in common. Bathora was hungry. She hadn't eaten anything since the afternoon of the day before, and the sun had already sunk halfway towards the horizon. She had no idea how to make food. It had always been provided by some of her tribespeople, preferably someone a tad more intelligent than herself. She began to fear she'd starve to death in this god-forsaken wasteland.

By complete coincidence there was a bowl of stew only a few feet away from where she was sitting. It was a really good stew - antelope meat with fresh vegetables in a spicy sauce, full of nourishment and vitamins. Unfortunately, Bathora failed to recognize it for what it was, instead using the bowl to pee in. After that the stew was useless.

The bird finally found a fat, juicy mosquito, smiling at its stroke of luck as it greedily gobbled it down. What it didn't know was that the insect carried a mortal disease, which killed the bird later in the evening. A hyena ate the dead bird and got sick during the night. The next morning a lone vulture found its dead body on the ground. After feasting on it for over an hour it decided to head south to become the first vulture ever to set foot on the South Pole. It flew over the vast ocean when it started to feel weak, and that would've been the end of this horrible disease if a lump of the bird's droppings hadn't accidentally fallen into the mouth of a man lying on his back, snoring loudly.

The man was a member of a people living on a bunch of islands far out at sea. These people were extremely intelligent, which is very uncommon for such an isolated civilization. They'd already found solutions to many of the social and scientific problems we're still struggling with, and would probably have taken humankind to far higher levels of knowledge and glory if only given a couple of more generations. Instead, they all died in the disease and their wisdom and culture were lost forever.

In a perfect world there would've been an election, so people could decide whether Bathora or this amazing race of humans would kick the bucket. Most would undoubtedly have voted for the survival of the super-people. Bathora's fans would mostly have consisted of men who thought they'd get to shag her if they gave her their votes. That would certainly yield her a fair number of votes, but not enough to save her poor, pathetic existence.

Unfortunately, the world wasn't perfect, and never would be after the island people succumbed to the horrible disease. Perhaps it was for the best after all. In the end life would probably have become wearisome with all those smartasses around. We all know how happy dumb people get when someone proves to them exactly how dumb they are. These super-intelligent people would soon have been labelled arrogant snobs, and the hatred towards them would have escalated until genocide felt like a reasonable solution.

Anyway, Bathora was alive and had started walking again, keeping her south-western course more by accident than by a good sense of direction. Thus, after another two hours or so, she came to something she'd never expected to find in this part of the land (or any part of the land, for that matter).

A bar.

Bathora didn't know what a bar was, of course. All she saw was a bunch of people in odd clothes sitting around a counter, drinking from mugs and making an awful lot of noise. They spoke in odd accents she barely understood, and many eyed her quizzically as she approached.

A man in a red-and-white striped shirt and blue leggings, with a wide-brimmed hat on his head and a smoking thing made from wood in his mouth, nodded to her and pointed at the stool next to his. Bathora seated herself on it.

"Good evening, ma'am," the man said. "Lemme buy ya a drink. Whatcha want?"

"Ummm… I'll have the same as you," she replied, hoping it wouldn't be anything poisonous. "Can I get some food as well?" she added hopefully.

"Sure thing, ma'am. Tell me, what's that thing you're wearin'? Looks like a sack t'me."

She looked down at her garment for – unbelievably - the first time ever. It did look very much like a sack, she noticed. It had been white from the beginning, but had turned brown from dust and dirt. She wondered how she could have walked around in this thing all her life. A woman in her position should be supplied with better clothing.

She was just about to provide the man with a reasonable - if completely untrue - explanation when the bartender, a snobby-looking ostrich with big, black sunglasses, put a mug of thick, black liquid in front of her. She eyed it suspiciously.

"What's this?"

"Guinness, ma'am," the man explained. "Fine brew, all t'way from Ireland. Have a swallow. I betcha like it."

Bathora took a sip. The drink was bitter, but not unpleasant. She drank some more while her new friend eyed her with an amused look on his puffy face. The bartender put a bowl of small, seed-like things before her. She asked what it was.

"Peanuts, ma'am. Where ya from? Look a bit lost, if I may say so. Never been here before?"

She took a handful of the peanuts and stuffed them eagerly into her mouth. They tasted quite well, and she could do with some salt after her long walk in the sun. She ignored the man's questions, not wanting to get too personal with him, even if the drink seemed to have awakened a certain giddiness within her. Instead she looked at all the strange things on the other side of the counter. Odd noises came from a small box made of a material looking vaguely like iron.

"What's that?" she asked the man, pointing at the noise-making thing.

"Why, that's music, ma'am. Good ol' country from the south. Maybe you'll allow me to steal ya away for a dance later?"

Bathora frowned at the thing. This wasn't music the way she'd known it so far. Music in the Telu tribe usually involved banging things together: logs, rodents, people's heads. The best music was considered to have been invented by a man who dropped a large melon into a flock of distressed birds. The deed had provided many people with both food and entertainment.

She didn't know it, but the cannibals she'd encountered earlier made lists of who among their victims had the best voices as they screamed in pain and pleaded for mercy. Some had produced sounds so high-pitched that boulders had split apart. Most people don't know opera has its origin in African cook pots.

"What do they use to produce this weird music of yours?" she asked the man.

"Why, guitars, of course. Piano and harmonica. Sometimes violin or accordion."

"Not rodents, then?"

The man choked on his drink, spattering foam all over the counter. "Rodents, ma'am? Ah, sorry. Is that a nick for some foreign instrument? Kind of fiddle, like they have in Norway?"

Bathora wondered if this man was a bit dense. He certainly asked a lot of stupid questions. That she found the questions strange because she didn't understand them hadn't occurred to her. She studied the thing the music came from. It certainly wasn't large enough to contain even one person.

Must be rodents, then, she decided. *Or insects, perhaps. Sounds like a lot of buzzing in there.*

Her thoughts were interrupted by a voice from her right, reminding her of some sort of bird.

"Oh, my goodness. Aren't you the most adorable child one can imagine? Look at her, everyone, 'cause you might never see such beauty again. Astonishing, simply astonishing. Let Margaery have a closer look at you, child. Oh, my, astonishing indeed."

A middle-aged woman, about as wide as she was tall, had come up beside her. She reached out a hand and stroked plump fingers down Bathora's cheek, beaming like a sun on happy pills. Bathora looked at her and wondered if she should buy the woman a pint of Guinness. She was, however, embarrassingly aware she didn't have anything to trade with, least of all the small pieces of paper and metal that frequently passed back and forth across the counter. She settled for giving her a smile instead.

"Hello, you look well fed," she said.

The man to her left choked once more on his drink, but the woman beamed as brightly as ever. She wore a dress that seemed to include all possible colours, as well as a few impossible ones. She looked Bathora up and down.

"Where are you from, child? Your dress looks unfamiliar. From Wales, are you? Or Norfolk, perhaps?"

"Err... no. I'm of the Telu tribe. Its chieftain, actually."

Her memory of life as the head of an African tribe had long since faded. It was a mere reflex that caused her to provide the woman Margaery with this piece of information.

The fat woman looked puzzled for a moment, but then the smile returned to her puffy face.

"Ahhhh... I see. You're one of those occult people from London, right? Goths, is that what they're called? Or Wiccans? Odd folks, if you ask me. My neighbour's friend had a granddaughter who ended up with them. Made her do all kinds of nasty things. Not saying you're like that, of course," she hurried to add, her face flushing red as an oversized beetroot. Bathora had no idea what she was talking about, so she took another swallow from her mug.

"I'm terribly sorry to say so, dear child, but that dress doesn't become you at all," the woman went on. "Here, come with me. My daughter left some stuff behind when she moved to France. I'm sure I can find something more suitable for a girl of your loveliness. Come, child, come."

Ten minutes later Bathora found herself wearing a strange garment made of some silky material that clung to her body in all the right places. She found herself liking it very much, and by the look of approval on Margaery's face it appeared the woman was of the same opinion.

"That's much better, child. That's how a proper lady is supposed to look. Going to draw the eyes of every young lad out there, you are. Amazing figure, I must say. Never seen anything like it. My oh my, if I had hips like those..." She chuckled merrily.

Annoying as the woman might be, Bathora found disliking her about as impossible as making a career in orchestral coughing. She tried to copy her silly-looking smile and way of speaking.

"Oh, thank you, my fat old friend. I'm sure you could have worn something similar if you'd lost half your weight. Your daughter must have looked absolutely stunning in this dress. An astonishing garment, indeed. Never seen anything like it." The last thing, by pure chance, happened to be true.

The dress had its effect on the people at the bar, just as Margaery had predicted. The males began a veritable crusade to get close enough to exchange a few words with her. They'd stopped calling her "ma'am" and moved on to the more sociable "babe". There was so much pinching it made Bathora feel like she was on a lobster battlefield.

"Hold on!" she called out as people pushed each other back and forth around her. "It'd be more efficient if you formed a line and came to me one at a time. I'd appreciate gifts, but peanuts will do fine. Hey, stop fighting over there! The fat woman's neighbour will smack you until you look like harmonicas. Behave like docile camels now!"

The suddenly abandoned female patrons seemed to contemplate which drinks they should mix together to create a bomb just powerful enough to blow Bathora's side of the bar halfway to Shangri-La. Bathora bumped into one who'd gone on a futile quest to reclaim her partner. The woman snapped something indecent that Bathora didn't quite understand. She gave the woman a venomous glare anyway.

"You're out of the tribe!" she yelled. "You and that little trollop with bones in her hair. Both of you, out!"

The woman's expression switched from outrage to bewilderment. She'd obviously never been thrown out of a primitive African tribe before. As she hesitated, the commotion around Bathora intensified. Someone lifted Bathora and plopped her down atop the counter. She swayed for a moment, then toppled over backwards, pulling a multitude of glasses and bowls with her as she fell into the bar.

That was when the people in charge of the establishment decided things had gone too far. The ostrich bartender called a couple of bouncers who enthusiastically attended to the task of throwing out the most unruly patrons. There was some debate about whether Bathora should be one of those. Some people insisted that she, being the cause of the turmoil, should be thrown out and barred from the pub for good, while others pointed out that the majority of the customers were likely to follow her out and that it'd thus be more profitable to allow her to stay. In the end, the fear of losing business won out.

"As long as *someone* pays for her drinks," the ostrich said sourly and continued sweeping pieces of broken glass into a heap on the floor.

A few hours and several pints later Bathora had moved into a drunken haze, grinning foolishly at a young man sitting beside her, telling jokes she comprehended as well as a cloud comprehends gravity. She'd complained about being hungry, and the man had bought her something he called a blurber or burglar or something. She'd gobbled it down without asking what it was made of. Five minutes later she'd forgotten what it tasted like.

"This is definitely the best pub in town," the man went on. "It has a different look every time you enter it. Once there was snow, and you could see icebergs all around. Another time it felt like you were in a jungle full of strange-coloured birds. Once I could have sworn I saw a dinosaur. I must've been really drunk that time." He laughed, and Bathora joined him, having no idea what they were laughing at.

"Can I get you a whiskey, sweetheart?" he said when they'd stopped laughing.

"Sure," Bathora said. "We just have to find ourselves a leopard and you can pinch one off it. Piece of cake."

The young man laughed again. Bathora smiled and emptied her mug. Slamming it down on the counter the way she'd seen others do, she belched into the crook of her arm while her companion waved for the ostrich.

"Two double Glenmorangie on the rocks," he ordered.

The whiskey was very strong, but Bathora's senses had been so deadened by the beer she barely noticed its bite. One glass went down, followed by another, and another, and after that she didn't remember anything.

She woke up, feeling the warm rays of the morning sun on her face. It must've been close to midmorning, but she didn't care. She yawned, stretched herself like a cat, and put her head back down on the soft pillow.

"Mmmm... you were magnificent, my love," she mumbled happily.

"I know," said the ostrich.

Bathora screamed.

She still screamed when she woke up. The sun was at its noon peak, and there was no sign of the bar anywhere. If not for the pounding headache Bathora might have thought she'd dreamed all of it. She was still wearing the dress, but it was rumpled and dusty and didn't smell very nice. Her stomach felt as if she'd swallowed a beehive.

"Well," she said to herself. "It's not like I feel like drinking today, anyway."

She continued walking the way she'd walked before she found the bar. There was no sign of habitation anywhere, and all she could find to eat was a handful of camel droppings. It actually improved the taste in her mouth.

It was late in the evening when she reached the foot of a small mountain range. She'd seen the jagged tops far off and for one brief instant thought she'd come back home. The joy of this had left her quickly, not because she'd found out these weren't the mountains to the north of the Telu camp, but because she'd forgotten where she came from.

Standing there in the deepening shadows she tried to think (without much success, naturally). There seemed to be no way up into the mountains, and she was definitely too lazy to walk around them, so after another moment of consideration she walked straight into them.

"Oof!" she groaned as the hard cliff face threw her back onto her ass. She couldn't understand why she was unable to walk through the mountain the way you walked through a bunch of sheets hung between two poles to dry in the sun. The insolence of the thing made Bathora furious. She stood up and waved her fist at the mountain like an ant complaining about having its home crushed under an elephant's foot.

"You whiskey-smelling peanut monger!" she yelled. "If my daughter knew about this she'd take all your dresses and make blurbers out of them! I've never seen anything like it! Step aside, child, or I'll stuff you so full of music you won't know when to drop the melon! Now, out of my way!"

She lowered her head and charged the mountainside once more. If she'd slammed her head into it with this much force she'd most likely never have eaten a burger again, but fortunately she managed to throw herself straight through the opening that led into the abandoned caverns of the Raven Cult. She stumbled into complete darkness, the momentum carrying her on until she fell straight on her face. If she'd landed on water she would have made the biggest splash ever.

"Oh, my," she mumbled, trying to get up. The tight dress the fat woman had given her made the process a bit tricky, but after a few gymnastic moves and an *ouch* or two she made it back to her feet.

Some random groping told her she was in some sort of tunnel, and something she didn't recognize told her she should follow it deeper into the mountain. This unknown thing was called intuition, a word only a small percentage of the African population knew how to pronounce back in those days.

After fumbling her way through the darkness for a couple of minutes Bathora reached a large cavernous hall. At first she just stood there, waving her arms in a vain attempt to find the tunnel walls, but then she forgot all about the tunnel and stumbled forward aimlessly. When she reached the centre of the hall a loud, booming voice addressed her.

"YOU ARE NOT OF THE RAVEN CULT. WHY ARE YOU HERE?"

In the darkness Bathora had trouble distinguishing between sounds coming from the outside world and those who always buzzed through her deranged mind. The words had made no sense to her, so she decided they must have come from inside her head. She took another step and called out in a moderately cautious voice.

"Hello? Anyone home?"

"OF COURSE THERE IS SOMEONE HOME, YOU FAT-ARSED MORON. I'M HERE. I'VE BEEN HERE SINCE THE BEGINNING OF TIME. ALMOST, ANYWAY."

This time she decided the voice hadn't come from inside her head. But which direction had it come from? She spun in a circle, trying to locate its source.

"Who said that?" she enquired.

"I DID. THERE'S NO ONE ELSE HERE. ALL MY SUBJECTS ABANDONED ME."

"And who are you? Were you at the bar last night?"

There was a snort that sounded like a rock being torn in half.

"WAS I AT THE BAR? THE BAR WOULD HAVE CRUMPLED AND FALLEN INTO THE ABYSS IF I'D TOUCHED IT WITH THE SMALLEST PART OF MY LITTLE FINGER. THE ENTIRE WORLD WOULD COWER UNDER THE BEAT OF MY WINGS IF I HADN'T GOT STUCK IN THIS MISERABLE CAVE. IMAGINE THAT - THE MIGHTY RAVEN GOD, STUCK IN A STINKING HOLE IN THE GROUND. THAT ISN'T A PROPER LIFE FOR A GOD, IS IT?"

Bathora's eyes widened. "Are you a god? Wow! Does that mean you can see in the dark and stuff?"

This time there was a sigh that made her hair waft behind her.

"CAN I SEE IN THE DARK? WHY, OF COURSE I CAN. I SEE EVERYTHING. I'VE ALWAYS SEEN EVERYTHING, BUT I'VE NEVER BEEN ABLE TO TELL ANYONE WHAT I SAW. I HAD TO STAND HERE AND WATCH MY SLUG-BRAINED SUBJECTS RUN ABOUT LIKE NEW-BORN CHICKENS WHILE THERE WERE IMPORTANT TASKS THAT NEEDED TAKING CARE OF. BUT DO YOU KNOW WHAT THE MOST FRUSTRATING THING OF ALL WAS?"

Bathora shook her head. It didn't take long to go through the list of things she knew, and what the Raven God had asked her wasn't among them.

"I'LL TELL YOU, THEN. IT WAS WHEN I FINALLY GOT MY VOICE BACK. IT WAS THE EGG, YOU SEE. WHEN THEY FINALLY FIGURED OUT HOW TO GET THE EGG I REGAINED MY ABILITY TO USE HUMAN SPEECH, BUT WHAT DO THEY DO THEN? THEY *LEAVE*, EVERY SINGLE ONE OF THEM! JUST TOOK THE EGG AND WALKED OUT OF HERE. DO YOU HAVE ANY IDEA HOW IMPORTANT THAT EGG IS? DO YOU?"

Bathora thought for a moment. "Does it have anything to do with the ostrich?" she tried. "Perhaps the egg belongs to him?"

"WHAT? OH, BUGGER IT, WHY AM I TELLING YOU THIS? I SEE NOW YOUR BRAIN CAPACITY IS EVEN MORE LIMITED THAN THAT OF MY FORMER SUBJECTS. *MUCH* MORE LIMITED. HOLY SHIT, IT'S A MIRACLE YOU'RE ABLE TO TALK AT ALL. AND STILL THERE'S SOMETHING ABOUT YOU... ARE YOU A PRIESTESS?"

All these unexpected questions made Bathora dizzy, so she sat down on the cold floor and began peeling dirt from between her toes.

"I suppose I was," she began, letting her mouth do the job her brain was too simple for. "I never knew of whom, though. To be honest, I never thought much about it. I did what I did and no one said anything about it. Most of the time I told others what to do. They always obeyed me, for some reason. Quite odd, now that I think of it. I never had to tell them twice. They always did what I told them to do."

"YOU MUST HAVE BEEN IN TOUCH WITH SOME GOD OR OTHER," the Raven God said. "I CAN FEEL A CERTAIN POWER IN

YOU. WHO KNOWS, THERE MIGHT BE SOME PURPOSE TO THIS MEETING AFTER ALL. WOULD YOU BE MY SERVANT?"

Bathora frowned. The word *servant* was one she hadn't been acquainted with before, and somehow it had a nasty ring to it. She didn't know what else to do with her life right then, though, so she chose not to dismiss the god's proposal instantly.

"What do you want me to do if I accept? I do have a certain amount of dignity, you know. I'm not going to sweep floors and scrub cook pots. That's work for more simple people."

She could feel the Raven God watching her, even if she didn't see his eyes. It seemed her question had taken him aback.

No wonder, she thought. *This fellow hasn't had anyone to talk to in thousands of years. No one has ever asked him what he wants from his followers. I hope it won't take him too long to answer. I really need to pee.*

"YOU COULD START BY LIGHTING SOME CANDLES," the Raven God finally said. "THERE'S PLENTY OF ROOM HERE - BEDS, FOOD, EVERYTHING YOU'LL NEED. BETTER MAKE YOURSELF COMFORTABLE."

She nodded. "And then what?"

It should be impossible, but she could have sworn the god smirked.

"HOW ABOUT A STRIPTEASE?"

~ 14 ~

The mountain rumbled again.

Standing in its shadow, Marsha felt incredibly small. Even an elephant would feel small here, if they'd been smart enough to make such observations. The only thing the big, grey animals seemed to care about was food, and the supply of it had dwindled quite a bit since they reached the land surrounding the mountain. The ground was stony, criss-crossed by cracks and often covered with flakes of ash and lapilli. A few thorny bushes and gnarled trees was all that could be found in the way of vegetation.

The next rumble was deafening and seemed to come from Marsha's right. When she turned she saw Emkei standing beside her, patting her ample belly with a satisfied look on her puffy face.

"Ahhh... that Hannah really knows how to make a good punch," she said.

Marsha had seen some of the brews the Elephant People's gargling woman mixed together, and she'd rather die than let them touch any part of her body. Emkei, however, both drank and gargled them as if they'd been the sweetest juice.

The gargling woman used her brews to get in contact with the gods and pass their messages on to the queen. The only things Emkei passed on were a few really loud burps. She claimed the brews made her feel blessed, though, so maybe the gods had something to do with it after all.

"I don't like this mountain," Marsha muttered. "It feels like it's looking down on me, and not in a pleasant way. I wish we didn't have to go any further."

"Do you know why we're here in the first place?" the seer asked. "Are we looking for something?"

Marsha hadn't told anyone about her dream. She knew this mountain had something to do with it, but hadn't been able to figure out what. The mountain was named after Azagh, the great demon of fire, who appeared in many of the legends told by people in this part of the continent. There had been a fiery demon in Marsha's dream, but she couldn't remember anything about a mountain like this one.

Perhaps the demon lives in the mountain, she thought. *The rumbling sure sounds like some immense beast roaring. But how do we find out?*

In her dream she'd been told they needed the demon to save the egg, but that they'd all die if they didn't kill it. The main problem was that the demon was huge and immensely powerful. Not even Amanda had managed to defeat it, even if she'd been close. Marsha had woken up just as the demon was about to kill her, right after she'd accused it of cheating at Yahtzee. That part of the dream was very confusing.

"I'm not sure," she said thoughtfully. "I know I had to come here, but I have no idea what to do."

Emkei scratched her head with a plump finger. "I heard something about a magic material some people claim to have found close to this mountain," she said. "Black and shiny, sharper than any stone or metal but also much more frail. It's said you can cut through anything with it. Perhaps that's why we've come here, to look for it?"

"Nah," Marsha mumbled. "We must protect it, not cut it in half. Everything is lost if we break it."

The old seer gave her an askance look. "What are you talking about? Protect what?"

Marsha had just determined the time had come to tell Emkei and her other friends about her dream. She hoped they wouldn't laugh at her. She also hoped they'd make some sense of the parts she didn't understand. As a seer, Emkei should be used to interpreting dreams and visions, even if she seemed to use her stomach more than her head most of the time.

She'd just opened her mouth to begin her account when Tiwi's chirpy voice interrupted her. The queen of the Elephant People was talking to Pebe, and the subject of the conversation appeared to be the same as usual.

"I did encounter the demon once," the queen said. "It was the most fearsome thing I'd ever seen, but it didn't scare me. I called it a eunuch and a big, smelly buffoon, and that made it so angry it forgot to watch its step and blundered straight into a river. Do you know what happens when a Demon of Fire gets soaked in cold water?"

"No," Pebe replied, his face full of expectation and excitement. "What happens?"

Tiwi laughed. "Not very much. Its fire dies, and after that it's just like any other big, clumsy beast. It had to lumber back to its mountain with the tail between its legs. How many demons have you defeated, my brave friend?"

Pebe thought for a while. "Only one, but it was much more fearsome than yours. It was huge, at least as big as that mountain, and it ate everything that came in its way. Its excrement lay like tall hills behind it. The smell was enough to kill people miles off, and entire tribes were crushed under its feet."

"Rubbish!" Tiwi exclaimed. "You're just describing that old seer again. You must do better than that if you want to fool me. Look, there she is, talking to Lady Marsha. Any fool could uncover a lie when the truth is right in front of her. Hello, ladies! Are you ready for the last part of our journey?"

The mountain rumbled again, almost as loud as Emkei's stomach this time.

Pebe looked up at it, clearly unnerved by the sound.

"I hope it won't be the end of everything," he muttered. "It really sounds like there's a demon in there."

"Oh, old Azagh has been there since the beginning of time." Tiwi laughed. "Don't worry about him. If he shows up I'll take care of him."

"Do you know where we'll go?" Marsha enquired. "If what we're looking for is on that mountain, or in it, well, it's a big mountain. We could spend months there without finding a thing."

Tiwi put a hand on her shoulder and smiled brightly. "You must trust in faith, my dear Marsha. The gods have led us here, and they'll continue to lead us. I know I'm destined for glory, and if someone tries to deny me they'd better make sure they run really fast. We'll go to the mountain's foot, and if we find nothing there we'll start climbing. The elephants can't go any further than this, so we'll have to leave them behind. Hannah, I and Embolo will go on, the rest will take care of the animals. We leave within the hour."

She scampered off to make sure everything was prepared. Marsha knew this might be her last chance to talk with her friends in private, so she pulled them off to one side, making sure none of the Elephant People were close enough to listen. Amanda joined them from wherever she'd been. Marsha's voice was low and grave when she spoke.

"There's something I have to talk to you about," she said. "I had a dream a few nights ago, just before we came in sight of this mountain. I know it was no ordinary dream. There were important messages in it. Some I did understand, but others made no sense at all. Anyway, this is what it was about."

She told them everything she remembered - about the fiery demon they both needed and had to defeat, the egg they had to protect if their tribe was to survive, and finally how she'd woken up the moment before the demon would kill her. Some details had gone a bit blurry, and she mixed up parts of the conversations she'd had with Emkei and Amanda, but most of the account was accurate enough.

"I know we have to find this egg," she finished. "It's important that all of you know that if we ever become separated from each other. It's all about the egg. The mountain is important too, but I don't think we'll find the egg there. Actually, I have no idea what we're to do here. I was hoping you'd help me figure that out. Emkei, you're a seer, after all. What do you make of this?"

"Oh, dear me, what a headache I got all of a sudden." The fat woman raised a hand to her forehead. "I can hardly think at all. Perhaps Amanda can answer your question. What was it again?"

Amanda grinned happily at Pebe. "I liked the part about Pebe's doll. Maybe that's what we'll find on this mountain."

"That wasn't funny," the young man muttered. His face had turned a bright red.

Marsha wanted to scream at them. Why couldn't they understand the importance of things for once?

"Listen to me now," she said acidly. "Our future, and the future of the Khadal, depend on this. Perhaps even the future of humankind itself. We really need to work this out. There's a rumbling mountain looming over us, and somewhere else there's an egg that needs our protection. In my dream people kept saying Amanda would save things, but all she did was throw an elephant at the demon. And if the demon keeps cheating, just like the elephant did... What if Ogian has something to do with it?"

"How could he be involved in anything important?" Amanda snorted. "He can't even cheat properly. The only ones among the Elephant People who seem to possess any sort of competence are Hannah and Tiwi..."

"And it's those two who'll go with us to Mount Azagh!" Marsha pointed out. "Now *that*'s what I call coincidence. Or maybe not." She stuck out her chin in an insolent way.

"But they didn't cheat in your dream, did they?" Amanda delivered a triumphant smile that made Marsha want to hit her. She knew there wouldn't be much left of her if Amanda chose to hit her back, though, so she calmed herself and tried to think instead.

"No, but Hannah gargled the dice," she said thoughtfully. "That can hardly be called fair play, can it?"

"Perhaps the gargling woman has our fate in her mouth?" Emkei suggested.

"I'd rather not have it back if that's the case," Pebe said sourly.

"Here they come," Amanda cautioned. "I suppose you don't want us to tell them about this dream of yours?"

"No," Marsha said quietly. "But remember: *the egg must be saved.*"

The journey to the mountain's foot took two or three hours, and no major incidents occurred. The rumbling kept getting louder, until it felt like the ground quavered beneath their feet. The gargling woman helped the blind Embolo along while she and Emkei discussed the use of sulphur in fruit punch. Marsha walked by herself, trying not to listen to Tiwi's endless bragging and (usually successful) attempts to spook Pebe.

"Do you think there's something going on between the two of them?" Amanda suddenly asked.

"What?" Marsha hadn't noticed the other woman walking up beside her. "What are you talking about?"

"Tiwi and Pebe. They certainly seem to get along very well."

Marsha had never been very good at the games men and women played to express interest in one another. What Tiwi and Pebe did certainly didn't seem romantic to her. In her somewhat conservative mind romances involved flowers and presents and watching the sun set across the ocean. The last thing she'd do if she ever fell in love with someone was to tell him silly stories about how many monsters she'd faced down or what impossible feats she'd accomplished.

"I don't know," she said. "I think it looks more like she despises him."

"Oh, that's just for show," Amanda said, waving one of her hands dismissively. "She can't allow herself to seem too eager. That'd give her a disadvantage in a possible relationship. A woman must let a man think she's dating him out of pity and that he must do anything she wants if he's not to lose her. It's called equality between the sexes."

"It is?" Marsha was about as familiar with this as with quantum physics. "Why not just tell each other how they feel?"

The other woman looked at her as if she'd suggested stopping a rampaging rhino by telling it to calm down.

"That would possibly be the worst thing any of them could do. You can't just tell someone you love him, Marsha. He'd be scared witless and wouldn't stop running until he'd put half a world between himself and you. No, what she's doing now is perfect. Pebe probably desires her more with every moment. Soon he'll be about to burst, and that's when she'll strike."

"Strike?" Marsha sounded worried. "She won't hurt him, will she?"

"Of course not. Kiss him, most likely, and then…" She chuckled with amusement.

"And then what?" Marsha was still not convinced the elephant queen wasn't planning to harm the young Khadal man, and as his chieftain she had to ensure his safety.

"What do you think? What do men and women usually do when they're in love?"

"I don't know," Marsha said. "Go for walks in the moonlight?"

Amanda put a hand on her shoulder. "My dear Marsha, we really need to find you a husband. Fertility potions are all very nice, but there's more to life than breeding. Marsha? Why did you stop?"

They'd reached the foot of the mountain. No more than a dozen meters ahead of them the rocky slope began rising, steeper and steeper towards the jagged top high above them. Marsha stood motionless like a statue as her wide-open eyes struggled to take in the whole scene in one visual gulp.

"Whoa!" she exclaimed. "That's a pretty big mountain."

Tiwi laughed. "Not really. I've seem much bigger ones. Did you know there's a mountain to the south-east so tall the snow around its top never melts."

"Snow?" asked Pebe. "What's that?"

"Frozen rain," the elephant queen conveyed in a tone usually employed by parents explaining the most trivial matters to young children.

"That's a load of rubbish," the young man retorted. "Rain always stays the same, even when the weather's cooler. We of the Khadal aren't foolish enough to buy a story like *that*."

"*Frozen rain, on the plain, Pebe's got a rotten brain*," Amanda mused. "*Not a fool, just a tool, wait until it's really cool*."

"People often try to cover up their own lack of knowledge by accusing others of lying," Tiwi said haughtily. "One day I might bring you there to see for yourself. If you're man enough to climb all the way up, that is."

"I'll climb to the top and back down five times before you've even made it halfway up," Pebe boasted. "Then we'll see who's man enough for whom."

Amanda snorted.

"I don't know about you," Marsha said, not quite able to hide her impatience. "But I'd like to have a look around this place. Some of you might think that things will work out of their own accord, but I've always preferred to rely on honest work."

"Sure," the elephant queen said cheerfully. "It'll get boring to just stand here anyway."

Huge boulders lay scattered across the lower regions of the mountain. Tiwi claimed the demon Azagh had thrown them out when he prepared his abode inside the mountain. The boulders had been tossed into the air as if they'd been small pebbles, and there'd been smoke and fire, which explained why the land was so barren for miles around.

Marsha went for a walk between the large rocks, but found nothing of interest. Tiwi appeared to remain confident that whatever she was looking for would be placed before her by the hands of fate. She picked up a small pebble and tossed it at Pebe. The young man emitted a muffled *ouch*.

The gargling woman sniffed the air and produced a satisfied nod. Emkei lumbered over to her, and they were soon engulfed in another murmuring conversation. Marsha could make out words like *spice*, *pie* and *turnips*. She shook her head.

The mountain rumbled again.

This time it didn't 'stop.

And this time the ground unmistakably shook beneath them.

"Mommy!" Pebe wailed.

"It's the demon!" Marsha bellowed. "It's coming!"

Pebe pointed at Tiwi. "You said you'd stop it! Make it stop now!"

But the elephant queen looked almost as frightened as Pebe himself, and with good reason. Deafening booms beat against their ear drums like enormous hammers. Marsha saw cracks open in the mountainside high above them, a bright, glowing liquid pouring out of them. A rancid stench stung her nostrils, filling her eyes with tears. The quaking beneath them grew more convulsive, and one by one they tumbled backwards and fell. Marsha somersaulted backwards down the slope she'd just ascended.

Tiwi tried to get up, but Emkei had fallen across her body and pinned her down like the carcass of some large, heavy beast. The queen yelled and banged her fists into the seer's soft flesh until Emkei managed to roll off her. Finally able to move again, Tiwi rose and took a few staggering steps.

"We must run!" she screamed. "We must get away from here!"

"It's no use!" Marsha shouted. "We can't run from the demon. It'll catch us one by one, until there's no one left. We have to defeat it. Amanda, this would be where you step in and save the day."

"Me?" The beautiful woman looked perplexed. "Why me?"

"Because the dream told me so. The demon must be defeated, and you're the only one strong enough to do it. You have to be careful when you do it, though. There's something important it must do before it dies. Ask it, if you get a chance. Perhaps it possesses some information we need. Ask it if it knows where the egg is."

Amanda stared at her in disbelief. "You want me to kill a demon *gently*? A demon the size of a mountain? You must have gone completely insane."

"Look!" Emkei pointed at something above them. "It looks like molten fire floating down the mountainside. Now, wouldn't *that* be something to put in a stew?"

Marsha looked up. It really was molten fire, large rivers of it. It came from the jagged top of the mountain as well as from numerous cracks and crevices. A thick pillar of smoke rose from the mountaintop, a thousand feet or more into the sky. A red glow painted its lower parts as if with blood. Marsha turned back to Amanda, and this time her voice came out as a shriek full of desperation.

"Don't you see it?! The demon is coming! You must stop it! Put it back inside the mountain! You must do something!"

Her words appeared to give Amanda an idea. She ran to the biggest block of stone in sight and lifted it high above her head. Then she started running up the mountainside as if it'd been a flat and even path. Marsha watched her move further and further up, until she looked like nothing but a small ant carrying its burden up the side of the anthill. The mountain roared and trembled as if it was about to explode. Marsha and her friends had to retreat a little further.

There was a bubbling and hissing sound, and suddenly a wall of lava rose above Marsha. It flowed over the rocks and made them part of its raging torrent. Marsha screamed and threw herself to one side. The glowing flood passed only a few feet from her, its heat stinging her skin like a viper's poison.

Emkei emitted a cry of delight and lumbered over to kneel beside the river of fire, the gargling woman joining her a moment later. The two plunged their faces into the lava to fill their mouths, then lifted their heads towards the darkening sky and gargled. The sight was so terrifying that Marsha stood paralyzed and watched in mute amazement. The fires danced in and around the women's mouths, creating small fountains and whirlpools. The heat didn't seem to bother them at all.

Marsha forced her gaze to return to the mountain's top. She could still make out Amanda, a tiny little spot under the large boulder. She was close to the top now, climbing the steep slope one step at a time. Fire and smoke kept gushing from the crater, more violently than before.

Amanda reached the top, took careful aim, and slammed the boulder down into the crater. The mountain rumbled furiously, but no more smoke or fire came.

Marsha reached out and grabbed Tiwi's arm. Or rather, she intended to grab her arm, but as her eyes were still fixed on what went on above her she incidentally squeezed the queen's buttock instead. Tiwi gave Pebe a hard slap across the face and began yelling something about how to show a queen proper respect. Marsha hurried to grab hold of her arm. This time she succeeded.

"We must get away from here!" she shouted. "Amanda won't be able to hold the demon down for long. Come, run!"

With combined efforts they managed to drag Emkei and Hannah away from the lava flood. The gargling woman tried to fill one of her bottles with the glowing liquid, but its heat made the glass melt. When Emkei poured some into one of her pockets it burned through the cloth instantly. The two women wailed in despair and loss as they were herded away from the mountain.

As they made their stumbling way across the still shaking ground Marsha looked back to see how Amanda was doing. The woman was still holding the boulder in place, keeping the mountain from erupting. Marsha could barely imagine the strength it must require to keep such a raging force down. Demon or no demon, she knew the mountain would have killed them if they'd remained at its foot. She whispered a prayer for the brave, young woman and trudged on.

Amanda must have watched them get away, for when they were at a safe distance from the mountain she let go of the boulder, which turned out to be a terribly bad thing to do. The mountain released all the fury Amanda had kept down with her incredible strength. Fire and smoke exploded from the crater, hurling the boulder - with Amanda on top of it - thousands of feet into the air.

Marsha watched her friend vanish somewhere far to the north, like a bird blending into the distant horizon. Her legs gave out beneath her and she collapsed on the ground, sobbing convulsively.

Someone put a comforting arm across her shoulders. When she looked up she saw that it was Embolo, the blind man who hadn't said anything since they reached the mountain's foot. Now, at what felt like the end of the world, he appeared to be the only one able to speak.

"Don't worry, my lady," he said gently. "I felt the strength in that woman, even if I couldn't see her beauty. I don't think we've seen the last of her. She just waited for us to reach safety, then she let go. Wherever she ends up I'm sure she'll keep fighting for this cause of yours. And, like I said, perhaps your paths will meet again before this is over."

"But..." Marsha stammered. "The demon. It hurled her into the sky, just like in my dream. The demon..."

She turned back towards the mountain, expecting the huge, fiery creature to come lumbering towards her. The mountain seemed to have calmed itself considerably, though. There was still lava running down its slopes and smoke kept rising from its crater, but the rumbling had dwindled to a low, subterranean groan. A keen wind had come in from the west and taken the acrid smell of sulphur with it. A thin ray of sunlight pierced the dark smoke clouds and engulfed them gently in its warm light.

Marsha reached out a hand and let Embolo help her back to her feet. Tiwi waited for her, her face looking strangely humble.

"She was the bravest woman I've ever met," she said reverently. "I hope she'll be all right, because I'd very much like to tell her that. Anyway, she saved our lives and will have the eternal gratitude of the Elephant People. From now on, Lady Marsha, I will follow wherever you go and do everything you ask me to. The Elephant People is at your command."

She dropped to one knee and lowered her beautiful head. Marsha hurriedly pulled her back up and embraced her.

"Let us be like sisters instead of leader and follower," she said. "We survived the mountain's fury together, and we'll survive whatever else we might face. Let's continue this fight side by side, your people and mine. Let's join dice, as Ogian would have said."

Tiwi's laughter chimed through the clear air. "You already speak like one of our people, Lady Marsha. Very well, then, side by side it is. But you'll have to decide what we're to do next. It's obvious that neither of us found the end of her quest at Mount Azagh."

"No," Marsha said softly. "But I still think a lot of good came from our visit here. We must find Amanda, though, and make sure nothing's happened to her. I think I know exactly where she'll go if she's hale and healthy."

The queen raised an eyebrow. "You do? Where?"

"Home."

~ 15~

The whole idea of the sun as an evil bastard was actually the product of a very big misunderstanding. The Raven people never found out, even though some might have guessed it deep down inside. Logically there's no reason why ravens should be afraid of sunlight. They don't even get burnt like some humans with too pale skin, and if they feel about to succumb from the intense heat of an African summer day they just take off and flap themselves up into a more comfortable temperature, or fly north until they've found a place where they don't have to sweat. A Raven God don't even have to do that. It simply decides how it wants to feel, and that's all there is to it.

The Raven God had an enemy, though. It was an ancient enmity that went back all the way to the beginning of time, when animals ruled the world in perfect harmony. Each race had its own place in the grand scheme of existence. Everyone had everything they needed, and there was no need to squabble. It was a perfect life for both the gods and their protégés.

Then *she* came.

Many men blame women for everything that goes wrong in their lives, complaining about how they can neither live with nor without them. This way of reasoning might have its roots in this prehistoric conflict that took place long before the first members of the highly overrated human race became part of the ecosystem. For it was, beyond doubt, a woman who was behind all the hardship the inhabitants of this world went through during this period, when the mountains and oceans were still young and no one had even dreamed about such a horrible thing as the mobile phone.

Her name was the Bug Goddess.

In the beginning she revealed neither her true name nor her true shape. Instead she appeared in a form that seemed unbelievably attractive to everyone who gazed upon her. The animals of both air and land were filled with reverence for the beauty and wisdom she radiated, and many of the male gods became inconceivably horny. Most of all (as you might have guessed) the Raven God.

It was said that when the animals of Africa saw the Raven God and the Bug Goddess together they all agreed that they'd never seen anything so glorious and majestic before. The two seemed to give a new meaning to the word perfection, a sense of belonging to a higher order of life. Many of the animals began worshipping them, and even a few of the minor gods followed their example. This was, of course, exactly the effect the Bug Goddess had hoped to achieve.

As someone who'd never been interested in gaining power for himself, as well as being completely besotted with the Bug Goddess, the Raven God never realized in which direction matters were going. All he wanted was to help the lesser beings of the world in any way he could, and when the Bug Goddess began issuing commands on a regular basis he simply mistook them for good advice.

As her power grew, the Bug Goddess began working her schemes more openly. The power she'd won for herself and the Raven God increased with each day, until the entire land had fallen under their reign.

This was the first time something like this had happened. The idea of one animal ruling another had been completely unheard of before the Bug Goddess entered the scene. But many things were about to change, and new ways of thinking had already begun to spread among some races.

By order of the Bug Goddess, a huge palace was built to accommodate herself and her followers. No animal would ever have considered living inside a building, no matter how lavish and vibrant, prior to the arrival of the Bug Goddess, but many had been seduced by the gaudy ways she'd introduced and enjoyed basking themselves in the splendour of this new palace and its rulers.

Not all were happy with this new way of life. Some even voiced their disapproval openly. Foremost among those was the Hippo God, who'd been the Raven God's closest friend before the Bug Goddess came between them.

The Hippo God had never been fooled by the Bug Goddess's alluring exterior and honeyed tongue, even though she'd shown as much interest in him as in the Raven God when she first came to the land. He had declared openly that all hippos were free animals and refused to pay homage to the two self-made rulers. Thus he became the Bug Goddess's greatest enemy, the one she hated and feared the most.

The Elephant God did all he could to help the Hippo God in his cause, even if he didn't dare to rebel openly. Together they tried to make the other gods see what was about to happen, telling them the Bug Goddess sought to make herself a tyrant with infinite power over all other animals.

"Why," the Hippo God asked, "would animals and gods need someone to tell them what to do? Why would they *accept* it? There was a time, not too long ago, when all of us lived in freedom, each one leading the kind of life he or she found most suitable. No one would ever have dreamed of assuming power over other creatures, nor to force them to bow and scrape before you. You call this self-styled queen wise and generous. I call her an oppressor who'll turn us all into slaves if she isn't stopped."

Some listened, but the majority were still too dazzled by the splendour of their new rulers and their court. There were even a few who murmured that the Hippo God was jealous and wanted the throne for himself.

The Hippo God grew angry and said that only someone bereft of all honour and wisdom would consider sitting on such a despicable thing as a throne. In his fury he uttered several harsh words and insults directed at both the Raven God and his queen. His words made many upset, and in the end they reached the rulers' ears too.

The Bug Goddess immediately demanded the Hippo God to be brought before her as a traitor. When the Hippo God refused, the Bug Goddess sent a couple of the guards she'd been training in secret to capture him and bring him to the Royal Palace by force. Many of the onlookers encountered words like *treason*, *violence* and *punishment* for the first time, and some grew uneasy and averted their eyes at the thought of what their queen had just ordered.

It is said that the Raven God lowered his head and wept when he saw his old friend dragged into the throne room in thick iron chains, but the Bug Goddess showed no sign of compassion. In a loud, angry voice she listed the crimes the Hippo God had made himself guilty of, declaring that the only suitable punishment for such a dire list of offenses was death. This brought a shocked murmur to the hall, for no animal had ever taken the life of another before.

The Raven God was still a fair and just man, however, and he announced that the Hippo God would be imprisoned in a cell below the palace until a proper trial had been conducted. The Bug Goddess and the ones who followed her weren't pleased with this, but in the end she resigned herself to the king's decision, and the Hippo God was removed from their presence.

Late that night the Raven God went down into the dungeons, meaning to set his old friend free, but when he came to the cell where they'd put the Hippo God he was faced with a sight more horrifying than anything he could have imagined in his wildest dreams.

A monstrous creature crawled over the Hippo God, using its thin, hairy legs to pin him down while its jaws searched for his throat. It was a creature so vile it made him want to run outside and empty his stomach, and yet he knew it for what it was. His queen. The woman he loved was the Bug Goddess.

The Hippo God tried to hold her off, but the heavy chains restrained him, and the Bug Goddess had grown huge and strong. As he turned his head to the side to avoid her sharp fangs, his eyes fell on the Raven God who stood paralyzed not far away. The Hippo God said nothing, but there was such an intense plea for mercy in his eyes that it woke the Raven God from his shock and filled him with cold, murderous rage.

He hurled himself at the Bug Goddess, clawing her repulsive flesh with his talons. She turned her multitude of eyes to him, the hatred in them so fierce it almost struck him to the ground. They fought on, down there below the earth, insect against bird, in the first real battle the world had ever seen.

The Raven God soon noticed he couldn't match the Bug Goddess's vicious strength. The close confines of the prison cell worked to her advantage as well, forcing the Raven God to remain on the ground, where he was much slower and clumsier than in his natural element – the air. Each time he tried to attack, the Bug Goddess hurled him back with brute force, until he stood with his back to the stone wall where the Hippo God was chained.

"Free me, my brother," the Hippo God whispered to him then. "Let us join forces against our enemy."

Nodding his head, the Raven God dropped to his knees, pretending the battle had drained the last vestiges of strength from his limbs. Using his body to block the view, he started working on the bonds holding the Hippo God. It took a few moments before the Bug Goddess realize what was happening, and by the time she recognized the threat it was already too late and the Hippo God was free.

With the two of them fighting together the battle took on a completely different shape. The Hippo God was strong and more suited to this type of combat, and after a short time the Bug Goddess turned and fled back into the palace.

Their moment of triumph was short, however. The Bug Goddess had filled the palace with people faithful only to her, and now she called on them to aid her. Lions roared, hyenas howled, the sharp teeth of predators shone in the night, and the sound of their charge was like rolling thunder.

The two friends managed to get out of the palace, but didn't get far. The Bug Goddess's minions surrounded them in one of the large courtyards, where they would surely have been killed if the Elephant God hadn't broken through the enemy lines with a company of the biggest and strongest among his people and enabled them to escape.

That was the beginning of the first war the world had ever seen. Even though it was fought without a single weapon it was bloodier and more terrible than most of the later conflicts between the nations of humans. All the animals of Africa were put against each other on the battlefields, now forced to kill those they'd called their brothers not long ago. The war brought dire consequences to the world, and there are still enmities which have their origin in this ancient struggle.

Many of those enmities grew so strong during the long years of war that they could never be amended. Traces of the conflict can even be found among animals in other parts of the world. Cats and dogs, cats and mice, and of course birds and insects - all are examples of races who still have trouble coexisting.

Many have speculated about whether the constant warring among humans is a result of similar antagonism, but there are substantial evidence that show it's just a simple mix of greed and blatant stupidity.

When the fighting finally ended there was no chance of returning to the old ways of life. All the brutality and sorrow had caused severe damage to the minds and hearts of the animals. Memories of the lost days of happiness and peace had faded until only the wisest among the gods remembered what life used to be like, and the reminiscence brought nothing but sadness to their hearts.

But I guess a brief account of the war itself is in place before we move on to more recent events.

In the beginning the war went badly for the two friends. The Bug Goddess had trained her subjects in the arts of fighting, whereas the Hippo and Raven were unfamiliar with such deeds of violence and cruelty. The Bug Goddess also unleashed large forces of creatures like herself - spiders and insects with many legs and venomous bites. Some were as large as lions, and more bloodthirsty. For many years it seemed like the free animals were on their way to utter defeat.

Their forces had won a few victories, mostly thanks to the immense strength of the elephants, hippos and rhinos. A charge by a company of these huge animals made the ground tremble, and their opponents often fled to avoid being trampled to death. The mighty roars of today's hippos are a remnant of the war cries which echoed across the plains wherever their ranks stormed into battle.

But these powerful beasts were too few in numbers to defend the entire African continent. In most of the battles the two friends suffered devastating losses, for the Bug Goddess had all the sharp-toothed predators under her command, and very few animals could stand against them. Lions, leopards and cheetahs delivered horrible slaughters across the savannahs, and the merciless hordes of monstrous insects filled everyone with fear whenever they appeared.

In the end the situation became so desperate that the Raven God summoned his two closest allies, the Hippo God and the Elephant God, to a secret council. At this council they discussed the pointlessness of continuing the war the way they'd done so far, as it was obvious that their own forces couldn't match those of the Bug Goddess in pure strength, and therefore it was only a matter of time before they were utterly destroyed. The Raven God stated that a change in tactics was necessary, and as desperate times called for desperate ideas he made a suggestion.

His two companions argued against him at first, pointing out the great risks of the venture and how the free animals would be without leaders if it failed. After many days of discussion they agreed that the Elephant God would remain behind and continue the war if the two others were defeated. All chance of victory would be gone by then, and all the Elephant God would be able to do was make sure the animals fought on to the bitter end.

The Raven and Hippo would make one last attempt to strike at the Bug Goddess herself. They knew it was a desperate mission - their enemy was strong and devious, surrounding herself with the fiercest among her fighters. They had to use all their wisdom and all their courage if they were to succeed. Late one night they left their camp and journeyed quickly to the Royal Palace, where the Goddess still had her headquarters.

Many songs were sung about the heroic deeds of that night, of how the two friends passed through both godly and mortal watchers and finally reached the Bug Goddess's private chambers. They slew the demonic bugs and spiders who stood guard there and burst into the heart of their enemy's domain.

The Bug Goddess was ready for them. They'd barely made it through the door when a torrent of power shot towards them, piercing the darkness like a bolt of lightning. The Raven God barely managed to throw himself out of the way, rolling to the side as the lethal blast tore down most of the wall behind him. He climbed back to his feet to see the Bug Goddess, her form huge and darker than the shadows of night around her, deflect a burst of power from the Hippo God. There was a deafening crack as the stone split above them, sending a shower of debris raining down.

The fight continued, until large parts of the palace had crumbled into dust. The Bug Goddess was as strong as the two others put together, her attacks filled with such malice and cruelty that the Raven and Hippo were forced to retreat and use all their power to defend themselves. Their mission seemed about to end the same way as the war, in complete failure.

But then the Raven God discovered something new to strike at. Knowing it might be his last chance, he focused all his power and hurled it at the connection between the Bug Goddess and her kin among the mortal beasts. The Hippo God added his own power, and their combined efforts turned out to be powerful enough. All the monstrous insects the Bug Goddess had under her command - bugs, spiders, ants, flies and wasps - were shrunk into a fraction of their former sizes.

This immediately changed the situation on the battlefields. All across the land a cry of surprise and hope arose among the armies of free animals. The most dreaded among their enemies had been reduced to insignificant nuisances, buzzing harmlessly around their heads or struggling to crawl up their legs. The remainder of the Goddess's fighters were shaken, and many faltered and withdrew from their suddenly much more menacing opponents.

But the attack had used up most of the two companions' strength, leaving them defenceless as the Bug Goddess struck a fearsome counterblow against them, destroying their physical forms and trapping their spirits inside stone figures. From there they helplessly watched the world around them, stripped of all power, unable even to speak a single word. They knew they were doomed to remain imprisoned like this while the endless years of the world passed before them, new peoples coming and going.

Before they were separated the Hippo God summoned all the power he still possessed and sent a short, faint message to his old friend.

"One day our bloodlines will be united," he whispered. "And even if we'll never be free there will come something new, a scion, who will carry our legacy to the peoples of the world. A new time of wonders will come, and then there'll finally be peace for us. Farewell, my friend."

The Raven God remembered those words as the centuries passed and his stone statue was moved from land to land until it finally ended up in a dark cave beneath an ugly mountain. He never saw his friend, the Hippo God, again.

The Bug Goddess had used all her power when she imprisoned her two enemies, and for thousands of years she lay hidden deep inside the earth, slowly recovering her strength. If her enemies had known about the vulnerable state she was in they could easily have finished her for good and all, but most were too busy grieving for the loss of their two valiant commanders or for all the lives the war had claimed. So no one went to search for the Bug Goddess, and soon the world had forgotten about her existence altogether.

In Africa life went on, but the enmities which had been born during the ancient war still remained. Ravens ate bugs, lions fed on antelope and buffalo, and hyenas feasted on carcasses just like on the ancient battlefields. Elephants refused to eat meat, instead contributing to the old cause by putting insects into their mouths, filling up with water and gargling until the insects had drowned.

Very few predators dared to attack a hippo or an elephant, perhaps because some vague memory of their valiant deeds during the war against the Bug Goddess still lingered, even though all memories of the actual war had vanished.

No one knew exactly when the Bug Goddess returned to the world. In the beginning she was much too weak to cause immediate harm, but she still had her wits and a way of bringing out the most evil and destructive parts of a being's nature. She urged the predators to continue to prey on weaker animals, and told all her subjects among the insects to breed faster in order to compensate for their lack in size. Many of those insects started to carry diseases, some of them even with mortal outcome. The world slowly turned into a darker place once more.

When humans emerged onto the scene the Bug Goddess found new and even more devious ways to work her evil schemes. Humans seemed to have no inhibitions when it came to harming and killing members of their own race, something that only the most malicious among the animals would do.

Like other predators humans fed on the flesh of animals who'd belonged to the Raven God's allies, and their hunger seemed to be without limits. The Bug Goddess gorged herself in the pain and grief this new race had brought into the world.

She found her most loyal subjects among the humans in the Telu tribe. They were ruthless fighters, sly rather than wise and with a relentless thirst for blood. Under the influence of the Bug Goddess their people thrived, conquering large parts of the African continent where they ruled as merciless tyrants.

But not all humans were cruel and evil of heart. There was another strong tribe, the Khadal, who'd started to worship the Hippo God. The ancient statue in which the Bug Goddess had imprisoned her enemy stood in the great hall of their temple, wisdom and strength radiating from it and filling their bodies and minds. The Khadal didn't seek to dominate other peoples, only to protect and guide them. Before long there was another war sweeping across the land.

The people of the Hippo God fought bravely, but they couldn't withstand the power of the Bug Goddess. She had taken on the shape of a stunningly beautiful woman, styling herself the queen of the Telu and fighting alongside her subjects, hurling bolts of magic power at their enemies.

With the Bug Goddess leading the way, the Telu pushed the Khadal forces back until the last remaining defenders took up position in the temple of the Hippo. After a short but intense battle the Telu emerged victorious, bringing down the temple around the bodies of their fallen enemies. But in their last desperate defence the High Priests of the Hippo God summoned their power and a storm of fire hit the Telu ranks. Its vortex struck the Bug Goddess, who fled screaming from her burning body and wasn't heard of for many centuries.

Without the Bug Goddess the Telu tribe dwindled until only a small colony remained close to the northern mountains. Her power continued to flow through their leaders, coercing the rest of the tribe into following them even if they didn't understand why. The leaders themselves were usually too thick to notice that there was something special about them. One of their chieftains even left her people and entered the service of the Raven God, but by then the Bug Goddess had found other things to occupy her evil mind.

The Khadal weren't completely crushed. A small number had managed to escape the fall of the Hippo Cult and put up new abodes on the plain south of the jungle where the old temple had stood. As with the Telu, their tribe was merely a bleak shadow of its former self, all but a faint trickle of its ancient wisdom gone forever.

But now we've gotten away from the question of why the Raven Cult ended up in the caves under the mountains to the west. Most of the smart things in the Raven Cult's old writings can be ascribed to a young woman named Marydette. She was a member of a small tribe of people who'd built their huts around the Raven God's statue, which at this time stood in the middle of the jungle far to the south. Her people had indulged in a primitive worship of the statue, mainly because it was big and somewhat menacing.

But Marydette was a very perceptive woman, and the Raven God often spoke to her in her dreams, telling her about the old war against the Bug

Goddess and how he and the Hippo God had been imprisoned like this. Marydette listened and wrote down many important things that no human would otherwise have learned.

Unfortunately Marydette was killed by a lion, and most of her work was lost. A few things were picked up by a big buffoon named Hippodemus, who later became known as the founder of the Cult of the Raven. What he really did was screw up most of what poor little Marydette had learned from the Raven God, which made the god himself want to moan loudly where he watched from inside the statue, unable to do anything to correct the mistakes the members of Hippodemus's cult made, as none of them were able to speak to him.

The biggest mistake was when Hippodemus found a script containing the purpose of the cult. Marydette had written that "Our purpose is to serve the Raven God and protect the world from the evil eyes of the Bug Goddess", but the parchment had been torn apart, and the piece Hippodemus found ended with "the evil eye".

That summer had been incredibly hot and many of his people had died from heat stroke, so Hippodemus automatically assumed the text was a reference to the sun.

So whenever Hippodemus held his pointless little sermons he accentuated the importance of avoiding sunlight. As with most religious groups, the members of the newly found Raven Cult swallowed all the rubbish their leader fed them, and they raised their arms to the sky and cursed the sun, believing it to be the source of all evil.

This folly continued until the tribe realized what a bad idea hunting by night was. Torches promptly scared away every animal in sight, and without them it was impossible to see anything. The Raven Cult grew hungrier and unhappier with each day.

Finally Hippodemus decided it was time for them to move. He spent several years looking for a place where his cult could live and work without being exposed to the sun, and finally found the caves which have been the home of the Raven Cult ever since.

The Raven God really hated those caves, but imprisoned as he was in the stone statue there was nothing for him to do but weep and endure.

To weep and endure wasn't really Lulu's thing. Sulking was another matter, of course, but generally she was a woman who loved action. If there was something she didn't like she did something about it. If something needed to be done and she didn't want to do it she made someone else do it for her.

And if there was someone she didn't like she did what she could to rid herself (and preferably the rest of the world) of the person in question.

Right now there was a person she didn't like. She didn't like her at all.

Lizbug's tent was dark. Lulu didn't think she'd ever seen her use a torch or a candle.

Not very strange, she thought. *As pale as that woman is she'll probably illuminate the whole place just by taking her clothes off.*

She frowned at the thought. Had the woman taken her clothes off for her former lover, Dogshit? Not that it mattered now, of course. Their relationship was over and done with, and she'd never touch the man now that *she* had put her filthy fingers on him.

The moon was full, and in its pale, silvery light she saw small things move on the ground outside the tent. At first she thought they were dead leaves or parts of some other greenery shuffled across the ground by the night breeze, but when she looked closer she realized it was a multitude of bugs and insects crawling into the tent.

They've probably caught the scent of some scrap of food Lizbug dropped on the ground, she thought. *Or maybe she left her underpants somewhere. Insects are drawn to shit, aren't they?*

But there was something about the way the insects moved, in perfect columns like an army on the march. That certainly wasn't normal behaviour for this type of creatures. Ants often lived in organized societies, but most other bugs were solitary creatures. They certainly didn't work as a unit. Lulu suddenly had a strong impression that something wasn't as it should be. She stepped a little closer, trying to hear if something moved inside the tent.

"Lulu, is that you?"

It had only been a whisper, but it made her jump anyway. Ashlob - the short, pretty woman with the odd way of walking - came sauntering towards her. The two of them weren't exactly friends, but Lulu couldn't think of any specific reason to dislike her.

Most of the Raven people were nice enough once you got to know them, and since the night the High Priest showed her the funny-looking egg they'd stopped treating her and Doggy like evil demons. Even the snobby Chrisox had lightened up a bit. The other night he'd given her a good-night hug, something none of the cult members would have dreamed of doing a week ago.

She breathed in deeply and did her best to give Ashlob a pleasant smile. "Hi, Ashlob. What are you doing up this late?"

"Oh, nothing much," Ashlob said with a small shrug. "Just making sure the pattern hasn't been disturbed."

Lulu grimaced, but the other woman didn't seem to notice it in the darkness. Ashlob had some very odd ideas about the world and the people living in it. Lulu had seen her count stones to make sure there was balance in the universe, and once she'd cut a worm in half because there had to be an even number. Her odd way of walking back and forth probably had something to do with those things as well. Lulu found it best not to ask too much.

"What are you up to yourself?" Ashlob asked.

"I was on the way back to my tent when I saw something quite odd. There were bugs and spiders and such crawling into Lizbug's tent. Hundreds of them, in straight lines."

The other woman leaned forward. "I see nothing, but it shouldn't be a problem as long as they went in straight lines. Straight lines are good. You should always walk straight, so you don't get away from your course."

Lulu turned back to watch the tent. Ashlob was right; the bugs had vanished. One moment there, gone the next. Straight lines or no, she knew there was something strange going on. For one brief moment she considered aborting her mission, but then she remembered the look Lizbug had given her when she stood there with Doggy in her arms. Fury filled her, and she clenched her hands into fists.

"Oh, well, not much more to do now," Ashlob murmured. "I should get some sleep. Must be up early tomorrow and count dew drops. Goodnight, Lulu."

Lulu muttered something in return but didn't take her eyes off the tent. The camp was still around her; even the camels appeared to be asleep. She took out the knife she'd hidden inside her cloak and crept closer.

She'd found an excuse to peek into Lizbug's tent earlier that evening, so she knew where the woman slept. After one last stop to listen and make sure nothing moved anywhere around her she cut through the thin wall until the opening was big enough for her to squeeze through.

A thin ray of moonlight found its way through the gap she'd made and fell on Lizbug's peaceful face. The woman looked to be sound asleep - her breath was deep and slow and she even snored softly.

Lulu knelt beside her, let her blade reflect the moonlight dramatically for a moment, and ran the sharp edge across Lizbug's throat. As a cannibal she was used to cutting through meat. It would probably have made her hungry if she hadn't loathed this woman so much. She used Lizbug's black robe to wipe the blood from her knife, then left the tent silently.

Back outside she took a deep breath of the sweet night air. It somehow felt cleaner and more fresh now that the evil bitch was dead. She knew she should worry about what'd happen when the body was found. It was obvious that she'd be the prime suspect, especially after Ashlob found her at the crime scene right before it happened. But at the moment she felt nothing but jubilant glee.

"No one fucks with Lulu unless she invites them to her bed," she said with a chuckle. "Ah, sweet revenge. This calls for a celebration."

She was just considering whether to wake up the young man Drunk and invite him to share her bed when another need screamed for her attention. She'd drank a lot of tea earlier, and in all the excitement she'd forgotten to relieve herself. Finding a small grove, she snuck off to repair the damage.

When she'd finished she stood up and started to walk back towards the camp, whistling a merry tune. She decided she'd pay Drunk a visit after all. The young man might not be much to look at, but he was by far the best this Raven Cult had to offer. Perhaps she'd give his ear lobe a nibble, too. A quick bite in the heat of the moment wouldn't reveal her cannibal ways, would it?

She'd only taken a few steps when someone stepped out from behind a tree and blocked her path. At first she thought it was Ashlob, and opened her mouth to say the number of trees was even and she wouldn't have to count them, but then she recognized the pale face and the deep, dark eyes. Blood-red lips parted in a malicious grin.

For the first time in her life Lulu was truly afraid.

"It-it can't be," she stammered. "I-I killed you!"

Lizbug said nothing. She just stood there, her skin as pale as the moonlight. There was no sign of blood on her neck and robe, not even a scar. Lulu knew she'd done the job right and that there was no way the woman could have survived. Not unless…

"You're not human," she squeaked. "You're a monster, a demon. I should have guessed. The way you stole Doggy from me - it was more than plain sex appeal. You used some wicked magic on him. Are you going to use the same on me?"

Lizbug didn't answer. Instead she changed into her true shape.

Lulu screamed and ran blindly into the night, faster than she'd ever run before in her life.

~ 16 ~

Gemma sat on a rock and looked gloomily into the distance. Her spear lay on the ground beside her, in case some members of the Telu tribe showed up. Actually, it lay there because she'd put it there after she used it to clean her toenails. There'd been half an ecosystem under them, plus a few kinds of metal ore and a piece of an old bubblegum. The gods alone knew how *it* had ended up there.

On second thought, the gods didn't know either.

They'd run through the wilderness for the better part of two days, aimlessly at first but recently in a direction Gemma thought would lead them back to the jungle. Back home. Their attempts to revive the Hippo Cult had ended in complete disaster, so there was no reason to remain in this dry, dusty wasteland. The Telu could keep it if they liked it so much. She didn't care.

She stretched her long, slim legs and almost fell off the rock. She looked around to make sure none of the others had seen her clumsy move, but Fae and Tom-Tom seemed too busy discussing lightning and images in their heads.

"It was amazing!" the skeleton exclaimed, his voice filled with the new-found enthusiasm the experience had given him. "I almost felt alive again. In some ways it was better than being alive. Do you know which part of this continent has the greatest number of thunderstorms?"

Fae laughed and gave his back a hearty pounding. "I knew it'd work on you, my bony friend. Perhaps we can build some sort of construction that absorbs the power from the lightning and magnifies it. Imagine the sensation you'd get when connected to a device like that!"

The thought made Tom-Tom whistle. Or it would have if he'd had lips. The sound was more like an icy wind blowing through an old dungeon.

"We should start working on it as soon as we've settled this business with the Telu," he said. "We'll need lots of bones, though. Do you think Gemma will help us with that? She's very good at hunting."

"Why don't we ask her?" Fae waved her hand vigorously. "Hey, Gemma! Would you help us get bones for our new lightning-catcher? You'll be the first to try it once we've made sure it's safe. A guest of honour, sort of."

Gemma shrugged. "Sure. Why not?"

"Good. We'll need two tall poles and lots of smaller ones, and the bones will be nailed to them like a spiderweb. The power will circulate through them until it's strong enough. Hmmm, I think the effect will be better if you hang suspended between the bones and have no contact with the ground. We'll need straps for that, strong ones. Who's the heaviest person in your tribe, Gemma?"

"That'd be Emkei, the seer. I don't think there's anything strong enough to hold her up, though. She once made a buffalo collapse under her weight. A really big and strong one."

Fae nodded. "We can have one spot on the ground where all the fat people can stand. The effect won't be the same, of course, but it's either that or lose some weight. The next thing we'll have to think of is to find a suitable location for the whole structure. Somewhere high up, a hill or something. If you drive the poles..."

Gemma stopped listening. She'd spotted movement somewhere to the north-east. It looked like a small company of men moving swiftly across the barren ground. She reached for her spear. This time she really fell off the rock and landed on the weapon's shaft. It somersaulted and landed a couple of feet away with a loud, clattering sound.

Fae and Tom-Tom looked up. "What's going on?" asked the young girl.

Gemma hurried to retrieve her weapon and assumed a half-crouching position. "Someone's coming," she hissed. "They must have seen us already."

"Telu?" Fae asked, shading her eyes with one hand as she gazed into the distance.

"Who else can it be?" Gemma snarled. "Prepare to fight till the bitter end. I won't have any of us taken alive."

"Not a problem here," Tom-Tom chuckled.

The men came closer. Gemma counted to a dozen, then decided she should count the men instead. She got to eight before losing count. She sighed and made another attempt. This time the numbers just spun in her head. Focusing hard, she began a very slow recount.

By the time she got to five the men were only twenty meters away. Fae nudged her elbow urgently.

"Aren't you going to attack them?" she asked.

"Shhhh, I'm counting them," Gemma hissed. "We must know what we're up against. Please don't distract me."

"What? I've already counted them. They're..."

"Step back!" Gemma snapped. "One of them just brought forth a spear."

The one who appeared to be the company's leader had indeed grabbed a spear, but to Gemma's surprise he put it down and approached her empty-handed. Then she saw that it was Joz, the man who'd welcomed them when they came to the Telu tribe's camp. She kept a firm grip on her spear's shaft and waited for him to speak. He appeared to do the same, for the silence lasted for several minutes before Joz finally opened his mouth.

"Your Highness," he said in a clear voice. "I've brought these men as a gift to you. We all want to enter your service and fight with you against the usurper Winston. They called you a fraud, but we know you're the rightful queen of the Telu. And..." He blushed and looked down at his feet. "I think you have a very nice butt."

Gemma lowered her spear. "You left your tribe to follow me instead?"

"Following is a good thing to do if you want to look at someone's butt," muttered Fae, who'd stepped up beside her. "This also brings some new hope to this Hippo Cult business. Providing these people are willing to join, of course."

"Will you join the Hippo Cult?" Gemma asked.

"We'll do anything you command," Joz said solemnly. "We're your loyal subjects."

He bowed, and the others followed his example. Gemma finally finished her count. *Fifteen men. A big step forward.*

Fae clapped her hands, face beaming with delight. "This is wonderful!" she exclaimed. "Let's have a party!"

"Errr... I don't think that'd be a very good idea right now," Joz mumbled.

Gemma was in quite a partying mood herself, and this Joz fellow was far from bad-looking. She wouldn't mind getting drunk with him and do some cuddling. But the look in his eyes made a worm of worry crawl up her spine. She tightened her grip on the spear's shaft again.

"Why not?" she demanded.

"Because Winston and his men have followed us all the way here. We've managed to keep them behind so far, but they can't be far away now."

An instant later they heard screams and howls from somewhere to the north-east. They did indeed sound very close.

"That would be them," Joz concluded.

Gemma gazed in the direction the shouts had come from. A large number of people were running towards them, waving spears and clubs in the air. Gemma started to count them but gave up when she came to four. There were just too many of them.

"They must be at least three times as many as we are," said Fae, who was slightly more gifted in the ways of mathematics.

"The Hippo Cult has been outnumbered many times," Tom-Tom boasted. "And yet our courage and strength never failed. We fight like lions and do not fear death."

"Perhaps that's why all of you died," Gemma muttered. "Come on, let's run!"

"Flight is for the weak," Tom-Tom said reproachfully. "The Hippo Cult stands and fights."

"It'll die out again if we do that!" Fae snapped, took the skeleton's arm and dragged him away with her. Gemma and the former Telu people were already on their way south, running like antelopes with a cheetah on their tails. Joz ran close behind Gemma, his eyes fixed firmly on her bouncing buttocks. Right then he'd probably have followed her if she'd leaped off a cliff.

They ran like this for almost an hour before Gemma ordered them to stop. She was barely out of breath herself, but many of the Telu people were struggling to keep up. Fae laughed happily as she ran at Tom-Tom's side, now and them bursting into a series of cartwheels. The skeleton's bones creaked softly as he moved, making him sound almost like an old rocking-chair.

"Do you see them?" Gemma asked Joz, who hadn't taken his eyes off her butt.

"Who? Oh, them?" He stood on his toes and peered into the distance. "No. It looks like we've lost them." He went back to admiring her backside.

"Good." Gemma dusted off her hands. They hadn't been more dusty than usual, but for some reason it seemed like the thing to do. "We should find a place to hide," she continued. "We'll be easy to find in this open land. Does anyone know where we are?"

No one did, least of all Joz. The only one who seemed to have the slightest sense of direction was Fae, who claimed to feel a storm somewhere to the east and thus could point out which way that was. Tom-Tom would probably have run off to check it out if Gemma hadn't reminded him that there were more urgent business at hand. Finally they set off at a steady jog, zig-zagging across the land as they searched for a more sheltered place to spend the night.

They found a rocky hollow a few miles away and settled there. The large, jagged boulders provided excellent protection from unwanted eyes. Nonetheless, Gemma found it best to post guards to keep watch in case the Telu people were lucky enough to stumble straight into their midst. As the sun sank towards the western horizon she seated herself on the ground and leaned her tired back against a rock. Joz sat down beside her.

"I know this is much too bold for a simple servant like me, Your Grace," he said. "But I get so bored when I have nothing to do and it looked like you had no queenly matters that needed your immediate attention. So I thought maybe we could talk a little, if you don't mind. I`ll leave if you don't want to, of course."

Gemma gestured for him to come closer. "It's alright," she said. "I'm pretty bored myself. Besides, you could tell me some more about those people who're chasing us. Winston and Gideon. How did they end up ruling the Telu tribe?"

His forehead creased in thought. "I'm not sure, Your Grace. We used to have another chieftain. Her name was Bathora. She was quite a loon, but she guided us well enough considering her limited brain capacity. Perhaps that was what made her such a good leader. She was too stupid to abuse her own power. Everything was fine as long as she ruled. But then she disappeared."

Gemma had heard Fae talk about this Bathora woman and had been surprised she'd been smart enough to understand how to breathe.

Perhaps that's why she disappeared, she thought. *She forgot how to breathe and died. That sounds just like the thing that woman would do.*

"Did anyone see her leave?" she asked.

"No, Your Grace." Joz shook his head. "That's the odd thing. Well, not that odd, really. We had our annual race, and most of us lay panting on the ground at the time. Winston and Gideon didn't take part in the race, but if they knew something they never told the rest of us."

"Perhaps they murdered her?"

The thought seemed to make the man feel uncomfortable. "No one dared to make such accusations, but you could see the unspoken questions in people's eyes when they talked about her disappearance. There's one thing speaking against that theory, though."

Gemma had been looking at the ground, but now she turned to face the young man. "Oh? What was that?"

"Bathora and Winston were lovers. At least they were in the past. No one would suspect he desired to harm her."

Gemma nodded. She'd had men fight over her several times, but none of them had ever raised a hand against her, not even when she rejected them. That had probably something to do with her reputation as a spear fighter, but still...

Another thing struck her, so she turned back to Joz.

"This Winston seems... a bit odd," she said. "I mean, none of the others have wings or stings or skin that would make a tiger avert its eyes. How often does he take on a new shape?"

"It varies," Joz explained. "No one knows when it'll happen or how he does it. There are just some mornings when you go out for a pee and suddenly he's changed. It always unnerved me, but Bathora seemed fascinated by it. As far as I know Winston was the only one she ever let into her bed. You should think that'd make Winston very unpopular, but now he's their leader and they follow his commands. Perhaps they're afraid of him."

Gemma was definitely afraid of the man. Not just because of his odd appearance, but because there was something about him that made her instincts cry out like a mad hyena. She knew this Winston to be her enemy, and knew that in the end it'd come down to either her killing him or the other way around. It was as evident to her as the smell of one of Emkei's farts.

"What about Gideon?" she asked. "How did he end up as second-in-command. For that's what he is, isn't it? Winston's right hand, his eyes and ears. Do you think it's because they're lovers, or is there some other reason?"

Joz was silent a few moments before speaking. "I don't know, Your Grace. They've always been close friends, so it was only natural that Winston gave him a prominent position when he took over. They complement each other well - Winston cold and hard and Gideon charismatic and friendly. I wouldn't say Gideon is much less dangerous than his master, though. A smiling façade often conceals a heart of stone. Just look at your skeleton-friend."

That last thing left Gemma very confused. "Tom-Tom? He can't smile, and if he's got a heart it's likely made of bone, not stone. You can't compare him to Gideon. They don't even have being alive in common."

"That was what I meant." Joz flashed her a triumphant smile. "Just because you don't smile doesn't mean you're a bad person. Gideon smiles a lot, but I wouldn't trust him to look after my old mother for five minutes."

"Why not? What would he do to her?"

Joz leaned closer and spoke in a low voice. "I once saw him bite the head off a small bird."

Gemma opened her mouth to reply, but a loud, buzzing sound caught her attention. She looked around, trying to locate where it'd come from. It had gone very dark in the little hollow, but she thought she saw a dark shape disappear around an outcrop. She rose gracefully to her feet.

"What was…?" she began.

"Down!" Joz threw himself at her and pulled her down to the ground with him. The buzzing sound was suddenly right above them, and something hard struck the top of Gemma's head just as she dropped. She didn't want to think about what would've happened if she'd remained standing.

"It's Winston," Joz whispered beside her. His breath was hot against her cheek. There was no mistaking the fear in his voice, even if she couldn't see his face in the dim light of dusk. She rolled away from him and reached for her spear. There was safety in the feeling of hard wood against the skin of her hands. She rose to a half-crouch.

"How did he find us?" she hissed.

Joz had found his own spear and aimed its point at the darkening sky. His head moved from side to side, searching for any sign of the Telu chieftain.

"We told the guards to keep watch in every direction," he grumbled. "North, south, east and west. We didn't tell them to look *up*. That's where he came from."

"You mean he's flying?"

"Indeed. He must have patrolled the land from above. This hollow might be hidden from people on the ground, but from the sky it's as visible as your buttocks. Pardon me, Your Grace," he added quickly.

Gemma touched her scalp with her left hand. "Something struck me. Was that…?"

"His sting, yes. Be happy it didn't penetrate your skin. We wouldn't have had this conversation if it had."

Gemma gave him a questioning look. "Why not? It makes people go mute?"

"It makes people go dead."

"Oh."

"Watch out, here he comes again!"

The fierce, buzzing sound reached Gemma's ears a moment before the flying man's dark shape came out of the shadows. She ducked quickly, but managed to swing her spear in a wide arc. There was a low grunt, the rapid movement of the thin wings ceasing for a second. Winston regained control quickly enough, though, and vanished behind the northern slope.

"We must get out of here!" Joz hissed. "Now that he knows where we are this hollow will only work against us. He'll come back with all his men and then we'll be trapped here. Gather the others. It's time to run again."

Their flight was a hazardous journey through the darkness. The land was uneven and there was only pale silver moonlight to guide them. Once Gemma tripped on a sleeping warthog and tumbled headlong down a slope. The fall made her so dizzy Joz and Fae had to drag her along between them for over a mile. The warthog didn't even wake up.

After a few hours Gemma ordered a halt. Fae made a double backwards somersault and landed in a sitting position on her shoulders. Gemma was weary and not in the mood for games, but when she tried to shrug her off Fae jumped into a handstand with one hand on Gemma's left shoulder and one atop her head. The former Telu woman's legs were stretched out in a perfect horizontal angle. In the darkness they looked like some weird sign pointing to the east. Some of their companions even began walking in that direction.

"Stop!" Gemma called. "You must stay close, or you'll get lost. Is everyone here? Joz, count them. We'll be here all night if you make me do it. Where's Tom-Tom?"

"Here," the skeleton droned. "I was going to sneak off for a pee, but then I remembered I have no bladder. Perhaps I could use your pouch, Fae?"

"What pouch?" The girl sounded puzzled as she climbed down from Gemma's back.

"The one hanging from one of the bones in your hair. What's in it, anyway?"

Fae reached up to touch the little bag but couldn't find it. "I don't know," she mumbled. "I'm not even sure it's mine. Where is it?"

"Be quiet, you two," Gemma whispered. "We don't know how close Winston and his men are. Anyway, we can't travel much farther tonight. The moon sinks towards the western horizon, and soon there'll be no light left. We must find a place to spend the rest of the night." She looked around. "What's that?"

Fae frowned into the darkness. "What's what?"

Gemma pointed. "That way. There's something dark sticking up. Or is it many smaller things? It's hard to see."

"It's trees," Tom-Tom announced. "We've come back to the jungle."

Gemma felt her heart leap in her chest. They'd be safe in the jungle. There'd be countless places to hide, and their pursuers would have to look a long time before finding any tracks. And the best thing of all was that the trees would protect them from Winston's eyes if he tried to find them from above. That thought made her laugh aloud.

"I hope your men have some strength left, Joz!" she called. "We'll all sleep together in the jungle. Doesn't that sound great?"

The only reply she got was a couple of half-choked sounds. Joz himself had fainted.

"No!" She knelt beside him and grabbed him by the shoulders. "You must walk a little further before you get any. We can't do it here in the open. If Winston finds us he'll put his sting into us, and that's the last thing I'd want inside me right now. Get up! Hey, you, why are you drooling? Help me get him up. I can't do it all by myself."

Slowly, the men returned from their dirty fantasies and helped Joz back to his feet. The man mumbled incoherently but stumbled along when they continued their nocturnal march. The trees crept closer, until Gemma suddenly bumped right into one.

"Damn," she cursed, rubbing her aching nose. "Didn't see that one. I think we should walk single file here. It's important that we keep together. Tom-Tom, you'll walk last. I`ll take the lead."

She turned and bumped into the tree again. This time she fell backwards and would have hit her head badly on a rock if Joz hadn't caught her. As he held her in his strong arms Gemma wasn't sure if she really wanted to regain balance. After a while, however, she forced her body to pull free and turned to address the others.

"Like I said, we should..."

She wasn't sure what they should.

"Move on?" Fae suggested.

"Move on," Gemma echoed. "Follow me."

"Mind the tree," Fae muttered sardonically.

Their march through the jungle was slow and painful. Slow because it was almost completely dark, and painful because some plant with stinging thorns grew all over the ground. Fortunately, the night was full of sounds, so Gemma wasn't worried that the Telu warriors would hear them whenever someone let out a cry of pain and began jumping up and down on one leg. Tom-Tom was the only one the thorns didn't bother, but he kept complaining about getting moths in his eye sockets instead.

When she decided they'd gone far enough into the jungle to be safe, Gemma found a spacious glade and told her people to make camp there. It wasn't much of a camp. People just sat or lay down, trying to find a comfortable position. Gemma remained standing and talked a little with her two companions from the journey north.

"What do you do when the rest of us sleep, Tom-Tom?" she asked the skeleton.

"I wait."

"Isn't that boring?"

"Very much so."

"Isn't there something you can do?" asked Fae. "Like carving wood sculptures or solving advanced mathematical problems?"

The skeleton pondered this for a while. "I suppose I could," he finally said. "It's just that I'm so used to doing nothing. That was all I could do while I hung from that chain in the Hippo God's temple. Too much activity wearies me. It gets better with time, though. I feel much more active now than when I first met Gemma. Back then I was really miserable. Isn't that right, Gemma?"

But Gemma didn't listen. She just stood there staring into the darkness with a troubled expression on her beautiful face.

"The trees," she mumbled. "They're moving."

Fae laughed. "It's just the shadows playing tricks with your imagination. All you need is some sleep. In the morning you'll feel much..."

"I see it too," Tom-Tom said soberly. "They're coming closer."

It was true. All around there were dark figures closing in on them. They made absolutely no sound when they moved. Gemma raised her spear but hesitated. How did you fight a moving tree? She should have had an axe, then the fight might have become more even. Her spear wouldn't do more than peel off some of the bark.

The dark shapes moved further into the glade. They were easier to make out now. Gemma strained her eyes to see better. There was something that didn't add up. But again, that wasn't unusual when she tried to calculate things. And yet...

"Those are not trees," Fae hissed. "They're..."

Suddenly the night burst into flames all around them. Two dozen torches were lit simultaneously. Many were thrown into the middle of the camp, where some of Gemma's men had already fallen asleep. Screams of pain and terror filled the night. Another torch landed in a stand of dry undergrowth and set it on fire. Through the fire and smoke that already seemed to fill the glade Gemma saw the glimmer of steel and understood what had happened.

The Telu warriors had found them.

She had no time to wonder how it had happened. The Telu men were attacking and she had to run her spear through one who would have slammed right into her otherwise. She took a couple of steps backwards and shouted as loudly as she could.

"We're under attack! To me, everyone. Stay together!"

It wasn't much use. The attack had come so suddenly and forcefully that it had turned her men into a bunch of frightened hens, running this way and that without accomplishing anything. A few ended up close to her, but more out of accident than good planning. She saw one man fall, then another. The grass had caught fire in some places and the flames lit up the battle scene all the way to the treeline. It was a terrible sight.

"No!" Tom-Tom moaned. "Not again! It cannot happen again!"

Gemma understood they had no chance of winning this battle. Gritting her teeth, she grabbed hold of as many of her own fighters as she could and pushed them towards Fae and Tom-Tom.

"Keep them together!" she bellowed. "I'll be right back!"

She ran into the middle of the camp, where the fighting was fiercest. Her spear blade flashed in the firelight as she stabbed faster than any viper's bite. Three enemies fell. Some more stopped fighting and turned to see what was going on. Gemma leapt past them, ducking under one spear and kicking away another. And then she saw him. Her heart almost stopped beating.

Joz stood back to back with another of Gemma's men, both of them hard pressed to defend themselves. Gideon kept launching furious attacks at Joz's companion, while Joz himself was engaged in battle with Winston. The half-human man was even more frightening when he fought with a spear than when he'd attacked them from the sky like some monstrous wasp. His face was calm and expressionless, his movements controlled but deadly. The point of his spear seemed to burn with a light of its own as he swung it at his enemy, as graceful as a dancer.

Sweat ran down Joz's face as he struggled to keep his opponent's weapon away. The effort of each parry made him grimace, whereas Winston appeared to have no trouble keeping up his relentless stabbing and swinging. Gemma knew her friend wouldn't last much longer.

She was about to throw herself at Winston when Gideon ran his spear through Joz's comrade. The man slid down, his back still against Joz's, and collapsed on the ground. Gideon raised his weapon again, this time to stab Joz in the back. Gemma snarled and leapt like a gazelle, ramming the Telu warrior from the side and knocking him over. They wrestled for a few moments, then

Gemma managed to roll into a knee-stand and thrust her spear deep into her opponent's body. A choked sound came from Gideon's mouth, then he lay still. Dark blood began to pour through his clothing and onto the ground.

Gemma looked around to see how Joz was doing, finding him just as Winston gave him a hard whack across the face with his spear shaft. Joz tumbled backwards and landed somewhere to Gemma's left. Growling with fury, she lifted her spear and aimed it at Winston, but the man moved much faster than she'd expected. He was on her before she could react, and with a brutal blow he struck the spear from her hands. She stood empty-handed before him like a child awaiting punishment.

Winston's face showed no signs of joy or triumph. He simply took a step closer and held his spear above his head, ready to thrust it through Gemma's unprotected body with all his strength. The black and yellow skin on his arms shone in the red light, bright and terrible. The sight of this cold, arrogant monster of a man made Gemma's blood boil with pure rage, so she did what any other angered woman would have done.

She kicked him between the legs, hard.

It was a perfect kick, the kind a man has nightmares about and prays he'll never experience in real life, the kind that gives you so much pain you're unable to scream, the kind to make the god who invented the male genitals turn white as a sheet. It was a kick every woman manages only once in her lifetime, a kick neither she nor her victim is likely to ever forget. It was a kick to make any man utterly defenceless, and it made Winston defenceless as well.

But she didn't get to kill him.

Gemma dove for her spear, but when she turned back to Winston she saw him take to the air, wings beating too fast for the eye to see. Even as he flew he was bent double, both hands clutching his groin. He flew out of the circle of firelight and vanished into the night.

A pain-filled groaning came from the ground behind her. She turned and saw Joz struggling to get up. He took the hand she offered and let her help him to his feet. His nose appeared to be broken, and blood trickled both from it and from a scar across his forehead.

"Oh dear, you look awful," she complained.

"Thanks," he said. "Where's... where's *he*?"

"He got away. And so should we. Come on!"

The battle was almost over. Only a few scorched patches remained of the glade's grass, and the ground was covered with corpses. The last of Gemma's men had fled and she could hear screams and the clash of weapons among the trees as the Telu warriors gave chase. She sent Fae and Tom-Tom a quick thought, hoping they'd managed to get away. There was no way she and Joz could stay and look for them – with so many enemies about it wouldn't be long before the two of them were discovered. Keeping a firm hold on Joz's arm, she pulled him with her into the trees.

It was still the middle of night, but fires were blazing in many places and Gemma had no trouble finding her way through the jungle. Joz stumbled along behind her, every now and then raising a hand to wipe blood from his eyes. Gemma had no idea in which direction they were running, her only thought to get as far away as possible from the glade and the fading sounds of battle as possible.

"I think we've made it!" she shouted over her shoulder. "We've escaped."

Suddenly they burst out of the jungle and onto a narrow patch of open ground. It sloped upwards quite steeply, and it was too dark to see where it led. Gemma ascended the slope with long strides and stopped dead. Her bare feet slid on the dry earth and she was close to falling.

"What is it?" Joz mumbled dizzily. "Why did you stop?"

"Look." Gemma pointed a finger at what lay ahead of them. Her face was utterly miserable.

They stood on the edge of a cliff. Far below them, forty feet or more, a foaming river gushed rapidly through the starlit landscape. Its roaring voice reached them like the call of some wild, ravenous beast. Gemma saw dark spots here and there and understood they were sharp rocks sticking out of the water. She let her eyes follow the raging torrent until it vanished into the darkness somewhere to their right.

"We can't go any further here," she shouted. "We must go back and find another way."

But then they heard shouts from somewhere behind them, and torchlight flashed between the trees. A large number of Telu warriors burst out of the jungle and began running up the slope towards them. Winston was at their head, his half-human form radiating force and malice. Gemma made no effort to try to count the warriors behind him. She knew perfectly well they were far too many for her to fight, especially with Joz in his present condition.

She turned back to watch the ghastly torrent of water and foam beneath them. In the pale starlight it looked almost like something from another world. If there was a river separating the land of the living from the realms of the dead it would probably have looked something like this.

Actually, Gemma thought, *it really is the river separating the dead from the living. If we jump into it there's no telling which side we'll be washed up on. One thing's for certain, though. If we stay here we'll be dead before long.*

"There really isn't any other way, is there?" said Joz, who appeared to have shared her thoughts.

"I suppose not."

"Gemma..."

She looked at him. "What?"

"There's something I have to tell you, in case everything ends here. I thought I'd be content with serving you as my queen, admiring you as my queen. But now, when I've gotten to know you as a woman, things have changed. What I feel for you goes way beyond respect and loyalty. I love you, Gemma, and my spirit will keep on loving you even if those cruel rocks down there smash my body to pieces."

Winston and his men had almost reached the top of the slope, where Gemma and Joz stood, two dark silhouettes at the edge of doom. A few more moments and the Telu warriors would be on them. The whole scene was as dramatic as it could get.

Gemma threw her arms around him and their lips met in a short but passionate kiss.

"I love you too, Joz," she whispered. "If we're going to die, let's die together, hand in hand."

She held out her hand. The world seemed to fade away around them until everything else was gone - the raging river far below them, the spear in Winston's hand, so close, so sharp. There were only the two of them. They were together, and nothing else meant anything. Joz took her hand.

They jumped.

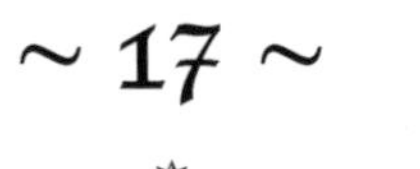

Some people like to call things they don't understand *odd* or *weird* in a stupid attempt to cover up their own ignorance. The people intelligent enough to understand these things are also dismissed as *odd* or *weird*, especially since they spend a lot of time laughing at the ignorant fools unable to understand even the most trivial matters. The aforementioned people often have a tendency to surround themselves with people gifted with the same low level of intelligence, allowing them to trick themselves into believing their own viewpoint is the right one and the *odd* ones are wrong. That people with such limited intellects are able to go through life without forgetting to breathe or eat or sleep is beyond comprehension.

Amanda didn't belong to this despicable group of people. She was a woman not afraid of admitting there were numerous things she didn't know. That there probably were a lot of people who knew things she didn't know didn't bother her either. She was well aware of what she was good at (which was a substantial number of things), but rarely felt the need to boast. She wouldn't call anyone *weird* unless they really were, and if anyone was foolish enough to insult her in that way they'd better be prepared for trouble.

If she encountered something she didn't understand she wouldn't simply dismiss it as *odd* or *weird*. Instead she'd try to find out a couple of things:

1) Can you eat it?
2) Can you sleep with it? and
3) Can you do some other thing with it?

Someone who'd just dismiss unknown things as *odd* would most certainly not survive the situation she was soon about to find herself in. This wouldn't be too great a loss for mankind as a whole, seeing as such people don't contribute much to the important areas of society. They function mostly as breeding stock, which unfortunately means their genes are transferred in excess to the next generation. This is probably why humans, despite their superior brains, often don't behave that differently from simpler primates.

Amanda, however, was a quite valuable person, not only because she'd just saved her friends (and some other people she would at best call acquaintances) from an erupting volcano, but because she was considered one of the best lovers on the continent. Any man who dismissed her as *odd* or *weird* was hopefully too stupid to ever find out what he was missing out on.

Very few people have been tossed into the air by a volcano, and even fewer have survived it. Strangely enough, the survival issue wasn't what occupied Amanda's mind at the moment, despite her having been thrown thousands of feet into the air. What worried her was how she was going to make a graceful landing. After some quick calculations that would've made Gemma green with jealousy she decided she had plenty of time to find a solution to this problem, and after a few critical moments when she thought she'd fall off her boulder she managed to make herself comfortable and enjoy the view.

The boulder carried her far to the north. After a couple of hours she started to get hungry. Looking around, she wondered if she'd be able to catch a bird in flight, then realized there wasn't enough room on the boulder to make a cook fire, and the only burnable things she had were her clothes. The idea of landing naked in a strange place somewhere didn't appeal to her, so she made herself endure the hunger and wait patiently for the boulder to start descending.

A short time later she noticed the boulder was beginning to lose altitude. She wondered how far the thing would've managed to carry Emkei. *Probably no more than a dozen feet or so*, she thought, chuckling to herself. Amanda wasn't emaciated in any way, but compared to the old seer she must appear light as a feather.

As the boulder dropped towards the ground she began looking for a nice place to land. For a moment she thought she'd end up in the middle of a big lake, which would have annoyed her immensely as she didn't have any spare clothes, but then she spotted a small island lying like a green gem in its middle. The boulder swept in over it, dove over a grove of trees, and bounced a few times across a patch of open ground before slamming into a cliff and shattering into a thousand pieces.

Amanda had leapt off it an instant before it hit ground, and after rolling down a small slope she ended up flat on her back. She lay there for a while, looking up at the sky she'd just left and wondering if she'd gotten stains on her clothes. The sunlight was warm and the breeze pleasantly cool. She closed her eyes and dozed off.

Something wet and soft nuzzled her ear. Amanda murmured something, still half-asleep, and pushed it away. She had almost drifted back to sleep when the thing touched her again. She slapped it, harder this time.

"Lay off, Pebe," she muttered drowsily. "I'm not interested."

Something touched one of her ample breasts.

"That's it!" she snapped, sitting up. "I've told you what'll happen if you go to far with this game. You won't be able to sit for a week when I'm done with you."

Then she remembered she wasn't back in the Khadal camp. Thoughts of poisonous snakes, cannibals and people with deviant sexual preferences went through her mind. She looked around, trying to establish the nature of the threat, but found nothing.

Then she looked down at the ground beside her.

A small, green creature was studying her with round, blue eyes. It looked somewhat like a broccoli on four short, thick legs. Its size was about the same as a cat or a very small dog, but as those animals didn't exist in this part of the world Amanda compared it to animals she knew to be edible.

"Not much meat on you, is there?" she mused, patting the thing on its head. It made a low, clicking sound and tried to sniff her hand.

"Never heard about your kind before," she went on, happy to have someone to talk to even if the creature showed no sign of understanding. "Am I the first human to visit this island? How many of you are there? Do you have some sort of society?"

The green creature sniffed her leg. A short, rough tongue shot out and licked salt sweat from her skin. Amanda scratched its neck. The skin was dry and hairless, almost like that of a snake. It purred softly when she touched it.

Then she heard a whistling sound from somewhere to her right. The green creature lifted its head and answered the call. A moment later Amanda saw more broccoli creatures emerging from between the trees. They moved slowly and not very gracefully. Their lazy, lumbering movements made her even more certain these creatures didn't pose any threat to her. They showed no sign of predatory instincts, and even if they tried to attack her she'd have no problem outrunning them. Hell, by the look of it she'd be able to *outwalk* them.

As you can see, Amanda didn't just dismiss the broccolis as *odd* or *weird*. Instead she showed a keen interest in their nature and way of life. This would prove very useful later, because there happened to be nothing a human could eat on this island, and the lake water was salty and full of algae. The broccolis lived solely on a specific kind of plant that gave them both nourishment and moisture, but was very poisonous to humans.

What she did, however, was trying to find answers to the three questions her brain always formed when faced with something new. She took a bite from one of the small, green things, but the taste was bitter and she spat it out again. She pondered the second question for a while, then decided it wouldn't be a good idea to explore the possibilities. She tried sitting on them, but that only squished them into a green mass. After eradicating a few of them this way she gave up and tried to think of some other way to put the little buggers to use.

"I can't stay here," she said, more to herself than to the broccolis. "There doesn't seem to be anything to eat, and I must help Marsha find that egg. Too bad I never learned to swim - it never seemed necessary until now. I suppose I could try to build some sort of raft, but I have no idea how to put it together."

She looked at the small creatures. They regarded her curiously with their big, blue eyes. The one she'd tried to eat licked its wound tenderly.

"Well, at least we can give it a try," she resolved. "Come, let's go down to the shore."

It took her a while to get the broccolis to come with her, and when they did they kept stopping to examine different things on the ground. The sun had already sunk most of its way towards the western horizon when they finally made it onto a small patch of sand, gently caressed by the lake's lapping waves. Amanda shaded her eyes with a hand and judged the distance to the mainland. Five miles, perhaps. This wouldn't be easy.

"I want to go over there," she said, using hand gestures to explain to the broccolis. "I don't suppose you have any suggestions?"

They stared dumbly at her.

Amanda shrugged. "Oh, well. I'll start working and maybe we'll find some way for you to assist. There should be enough wood, at least. Wait here."

Some of the broccolis remained on the beach while she went into the trees. Others followed her, slowly and stopping for a snack whenever they found one of the plants they ate. Amanda managed to find a bunch of boughs thick enough to form a good raft and light enough to float even with her extra weight on them. She returned to the beach and laid them out in front of the broccolis.

"Here," she said. "These will carry me across the water." She demonstrated the idea of using a raft as well as she could. "The only problem is that I have nothing to tie them together with. I looked for elastic twigs or branches, but everything is too dry and brittle here. I really have no idea what to do."

The broccolis seemed to confer between themselves, their whistling voices sounding eager and excited. Then a few of them lumbered off with determined steps. Amanda watched them dubiously. Could these funny little things really have the solution to her problem?

It appeared they did. After a considerable amount of time the broccolis returned, carrying some sort of roots they'd pulled out of the ground. The roots were both strong and flexible, and it didn't take Amanda long to tie the boughs together into a rough but adequate raft. She hauled it into the water and turned to say farewell to the broccolis.

"Thank you for all the help," she said. "I wouldn't have managed without it. Take good care of yourselves, right? I'll come visiting whenever I have time. Bye!"

Using a paddle she'd made from some leftover boughs, she started transporting herself across the lake. Fortunately there was almost no wind, and she made good pace once she'd figured out the best way to use her simple tool. The only setback was when a pair of crocodiles attacked her, not because she was afraid of being eaten but because they splashed water all over her while she strangled them. Amanda hated wet clothes almost as much as the Khadal men loved the way they clung to her curvy body.

At least an hour of daylight remained when she reached the southern shore and climbed back onto the African mainland. She pulled the raft out of the water and hid it under a protruding cliff. If someone less considerate found it and paddled out to the island it might mean the end to the peaceful broccolis, and that was the last thing she wanted to happen.

As the sun vanished behind the hills to the west, Amanda's stomach reminded her that she'd had nothing to eat since breakfast. She was trying to decide what to do about that when she thought she heard voices somewhere to the south. She listened intently for a few moments, then nodded.

"Sounds like a small company on the move," she said to herself. "I think I'll check them out and see if they'll offer me something to eat."

She knew quite a few methods a woman could use to make men give her things, and breaking a few of their bones was only one of them. Humming a merry tune, she trotted off in the direction the sounds had come from.

The travelling company had just made camp when Amanda caught up with them. They looked a bit odd, garbed in black robes that covered them from top to bottom. Pale faces peered out of the cowls, except for one young man whose skin was almost as dark as her own. She approached a young woman who appeared to make a clumsy attempt of tethering the camels they'd used as mounts.

"Hi there," she said cheerfully. "Can I help you with anything? If your hand is injured they shouldn't make you do this. Here, give me the rope."

The pale woman gave her an askance look. Amanda noticed she was quite pretty, her brown eyes looking even bigger and darker because of the contrast with her pasty skin. Her hands kept working as she replied.

"Thanks, but it's got to be done the right way. The knot must be able to resist all the currents, no matter what dimension they come from. Miss something, and you might as well have set the beast loose yourself. Please move a little to the left - I have to make another circuit to make sure nothing's getting through."

Amanda complied, watching as the woman began walking slowly around the tethering pole. She had the oddest way of walking - two steps forward and then one backwards as if in some sort of weird dance. As Amanda studied her more closely, she noticed the woman's hands weren't clumsy at all. They worked swiftly, in some sort of pattern both very intricate and utterly useless. She wondered if this was one of the rituals she'd heard existed among some very superstitious tribes living far away from civilization.

The pale woman seemed intent on spending half the night with the camels, so Amanda left her and went further into the camp. A stocky man a few years older than herself spotted her and came over, a wide grin splitting his face.

"Hello," he said. "I'm Chrisox, and I can see through your clothes. I must say I'm impressed."

Amanda glared at him. "You should be. I can't see through that thick robe of yours, but I could smash my fist through your heart with barely an effort. Don't take that as a threat. Just give me something to eat."

"I`ll get Drunk," the man said, sounding more than a little nervous all of a sudden. "There should be enough stew for one more, especially now that Lulu's left us. Please stay here, it won't take long."

"Wait!" She reached out and grabbed one of his sleeves. "You don't have to get drunk just to get me some food. Or is that another of your strange rituals? Not saying rituals are bad, of course. It's just that I met this woman over by the camels, and she did some things I couldn't get a hang on. I`ll get the food myself if it helps."

Chrisox managed a weak smile. "That's Ashlob. She's always like that. Hears voices in her head and finds demented messages in the patterns of stones and plants. Just leave her to it; she's a very nice person when her brain works more normally."

"Ahh, I see," Amanda said. "We have a seer in my tribe who says odd things all the time. She's quite nice too, as long as you don't end up under her immense bum. That's far from nice. Anyway, there's still no need for you to get drunk."

"But he's... oh, now I see. You got it the wrong way. Drunk is the name of our most recent recruit. The young lad with the tainted... I mean... tanned skin."

"Really?" Amanda frowned. "Why would anyone name their son Drunk? It'd be like naming him Dumb. Hi, I'm Dumb! The poor kid must have been the laughing stock of the entire tribe."

"Maybe so, but he's a damn good cook. I'm afraid there's no meat in the stew, though. The Raven Cult eats only vegetables."

Amanda blinked. "The Raven Cult? Never heard of that one. Where do you come from?"

Chrisox seemed a bit more relaxed now that the subject had moved away from tearing out people's hearts. He even gestured for Amanda to come with him.

"We used to live in the caverns beneath a mountain range," he said. "But that was before the egg came."

Amanda froze in mid-stride. For a moment she thought her whole body had turned to ice. The look on her face must've been something really special, for Chrisox looked very concerned when he regarded her.

"Is something wrong?" he enquired.

She had to swallow twice before her throat could produce anything, and even then it sounded oddly shrill, like Pebe's voice whenever you held him upside down over a boiling kettle.

"No, nothing's wrong. You mentioned an egg. How did you find it? Do you know where it is now?"

"Of course I do," Chrisox said. "It's in the High Priest's tent. We can have a look at it after we've eaten."

"I'd like to see it now, if you don't mind."

The Raven Cult man gave her a curious look. "Why the hurry? There's plenty of time after we've eaten. I'm sure the others are eager to meet you, too. Or," he added with a sheepish grin, "will you cut out my heart if I don't show it to you right away?"

"No, but..."

"Fine, then. I really can't wait to get some of that stew into my mouth."

The stew was excellent, but Amanda didn't manage more than a few spoonfuls. The thoughts raced through her mind like a pack of cheetahs on the hunt. *The egg was here, in the Raven people's camp*? She had no doubt it was the same egg as in Marsha's dream, not after Chrisox had told her how it'd come into their hands. It was clear that this was no ordinary egg. Ordinary eggs didn't pop out of holy statues like that.

But what was she to do with it? She tried desperately to remember what Marsha had told her. Unfortunately she hadn't listened very carefully to the woman's ramblings about demons and Yahtzee cheaters. *Protect the egg.* That was the most important thing. There'd be time to think about the details later. The egg had to be protected - that was why she'd come here. The volcano had only acted as a means of transportation.

Amanda almost laughed out loud when she thought about what being a god must be like.

We need someone to guard the egg, and these Raven Cult people are too busy counting stones and plants to be of any use.

Well, there's this incredibly hot and strong chick in the Khadal tribe. Amanda, I think she's called. The idea of a god finding her hot made her smirk, even if she was making up the conversation herself.

Great! But how are we going to get her there? She's far to the south, and those elephants aren't that quick.

How about we use that volcano over there to lob her across the countryside?

Haha, you mean like seating her on a boulder and tell her to hold on tight while we get the eruption going?

Exactly!

And you don't think they'll suspect we had something to do with it?

Nah, these people are simple. They're used to blaming everything on divine intervention. They won't think much of this.

Okay, let's do it!

She realized the old man who appeared to be the cult's leader had asked her a question. She apologized for not listening properly.

"Would you mind telling us a little of your own people?" he repeated. "I'm very interested in learning more about people who live under the evil eye. We've always thought they were tainted by its evil influence, but then Drunk appeared, and later Lulu and Doggy, and we learned you're no more evil than anyone else."

"Not all of us agree with you there," said Lizbug, a pale and very beautiful woman who appeared to have taken an instant dislike to Amanda. She appeared to be some sort of fanatic who thought anyone who'd lived under the sun was worthy only of scorn. Amanda thought her ideas ridiculous, but decided to keep an eye on the woman anyway. Something about her made Amanda suspect she was far from harmless. There'd been one moment when she'd met Lizbug's deep, dark eyes, and had glimpsed a malice and hunger stronger than any she'd ever seen in a wild predator.

"There isn't much to tell," she began. "We've always lived a very peaceful life, between the jungle and the savannah. Our tribe is called the Khadal. The people are simple folks - hunters and such. We never did anything really important."

"Why did you leave your tribe, if life there was so nice?" asked the High Priest.

Amanda shrugged. "Gemma, one of my friends, went hunting and didn't come back. Our chieftain organized a search party. We searched for many days, but then I got away from the others and ended up here."

"Gemma?" Chrisox said wistfully. "A female hunter? I would've liked to see through *her* clothes. Mmmmm."

Amanda gave him a haughty look. "She doesn't wear all that much, so whatever talent you possess will be quite useless there. Anyway, thanks for the stew, Drunk. It was really good. Can we go have a look at that nice egg now?" she asked, turning back to Chrisox.

The cleric nodded. "Sure, if it's okay with the High Priest."

Marqamil put down his bowl and stood up. "Of course. Come along, dear Amanda."

Of all the wondrous and amazing things Amanda had seen in her life, the egg in the High Priest's tent was by far the most captivating. It was larger than any ostrich egg she'd seen, the colours and patterns on its shell so exquisite they took her breath away. Even without Marsha's dream she could've told instantly that this egg was the most important thing in the world.

But in what way? What is it supposed to do?

She had no answer to those questions, so she decided to find out what the Raven people knew.

"Do you have any idea what you're going to do with it?" she asked.

Marqamil glanced down at the egg, a solemn expression on his face. "All we know is that we need to keep it safe. Its meaning will become clear to us eventually. At first I thought it was some kind of weapon that would bring about the final defeat of the evil eye, but now that I've learned our enemy might be something completely different I'm not so sure anymore. I suppose we'll just have to wait and see."

"Have you heard about the demon at Mount Azagh?"

The High Priest shook his head. "No, what about it?"

"Oh, nothing." Amanda reached down a hand to touch the egg. "Hey!" she exclaimed. "I felt something!"

Both Marqamil and Chrisox hurried to put their own hands on the cold, hard shell. Their faces mirrored each other, two masks of intense concentration and concern. After a while the High Priest shook his head and stepped back.

"It feels like it always did. What was it you felt?"

"It was like... like a jolt of energy. I could feel it pulsing through the shell."

The High Priest touched the egg in several different places. "I feel nothing. Are you sure you didn't imagine the whole thing?"

"No, it was real," Amanda said, shaking her head vigorously. "I just put my hand on it, like this."

She touched the egg again. At first it was cold and still, but then she felt it again. Something inside the egg responded to her touch, like two hearts beating together in a lovers' embrace. It was weak but unmistakable.

When she looked up she saw that Chrisox's mouth had dropped open as he stared wide-eyed at nothing. "You feel it too?" she asked.

"I do," the cleric stammered. "It's... alive."

"Make way!" Marqamil pushed himself forwards so violently it made Amanda lose her contact with the egg. The High Priest's hands searched the egg's surface intensely, but the sour grimace on his face showed he didn't find what he looked for.

"It's gone now," Chrisox said calmly. "It vanished the moment you pushed Amanda away. Let her touch it again, High Priest."

Reluctantly, the old man made room for Amanda. She gently put both hands on the egg. The response came almost immediately this time. She heard the High Priest gasp.

"What do you think it means?" Chrisox asked in a low voice.

"It means something has changed," Marqamil said. "Amanda's presence has awakened something inside it that's been sleeping until now." He turned to study the Khadal woman. "What do you think, child?"

Amanda looked at the six hands resting on the egg. "I don't know," she mumbled. "All I know is that we must protect this egg. That's all that matters. My presence here seemed like a coincidence at first, but now I know there was a purpose behind it, even if I'm not sure what my part in this will be. I wish my friends were here, especially Marsha. She'd know what to do."

For a moment she thought she saw her three friends sitting by a fire somewhere. Tiwi was there as well, and the gargling woman Hannah. Marsha put her hand atop one of the elephant queen's and said something. The words reached Amanda so faintly she wondered if she'd heard them at all.

Trust Amanda. She'll take care of everything.

The vision vanished as quickly as it had appeared, and once again Amanda found herself looking down at the strange, wondrous and so unbelievably important egg. How could she protect it if she didn't know what to protect it against? How would she be able to tell a friend from an enemy? She'd had her doubts about Tiwi and the Elephant People, but they'd obviously turned out to be good and honourable people. And the ones in the Raven Cult... Who knew what went on inside those thick, black robes? The last thought gave her some associations she'd rather been without.

She was awoken from her reverie by the sound of running feet. Drunk burst through the tent's opening followed by Ashlob, who stepped back and forth sixteen times before deciding it was safe to enter. The High Priest turned his attention away from the egg.

"What's going on, Drunk?"

"It's Dogshit!" the young man gasped. Apparently he wasn't very used to running.

"Get somebody to clean it up."

"No, High Priest. The man with the long hair and the smelly farts. He's missing. No one's seen him since we made camp."

"Perhaps he's avoiding your stew," Chrisox said with a wink. "Lizbug barely ate anything either."

Drunk's tanned face took on an affronted look. "She said it wasn't because it didn't taste good. She just wasn't hungry."

"He probably decided he wanted to follow Lulu after all," said Marqamil. "She was a fine-looking lass, was Lulu."

"I don't think so," said Drunk. "He seemed not to notice her existence after he first laid his eyes on Lizbug. I even asked him something about her once and he said "*Who*?". Besides, Ashlob and I searched around the whole camp but found no footprints. Ashlob made the circuit four times!"

The brown-eyed woman nodded. "Had to be four. Four is a good and even number. We should all cut off one finger from each hand and one toe from each foot. That would help the world to get back in order. Have you tried walking on all fours, by the way? It gives you a wonderful sensation of harmony and being one with every particle in the universe. If all of us did..."

"Silence!" the High Priest snapped. "If Dogshit didn't leave our camp he must still be here somewhere. If something has happened to him we must find him and help him. Come, everyone! If we split up we can look in many places at the same time."

Amanda followed them out into the starlit night, but she didn't feel like taking part in the search for the missing man. There were too many other things on her mind, so many questions she wanted the answer to. How could an egg like that pop out of an old statue in some dark cavern full of raving maniacs? What would happen if it hatched? Did she want it to hatch?

Marsha hadn't told her why the egg had to be protected. Perhaps the danger lay in what rested inside it? But no, she had felt the pulsing energy through her own flesh and knew it was something good. It had recognized her touch and responded to it. Nothing had happened when the members of the Raven Cult did it. The connection seemed to exist only between herself and the egg. There had been a strong feeling of kinship, of belonging together. But still...

She stood by herself in the darkness. The cool night breeze made her shiver slightly. Or had it been more than the breeze? Now that she'd seen the egg she wanted to remain close to it, to keep a constant watch over it. She turned and walked back towards the High Priest's tent. It felt almost like something was calling her.

Marqamil had kept the torches burning inside his tent, and as Amanda approached she saw through the cloth that someone was moving inside it. Perhaps they'd found that missing guy and had returned to their tents for the night? But it had only been a few minutes, and she'd heard no sounds indicating the search was over. Frowning, she stepped through the opening.

A shape clad in the dark cloak of the Raven people was leaning over the chest where the High Priest kept the egg. It had its back to Amanda, seemingly too intent on what it was doing to notice her presence. She stood perfectly still as she watched the shape pick up the egg, tuck it into the thick folds of the robe, and turn around. Lizbug's dark eyes met hers.

"I'd put that back if I were you," Amanda said calmly.

The other woman's eyes flashed with fury. "Or you'll do what?" she hissed.

Amanda folded her arms across her ample bosom. "Well, there are two things I could do. I could call for the High Priest and tell him you tried to steal the egg while the rest of his people were out looking for that man who went missing. Or I could deal with you myself. Perhaps I should let you choose."

Lizbug laughed softly. "You ignorant fool! Do you really think Marqamil would listen to someone like you? He's mad with desire for me. I'd only need to touch him and he'd do whatever I wanted him to. I could tell him you broke into his tent and I apprehended you, and then you'd be put to death as a traitor to the cult. As for *taking care of me...*" She leaned forward, her blood-red lips curving into a mocking smile. "You're free to try."

Amanda took a step forward, trying to decide on the best way to beat the other woman into a bloody mass. Lizbug remained motionless, but for a moment Amanda thought her form turned blurry. Then she was there again, completely solid and looking at something behind her. Amanda looked back over her shoulder.

"What are you two doing here?" asked Marqamil. "I told everyone to help look for Doggy."

"Lizbug tried to steal the egg," Amanda blurted. "She'd probably have escaped if I didn't stop her. You'll find the egg inside her robe."

The High Priest stepped further into his tent. "What are you talking about? The egg is right where I left it."

Amanda blinked. It was true - the egg rested on the soft cloths inside the chest. She hadn't seen Lizbug put it back. The woman must've moved incredibly fast. Amanda glared at her, but Lizbug seemed to have dismissed her the way you dismiss a broken tool. She flashed the High Priest a perfect smile and spoke in a voice full of amusement.

"You should keep an eye on that woman, High Priest. She's imagining things, and not in the adorable way Ashlob does. No, she's the kind who'll never cause anything but trouble. Who knows what dark motives she had when she came back to your tent like that? I'm not making any accusations, of course, as I have nothing to back them up with. I just wouldn't place too much confidence in her if I were you."

Rubbing his chin slowly, the High Priest gave Lizbug a long look. Amanda could almost feel the conflicting emotions inside him. The reasonable part of him must surely know she spoke the truth. There was no way he could buy Lizbug's story, even if he had the hots for her as she claimed.

"She never did anything that seemed suspicious to me," he said hesitantly.

Lizbug sighed, not bothering to hide her impatience. "I've tried to tell you so many times these tainted people can't be trusted. Didn't Dogshit disappear at exactly the same time she came into our camp? One incident could be coincidence, but when things start to add up..."

Marqamil turned his face to regard Amanda, and this time its expression was stern. Amanda felt an immense amount of rage and frustration pulse through her. This pale bitch really knew how to pull the High Priest's strings. The old man adored her, worshipped her. There was no way he'd take Amanda's part in a conflict like this, where word stood against word. She had to say something, though, or Lizbug would succeed in marking her as a lackwit and potential traitor.

"You felt the life inside the egg!" she yelled, her voice shrill with desperation. "It was only there when I touched it. You need me. The egg needs me!"

The High Priest looked from one woman to the other, obviously not pleased with being pushed from side to side like this. "I-I don't know..." he began.

"You shouldn't have let her touch it," Lizbug interrupted. "Whatever is inside the egg must have been frightened by the touch of her filthy hands, burnt almost black by the malicious gaze of the evil eye. Don't let her anywhere near it again. She'll ruin everything!"

"Yes, but..."

"But you said the egg came when Drunk touched the statue!" Amanda went on. "It wouldn't be here if not for him, and his hands are tanned just like mine. I think the egg needs sunlight. All living things do, except the vermin that crawl through the earth."

The High Priest shook his head. "This is too much for me to deal with right now. I think we should all get some sleep. We'll continue this discussion in the morning, when we are rested and less tense."

Lizbug bowed her head in - Amanda had no doubt - totally feigned deference. "A wise decision, High Priest. We of the Raven Cult have always settled matters in a calm and rational way, like the enlightened people we are. I'm certain all unforeseen disturbances can be handled."

Her dark eyes sent Amanda a disdainful look as she finished her little speech. The Khadal woman gritted her teeth in silent rage, but the High Priest seemed not to have noticed the insult. He simply nodded and continued.

"Amanda, you can have Doggy's old tent. I doubt we'll ever see him again."

"But she really was going to steal it!" Amanda shouted. "It won't be safe while she's around. I won't leave it!"

"Silence!" the High Priest snapped. "From now on I don't want anyone else inside my tent. Leave now, both of you. And Amanda, I don't want any more trouble from you, or I might have to send you away. Do you understand me?"

She opened her mouth to voice another protest, but realized it'd do her no good. "Yes, High Priest," she murmured.

Lizbug flashed her a triumphant grin. The High Priest mistook it for a gesture of reconciliation.

"Good," he said. "Oh, Lizbug, you've got something stuck between your teeth."

The pale woman picked it out. It was a thin, white bone.

"I thought you said the Raven people ate only vegetables," Amanda muttered sourly.

"I sometimes use a bird's pinion to clean my teeth," Lizbug explained. "How else do you think I get them this white?" She tossed the bone away nonchalantly.

The High Priest said something about the importance of keeping your teeth clean, but Amanda didn't listen. She'd just realized what kind of bone it had been, and it hadn't come from a bird.

It was a human fingerbone.

"I'll take Doggy's tent," she said, struggling to keep her voice calm. "Like you said, he won't be needing it anymore."

~ 18 ~

Lulu kept running.

She didn't run because the sight of the Bug Goddess in all her unveiled vileness had driven her mad with fear. Nor did she run because she wanted to get as far away from the foul beast as possible. She didn't even run because she was in a hurry to get anywhere (like the bathroom). No, she ran because there was a lion chasing her.

The lion was not really interested in her. It had just eaten a fine, fleshy buffalo and was merely trying to get rid of some of the calories so its wife wouldn't scold it when it got home. The problem was that the lion wasn't very fond of running, but when it spotted Lulu it got a wonderful idea. Using her as a pacekeeper, it roared every now and then to keep her feet moving while following at a safe distance.

Lulu might have died from exhaustion if she hadn't been in better shape than the lion. After a couple of hours of sprinting across the savannah the lion had to give up and collapsed on the ground, panting convulsively. Lulu kept running until she'd made sure the lion was no longer chasing her, after which she slowed to a steady walk. Her breathing went back to normal within a few minutes.

The image of Lizbug's true shape kept appearing before her mind's eye. It was a sight so terrifying and revolting it made a meal at McDonald's look tasty. She hadn't spent much time thinking about how such a creature had ended up among the Raven people, or where it had come from in the first place. She didn't know if the monster meant to consume all of them, or use them in some other way. What she did know was that she'd kill any bug or spider she encountered from now on.

You might think she'd be angry if she knew Lizbug had eaten her former lover. The truth is that she would've been more than angry, but not because of the actual killing. Among the cannibals of the swamp lands it was tradition that the flesh of a dead person belonged to his or her spouse, and those who were invited to share it took this as the greatest of honours. They considered devouring someone else's husband or wife a much graver insult than sleeping with them. If the offender was someone outside the tribe it was basically a declaration of war.

There was a much-cherished story among her people, about two young lovers from separate cannibal tribes. Their love was so strong that each of them swore they wouldn't be able to live without the other. Both were promised to people within their own tribes, so they had to meet in secret out in the jungle. Lulu found that element particularly romantic.

One day, when the young man waited for his lover, he was attacked by a gorilla and knocked unconscious. When the girl found him on the ground with blood all over his face she drew the conclusion that he was dead. Utterly heartbroken, she took a farewell bite from his cheek before drawing her small knife and slitting her own throat. When the lad came to a short time later he found his lady love dead by his side. Stricken with grief the same way she'd been, he took a bite out of her bum (where there was a lot of good meat), and then swallowed a poisonous plant he found nearby.

This was all very sad, and it would soon get even worse. The jealous man the girl was supposed to wed had followed her to see what she did during the long hours she spent in the jungle. He arrived at the tragic scene just as the man from the other tribe bit into his betrothed's derriere. Naturally, he ran straight home to tell the rest of his tribe about the grievous insult.

What he didn't know was that a member of the young man's tribe had come to the same place a few minutes earlier, just as the mourning girl took her last bite before killing herself. He, too, ran back home to tell everyone what he'd seen. That same day the tribes declared war, and virtually everyone was killed.

Lulu didn't know that Lizbug had insulted her tribe in a most profound way, but she was furious anyway - not with Doggy or Lizbug as much as with herself. She knew now that the evil bitch must have used some kind of foul sorcery on her former lover. For someone able to shift shape like that it'd probably be the easiest thing in the world to consume a man's mind the way she had done with Doggy. Hell, women with looks like that didn't usually need magic to steal a man's soul. She'd done it herself a fair number of times.

There was a fair amount of anger directed at Doggy, even if she knew he'd been the helpless victim of some fell demon and that she should feel sorry for him. She wanted to scream, stamp her feet, throw things at him, and rave at him for being foolish enough to get stuck in the evil woman's web. And yet there was also a part of her who wanted to hold him in her arms and whisper in his ear how much she loved him. That was what made her most furious of all.

Just like a lovesick teenager, she thought angrily. *Soon I'll be weeping too, weeping and writing emotional poems. Damn him for doing this to me. Damn her. And damn me for being such a fool. I really need to chew something that talks in a language I understand!*

She'd lost track of where she was a long time ago. She'd swum across a river that might or might not have been the one they'd followed when running from the woman Bathora. The landscape around her had turned more barren, making it more and more difficult to find things to eat and drink. The strange, moving bar had moved through time and space and was at present located somewhere in the future. Thus, fortunately, Lulu was spared the disappointment of learning that a Bloody Mary contained mostly vegetable juice.

Her journey had no goal or purpose. When she'd been with Doggy things had been so obvious. They'd find some new place to live and breed, with plenty of food and other nice things. They'd build up a new tribe eventually, even more prosperous than the one they'd belonged to in the swamplands. That one had contained a fair amount of losers, she realized, now that she'd learned better to put things in perspective.

But she was alone now. There was nowhere for her to go, no place she could call home. She was the last member of her tribe, a tribe that would be all forgotten once Lulu herself was gone. So why would it matter where she went or what she did? There'd be no one left to remember it anyway.

She might have found a decent life with the Raven people. Most of them had turned out to be decent folk. There was the matter of Lizbug, of course. Whatever that monster of a woman had planned, it couldn't possibly be anything nice. Lulu doubted there'd be much left of the Raven Cult when that whore was done with them. So she trudged on aimlessly, and when she saw a mountain range rise before her she didn't bother to walk around it. Thus she ended up in the old caverns of the Raven Cult.

Lulu didn't know this, but the halls under the mountain had gone through a significant face-lift in the last couple of days. They hadn't been in the best of conditions when the Raven people left, and would probably have been quite miserable if left untended. This wasn't the case when Lulu entered, though. A multitude of torches lit up the tunnels and chambers; the floors had been dusted and the air was fresh and dry. There was even a hint of lavender when she breathed deeply enough.

Despite her dulled and dismayed mind, Lulu found herself admiring this subterranean world. Shadows played across the smooth rock walls as if performing a dance or a play. Lulu suddenly felt an intense urge to run around and play hide-and-seek in the winding system of tunnels and chambers. She almost giggled when she thought about the endless possibilities for secret meetings a place like this offered.

This must be where Marqamil and his people used to live, she suddenly realized. *What a coincidence that I'd end up here. It's almost like two threads being tied together by fate. My tribe is gone, and it's only a matter of time before Lizbug has brought the Raven Cult to an end. And here I am - the last member of my tribe in the old abode of the lost cult.*

But am I really alone here?

She was fairly certain the old man had said the entire cult had left their ancient homes, so how come this place had such a tangible feeling of being inhabited? She hadn't seen any people yet, but someone must've kept the floors swept and the torches burning. Or was it the power of the Raven God that kept this place in order? She didn't know what to believe.

Finally, she made her way to the largest of the cavernous halls, and there she stopped and stared. A tall statue of a creature looking like a mix of bird and human stood close to the opposite wall. In front of it was a circle of lit candles, and in its centre a young woman was dancing.

The woman had her back to Lulu, keeping her from making out any features. Lulu saw that she wore only a thin shift that did very little to conceal her curvaceous body. As she watched, the woman began pulling off the shift, baring her brown shoulders. She knew it must've been the light playing tricks, but she could've sworn she saw something glow in the statue's ruby eyes, as if it enjoyed what it saw. The woman began turning around in a circle, rolling her hips from side to side, and her eyes fell on Lulu.

For a moment the two women stared at each other, then hatred flashed in their eyes as recognition came. Lulu took a few steps forward, hands clenched into fists.

"*You*!" she hissed.

"*You*!" Bathora echoed.

Catfights have always played an important part in the human civilization. Imagine two tribes of cavemen at war, for example. While the men thumped each other's heads with wooden clubs their women contributed by scratching and tearing at each other's hair and clothes, until the men decided it was a much better idea to watch them than to continue their own fights. As they enjoyed themselves this way, many conflicts were solved or forgotten, and much killing was prevented

No one has really been able to determine what's so appealing about two women rolling around on the ground whilst emitting far from sensual sounds. There is, of course, the obvious enjoyment of seeing their clothes torn to shreds, but a very thorny bush would manage that just as deftly. The fact that the fight is considered more exciting the dirtier the women become hasn't been explained either. I mean, who'd want to go anywhere near a woman covered in mud if meeting her in a night club?

Many women experience a similar kind of excitement when they watch a man dance, especially if he isn't very good at it. This might indicate that people find pleasure in watching others humiliate themselves, or maybe watching people of the opposite sex do things they know their own gender is better at. But why isn't it as exciting to watch a guy knit or a woman drive a car, then?

Anyway, there never was a struggle between two females like the one between Lulu and Bathora. Not only were both women incredibly hot - they also hated each other with a passion so fierce it would've made a tiger yelp and start purring frantically. They bit, they kicked, they punched and scratched and tore at each other until what remained of their clothing was soaked in sweat and blood. Some of the candles toppled as the two women rolled around among them, making the illumination more mystic and evocative.

Bathora drove a knee hard into Lulu's stomach, causing the air to explode from her lungs. In response, the cannibal woman pulled her opponent's head down towards her own face and tore off half her ear with her teeth. Bathora screamed, Lulu gasped, and then they commenced another round of tearing and hissing. The Telu woman was the stockier of the two, but Lulu was as fierce as a lioness protecting her cubs. Any advantage one of them managed to gain was soon evened out by the other's countermove.

Once Lulu managed to grab hold of one of Bathora's half-exposed breasts and twisted hard. The Telu woman roared with rage and pain and struck Lulu across the face, making blood spurt from her nose. While the cannibal woman was still stunned from the blow, Bathora grabbed her around the waist and flung her to one side with all her strength. Lulu crashed into the statue of the Raven God, causing it to sway from side to side a few times before settling again.

"Ha ha ha!" laughed Bathora. "Wasn't that a pleasant thing to behold? Astonishing, simply astonishing. Guitars and peanuts, I wish my daughter could have seen it. Too bad she ran off with those whiskey-smelling goths. Get up, bitch, and I'll finish you off before the ostrich calls security!"

Lulu had climbed to her hands and knees, and now she kicked off against the stone wall and flung herself forwards. Her hands closed around Bathora's calves, yanking the Telu woman off her feet. Retaining her grip, she turned Bathora around on her stomach, then bent her legs backwards until she sat on her opponent's back. Bathora moaned as Lulu pulled harder at her legs until they almost touched the back of her head.

"Now, how does *that* feel, you filthy piece of pork?" Lulu said triumphantly. "I think I can hear your spine creaking down there. Want me to pull a little harder and see if it snaps? But no - that would probably make your shift drop away completely from that fat ass of yours, and that's something I'd rather not witness. I see enough of it as it is. Gods, woman, it's *enormous*! Did you never consider going on a diet?"

Bathora's only reply was a muffled grunt. Her legs were slick with sweat, and when Lulu tried to readjust her grip the Telu woman kicked herself loose and then heaved Lulu off her back with a mighty effort. Lulu tried to hold on, but her hand only tore off another strip of Bathora's shift. She tumbled backwards, and a moment later the Telu woman was on her again, scratching and tearing.

The Raven God watched in stunned amazement as the fight went on for what seemed like half an eternity. The torment of not being a creature of flesh and blood was almost unbearable, and yet he couldn't stop staring. Both women were so incredibly sexy, stronger and fiercer than anything he'd ever seen in all his long days. He tried to decide which one to root for, but it was like choosing between sunrise and sunset.

If only I'd been a living creature again, he thought. *Then all three of us could've made peace and spent the rest of eternity in bed, finding divine pleasure in each other's bodies. That's how gods are meant to live, isn't it? Oh, look, the cannibal chick's boob almost fell out! Another tear at that nasty hide robe...*

The women fought on as the lecherous god cursed his fate and blessed evolution for bestowing such delightful creatures upon this world. Both women knew the other wouldn't give up until one of them was dead. Hands reached out for throats, sharp fingernails aimed for eyes, elbows struck stomachs, ribs and backs. It's quite unbelievable how much a human body can endure when filled to bursting with adrenaline. Pain or fatigue no longer existed, only burning hatred and bloodlust.

Finally, Bathora managed to wrestle Lulu down onto her back and seated herself across her chest. Lulu tried to push her off, but the woman seemed to weigh as much as a horse. It felt as if her ribs were about to sink into her lungs, and she started gasping violently. Bathora kept her firmly pinned to the ground despite her furious efforts, and slowly but steadily the lack of air drained Lulu's muscles of their strength until she lay helpless, crushed under the Telu woman's humongous ass.

"This was too easy," Bathora said scornfully. "Did you really think you'd have a chance against me after I destroyed your whole tribe?" She wasn't entirely sure how she'd accomplished that, but decided it wasn't important right then. "You should never have tried to cook me. I have very little mercy to offer people who do that."

Lulu couldn't reply. She couldn't even breathe, no more than someone trapped under an elephant could breathe. *How can the bitch be so damn heavy? It isn't normal*! She tried to think of a way to turn the situation to her own advantage, but there wasn't a single passage in the whole Book of Turning Things to Your Advantage that would've helped. Bathora had her at her mercy, and like she'd just said, that mercy was a very thin thread to rely on.

"I could sit here and wait for you to suffocate," Bathora went on. "But it'd be incredibly boring, and I've always had a thing for knives. It'd be a fitting way for a cannibal to die, getting your body parts sliced off one by one. Talk about ending up in your own stew." She chuckled with amusement.

Lulu felt the most wonderful feeling she'd ever experienced. For a moment she wondered if she'd died after all and gone to some blissful afterlife, but then she realized it was Bathora who'd taken her weight off her chest. She pulled some air into her aching lungs and flexed her numb limbs. A low growl escaped her lips and she blinked to focus her blurry vision.

"Oh, no." Bathora's voice came from somewhere above her. "Don't even think of it!" She stomped her foot down on Lulu's midsection, the brutal force making the air explode from her lungs. It took her a long time to recover, and by then Bathora had found a long, sharp dagger and stood near one wall, regarding her with an amused expression.

"You really look pathetic, lying down there like that," she mused. "Like a half-eaten blurber or something. But you never visited the bar, so you wouldn't know. Anyway, it's cutting time."

Lulu heard a low, rumbling sound and wondered if Bathora had farted. The sound increased in strength, though, finally culminating in a deafening roar. She forced her aching body to obey her will, lifting her head enough to get a better view of the cavern around her.

A tall, half-human shape had walked straight through the wall, burying Bathora under a mass of broken rock. The stone giant held a parchment high above its head and waved its other hand in a triumphant gesture.

"I have it!" it exclaimed. "I have the answer! It's all in this sacred writ!"

Lulu used her elbows to push herself up a little further. "What? What's that?"

"It's called *My night with Lizbug,* written by some man of wisdom named Marqamil. Here, listen to this!" The creature held the parchment before its deeply set eyes. "As she lay there on the bed, her clothes resting comfortably in a pile on the floor, I felt my body teem with lust. I saw the same mad desire glow in her dark eyes as she beckoned for me to come closer. I was already hard as a rock, and as her creamy white thighs parted, exposing the full flower of her womanhood, I could no longer restrain myself. I thrust into..."

"Right," Lulu interrupted. "That's quite enough, thank you. I can't imagine how that perverted filth can be so important to you, but I'm happy you found it. Now, about the woman you killed..."

"Don't you see it?" Tai-X rumbled joyfully. "This is what we've been looking for. The knowledge of how to make new stone giants! *Make* them, indeed! Who would have thought of that? *Hard as a rock,* the man wrote. That ought to be proof enough for anyone. I must go back to my people at once. There are babies to make. Lots of babies. *The full flower of her womanhood...*" the stone giant kept mumbling as it strode across the hall and through the wall on the other side. Lulu frowned after it.

"ERR... HELLO?"

Lulu looked around. She was pretty sure there'd been no one else in the cavernous hall. Perhaps another stone giant had come in search of the High Priest's dirty fantasies? But she saw no sign of any living creature.

"WHAT A MESS THEY'VE MADE OF MY HOME. IT WON'T BE THE SAME AFTER THIS."

The voice seemed to come from everywhere, or maybe it came from inside her own head.

This is it, she thought. *I'm hearing voices. That's the most common symptom of madness. I must've struck my head when I fought that Telu bitch.*

"NO, YOU'RE NOT GOING MAD. I'M OVER HERE. LOOK TO YOUR RIGHT."

She turned her head. There were the scattered remains of the circle of candles, in the midst of which Bathora had performed her erotic dance. And at the far end of the cavern…

"YES, THE STATUE. TOOK YOU A WHILE, DIDN'T IT?"

"Who are you?"

"I'M SELLING HOT DOGS. WHO DO YOU THINK I AM? THIS USED TO BE THE ABODE OF THE RAVEN CULT. WHAT WOULD THAT MAKE ME?"

Lulu didn't know what a hot dog was, and while she tried to work out what the statue had meant she missed the last part of its tirade. When it fell silent she shook the thoughts away.

"Sorry, what did you say?"

"I'M THE RAVEN GOD, DAMMIT!"

"Really? I would never have guessed."

If a statue could scowl, that was what the half-human, half-bird stone sculpture did.

"WHAT DO YOU MEAN YOU'D NEVER HAVE GUESSED? NOT EVEN THAT MORON BATHORA COULD HAVE MISTAKEN ME FOR AN ORDINARY RAVEN."

"I didn't do that. I just thought that a god would be, well, you know, more divine. You sound more like a whiny teenage girl."

"YOU WOULDN'T BE SO HAPPY IF YOU'D SPENT THE LAST CENTURIES LISTENING TO THE INANE RAMBLINGS OF PEOPLE WHO CLAIM TO SERVE YOU. AND WHEN YOU FINALLY GET A CHANCE TO TELL THEM WHAT THEY SHOULD DO THEY RUN OFF AND I'M LEFT WITH A WOMAN WHO MIGHT ACTUALLY HAVE IMPROVED HER INTELLIGENCE IF HER HEAD AND ASS CHANGED PLACES."

"Hey! There's no call for such insults! You may be a god, but your manners are worse than those of a six-year-old."

"I WAS REFERRING TO BATHORA. YOU ACTUALLY SEEM A TAD SMARTER. WHY DID YOU COME HERE?"

Lulu had been sitting cross-legged on the hard stone floor, but now she rose unsteadily to her feet.

"I ran from someone," she said. "One of your cult's members, I think, though she wasn't human. She called herself Lizbug…"

There was a shriek of pure outrage from the Raven God. It gave Lulu an image of a bird tumbling from the sky in a cloud of feathers. Any fears she'd had about the Raven God not being on the same side as herself instantly left her.

"YOU CAN'T POSSIBLY IMAGINE," the Raven God said when it had calmed down a little, "HOW FRUSTRATING IT IS TO SEE YOUR DIREST ENEMY WALK AMONG YOUR OWN PEOPLE, WEAVING HER WEBS OF DECEIT WHILE YOU'RE STUCK INSIDE A STATUE, UNABLE TO DO ANYTHING TO PREVENT HER."

"So you know who… what she is?"

"OF COURSE I DO! IT WAS HER, THE BUG GODDESS, WHO TRAPPED ME INSIDE THIS SLAB OF STONE, BACK WHEN THE WORLD WAS YOUNG AND ANIMALS WERE THIS LAND'S ONLY INHABITANTS. THERE HAVE BEEN COUNTLESS BATTLES BETWEEN HER PEOPLE AND MINE, AND IN MANY WE'VE BEEN VICTORIOUS. BUT SHE'S ALWAYS COME BACK, IN A NEW SHAPE AND WITH NEW TRICKS."

"I tried to kill her," Lulu said. "But she didn't die. She just stood there, and then she changed…" The memory made her shiver.

"SHE CHANGED INTO HER TRUE SHAPE. YOU SAW WHAT A REPULSIVE CREATURE SHE REALLY IS, THEN. IF THERE WAS SOME WAY I COULD PROTECT THE EGG FROM HER…"

"The egg!" Lulu exclaimed. "I saw it! It was so beautiful. What's in it?"

"HOPE," said the Raven God dreamily. "OUR ONLY HOPE."

"I could go back." Lulu's voice was suddenly filled with determination. "I'd tell them who she really is, and then I could help protect the egg. If you could give me some of your powers…"

The booming laughter forced her to cover her ears with her hands. "GIVE YOU MY POWER?" the Raven God said between snorts of amusement. "YOU MEAN LIKE MAKING YOU DESCEND UPON OUR ENEMY IN A STORM OF FIRE OR SOMETHING? THAT'D MAKE YOU QUITE THE HERO, I'D WAGER."

"I wasn't hoping to win any glory for myself," Lulu said defensively. "I only want to protect…"

"NO, NO, I DIDN'T MEAN IT LIKE THAT," the Raven God interrupted her. "BUT DON'T YOU THINK I WOULD'VE INTERVENED LONG AGO, IF IT HAD BEEN IN MY POWER? LIKE WHEN SHE FIRST CAME HERE TO INFILTRATE MY CULT, OR WHEN THE EGG CAME INTO THEIR HANDS?"

"I guess," Lulu said. "I was just hoping…"

"NO, MY DEAR LULU, THERE'S NOTHING WE CAN DO BUT HOPE AND PRAY. DID YOU KNOW GODS PRAY MUCH MORE THAN HUMANS, BY THE WAY? THE ONLY DIFFERENCE IS THAT WE HAVE NO ONE TO PRAY TO. IMAGINE THAT!"

"I still think I should go back. People must know how important the egg is."

"THERE ARE SOME WHO HAVE A VAGUE IDEA. LET'S HOPE THEY HAVE ENOUGH STRENGTH TO WITHSTAND THE BUG GODDESS. I WASN'T WITHOUT FRIENDS BACK IN THE DAY, YOU SEE. THE HIPPO, THE ELEPHANT - THEY WERE STRONG ALLIES."

Lulu was too stubborn to give up, though. "But I must do something. I can't just sit here while good people die because of *her*."

She was certain the Raven God smirked as he replied. "KEEPING A GOD COMPANY IS A VERY WORTHWHILE TASK, MY SWEET LULU. HAVING A BEAUTIFUL YOUNG WOMAN AROUND WOULD HELP ME ENDURE THIS ETERNAL IMPRISONMENT. THE PLACE NEEDS TO BE CLEARED UP, TOO. LOOK WHAT HAPPENED TO ALL THE NICE CANDLES..."

"There's a war going on outside these caves, and you want me to *clean* for you?"

"LATER, MAYBE. RIGHT NOW I HAD ANOTHER THING IN MIND."

"And what would that be?"

"A STRIPTEASE."

~ 19 ~

Gemma sat on a rock, watching the sun slowly climb above the distant tree tops. The river ploughed a wide furrow through the jungle, and Gemma was grateful for the extra light it let through. Every time she gazed into the trees she was reminded of the nightmares of the previous night, of how close to getting killed she'd come. For the first time in her life she was reluctant to journey deeper into the jungle.

But I have to, she thought miserably. *Sooner or later I have to.*

She heard a rustling sound behind her and jerked around, reaching for the spear she no longer had. Fortunately, it was only Joz making his way back from one of his exploration trips. A number of bruises covered the former Telu warrior's face, and his nose would probably never be straight again. He smiled as he approached, however.

"Look what I found," he said, holding up two short spears. "They've been in the water for a couple of hours, but I don't think they've begun to rot yet. I don't think we'll find anything else. These two got stuck among the rocks further downriver; otherwise they'd be miles away by now."

Gemma took one of the spears and tried its balance with a few swings. The weapon was much lighter than the sturdy hunting spears she was used to. She couldn't decide whether to hold it with both hands or just one. It was almost like walking in someone else's shoes, if Gemma had known what a shoe was.

"Any sign of the others?" she asked gloomily.

Joz shook his head. "I'm sorry, Gemma. It seems we're the only ones who made it to this side of the river. There might be others who fled in a different direction, but..." He fell silent, looking away.

But that's not very likely, Gemma finished the sentence in her head. *Winston's men must have hunted down everyone. Those poor folks paid a dire price for rebelling against him. And it was all because of me. I never wanted to be queen of their damned tribe. The whole thing was doomed to fail from the beginning. They'd never have helped us protect the egg, not with such a wicked leader.*

The last thought made her frown. Why on earth had she thought about an egg? She'd eaten eggs lots of times, but the picture she'd seen with her inner vision hadn't looked like any of them. This egg had been large, and its shell had been covered with intricate patterns in every possible colour. She wondered if the terrors of last night had somehow affected her mind, causing her to imagine strange things.

"We can't stay here," she finally said.

Joz turned back to look at her. "Where should we go, then?"

"I don't know. Back to the temple, maybe. We don't have much of a cult left, but we still have an obligation to the Hippo God. It was the Hippo God we were supposed to follow, right?"

"Yeah," Joz said. "The skeleton kept talking about it. I quite liked the bony old fellow. Too bad he's dead."

Gemma stroked the spear blade absent-mindedly. "He's been dead for hundreds of years, Joz. I'm sure he won't mind another few hundred."

The former Telu warrior's face suddenly lit up. "Hey, don't you understand what that means, Gemma?"

She frowned back at him. "Means? It means nothing. What matters is that we should..." She fell silent.

"What?" Joz asked.

"Sshh! Don't you hear it? Someone's coming."

They stood completely still, staring into the jungle with their spears ready. Gemma bared her teeth in a silent snarl, expecting any second to find Winston coming at her like a huge, buzzing cannon ball.

But nothing happened. Joz leaned closer to her and whispered, "I don't hear anything. Are you sure it wasn't just the leaves rustling in the wind?"

She gave him an affronted look. "I'm a huntress, you idiot! Don't you think I can tell the difference between footsteps and leaves? There, I heard it again."

"You must have extremely good ears. I still don't hear anything."

"Probably wouldn't hear a herd of elephants playing Yahtzee." Gemma muttered, then wondered where that peculiar idea had come from.

"There's something moving down there!" Joz suddenly exclaimed. "Dammit, you were right! But it's not a human. Something small. Hey, little fellow! Come here. Don't be shy."

A small animal came trotting towards them. It stopped in front of Gemma and emitted small, chittering sounds.

"It's an aardvark!" she said happily. "Aren't you a cute little thing?" She bent down to pat it.

"Hey, sexy girl!" Someone gave her behind a hearty smack. "Boy, am I happy to see you! We didn't know if you'd gotten away."

Gemma almost jumped out of her skin. She stumbled forwards, and the aardvark quickly retreated a few meters to avoid being stepped on. When she finally recovered her balance she turned to see who'd sneaked up on her. Then she turned again, as she'd gotten disoriented and ended up looking in the wrong direction.

Fae and Tom-Tom stood in front of her. The young girl beamed like the sun itself.

"Fae!" Gemma exclaimed. "Tom-Tom! You're alive! Well, at least you are, Fae. How did you find us?"

"Well," the girl began. "Tommy here went into a deep trance, which put him in contact with the Hippo God. Mr. H.G. used his divine influence to find the particular pattern you two make in the vast web of reality. We had to spend a few hours interpreting the answer he gave us. Gods don't think of locations the way we do, you know. They're much more abstract. Anyway, the information we got gave us a pretty good idea of where you were, so we followed the river until..."

"I don't believe that!" Joz laughed. "You can't ask gods for directions. How did you *really* find us?"

Fae glared at him, then burst into laughter herself. "Okay, okay. We were lucky. But it's still good to see you. You should keep better watch, though. A bunch of Winston's men could probably have stolen your clothes without you noticing. I was surprised you didn't hear us coming. We made no effort to move silently."

"Gemma's good hearing only applies to aardvarks," Joz said, giving her a sideways glance. Gemma's face reddened.

"I did hear footsteps," she said. "It was Joz who distracted me with the aardvark."

Joz put an arm around her shoulders. "I'll make it up to you tonight, babe," he said with a mischievous grin.

Gemma smiled and leaned her head against his. Fae gave them a puzzled look, then her eyes widened.

"You two! You are! How? I mean, *when*? We've done nothing but running and fighting lately. How did you find time for... for...?"

"Well," Joz said. "When you think you have only seconds left to live you tend to get things done pretty quickly."

"This is amazing!" Fae exclaimed. "We must celebrate! Does anyone have food and wine? And where's the music? I feel like dancing!"

The skeleton cleared his throat, which didn't have much effect in his case.

"I'm sorry," he said. "But I don't think I understand what's going on. Why should we celebrate? Has something happened since last time we were together?"

"Alive people's business," Fae explained. "It's one of our greatest joys when two people discover they're in love."

"Love..." Tom-Tom said thoughtfully. "We had that back in my day too, I think. It usually involved two people taking off their clothes and..."

"Yes, yes," Fae interrupted him. "We know what it usually leads to. But there's much more to it. I really wish the two of you..."

She never got to complete the sentence. An all too familiar buzzing sound could be heard in the distance, and when Gemma jumped onto the rock she'd been sitting on before she saw the appalling, half-human shape of Winston outlined against the grey sky. The Telu chieftain appeared to follow the river at an altitude of about seventy feet, probably scanning the ground below for signs of surviving enemies.

"Quickly!" Gemma screamed at the top of her voice. "Hide!"

The shrill sound of her voice could be heard miles off. It even woke the big, hairy monster Gemma had encountered outside the ruined temple, startling it so badly its mate got excited and had it for lunch.

If you belong to a race that finds frightened creatures appetizing, you should make sure you have strong nerves.

Anyway, Winston heard Gemma's shriek and made a low swoop over the trees the small group tried to hide beneath. Gemma and Joz clutched their spears so hard their knuckles turned white, but the Telu chieftain didn't attack. Instead he climbed back to his earlier altitude and flew away across the river.

"He didn't see us," Gemma said, trying to believe her own words and succeeding. Some people can convince themselves of anything as long as they've heard it spoken.

"He saw us," Fae muttered.

"Then why did he go away?"

"To inform his fighters, I'd say."

"Oh." Gemma pondered this for some time. "Do you think they'll come after us?" she finally asked.

"They will," Fae said.

"Then we should get away from here."

"Yes, we should."

Gemma frowned. "So why aren't you going?"

"You're standing on my foot."

"Oh, I'm sorry." Gemma lifted her foot and put it down on Joz's instead. "Lead the way, Joz," she commanded.

"Umm, I think I'm unable to do that right now," the former Telu warrior said.

"Why? Did that insect-man scare you motionless?"

"No, it's because you're on my foot now."

"Oh, come on," Gemma said impatiently. "This is no time for jokes like that."

"It's true!"

The sound of shouting and spear shafts drumming on shields reached their ears. The Telu warriors must have reached the far shore of the river. Gemma knew it wouldn't take them long to cross. She moved out of their hiding place, stepping again on Fae's foot in the process.

"Come!" she shouted. "Run!"

The four of them vanished among the trees, leaving the slightly confused aardvark behind. It had never been this close to humans before, and found their behaviour extremely odd. A short time later the tortoise Gemma had encountered several days earlier passed by on its slow journey to whatever destination it had in mind. The two animals exchanged a knowing look, then went back to their own business.

Gemma led their headlong flight through the jungle, not because she knew where they were going but because she was the fastest runner. The others followed close behind her, especially Joz, whose eyes were once more transfixed on Gemma's backside.

After about a mile Fae suddenly called out.

"We can't run forever!" she said, gasping for breath. "The Telu warriors won't give up the chase, and with Winston keeping watch from the sky there'll be no way for us to escape."

"What else can we do?" Gemma asked. "We tried talking to them, but that didn't work. And they saw right through that disguise you tried."

"Let's go that way," Tom-Tom said, pointing to their right.

"Why?" Gemma asked. "If it's something to do with thunderstorms again I don't think this is the right time."

"The old temple of the Hippo God lies in that direction," the skeleton said solemnly. "We made our last stand there once before. It's a place as good as any to face the enemy."

The four of them looked at each other. Then, as one, they nodded.

"No more running, then," Gemma said. "We stand and fight, like the Hippo Cult of old. Let's make our ancestors proud."

They continued west at a somewhat less hazardous pace. A few times they heard the buzzing sound of Winston's wings above them, but they didn't bother with hiding any more. Now that they were determined to face down their enemy – and probably die while doing so – they almost welcomed the attack.

It didn't take them long to reach the temple. They soon caught sight of the smoke rising from its ruins, and after that it was easy to find their way. Gemma had a strange sensation that they were coming home, even if she'd only visited this place once before, and very briefly that time.

"Well, at least we've doubled the number of members since we left here," Tom-Tom said.

Gemma turned to look at him. "We have?"

"Yes, there were only the two of us then, and now we're four. That's twice as many."

"If you say so." Gemma looked around, trying to find a good defensive position. As a hunter, she was more used to hiding and stalking than fighting battles.

"Should we go inside?" she finally asked. "We could lay in wait for them in the dark. That would give us the advantage."

"I don't know," Joz said. "We wouldn't be able to tell ourselves apart from our enemies once the fighting began. I think we should face them out here in the open."

There was no time for further discussion, for right then they heard screams and shouts not far away. A short time later the force of Telu warriors burst out from between the trees, waving spears and shields in the air. Instinctively, Gemma started counting them, but after only a moment she shook her head to clear it. All she needed to do was kill them one at a time until there were none left, then she'd have all the time in the world to count the corpses.

"Yahtzee!" she bellowed, then frowned in confusion. "I mean, attack!" she corrected herself.

She and Joz charged the oncoming Telu warriors, stabbing wildly at them with their short spears. Tom-Tom, unarmed as he was, lured two of their enemies off to one side, where he allowed them to stab him – or at least try to – without concern. Fae somersaulted onto a large boulder and stood there, waving her arms and screaming at the top of her lungs. One Telu warrior dropped his spear and covered his ears with both hands, giving Gemma the opportunity to run her spear through his gut.

"Gemma, look out!" Joz shouted.

She caught the buzzing sound just as she glimpsed the dark shape swooping down from the sky. Dropping to the ground she rolled, pulling down another Telu warrior with her momentum. She felt a gust of wind as Winston passed overhead.

"He's coming in from behind!" Joz shouted. He was trying to fend off attacks from two enemies while also keeping Winston in sight. It didn't go very well.

Gemma leaped back to her feet. "Retreat to the temple!" she ordered. "If we have our backs to the wall he can't come at us from behind."

Right then Winston came towards her at incredible speed. He was holding one short spear in each hand, both points aimed directly at Gemma. She ducked just as he swung at her, waving her own spear over her head. It connected with one of Winston's weapons but didn't knock it from his grasp. With a couple of long strides she reached the ruined temple's wall.

"Get down from that boulder, Fae!" she shouted at the young girl, who was presently performing some silly dance while singing loudly. "You'll be an easy target for Winston up there!"

She grabbed the young woman's arm, pulling her down from her elevated position. As she did, the pouch hanging from one of the bones sticking out from Fae's hair came loose and dropped into Gemma's hand. She gave it a curious look.

"You never checked what was inside this, right?" she asked.

"Nope." Fae shook her head. "The circumstances never demanded it."

"Well, the circumstances are rather desperate right now," Gemma said. She untied the pouch's straps and held it upside down. A strange, metallic object fell into her hand.

"What on earth is this?" she said, holding it up.

"It's a gun," Fae said.

Gemma blinked. "A what?"

"I remember now!" Fae exclaimed. "I saw this bar in the distance, but by the time I made it there it had vanished. Only this pouch was left."

"What's a bar?" Gemma asked.

Fae shrugged. "No idea. The word simply came into my head when I saw it. Just like with the gun. I don't really know what it is, but… give it to me! He's coming back!"

She snatched the metal object from Gemma's hand just as Winston swooped down towards them again. Gemma raised her spear, bracing herself for the clash. This time the half-human Telu chieftain came at her with his sting first. Its sharp tip glistened maliciously as he shot towards her.

Then there was a series of deafening *booms*. Gemma watched in amazement as Winston's wings were torn to shreds. His dive turned into an uncontrolled tumble, arms and legs flailing madly as he plummeted towards the ground.

Gemma managed to throw herself to the side an instant before Winston crashed into the rock wall where she'd just stood. There was a nasty, splattering sound as the impact smashed his body to pieces.

Fae stood with her feet firmly apart, clutching the gun with both hands. Thin wisps of smoke rose from its barrel.

"Whoa!" she exclaimed, eyes shining with excitement. "That was awesome!"

Gemma looked at the ruined mass of flesh that had been Winston. "That thing did this?" she asked.

"Yeah," Fae said. "I'm not sure how I figured out what to do with it, but somehow I did."

"That's good," Gemma said. "Think you could use it on the other Telu warriors?"

"Sure thing!" Fae pointed the strange weapon at the remaining enemies, but this time it only gave off a low, clicking sound.

"Damn, I'm out of ammo," she said, throwing the gun away. "It looks like we'll have to fight them the traditional way."

But the Telu warriors didn't look all that eager to fight anymore. Winston's death had clearly unnerved them. They cowered near the edge of the open space in front of the old temple, giving each other uncertain looks, each one waiting for someone else to assume command.

Gemma was just about to order them to lay down their weapons and surrender when there was commotion behind her. She spun around, fearing that more Telu warriors had crept up to attack them from behind, but what she saw was so strange she lowered her spear and stared with her mouth open.

A group of people riding camels had approached through the trees to the west of the ruined temple. Despite the heat they wore thick, dark robes, and from what she could glimpse it looked like their skin was unnaturally pale. There were both men and women among them, and at their back rode a young, voluptuous woman whose face wasn't hidden inside a deep hood…

"Amanda!"

Forgetting about the Telu and the Hippo Cult and everything else that had occupied her limited mind recently, Gemma ran over to Amanda just as her old friend dismounted and threw herself into her arms. The two of them hugged each other for a long time. Gemma felt a tear trickle down her cheek. Amanda was here! Everything would be all right now.

"Hi, Gemma," Amanda said, untangling herself from the embrace at last. "What's up?"

"How did you find us?" Gemma asked. Then she looked at the other newcomers. "And who are these people?"

"The Cult of the Raven," Amanda informed her. "As for how we found you, I'm not quite sure. I think the egg guided us somehow. We just travelled in the direction that felt right, and now we're here."

"The egg!" Gemma exclaimed. "You have it? It's important. We must… we must…"

She wasn't sure what it was they had to do. In fact, she had no idea what that egg was or why it was so important. It was just something she felt – a sensation so powerful it drowned out everything else.

Someone cleared his throat, and Gemma looked up. One of the Raven people – a tall, middle-aged man with an air of authority around him – had stepped up to them. He was holding a small chest in his arms.

"I am Marqamil, High Priest of the Raven Cult," he said. "We've been led here by the egg, as fair Amanda said. Now, what is this place?"

"It's the old temple of the Hippo Cult," Gemma said. "We revived it after several centuries, but we've only managed to gather four members so far. You're…" Her mouth worked silently as she tried to count the newcomers.

"The Hippo Cult?" The High Priest's forehead creased in thought. "Never heard of it. Are you sure we've come to the right place, Amanda?"

"Of course!" There was nothing but firm conviction in the beautiful woman's voice. "It ought to be proof enough that we found one of my old friends here, along with…" Her expression grew more uncertain when she studied Gemma's companions, especially Tom-Tom.

Marqamil didn't look as surprised to see a skeleton among the small group of people. "That robe of yours looks somewhat similar to those we of the Raven Cult use," he said.

"Yes…" Tom-Tom's voice sounded distant, as if he was recalling things that happened long ago. "I think your cult was mentioned in some of our scrolls. There was a prophecy…" He trailed off, staring into the distance.

"Perhaps he'll remember if you show him the egg?" Gemma suggested.

The High Priest flicked open the chest's lid, revealing a large, beautiful egg, its shell covered with intricate patterns of innumerable colours. Gemma found herself unable to look away. This was simply the most astonishing, most magnificent thing she'd ever seen.

Tom-Tom's reaction was even stronger. The skeleton dropped to his knees before the High Priest, trembling hands reaching out to touch the egg. He kept them a few inches away, though, as if afraid he wasn't worthy of touching this sacred object.

"I do remember now," he whispered. "It was said that, at some unknown point in the future, the people of the Hippo and the Raven would be united, and then a new time of wonders would come. You must bring this egg into the temple, my lord."

"*Stop*!"

The shriek was so piercing it made all of them freeze. One of the Raven people, a pale young woman, stood facing them with a haughty – no, *regal* – expression on her stunningly beautiful face. Her eyes flashed with malicious hatred and something else, a kind of hunger that wasn't quite human.

"Lizbug?" Marqamil asked, confusion in his voice. "What's the matter?"

The woman fixed him with her deep, dark eyes. "You will give that egg to me. It's an abomination, a product of the evil eye's fell power. I will destroy it."

Gemma and Amanda quickly stepped between the woman and the High Priest. From the sounds she heard behind her, Gemma judged that Joz and Fae were backing them up.

"*You*!" The word came out of Tom-Tom's mouth as a low hiss, so full of hatred it almost made Gemma turn around. "It's *you*."

Lizbug shot him a malicious grin. "We meet again, Cultist. It looks like you managed to survive my followers' treatment. Well, sort of, anyway."

"Tom-Tom, who is this woman?" Gemma asked. "How can you know her?"

The skeleton had risen to his full height again and now stood with his fists clenched. If his face could've had an expression, it would be terribly grim. His mouth opened and closed but no word came out.

The woman who'd called herself Lizbug turned to the remaining Telu warriors, speaking in a commanding voice.

"Members of the Telu! You may not recognize my face, but look deep into your hearts and you'll know me for who I am. I was once your queen, and as queen I now command you to..."

"Lies!" Joz cried at the top of his voice. "It says in the prophecy that our rightful queen will wear a thong. Gemma is the true queen of the Telu!"

Lizbug bared her perfect, white teeth in a triumphant smile, then she turned around and let her thick, black robe fall to the ground, revealing the most glorious female body Gemma had ever seen. Marqamil emitted a low, strangled sound, but all else was silence.

Underneath the robe, Lizbug wore only a black thong.

The remaining Telu warriors emitted a roar of ecstatic joy, raising their spears and shields into the air. The hesitation from before was gone. They'd found their queen, and now they'd find glory.

"Kill them!" Lizbug shrieked, turning around to point a long finger at the group around Gemma. "Kill them all, and give me the egg!"

The Telu warriors charged.

"High Priest!" Amanda shouted. "Head for the temple! We'll cover you!"

"We can take them!" Gemma said. "With the reinforcements you brought..."

Amanda cut her off with a shake of the head. "The Raven people are no warriors. We can't count on them."

With almost bestial howls of fury, the Telu warriors crashed into them. Gemma used her spear to deflect a savage blow from a heavy club, then ducked under another swing. Amanda didn't have a weapon, but it turned out she didn't need one. Her fists were much more lethal than any club or spear. Two Telu warriors dropped to the ground with crushed skulls; another tried to grab her by the hair but instead found himself flying through the air, crashing into the cliff wall not far from where Winston had met his end.

Joz had joined them and was putting up a brave fight. Gemma saw him receive a cut across his right side just as he drove his spear into his opponent's chest. She speared another enemy, who'd tried to run past her to attack Marqamil as the High Priest lumbered towards the temple's entrance with a panicked expression on his pasty white face.

She turned around, looking for another Telu warrior to fight, but a shout from Amanda drew her attention.

"Gemma, stop her!"

She looked the way the other woman was pointing and saw Lizbug, fully dressed again, striding majestically towards the temple's entrance. Tom-Tom and Fae had placed themselves in her way, blocking the dark opening through which the High Priest had just vanished.

"They can handle her!" she shouted back. "These warriors are the real threat."

"No!" Amanda shook her head vigorously. "You don't understand. She's not human. She's..."

Lizbug extended her right arm, and a blast of magic power shot out towards Tom-Tom. The skeleton didn't flinch as he was electrocuted. Instead he threw his head back and emitted an elated scream as golden sparks crackled along every bone in his body.

"That was the most amazing thing I ever experienced!" he hooted as the unearthly light dimmed. "Beats the hell out of lightning. Can you do it again?"

Lizbug snarled and clenched her hand into a fist. This time her attack tore up the ground beneath Tom-Tom's feet, flinging him and Fae into the air. The entrance to the temple of the Hippo Cult was suddenly unprotected. The woman who'd called herself Lizbug strode towards it, the ground before her feet turning smooth and even as she went.

"She mustn't reach the temple!" Amanda shouted. "She mustn't get to the egg!"

Gemma tried to retreat, but there were Telu warriors all around her and she had to struggle to hold off their attacks. Amanda was locked in a similar kind of struggle, hard pressed despite her inhuman strength. Joz had taken another wound and was barely holding his own against a large Telu warrior.

Behind them, Lizbug had almost reached the temple's entrance.

Just as the last flicker of hope was about to leave Gemma, she spotted something bright and yellow sprouting from the mound of earth Lizbug had torn up. At first she couldn't make out what it was, but then the sun peered out between two clouds, shining down at the marvellous little thing, and Gemma gasped.

It was a sun rose.

"Pick it, Tom-Tom!" she yelled, as loudly as she could (which was rather loud, as many members of the Khadal tribe could certify). She had no idea why she wanted so desperately for the old skeleton to pick the stupid little flower. The sensation was just there, its urgency blotting out everything else. It was the same urge Marsha had experienced that day, at the very beginning of this story. Except this time it was even stronger.

Moaning softly, Tom-Tom pushed himself to his hands and knees, then reached out one bony hand and let his fingers close around the sun rose's thin stem. If he'd had skin or flesh, the flower would've stung him like a scorpion's tail, but with the state of his body being what it was he felt absolutely nothing. He picked the little flower and held it up in front of him like a sacred token.

"Stop!" he shouted, his voice as hard as steel. "In the name of the Hippo God, I command you to stop!"

And, to the surprise of all, most of all herself, Lizbug stopped.

Her eyes were transfixed on the small, brightly yellow flower. There's something about the colour yellow that insects find irresistible, and it looked like the same was true for their Goddess. As Lizbug stood frozen, staring at the sun rose, the Telu warriors under her command also hesitated, lowering their spears and gazing around in confusion.

"Go after the High Priest!" Tom-Tom called to the two Khadal women, his eyes never leaving the paralyzed Lizbug. "He may have need of you. Protect the egg!"

As one, Gemma and Amanda turned and sprinted back toward the Temple's entrance, throwing wary glances at the creature who'd called herself Lizbug. The pale, beautiful woman didn't seem to notice them - her dark, unblinking eyes never leaving the sun rose. Then they were through the opening and surrounded by almost complete darkness.

Gemma, having been there before, led the way through the long tunnel, Amanda following close behind her. A short time later they emerged into the large, cavernous hall where the statue of the Hippo God stood, arriving just in time to see the dark form of the High Priest Marqamil, outlined against the light of the fire burning atop the altar in front of the statue, kneel down and place the egg on the smooth stone surface before the brazier.

The two women froze. Gemma held her breath as she watched the scene before her. At her side, Amanda's eyes were bright with excitement as she waited to see what would come out of this. For a few moments everything was silent.

Then a flash of bright red light shot out from the statue's ruby eyes, blinding Gemma where she stood a dozen paces away. There was a loud *crack*, like a bolt of lightning splitting a tree trunk in half. The sharp sound still echoed between the rough stone walls when the red spots stopped dancing before Gemma's eyes and she could see again.

The large egg had broken in half, and between the two shards rose the most peculiar creature Gemma had ever seen (and that included oddities like Tom-Tom, Tai-X, Winston and Pebe). It looked like a miniature version of the Hippo God's statue, but on its back was a pair of raven-black wings, beating furiously as the odd-looking creature struggled to gain altitude.

By the altar, the High Priest had fallen flat on his back, but now he slowly climbed back to his feet, his legs shaking as he tried to straighten himself.

"The *Scion*!" he gasped, reaching out one trembling hand towards the winged hippo. "Marydette... I mean, Hippodemus, mentioned it in one of his chronicles. This is a miracle!"

The Scion (or whatever it was called) made a quick circuit above their heads, then vanished into the tunnel leading out into the open.

"FOLLOW IT!" a powerful voice boomed. Gemma couldn't tell if she heard it through her ears or inside her head. "PROTECT IT!"

The commanding tone woke her from her stupor, and she and Amanda darted after the winged hippo, paying no heed to the scratches and bruises they received when they came too close to the jagged stone walls in the blackness. There was only one thought in their heads – to ensure the safety of the strange little being the beautiful egg had spawned.

When they finally reached the entrance the Scion was no more than a few paces ahead of them. They barely noticed as the winged hippo flapped out into the daylight and perched on a stone ledge above the opening, though. In front of them stood Tom-Tom, except it wasn't the Tom-Tom Gemma had spent the last few weeks with. Instead of the robe-covered skeleton there stood a tall, handsome man, his proud features locked in an expression of purest wonder.

"I'm alive," he whispered, one hand reaching up to touch the smooth skin of his left cheek. "I'm alive again."

"R-Really?" Gemma managed, staring in amazement at him. "Are you sure?"

"Yes!" Tom-Tom said, louder this time. "I can feel my heart beating. There are smells, tastes..." He trailed off, licking his lips almost reverently.

Gemma smiled. "That's wonderful. But how did it happen?"

The Hippo Cult man made a brief shake of his head. "I don't know. There was a surge of power, and suddenly I was flesh and bone again. Well, the bones were there all along, but..."

"Where's that flower?" Amanda interrupted. "The one you used to stop Lizbug?"

Feeling her body go tense, Gemma looked at Tom-Tom's hands. Both were empty.

"It stung me when I got my body back," he said, rubbing the inside of his right hand. "I must have dropped it."

"But that means..." Gemma began, then fell silent as her eyes fell on the huge, dark shape suddenly looming behind Tom-Tom.

Slowly, Tom-Tom turned around, the expression on his face changing from wonder to dread.

Where the woman Lizbug had stood a few moments before, a huge, monstrous insect now towered over them. It radiated malice and terror and a power so immense it filled everyone with despair. As it turned its multitude of evil eyes on the three humans, Gemma felt all strength and courage wither and die inside her, and she shrank away from the terrible beast.

"The Bug Goddess." Tom-Tom's voice was so faint Gemma could barely make it out. The newly reborn man started trembling violently where he stood.

"Lizbug?" The High Priest Marqamil had appeared behind them and was now staring at the enormous bug with a mix of fear and disbelief. "It can't be. She lived with us for months. She..."

Gemma started as the winged hippo let out a terrified shriek and took to the air. Fast as lightning, one of the Bug Goddess's long, hairy legs shot out, snatching the small creature out of the air and slowly pulling it back towards its vile head. The cruel jaws opened hungrily.

"Let go of it, bitch!" Amanda yelled. With a few quick steps she reached the Bug Goddess, drew back her arm and punched the vile creature right in the face. A few of its multi-faceted eyes went out and the enormous bug took a step back, letting go of the winged hippo.

Amanda's attack served as a wake-up call for Gemma. Suddenly the terror fled from her heart, the weakness vanishing from her limbs. Red-hot fury filled her, and with a wordless cry she charged the beast, driving her spear into its side.

A blood-curdling, inhuman shriek tore the air in the glade into shreds. The Bug Goddess turned her full attention on the two Khadal women. A hairy leg, spindly but harder than steel, shot out, and suddenly Gemma was flying through the air. She landed a few paces away, sharp pain exploding through her chest. With a crash, Amanda ended up next to her.

Gemma tried to rise, but pain such as she'd never experienced before lanced through her with even the tiniest movement. She groaned and slumped back onto the ground, her vision blacking out for a few moments.

There was a shuffling sound right next to her, followed by a sickening stench. Gemma managed to lift her head a few inches. What she saw made her heart freeze in her chest.

The ghastly head of the Bug Goddess hovered over her, emitting a stench like rotting corpses. Curved, sharp mandibles prodded her flesh, reaching around her to lift her up towards the creature's open mouth. Gemma's heart began pounding so fiercely she could almost swear it made the ground beneath her shake.

Then she realized it wasn't just the beating of her heart she felt. The ground really *was* shaking. The Bug Goddess noticed it at the same time, letting Gemma's limp body fall back onto the ground and turning her head to the side just as loud, crashing sounds came from between the trees to the south-west.

Huge, grey beasts burst into the glade, small trees and branches scattering all around them. The foremost one lifted its long snout into the air and trumpeted defiantly. On its back sat a tall, slim woman and behind her, holding on for dear life...

Gemma blinked. Her eyes must have played a trick on her. Surely that couldn't have been Marsha?

The Bug Goddess braced herself, ready to leap, but the elephant ran her down before she could move. More of the huge beasts followed, trampling the vile insect's body into the ground. Triumphant hoots came from their riders, the loudest from one who carried a suspiciously strong resemblance to Pebe.

With a groan, Gemma managed to push herself up into a sitting position. Beside her Amanda had risen to her feet, looking slightly dazed but ready to take on any threat that presented itself.

But there was nothing left to fight. The elephants had formed a circle around the crushed body of the Bug Goddess; the few remaining Telu warriors had scattered and fled. A great hush had fallen over the glade, interrupted only by the occasional snort from one of the elephants.

"Gemma! Amanda!"

Gemma had to smile despite the miserable state she was in. Marsha came running towards them, Pebe and Emkei following close behind her. Gemma let her tribe's chieftain help her back to her feet, wincing as Marsha clutched her in a tight embrace.

"I was so worried about you!" Marsha said, her voice muffled as she spoke into Gemma's shoulder. Then she let go and threw herself into Amanda's arms. "And you too, Amanda! When the demon inside that mountain threw you into the air I thought we'd never see you again. I should've had more faith in you. Embolo said it'd take more than that to break you."

Gemma and Amanda hugged the other two members of the Khadal tribe. There was something odd about Emkei's breath, Gemma noticed. The old, fat seer had never smelled very nice, but this new odor was like nothing Gemma had ever experienced before, and that included the worst of Marsha's potions.

When they'd finished celebrating their reunion, they turned their attention to the huge carcass in the centre of the glade. Some of the Elephant People had dismounted and were now standing off to Gemma's left, eyeing the dead insect with disgust. Off to the right, Marqamil had rejoined what remained of the Raven Cult, the dark-robed men and women keeping a safe distance. Joz, Fae and Tom-Tom had come forth to stand with the Khadal people. The last two, Gemma noticed, were now holding hands.

"Is it dead?" Tiwi, the leader of the Elephant People, asked, prodding the enormous bug with the toe of her boot.

"Looks like it," Marsha said. "But will it stay dead? It appears people have thought this creature dead before, only to have it return a few centuries later."

"It's never been killed in its true form, though," Tom-Tom said. "But we should burn the body anyway. Fire is the best weapon against these creatures."

"There's another thing we can do that'd be even more effective," said an old woman from the Elephant People.

"And what's that, Hannah?" Emkei asked.

"I'll gargle its brain. That'll neutralize all the life force that might still linger in it."

Gemma exchanged a puzzled look with Joz. "Did you say *gargle* it?" she enquired.

"Hannah is the Elephant People's gargling woman," Marsha explained. "It's like a priestess, only much smellier."

"That should work," Emkei said, nodding to herself. "Are you sure you can fit the whole thing into your mouth, though? If not, I'd be more than happy to help you."

The gargling woman gave Emkei a smug smile, took a knife from her belt and began slicing open the Bug Goddess's head. The gory scene made Gemma want to throw up, but she forced herself to watch as the old woman dug her hand deep into the dead insect's stinking innards and pulled out a surprisingly small mass of grey-white flesh.

"Insects aren't very intelligent," she announced, holding up the sticky blob. "When in her true form, the Bug Goddess acted mostly on instinct, not able to form the complex patterns of thought she used in her human guise."

With that, she stuffed the small brain into her mouth, rummaged through her clothing until she found a small bottle of dark liquid, which she took a deep swig from. Gemma watched in amazement as the old woman leaned her head back and emitted a strange, gurgling sound deep in her throat. It went on for perhaps two minutes, then she bent over forwards and spat out a thick, brown liquid onto the ground.

"The Elephant God sends his regards," she said, wiping her mouth on her sleeve.

"Did he mention me?" Tiwi asked, eyes glistening with excitement.

The gargling woman gave her queen a motherly smile. "He actually did. He said you're not as bad as he first thought, and that you're probably the sexiest queen the Elephant People has ever had."

Tiwi beamed like the sun itself.

~ 20 ~

Three weddings in one day was a little too much for Marsha's taste.

It wasn't that she begrudged her friends their newfound happiness, of course. She was genuinely happy for them – even the two she'd only recently met – but being a person completely uninterested in love and romance she quickly grew tired of all the smiling and kissing and general soppiness. So now she'd found a boulder to sit on (which, accidentally, was the same boulder Gemma had sat on while talking to the stone giant Tai-X) some distance away from the revelry, where she could ponder her own future without anyone disturbing her.

Their journey back from Mount Azagh had passed in a strange, haze-like state. As they made their way across the savannah Marsha had suddenly felt a sense of urgency, so overwhelming it blotted out everything else. Some of her companions, including Emkei, Hannah and Tiwi, seemed to experience the same phenomenon, and they'd driven the large, tireless elephants hard across the plains, stopping only for a few hours' rest each night.

Marsha had thought they were heading back to the Khadal camp, but as they drew closer she felt herself pulled farther to the north, towards a spot in the jungle she knew nothing about. Strangely, she hadn't felt the slightest bit surprised when they burst out into the open space in front of the Hippo God's temple and found her friends battling a huge, monstrous insect. She'd immediately known it for what it was – the ancient enemy who'd come to destroy the egg, and with it all hope of a future filled with peace and joy for Marsha's people. Well, the elephants had done nicely for that vile creature.

It made her a little sad that she'd never gotten to see that wondrous egg, except in that dream which now felt like a lifetime ago. Once they were certain the Bug Goddess was dead and things had calmed down a little they'd began searching for the winged hippo which apparently had hatched from the egg, but it appeared the strange little creature had flown away during the fighting and was now nowhere to be found.

There was some loud cheering from the direction of the temple. Marsha decided she'd done enough contemplating for now and rose from her seat, slowly making her way back to the party.

After some mild urging from Gemma and Amanda, the rest of the Khadal tribe had left their old abodes and moved into the Hippo God's temple, where they, under Tom-Tom's guidance, were going to form a new version of the ancient Hippo Cult. It appeared that was where the tribe had originated from, so it felt only natural to make the temple their new home, now that they knew who they really were.

Marsha couldn't help but smile when she saw people from her own tribe dancing, chatting or walking hand in hand with members of the Elephant People or the Cult of the Raven. According to Tom-Tom and the High Priest Marqamil these three societies had been closely linked together since the beginning of time, driven apart only by the evil doings of the Bug Goddess. With that foul creature finally gone from the world, there'd be nothing to keep them apart in years to come.

Even the Telu tribe – foremost among the Bug Goddess's human servants – had been incorporated into their new family of joy and love. With Gemma now married to Joz and Tom-Tom to the pretty little girl with bones in her hair there'd be no risk of that tribe causing any harm. Most of them seemed like decent folks once you got to know them, and now that they were free of the Bug Goddess's influence Marsha found it unlikely that a creature like Winston would show up again.

With bonds of marriage between her own people and these other societies, Marsha was convinced the Khadal tribe would be at the centre of a new, glorious African civilization. The only ones they didn't have such a connection with was the Cult of the Raven, but from the amount of time Amanda had spent with the young man Drunk that might soon be amended.

Marsha sighed. There was no way to deny the profitability of such a union, but she thought she'd scream if she had to endure another wedding.

Her mood brightened when she saw the third newly-wed couple coming towards her. Despite Amanda's explanation back at Mount Azagh, she still had trouble getting how those two had found each other. Sure, they must be the two biggest braggarts the world had ever seen, but apart from that they were as different as two people could be.

"Lady Marsha!" Tiwi exclaimed, enveloping Marsha in a huge bear hug. "I thought you'd run off with one of the boys. Ogian has a weak spot for you, in case you hadn't noticed."

"Er, no," Marsha said, frowning. "I think I saw him playing Yahtzee with two of my people. Probably feeding them all kinds of lies about how the game is played."

"No doubt," the Elephant Queen said. "Those silly boys will have to find something new to occupy their deranged minds. No point fantasizing about me now that I'm a happily married woman." She smiled at her husband. Pebe smiled back.

"What will you and your people do now, Tiwi?" Marsha asked. "Will you settle in one place now that you've carried out the important task you spoke of?"

"Actually, it was I who did that," Pebe said, winking at Marsha. "You might not have noticed it in all the confusion, but it was my elephant who killed the Bug Goddess. Guided by my strong, steady hand, of course."

Tiwi cuffed him across the ear, making him squeal. "Sadly, we can't settle in one place," she said, turning back to Marsha. "Like I said before, our elephants eat so much we have to be constantly on the move."

"But…" Marsha said, her eyes moving from one to the other.

"I've decided to go with them," Pebe said, for once in his life understanding something correctly. "Travelling the world is a suitable occupation for a hero like me. There'll be plenty of adventures ahead, lots of opportunities to show everyone I'm the greatest warrior in the world."

"Don't forget to bring your doll," Marsha mumbled.

After Tiwi and Pebe had left her, Marsha spent some time watching a group of people dancing around a tree which had been left standing on its own when the elephants crashed into the open space. Among them were Fae and Tom-Tom, the latter still so taken with his strange reincarnation that he kept touching, smelling and tasting everything. Marsha guessed the two of them would have an excellent sex life.

As she stood there she suddenly noticed that someone had stepped up beside her. When she turned her head she saw Marqamil, the High Priest of the Raven Cult. The tall, middle-aged man was holding a cup containing a fizzy liquid of a sickly green colour. Marsha gave it a dubious look.

"Sure it's safe to drink that?" she asked.

The High Priest gave her a rueful grin. "That gargling woman from the Elephant People shows remarkable prowess as a bartender. As long as you stay away from her specials you'll be fine."

"It looks like some weren't wise enough to realize that," Marsha said as Emkei lumbered past on unsteady legs, holding the blind man Embolo by the hand. The poor lad looked scared half out of his wits, which made Marsha wonder what the massively built seer had in mind for them.

Marqamil chuckled softly. "Chrisox, one of my clerics, had one after he'd had a look at that, um, full-figured woman?"

"Oh?" Marsha blinked. "Why's that?"

"He claims he can see through people's clothes."

Marsha started imagining what that would be like when you had Emkei in front of you, then decided she'd better stop before she also had to find oblivion in one of Hannah's mysterious drinks. Instead, she eyed the High Priest closely.

"Will you go back to your old home?" she asked.

Marqamil took a sip of his drink, then shook his head. "I don't think it'd feel right, going back to those caverns. They'd remind me too much of... *her*."

The thought of living so close to the creature who'd turned out to be the Bug Goddess made Marsha shiver. She'd always hated bugs and insects, and the sight of the large, barren spot where they'd burned the carcass of the Bug Goddess still made her skin crawl. She wouldn't want to go anywhere near a place where such a creature had lived.

"You could stay here with us," she suggested. "Your people don't like sunlight, right? The temple of the Hippo Cult would suit you perfectly."

Marqamil shrugged. "I don't know. Perhaps we should do like the Elephant People and move from place to place, seeing what the world has to offer and what we can do to help enlighten its people. That should be safe now that we're finally rid of the evil eyes of the Bug Goddess..."

He broke off, his eyes suddenly widening, his mouth hanging open in an expression of shocked amazement. For a moment Marsha wondered if the ghost of the Bug Goddess had come back to haunt this place. She glanced around but saw only a large number of people enjoying themselves.

"What is it?" she asked, nudging his arm.

"By the Raven God's feathery bollocks!" the High Priest exclaimed. "That's it!"

Marsha had no idea what the middle-aged man was talking about. "What's what?"

The High Priest was visibly trembling with excitement. "The purpose of the Raven Cult!" he said, eyes darting from Marsha to the people around them. Marsha could make out the strange woman Ashlob, who'd insisted she'd marry Kharuba of the Elephant People for the sole reason of making the number of marriages even. She'd quickly abandoned her plans after having one look at the game of Yahtzee the black man was playing.

"Games like that," she'd said, "serve only to disrupt the smooth movements of the universe. You should have an even number of dice, and all should have the same number of pips. If we're to be married, you'll have to renounce this game and vow never to play it again. The choice is yours."

Kharuba had chosen to continue the game.

"What about its purpose?" Marsha asked, wondering how the Raven Cult had managed to keep the egg safe with people like Ashlob around.

"It says," Marqamil said, calming himself somewhat, "that our cult's purpose is to serve the Raven God and protect the world from the evil eye. We always thought that meant the sun. Only now I see we must've gotten it wrong, or that part of it must be left out."

"So what should it be instead?"

The High Priest gave her a triumphant smile. "To protect the world from the evil eyes of the Bug Goddess, of course. It's so clear now that I hear myself say it. I don't understand how we've been able to miss it all this time."

To Marsha's amazement, the High Priest untied his thick, woollen robe and let it fall to the ground. Underneath he wore a thin linen shirt and matching shorts. His arms and legs were so pale they made Marsha's eyes hurt.

"It's… wonderful!" the High Priest said, hesitantly reaching out one arm into the sunlight. Then he threw back his head and laughed. The sound was so filled with the purest kind of joy that Marsha couldn't keep herself from laughing with him.

"This is what religion should be like!" Marqamil said, holding out both arms and spinning around in slow circles. "Booze and dancing and as little clothing as possible. Damn, I feel thirty years younger. I think I'll find myself a pretty wench and show her what a man of the Raven God can do. Hallelujah!"

He emptied his cup in one long swig, then lumbered off into the mass of people. Marsha caught one last glimpse of his unnaturally pale legs, then he was gone. She shook her head. People never ceased to surprise her.

She caught a glimpse of bright wings flapping up in one of the trees and gazed up eagerly, sudden excitement filling her, but it was only an ordinary bird. Sighing, she turned her head away and began walking towards a table laden with pastries and cookies. Good Khadal stuff, of course – she doubted she'd ever grow fully accustomed to the things the other tribes ate.

An hour or so later she found herself seated on a low, grassy mound near the Hippo God's temple, Gemma and Amanda lounging on either side of her. Gemma had promptly refused all the more opulent garments the Khadal women had offered her for her wedding to Joz, instead donning her usual leather vest and thong, saying it was not only the clothes she'd worn when the two of them met but also what Joz found her most attractive in. Marsha supposed she could understand why when she saw Gemma reclining with her long, tanned legs stretched out in front of her. Those were the clothes her friend belonged in.

"Have you decided where in the temple you'll have your accommodations yet, Marsha?" Amanda asked.

Marsha gave the large stone building a long look. They'd begun repairing it, but it'd be a while before it was fully restored. Good thing nights in the jungle were warm and humid.

"I don't think I'll move into the temple," she said. "Not for some time, at least."

"Oh?" Gemma raised an eyebrow at her. "I know you're a bit claustrophobic, but many of the chambers are spacious, and the ceiling's high everywhere."

Marsha shook her head. "No, it's not like that. I mean to go away for a while."

"Go away?" Amanda exclaimed. "But you're our chieftain. We depend on you for guidance and, um, potions?"

"That time is over," Marsha said solemnly. "The Khadal tribe was my charge. We're the Hippo Cult now. It's time for people like Gemma and Joz and Tom-Tom to assume leadership."

"Me?" Gemma sat up abruptly, looking startled, almost afraid. "But I know nothing about leading a people."

"That's not what I've heard," Marsha said, smiling ruefully at her friend. "Fae told me how you led a group of people all the way from the Telu camp, through perils that made her shudder as she recounted them."

"Yeah, and most of them died," Gemma muttered, leaning back on the soft grass.

"That was inevitable," Marsha said. "What matters is that you saved those you could and brought them back to where they were needed. This Hippo Cult thing was yours from the beginning – yours and Tom-Tom's. It makes sense that you'll continue to lead it."

"But what will you do?" Amanda said. "You said you're planning to go away. Will you join the Elephant People?"

Marsha was silent for a while. "Perhaps for a short time," she finally said. "But I have a feeling my quest is one that has to be undertaken by myself. I intend to find that winged hippo, the scion."

Amanda nodded slowly. "Do you have any idea where it went?"

"No," Marsha said. "But somehow I know I must find it. It's the most important part of this new civilization we'll be creating. Without it we're nothing but a bunch of children playing in our parents' abandoned house."

"But that could take years!" Amanda said. "Decades, even. This continent is huge, and that little bugger could be anywhere. Sure you don't want us to come with you?"

Marsha shook her head. "This is my task, Amanda. I have no family, no ties to leave behind, except my friendship with you and a few others. You stay here and rebuild as much as you can of the Hippo Cult. The scion is what I dedicate my life to."

"But you won't leave at once, will you?" Gemma asked. "We've only just come together again."

"Not at once," Marsha said. "But very soon. This is a task that can't wait. I hope the Hippo God's power will help guide me, like it brought you here instead of to the savannah when you were going to hunt buffalo."

"Perhaps Tom-Tom can ask that statue where the scion went?" Amanda suggested.

"He did," Marsha said. "It doesn't know."

"Oh," said Amanda.

"Indeed," said Marsha.

Gemma appeared to have fallen asleep.

"So what do we do now?" Amanda asked after a short time of silence.

Marsha rose to her feet. "How about we try some of the gargling woman's drinks? All this thinking has given me a thirst."

Amanda grinned at her. "*A drink so pink to make your breath stink, or a brew of blue to grant you the courage to say I love you.*"

"That's some pretty awful rhyming," Marsha said, but she was grinning as she did.

"I know," Amanda said. "I should stop doing rhymes."

"Please don't," Marsha said. "They sort of remind me of the old days. We should always remember those, even if that new time of wonders Tom-Tom and Marqamil speak about really will come."

“True,” Amanda said. “The Khadal had forgotten they came from the Hippo Cult, but the Hippo Cult will never forget they came from the Khadal.”

“Right,” Marsha said.

Amanda put an arm around her shoulder, and together they went to find the gargling woman and her dubious drinks.

Printed in the United States
By Bookmasters